国内外经典教材辅导系列·英语类

常耀信《美国文学简史》(第3版)
笔记和考研真题详解
(修订版)

主编：圣才考研网
www.100xuexi.com

中国石化出版社

内 容 提 要

本书是英美文学经典教材《美国文学简史》（第3版）（常耀信主编）的学习辅导书。全书完全遵循该教材的章目编排，共分26章，每章由两部分组成：第一部分为复习笔记（中英文对照），总结本章的重点难点；第二部分是考研真题与典型题详解，精选名校经典考研真题及相关习题，并提供了详细的参考答案。

圣才考研网（www.100xuexi.com）提供常耀信《美国文学简史》辅导方案【视频课程、电子书、题库】。购书即可享受大礼包增值服务【本书电子书（电脑版、手机版）+全国名校真题汇编电子书】。手机扫码（本书封面右上角）领取本书大礼包。

图书在版编目（CIP）数据

常耀信《美国文学简史》（第3版）笔记和考研真题详解：汉英对照/圣才考研网主编．——北京：中国石化出版社，2017.7（2021.4 重印）
国内外经典教材辅导系列·英语类
ISBN 978-7-5114-4592-6

Ⅰ.①常… Ⅱ.①圣… Ⅲ.①文学史-美国-高等学校-教学参考资料-汉、英 Ⅳ.①I712.09

中国版本图书馆CIP数据核字（2017）第184531号

中国石化出版社出版发行

地址：北京市东城区安定门外大街58号
邮编：100011　电话：（010）57512500
发行部电话：（010）57512575
http://www.sinopec-press.com
E-mail：press@sinopec.com
武汉市盛宏源印务有限公司印刷
全国各地新华书店经销

*

787×1092毫米 16开本 15.75印张 394千字
2017年8月第2版　2021年4月第2次印刷
定价：56.00元

序　言

我国各大院校一般都把国内外通用的权威教科书作为本科生和研究生学习专业课程的参考教材，这些教材甚至被很多考试(特别是硕士和博士入学考试)和培训项目作为指定参考书。为了帮助读者更好地学习专业课，我们有针对性地编著了一套与国内外教材配套的复习资料，并提供配套的名师讲堂和题库。

《美国文学简史》(第3版)(常耀信主编)一直被用作高等院校英语专业英国文学教材，被许多院校指定为英语专业考研必读书和学术研究参考书。作为该教材的学习辅导书，本书具有以下几个方面的特点：

1. 梳理章节脉络，浓缩内容精华。每章的复习笔记以该教材为主并结合其他教材对本章的重难点知识进行了整理，并参考了国内名校名师讲授该教材的课堂笔记，因此，本书的内容几乎浓缩了经典教材的知识精华。

2. 中英双语对照，凸显难点要点。本书章节笔记采用了中英文对照的形式，强化对重要难点知识的理解和运用。

3. 精选考研真题，补充难点习题。本书精选名校近年考研真题及相关习题，并提供答案和详解。所选真题和习题基本体现了各个章节的考点和难点，但又不完全局限于教材内容，是对教材内容极好的补充。

与本书相配套，圣才考研网提供常耀信《美国文学简史》网授精讲班、电子书、题库。

购书即可享受大礼包增值服务【本书电子书(电脑版、手机版)+全国名校真题汇编电子书】。手机扫码(本书封面右上角)领取本书大礼包。

圣才考研网(www.100 xuexi.com)是圣才学习网旗下的考研考博专业网站，提供考研公共课和全国500所院校考研考博专业课辅导【一对一辅导、网授精讲班等】、电子书、题库、全套资料(历年真题及答案、笔记讲义等)、国内外经典教材名师讲堂、考研教辅图书等。

考研辅导：kaoyan.100xuexi.com(圣才考研网)

资格考试：www.100xuexi.com(圣才学习网)

圣才学习网编辑部

目　录

第 1 章　殖民地时期的美国

1.1　复习笔记

I. American Puritanism The British began to immigrate to North America in the first half of the 17th century. The first permanent English settlement in North America was established at Jamestown, Virginia in 1607. In 1620, the ship Mayflower carried about one hundred Pilgrims arrived at Plymouth, Massachusetts. Many early American immigrants were Puritans, and they came to the United States for a variety of reasons. The Puritanism they believed in later took root in the New World and had a profound impact on American thought and American literature.	**Ⅰ. 美国清教主义** 英国向北美的移民活动开始于 17 世纪上半叶。英国于 1607 年在北美建立了第一个永久性海外殖民区：弗吉尼亚州的詹姆斯敦。1620 年“五月花”号载运 100 余名移民抵达马萨诸塞州的普利茅斯。很多美国早期的移民是清教徒，他们出于多种原因来到美国。他们信奉的清教主义后来在新大陆生根发芽，并对美国思想和美国文学产生了根深蒂固的影响。
1. Doctrines of Puritanism The Puritans believed in the doctrine predestination put forward by the theologian John Calvin, including original sin, complete depravity, and limited redemption.	**1. 清教主义的教义** 清教徒信奉神学家约翰·加尔文宣扬的预设定论，原罪，彻底的堕落，有限制的救赎等神学主张。
2. The influence of Puritanism on American literature **(1) The idealism of Puritan had exerted a great influence on American writers.** Overall, American literature, at least white American literature, is based on the myth of the Garden of Eden in the Bible. To a large extent, it is a literary form of pious idealism as the legacy of American Puritanism. The Puritans longed to live in a perfect order. With great courage, they hope to establish a new Garden of Eden in the United States so that they can finally live an ideal life. Encouraged by this sense of mission, they were very optimistic in the face of difficulties and obstacles. These have become important nourishment for the production and development of American literature. Optimism is embodied in the works of many American writers.	**2. 清教主义对美国文学的影响** **(1) 清教徒的理想主义对美国作家的文学创作产生了深远的影响。** 从总体来看，美国文学——至少是白人的美国文学——是建立在《圣经》伊甸园神话基础上的文学。在很大程度上，它是美国清教主义遗产——虔诚理想主义的一种文学形式。清教徒梦想着生活在一种完善的秩序之下，怀着勇气和希望在美国建立新的伊甸园，以使得他们能最终过上理想的生活。在这种使命感的鼓舞下，他们面对艰难险阻却充满乐观主义情绪。这些都成为美国文学产生发展的重要滋养。乐观主义弥漫在许多美国作家的作品里。

(2) American Puritans' metaphorical way of observing things led to the emergence of symbolism, which is typical in American literature.

Puritan theology and Puritan literary practice are the main reasons for the development of native symbolism in the United States. To the pious Puritans, the reality of the world is just the symbol of God. All phenomena in life are part and concrete manifestation of God's intention. It is easy to spot this symbolic process which often occurred in Puritan thinking. Over time, this process became part of the cultural traditions on which the American people and writers grew up. Symbolism is commonly used by Jonathan Edwards, Emerson, Hawthorne, and Melville. This unique way of observing the world by the Puritans is a basic component of their education

(2)美国清教徒形象地观察事物的方式导致了具有典型美国文学特点的象征主义的产生。

清教神学和清教徒的文学实践是美国本土象征主义发展的主要原因。在虔诚的清教徒看来，现实的大千世界只是上帝的象征而已。生活中的一切现象都是上帝意图的组成部分和具体表现。很容易发现这种在清教徒思维中经常发生的象征过程。随着时间的推移，这一过程便成为美国人民和作家赖以成长的文化传统的一部分。对乔纳森·爱德华兹，爱默生，霍桑，麦尔维尔来说，象征主义已成为一种常用的技巧。清教徒这种独特的观察世界的方式是他们所受教育的一个基本构成部分。

(3) In terms of the writing skills, the conciseness of Puritan works also profoundly affected American literature.

The works of Puritan writers show a fresh and concise style. They use simple and sincere rhetoric, with the noble temperament under the direct influence of the Bible. Their works have left a lasting influence on American literature.

(3) 在写作技巧方面，清教徒作品的朴实无华也深刻地影响了美国文学。

清教徒作家的写作风格是语言清新、简单、直接；修辞简朴、诚挚，带有《圣经》直接影响下的高贵气质。这些都给美国文学留下了持久的印迹。

Ⅱ. Overview of the colonial literature

American literature grew out of humble origins. Diaries, histories, journals, letters, commonplace books, travel books, sermons, in short, personal literature in its various forms, occupied a major position in the literature of the early colonial period.

Ⅱ. 殖民地文学简介

美国文学由很多粗糙的文体发展而来。日记、稗史、札记、书信、备忘录、游记及布道文稿等在内的各种形式的私人文字，在早期殖民时期的文学中占据着主要地位。

1. Major writers of colonial period

(1) John Smith (1580 –1631)

Captain John Smith was one of the founders of the colony Jamestown, Virginia. His writing about North America became the source of information about the New World for later settlers.

In *The General History of Virginia* he wrote about his capture by the Indians and his rescue by the famous Indian Princess, Pocahontas.

Another thing he wrote about that became historically important was his description of the fertile and vast new continent in his *A Description of New England*.

1. 殖民地时期主要作家

(1) 约翰·斯密斯

约翰·斯密斯上校是弗吉尼亚州詹姆斯敦殖民地的建立者之一。他的作品中有关北美的叙述成为后来移民了解北美新大陆的信息来源。

约翰·史密斯在《弗吉尼亚通史》中讲述了他被印第安人俘虏及被著名的印第安公主郎波克杭特丝营救的故事。

他的另一部具有重大历史意义的作品是《新英格兰概览》，其中描述了肥沃且广袤的美洲新大陆。

(2) William Bradford (1590 – 1657) In 1620 William Bradford led the Mayflower endeavor and became the first governor of the Plymouth Plantation with his group of pilgrim fathers. His major work is *Of Plymouth Plantation.*	**(2) 威廉姆·布雷福德** 在1620年威廉姆·布雷福德率领清教徒前辈移民乘"五月花"号到达美洲，他后来成为普利茅斯的首任总督。 他的主要作品是《普利茅斯开发史》。
(3) John Winthrop (1588 – 1649) John Winthrop was the first governor of the Massachusetts Bay colony. In his famous speech *A Model of Christian Charity* he states that "we must consider that we shall be as a city upon a hill, the eyes of all people are upon us." The two major poets in the colonial period were Anne Bradstreet and Edward Taylor.	**(3) 约翰·温思罗普** 约翰·温思罗普是马萨诸塞湾殖民地的首任总督。 在其著名演说《基督教博爱的典范》中他说到"我们将成为山巅之城，全世界人民的眼光都在注视着我们。" 殖民时期的两大诗人是安·布雷兹特里特和爱德华·泰勒。
(4) Anne Bradstreet (1612 – 1672) Anne Bradstreet was known as the "Tenth Muse" who appeared in America. **① Major works** *The Tenth Muse Lately Sprung Up in America* *Contemplations* "Upon the Burning of Our House" "To My Dear and Loving Husband" "In Reference to Her Children" "The Flesh and the Spirit" "As Weary Pilgrim"	**(4) 安·布雷德斯特里特** 她被称作在美国出现的"第十个缪斯"。 **①主要作品** 《美洲最近出现的第十位缪斯》 《沉思录》 《写在我家失火之际》 《献给我亲爱的丈夫》 《关于她的孩子们》 《灵与肉》 《疲惫的朝圣者》
② Analysis of her major works ◆"Contemplations(9)" When the poet heard the grasshopper and cricket sing, she thought of this as their praising of their Creator and searched her own soul accordingly. It is evident that she saw something metaphysical, inhering in the physical, a mode of perception that was singular Puritan. ◆"The Flesh and the Spirit" This poem depicts two sisters arguing about their values. What "flesh" represents is the seductive power of secular materials. The "spirit" tries to persuade the "flesh" to believe in the divine majesty of God. The twin sisters are evidently the integral parts of one Puritan mind.	**②主要作品分析** ◆《沉思录》第九首 当诗人听到蝈蝈和蛐蛐同时鸣叫，她感到这是它们对上帝恩惠的赞扬。她由此开始反思自己。这首诗突出地表现出清教徒形象地观察世界的方式。 ◆《灵与肉》 这首诗描述了两姐妹的争论。"肉"所代表的是世俗的物质的诱惑力。而"灵"则试图说服"肉"相信上帝的神圣伟大。两姐妹代表了一个清教徒的完整思想。

(5) Edward Taylor (1642 – 1729)

Edward Taylor was a Puritan poet, concerned about how his images spoke for God.

① Analysis of major works

◆ "Huswifery"

This poem indicates that the poet saw religious significance in a simple daily incident like a housewife spinning. The spinning wheel, the distaff, the flyers, the spool, the reel and the yarn have all acquired a metaphysical significance in the symbolic, Puritan eyes of the poet.

◆ "Upon a Spider Catching a Fly"

The poet sees the spider as a symbol of Hell. Obviously, Taylor believes in God and thinks that God can save people who have made mistakes, even the guilty, from the dark trap of hell.

(6) Thomas Paine (1737 – 1809)

Thomas Paine was born in England and came to America in 1774. His life was one of continual, unswerving fight for the rights of man. He was a major influence in the American Revolution.

① Major works

Common Sense

The American Crisis

"The Times that Try Men's Souls"

The Rights of Man

The Age of Reason

②Analysis of his major works

◆ *Common Sense*

Common Sense criticized the British monarchy and promoted the development of the upcoming struggle to overthrow colonial rule. Paine asserted that only by following the call of human intuition, common sense, and conscience, the crisis faced by the North American colonies could be resolved. This pamphlet was popular in the colonies. It was not only a manifesto for the legalization of the independence, but also a spiritual encouragement to people who were struggling with the pain.

◆ *The American Crisis*

The American Crisis is made up of 16 pamphlets written between 1776 and 1783. The first pamphlet "The Times that Try Men's Souls" came out at one of the darkest moment of the revolution. "The harder the struggle, the more glorious the triumph," when Washington had it read to the troops, it proved a heartening stimulus, a spurring excitement to further action with hope and confidence.

(5) 爱德华·泰勒

爱德华·泰勒是个清教徒诗人，他的诗歌形象主要为上帝辩护。

①主要作品分析

◆《家务》

这首诗中，诗人从家庭主妇纺织这一普通的日常事件上看到强烈的宗教意味。在诗人这个清教徒的眼里，纺车、线杆、梭子、线筒及线卷，这些意象都具有抽象的意义。

◆《蜘蛛捕蝇有感》

诗人认为蜘蛛是地狱的象征。显然，泰勒信仰上帝，认为上帝能把犯错之人，甚至是有罪之人从地狱的邪恶圈套里拯救出来。

(6) 托马斯·潘恩

托马斯·潘恩出生于英国，于1774年来到美国。他的一生堪称为人的权利而坚持不懈、努力奋斗的一生。他是美国独立革命时期最有影响力的人物之一。

①主要作品

《常识》

《美国危机》

《考验人的灵魂的时代》

《人的权利》

《理性的时代》

②主要作品分析

◆《常识》

《常识》抨击了英国的君主制，推动了即将到来的推翻殖民统治的斗争的发展。潘恩宣布只有通过听从人的直觉、常识和良心的召唤，北美殖民地面临的危机才能得以解决。这个小册子在殖民地受到热捧，它既是独立事业合法化的宣言书，也是对深陷痛苦斗争中的人们的精神鼓励。

◆《美国危机》

《美国危机》由16篇写于1776年至1783年的小册子组成。其中第一篇《考验人的灵魂的时代》写于美国独立战争最灰暗的时刻。"战斗越艰苦，胜利越光荣，"当华盛顿把这篇文章念给士兵听时，它宛如一剂兴奋剂，鼓舞军民满怀信心和希望勇往直前。

(7) **Philip Freneau**	(7) **菲利普·弗瑞诺**
Philip Freneau's great position in the history of American literature is reflected in many aspects. He dedicated his poetry creation ability to the country's struggle for independence. His poems praised the justice of the people and exposed the atrocities of the British colonists. In addition, he is also one of the prominent representatives of initiating American literary nationalism. Freneau was the first to give up imitating English poems and directly observe and describe everything around him. He admired the style and features of the American land and Indian civilization.	菲利普·弗瑞诺在美国文学史上的重要地位体现在很多方面。他把自己的诗歌创作才能奉献给了国家的独立斗争事业，其诗歌歌颂了人民的正义事业，揭露了英国殖民者的暴行。除此之外，他还是开启美国文学民族主义的突出代表之一。弗瑞诺率先摆脱模仿英国诗作的羁绊，直接观察和描写四周的一切。他崇尚美洲大地的风貌和印第安文明。
① **Major works**	①**主要作品**
"The Wild Honey Suckle" "The Dying Indian: Tomo Chequi" "The Indian Burying Ground"	《野生的金银花》 《奄奄一息的印第安人：托姆·柴吉》 《印第安人墓地》
② **Analysis of major work**	②**主要作品分析**
◆"The Wild Honey Suckle"	◆《野生的金银花》
In this poem, the lyric beauty, the heartfelt pathos, and the multiple emotional responses and echoes that the sight described are simply amazing. Here we can see the poet enjoys the beauty that the American landscape is capable of offering. This poem is an indication of the poet's dedication of American subject matter.	这首诗旋律优美，伤感之情动人心扉，其中描写的景色引发复杂的情感激荡和共鸣。诗人尽情享受着美国土地所拥有的美丽风景。该诗显示了诗人致力于描写美国本土的题材。

1.2 考研真题与典型题详解

I. Fill in the blanks.

1. The term "Puritan" was applied to those settlers who originally were devout members of the Church of ________.
2. The most enduring shaping influence in American thought and American literature was ________.
3. Hard work, thrift, piety and sobriety, these were the ________ values that dominated much of the early American writing.
4. Many Puritans wrote verse, but the works of two writers, Anne Bradstreet and ________, rose to the level of real poetry.
5. *The Tenth Muse Lately Sprung Up in America* is a collection of poems composed by ________.
6. On January 10, 1776, Thomas Paine's famous pamphlet ________ appeared.
7. Except *Common Sense*, Paine's the other two famous works were ________ and ________.
8. Thomas Paine's second most important work ________ was an impassioned plea against hereditary monarchy.

9. Thomas Paine, with his natural gift for pamphleteering and rebellion, was appropriately born into an age of __________.

10. Philip Freneau was noteworthy first because of the nature of his poems. They were truly American and very patriotic. In this respect, he reflected the spirit of his age. Therefore, he has been called the " __________ of American Poetry".

Ⅱ. Multiple Choice

1. Anne Bradstreet was a Puritan poet. Her poems made such a stir in England that she became known as the " __________ " who appeared in America. (北二外 2016 研)

   A. Ninth Muse　　B. Tenth Muse　　C. Best Muse　　D. First Muse

2. The first permanent English settlement in North America was established at __________ (北二外 2009 研)

   A. Jamestown　　B. New York　　C. Boston　　D. Concord

3. The first settlers who became the founding fathers of the American nation were quite a few of them __________. (北二外 2008 研)

   A. Quakers.　　B. Anglicans　　C. Catholics　　D. Puritans.

4. It is a critical commonplace now that American literature is based on a myth, that is, __________. (北二外 2008 研)

   A. the ancient Greek myth of Zeus

   B. the British myth of the Saint Grail

   C. the Biblical myth of the Garden of Eden

   D. the legend of the Sleepy Hollow

5. The common thread throughout American literature has been the emphasis on the __________.

   A. Revolutionism　　B. Reason　　C. Individualism　　D. Rationalism

6. The ship " __________ " carried about one hundred Pilgrims and took 66 days to beat its way across the Atlantic. In December of 1620, it put the Pilgrims ashore at Plymouth, Massachusetts.

   A. Sunflower　　B. Armada　　C. Mayflower　　D. Titanic

7. The English colonies in North America rose in arms against their parent country and the Continental Congress adopted __________ in 1776.

   A. the Declaration of Independence　　B. the Sugar Act

   C. the Stamp Act　　D. the Mayflower Compact

8. What style did the seventeenth century American poets adapt to the subject matter confronted in a strangely new environment?

   A. The style of their own.

   B. The style mixed with English and American elements.

   C. The style mixed with native-American and British tradition.

   D. The style of established European poets.

9. Anne Bradstreet was a Puritan poet. Her poems made such a stir in England that she became known as the __________ who appeared in America.

   A. Ninth Muse　　B. Tenth Muse　　C. Best Muse　　D. First Muse

10. It was not until January 1776 that a widely heard public voice demanded complete separation from England. The voice was that of __________, whose pamphlet *Common Sense*, with its heated language, increased the growing demand for separation.

A. Thomas Paine　　B. Thomas Jefferson

C. George Washington　　D. Patrick Henry

11. Which is not connected with Thomas Paine?

A. *Common Sense.*　　B. *The American Crisis.*

C. *The Rights of Man.*　　D. *The Autobiography.*

12. "These are the times that try men's souls", these words were once read to Washington's troops and did much to spur excitement to further action with hope and confidence. Who is the author of these words?

A. Benjamin Franklin.　　B. Thomas Paine.

C. Thomas Jefferson.　　D. George Washington.

13. Which work is written by Freneau?

A. *The Rights of Man.*　　B. *The Wild Honey Suckle.*

C. *Poor Richard's Almanac.*　　D. *The Day of Doom.*

Ⅲ. Explain the following term.

1. American Puritanism（南开大学 2008 研）

Ⅳ. Read the following quotations and answer the questions.

Passage 1

I heard the merry grasshopper then sing,
The black-clad cricket bear a second part;
They kept one tune and played on the same string.
Seeming to glory in their little art.
Small creatures abject thus their voices raise,
And in their kind resound their Maker's praise,
Whilst I, as mute, can warble forth no higher lays?

Questions:

(1) This is the ninth of the "Contemplations" written by an early American woman writer. What is her name?

(2) Make a brief comment on this short poem.

Passage 2

Huswifery

Make me, O Lord, thy spinning wheel complete.
Thy holy word my distaff make for me.
Make mine affections thy swift flyers neat,
And make my soul thy holy spool to be.
My conversation make to be thy reel, and reel,
the yam thereon spun of thy wheel.

Questions:

(1) Identify the poet of this poem.

(2) Make a brief comment on this poem.

Passage 3

These are the times that try men's souls: The summer soldier and the sunshine patriot will in this crisis, shrink from the service of their country; but he that stands it now deserves the love and thanks of man and woman. Tyranny, like hell, is not easily conquered; yet we have this consolation with us, that the harder the conflict, the more glorious the triumph. What we obtain too cheap, we esteem too lightly: This dearness only that gives everything its value. Heaven knows how to put a proper price upon its goods.

Questions:

(1) Which book is this passage taken from?

(2) Who is the author of this book?

(3) Whom is the author praising? Whom is the author criticizing?

(4) What do you think of the language used in the book?

Passage 4

From morning suns and evening dews
At first thy little being came:
If nothing once, you nothing lose,
For when you die you are the same:
The space between, is but an hour,
The frail duration of a flower.

Questions:

(1) Who is the writer of these verses?

(2) What is the title of this poem?

(3) Give a brief comment on this poem.

V. Short answer questions

1. Who was Anne Bradstreet? What were her literary achievements?
2. What are the basic Calvinist tenets?（国际关系学院 2007 研）

Ⅵ. Essay question

1. What is the significance of American Puritanism in American literature?

参考答案及解析

I. Fill in the blanks.

1. England

（清教徒(Puritan)，是指要求清除英国国教 Church of England 中天主教残余的改革派。其字词于 16 世纪 60 年代开始使用，源于拉丁文的 Purus，意为“清洁”。）

2. American Puritanism

（美国文化源于清教文化，由清教徒移民时传入北美。美国主流价值观都可以追溯到殖民地时期一统天下的清教主义，并且清教思想对美国文学有着根深蒂固的影响。）

3. Puritan

（清教主义，起源于英国，在北美殖民地得以实践与发展。清教徒强调艰苦奋斗、勤俭节约、虔诚和淡泊。这些价值观也影响了早期的美国文学。）

4. Edward Taylor

（美国殖民时期最著名的诗人是安·布莱德斯特律和爱德华·泰勒。）

5. Anne Bradstreet

（安·布莱德斯特律是美国殖民时期著名的诗人。其代表作是诗集《最近在北美出现的第十位缪斯》（*The Tenth Muse Late Sprung up in America*）。）

6. *Common Sense*

（1776 年美国独立的风潮开始，托马斯·潘恩支持美国独立，反对英国的殖民专政，撰写了他的成名小册子《常识》，为美国从英国殖民中独立出来辩论，批评英国国王残暴无能，认为独立后的美国应该建立共和国。）

7. *The Rights of Man*, *The Age of Reason*

（潘恩著名的作品包括，《常识》《人的权利》《理性的时代》。）

8. *The Rights of Man*

（1791 年 3 月，托马斯·潘恩在伦敦出版《人权论》，激烈抨击埃德蒙·伯克（Edmund Burke，1729—1797）的《法国革命感言录》（*Reflections on the Revolution in France*）（1790）。《人权论》的可贵之处还在于，它冲破了当时笼罩于整个西方思想界对英国君主立宪政体的迷信，深入骨髓地批判了这一政体，给当时还处于摸索状态的法国革命指明了共和主义的崭新方向。）

9. Revolution

（潘恩是美国独立革命时期著名的作家之一。）

10. Father

（菲利普·弗瑞诺是开启美国民主主义的突出代表之一，他被称为"美国诗歌之父。"）

Ⅱ. Multiple Choice

1. B　安·布莱德斯特里特，清教徒诗人，1630 年从英国来到新大陆马萨诸塞湾殖民地，以《第十个缪斯在美国出现》闻名。
2. A　詹姆斯敦是英国人在北美的第一个永久定居地。
3. D　早期来到北美的殖民者有不少是清教徒，因而殖民时期的文学深受清教思想影响。
4. C　由于深受清教主义的影响，美国文学——至少是美国的白人文学——是建立在《圣经》伊甸园神话基础上的文学。
5. C　美国价值观的核心是个人主义，因而，个人主义也成为贯穿美国文学史的主线。
6. C　1620 年 100 多名清教徒前辈乘坐"五月花"号船到达美国马萨诸塞州的普利茅斯。
7. A　1776 年 13 个英属北美殖民地奋起反击英国的殖民统治，并且 1776 年 7 月 4 日，大陆会议通过了一份由托马斯·杰弗逊起草的《独立宣言》（*Declaration of Independence*）。
8. D　17 世纪美国诗人大多沿袭英国诗歌的风格。
9. B　安·布拉德斯特里特被誉为"美国出现的第十个缪斯"。
10. A　潘恩的《常识》号召美国摆脱英国的统治。
11. D　《自传》是本杰明·富兰克林的代表作，其余三项都是潘恩的主要作品。
12. B　"这是考验人的灵魂的时刻"，这句话选自潘恩的《美国危机》。

13. B 《野生的金银花》是弗瑞诺最具代表性的作品。

Ⅲ. Explain the following term.

1. The word Puritanism is originally used to refer to the theology advocated by a party within the Church of England. The term Puritanism is also used in a broader sense to refer to the attitudes and values considered characteristic of the Puritans. It has been employed to denote a rigid moralism, or the condemnation of innocent pleasure, or religious narrowness adhered by the early New England Puritans. The American Puritanism as a cultural heritage exerted great influence over American moral values. And this Puritan influence over American Romanticism was conspicuously noticeable. In addition, a preoccupation with the Calvinistic view of original sin and the mystery of evil marked the works by such famous writers as Hawthorne and Melville.

Ⅳ. Read the following quotations and answer the questions.

Passage 1

(1) Anne Bradstreet.

(2) This short poem offers the reader an insight into the mentality of the early Puritan pioneering into a new world. When the poet heard the grasshopper and the cricket sing, she thought of this as the praise to their creator and searched her own soul accordingly. It is evident that she saw something metaphysical inhering in the physical, a mode of perception which was singularly Puritan.

Passage 2

(1) Edward Taylor.

(2) The poem indicates that the poet saw religious significance in a simple daily incident like a housewife spinning. In his symbolic Puritan eyes, the spinning wheels, luggage racks, flyers, spools, reels and yarn all have certain metaphorical meanings.

Passage 3

(1) *The American Crisis*

(2) Thomas Paine

(3) Paine is praising those who stand "it", it referring to "the service of their country". In the meantime, Paine is criticizing those who shrink from the service of their country in this crisis.

(4) The language is plain, impressive and forceful. Paine himself once said that his purpose as a writer was to use plain language to make those who can scarcely read understand.

Passage 4

(1) Philip Freneau.

(2) "The Wild Honey suckle".

(3) Here Freneau offers a version of an abundant America with potential for providing a good life for all. The poem is also an indication of his dedication to American subject matter as he examined peculiarly American characteristics of the countryside.

V. Short answer questions

1. Anne Bradstreet (1612 ~ 1672) is one of the most important figures in the history of American Literature. She is considered by many to be the first American poet, and her first collection of poems, *The Tenth Muse Lately Sprung Up in America, By a Gentlewoman of Those Parts*, was the

first book written by a woman to be published in the United States. Mrs. Bradstreet's works also serve as a document of the struggles of a Puritan wife against the hardships of New England colonial life.

2. Calvinist theology is sometimes identified with the five points of Calvinism, also called the doctrines of grace. In English, the five points are sometimes referred to by the acronym TULIP, which means Total Inherited Depravity, Unconditional Election, Limited Atonement, Irresistible Grace and Perseverance of the Saints England colonial life.

VI. Essay question

1. The settlement of the North American continent by the English began in the early part of the 17th century. Many early American immigrants were Puritans, and they came to the United States for a variety of reasons. The Puritanism they believed in later took root in the New World and had a profound impact on American thought and American literature.

   The American Puritans were idealists, believing that the Church should be restored to the "Purity" and religion was a matter of primary importance. They accepted the doctrine of predestination, original sin, total depravity and limited atonement. Overall, American literature, at least white American literature, is based on the myth of the Garden of Eden in the Bible. With great courage, they hope to establish a new Garden of Eden in the United States so that they can finally live an ideal life. Encouraged by this sense of mission, they were very optimistic in the face of difficulties and obstacles. These have become important nourishment for the production and development of American literature. Optimism is embodied in the works of many American writers, such as Emerson, Whitman, etc.

   Puritan theology and Puritan literary practice are the main reasons for the development of native symbolism in the United States. To the pious Puritans, the reality of the world is just the symbol of God. All phenomena in life are part and concrete manifestation of God's intention. It is easy to spot this symbolic process which often occurred in Puritan thinking. Over time, this process became part of the cultural traditions on which the American people and writers grew up. Symbolism is commonly used by Jonathan Edwards, Emerson, Hawthorne, and Melville. This unique way of observing the world by the Puritans is a basic component of their education

   Regarding the technique, simplicity characterizes the Puritan style of writing. The style is fresh, simple and direct; the rhetoric is plain and honest, without a touch of nobility often traceable to the direct influence of the Bible. All this has left an indelible imprint on American writing. Thus, American Puritanism has been, by and large, a healthy legacy to the Americans.

第2章 爱德华兹·富兰克林·克里夫古尔

2.1 复习笔记

American critic Van Wyck Brooks, when commenting on the 18th century America and American character, noted that Jonathan Edwards and Benjamin Franklin together represent the 18th century. The American Puritan tradition is characterized by both religious piety and dispassionate pragmatism Jonathan Edwards represents the former and Franklin the latter. Both men were devout Puritans.

I. Jonathan Edwards (1703–1758)

1. Life

Born into an extremely religious family, Edwards entered Yale College at the age of 13 and received his master's degree in 1723. He later became a pastor in the suburb of Northampton, Massachusetts. In his sermons he focused on describing the awesome power of God, the fall of man, and the need for man to communicate with the Holy Spirit and to receive God's favor.' He was one of the key figures in the emergence and development of the Great Awakening movement in North America. He became famous not only in North America, but also in Europe.

2. Ideas

(1) He was the first modern American and the country's last medieval man.

His works reveal the modern consciousness of the man. He was influenced to no small extent by Newton's mechanical view of the universe and the Lockean thesis. He tried to reconcile Puritan ideas with the new rationalism of Lock and Newton.

His works also show his mentality as a medievalist. He loved to walk alone in the woods, having a pleasant conversation with Christ, with his body and mind deeply placed in the surroundings of God. This is what is called "the communion of the soul with God". This communication comes from a heartfelt "conversion" rather than from rational considerations.

美国评论家范·威克·布鲁克斯在评述到18世纪美国及美国人性格时指出：乔纳森·爱德华兹和本杰明·富兰克林一起代表了18世纪。决定美国人性格的清教主义传统具有宗教虔诚和冷静务实两个特点；乔纳森·爱德华兹代表前者，富兰克林代表后者。两人都是虔诚的清教徒。

I. 乔纳森·爱德华兹

1. 生平

爱德华兹出生于一个宗教气息极其浓郁的家庭里。13岁，他进入耶鲁大学学习，于1723年获得硕士学位。后来他成为马萨诸塞州北安普敦郊区的牧师。他在布道时着重描述上帝的威力、人的堕落以及人与圣灵的交流、接受上帝恩惠的必要性等。他是促进北美"大觉醒"运动发生和发展的关键人物之一。他不仅扬名北美，而且饮誉欧洲。

2. 思想

(1) 他是美国第一位具有现代思想的哲学家，美国最后一位思想依旧停留在中世纪的神学家。

他的作品显示出他思想的强烈现代意识。他深受牛顿机械宇宙观和洛克哲学思想的影响。他竭力调和清教思想和洛克、牛顿的理性主义。

他的作品也显示出他作为一个中世纪人的心态。他喜欢在林中独自漫步，和基督愉快的交谈，身心都深置于上帝的包围中。这就是所谓"灵魂与上帝的交流"，这种交流由发自内心"皈依"而来而不是出于理性的考虑。

(2) **He was a good deal of a transcendentalist.**

He believed that God is everywhere. God manifests himself through nature and man, who is both a part of God and therefore divine.

His work "*The Shape of Sacred Things*" is considered to be the forerunner of the transcendentalist nature symbolism in the 19th century. And his Puritan mysticism is fully and clearly stated in the writings of Ralph Waldo Emerson in the 19th century.

3. Major works

The Freedom of the Will

The Great Doctrine of Original Sin Defended

The Nature of True Virtue

"Sinners in the Hands of An Angry God"

"Personal Narrative"

Images or Shadows of Divine Things

(2) 他在很大程度上是一位超验主义者。

他认为上帝无处不在。上帝通过自然界和人体现自己，人是上帝的一部分，因此也是神圣的。

其作品《神圣事物的形影》堪称19世纪超验主义自然象征论的先导。而他的清教神秘主义在19世纪爱默生的著作中得到了全面而明确的陈述。

3. 主要作品

《自由的意志》

《伟大的基督教教义的原罪说辩》

《真正美德的本质》

《发怒的上帝手中的罪人》

《自述》

《神圣事物的形影》

Ⅱ. Benjamin Franklin (1706 – 1790)

Being a rare genius in human history, Franklin was a "Jack-of-all-trades" —printer, postmaster, almanac maker, essayist, scientist, orator, statesman, philosopher, political economist, ambassador.

1. Life

Franklin was born into a poor family of candle makers.' He was very industrious. At the age of 16, he began publishing critical articles under the pseudonym "*Silence Dogood*", and at the age of 17, he fled to Philadelphia to make a living, where he later became a publisher. He helped establish the University of Pennsylvania's predecessors, the Medical College of Pennsylvania and the North American Philosophical Society. He was also a renowned scientist of his time. He was one of the founding fathers of the United States because he signed the Declaration of Independence, the Treaty of Alliance with France, the Treaty of Peace with England and the U. S. Constitution. Franklin's literary stature is largely due to two of his literary achievements, namely, *Poor Richard's Almanac* and *The Autobiography*.

2. Analysis of major works

◆*Poor Richard's Almanac*

Franklin first issued *Poor Richard's Almanac* in 1732 and it continued to be issued for 25 years. 'The almanac contains poetry, prose, and many idiomatic sayings that soon became household

Ⅱ. 本杰明·富兰克林

富兰克林是人类历史上少有的天才。他是出版家、邮政总长、历书作者、散文家、科学家、演说家、政治家、哲学家、政治经济学家、大使、业务员等等。

1. 生平

富兰克林出生于一个贫穷的蜡烛制造匠家庭。他非常勤奋好学。16岁时开始以笔名"静行善"发表评论文章。17岁时只身逃往费城谋生。后成为出版商。他帮助建立了宾夕法尼亚大学的前身——宾夕法尼亚医学院和北美哲学学会。他也是当时著名的科学家。他签署过《独立宣言》《美法同盟条约》《英美和平条约》和美国宪法。他是美国的缔造者之一。富兰克林在文学上的地位主要由他的两项文学成就确定，即《穷查理历书》和《富兰克林自传》。

2. 主要作品分析

◆《穷查理历书》

富兰克林于1732年首次发行《穷查理历书》，并且这本历书持续发行长达25年之久。历书中有诗歌，散文，以及许多成语箴言，

words, many of which became mottos for people in the world. Many of his aphorisms come from other writers. But he enriched them with his own humorous wisdom, which makes *Poor Richard's Almanac* entertaining and educational. '

◆*The Autobiography*

(1) *The Autobiography* is one of the finest works of autobiographical literature. It is a concise and extremely engaging account of Franklin's leap from poverty and humility to wealth and fame. It is a faithful account of the glorious career of America's first self-made man. ' The whole book consists of four parts, written in different periods.

(2) *The Autobiography* is, first and foremost, a Puritan document because it records the Puritans' self-reflection and self-improvement. It is also the best illustration of the Puritan moral principle that in order to be successful, one must be hardworking, simple, and prudent.

(3) *The Autobiography* amply illustrates that Franklin was the voice of the American Enlightenment in the 18th century. He represented that in America, man is essentially good and free, with the God-given inalienable right to freedom and the pursuit of happiness. The book celebrates the realization of the American dream by telling the story of success through self-reliance.

(4) The style of *The Autobiography* reflects the simple, straightforward and concise style of the Puritans.

Ⅲ. Hector St. John de Crevecoeur (1735 –1813)

Crevecoeur was a French settler. His famous work is *Letters from an American Farmer*.

◆**Analysis of *Letters from an American Farmer***

Crevecoeur wrote back to Europe about the nature and significance of the new nation of the United States to help the world understand it better. *Letters from an American Farmer* contains 12 letters. The first eight letters illustrate the pride of being an American. However, from the 9th letter onward, the author's tone begins to become subdued. He realized that America also had all kinds of evils that were thought to be found only in the old world of Europe. A pessimistic tone lingers in *Letters from an American Farmer*.

这些成语箴言很快便家喻户晓，其中许多成为为人处世的座右铭。他的许多格言来源于别的作家。但是他充分运用自己的幽默智慧简化丰富了这些格言，这使得《穷查理历书》寓教于乐。

◆《自传》

(1)《自传》是自传体文学中的上乘佳作。它简明而极其引人入胜地叙述了富兰克林由穷苦卑微而跃至富有、闻名的故事。它忠实地记录了美国第一位自力更生者光辉灿烂的职业生涯。全书由四部分组成，分别写于不同时期。

(2)《自传》首先是一本清教文献。它记录了清教徒的自我反省和自我完善。它也是清教道德原则的最好说明，为了取得成功，人必须勤劳、简朴、谨慎。

(3)《自传》充分说明了富兰克林是18世纪美国启蒙运动的代言人。他代表着，在美国，人本质是善良自由的，拥有上帝赋予的不可剥夺的自由及追求幸福的权力。该书通过讲述自力更生而获取成功的故事，歌颂了美国梦的实现。

(4)《自传》的文体体现出清教徒朴素、直爽、简洁的风格。

Ⅲ. 克里夫古尔

克里夫古尔是法国移民。其著名作品是《来自一个美国农夫的信》。

◆**《来自一个美国农夫的信》作品分析**

克里夫古尔写信到欧洲介绍美国这个新国家的性质和意义，以帮助世界了解美国。《来自一个美国农夫的信》包括12封信。前8封信流露出作为美国人自豪的心情。然而，从第9封信开始，作者的语调开始变得低沉。他意识到美国也存在着被认为只有欧洲旧世界才有的各种罪恶。《来自一个美国农夫的信》中萦绕着悲观主义的基调。

2.2 考研真题与典型题详解

I. Fill in the blanks.

1. In his ________ Benjamin Franklin creates the image of a boy's rise from ________ to riches and demonstrates his belief that the new world of America was a land of opportunities which might be met through hard work and wise management.（天津外国语学院 2008 研）
2. If we say Jonathan Edwards represents the upper levels of the American mind, ________ represents the lower levels.
3. Before his death, ________ had gained a position as America's first systematic philosopher.
4. Jonathan Edwards' work *Images or Shadows of Divine Things* anticipated the nature symbolism of ________ in the 19th century.
5. Franklin's claim to a place in literature rests chiefly on his ________ and ________.
6. Benjamin Franklin's best writing is found in his masterpiece ________.
7. Franklin was the epitome of the ________, the versatile, practical embodiment of national man in the 18th century.
8. Eighteen-century America experienced an age of ________, of ________, and ________ like England and Europe.

II. Multiple Choice

1. The first symbol of self-made American man is ________.（北二外 2009 研）

   A. George Washington　　B. Washington Irving
   C. Thomas Jefferson　　D. Benjamin Franklin
2. At the Reason and Revolution Period, Americans were influenced by the European movement called the ________.

   A. Charitist Movement　　B. Romanticist Movement
   C. Enlightenment Movement　　D. Modernist Movement
3. In American literature, the eighteenth century was the age of the Enlightenment. ________ was the dominant spirit.

   A. Humanism　　B. Rationalism　　C. Revolution　　D. Evolution
4. Jonathan Edwards' best and most representative sermon was ________.

   A. *A True Sight of Sin*　　B. *Sinners in the Hands of an Angry God*
   C. *A Model of Christian Charity*　　D. *God's Determinations*
5. The secular ideals of the American Enlightenment were exemplified in the life and career of ________.

   A. Thomas Hood　　B. Benjamin Franklin
   C. Thomas Jefferson　　D. George Washington
6. From 1732 to 1758, Benjamin Franklin wrote and published his famous ________, an annal collection of proverbs.

   A. *The Autobiography*　　B. *Poor Richard's Almanac*
   C. *Common Sense*　　D. *The General Magazine*

Ⅲ. Explain the following term.

1. the literary form of autobiography (北二外 2008 研)

Ⅳ. Essay questions

1. Analyze *The Autobiography of Benjamin Franklin.*
2. Analysis of *The Poor Richard's Almanac.*

参考答案及解析

I. Fill in the blanks.

1. *Autobiography*, poor
   (富兰克林在《自传》中讲述了其白手起家、自力更生的故事，平凡却生动的讲述表明他坚信通过努力就能实现美国梦。)
2. Benjamin Franklin
   (美国文学评论家范·威克·布鲁克斯(Van Wyck Brooks)在《美国的成年》(*America's Coming Age*)中指出乔纳森·爱德华兹和本杰明·富兰克林是美国18世纪的两位重要的哲学家，他们是不同层次思想的代表。)
3. Jonathan Edwards
   (乔纳森·爱德华兹(1703－1758)是美国"大觉醒"(the"Great Awakening")的领军人物，他生前赢得了"美国第一位系统的哲学家"称号。其著名作品是《意志自由》(*Freedom of the Will*)。)
4. Transcendentalism
   (乔纳森·爱德华兹的作品《神灵的形影》(*Images or Shadows of Divine Things*)对19世纪的超验主义对象征主义的运用产生了很大的影响。)
5. *Poor Richard's Almanac*, *Autobiography*
   (富兰克林在文学上的地位主要取决于《穷查理历书》和《自传》。)
6. *The Autobiography of Benjamin Franklin*
   (本杰明·富兰克林文学上最大的成就体现在他的作品《本杰明·富兰克林自传》上。该书以平易的文风叙述了富兰克林艰苦创业、自学成才、坚持不懈的奋斗历程。)
7. Enlightenment
   (富兰克林是启蒙思想的缩影，是18世纪理性的代表。)
8. enlightenment, reason, order
   (18世纪的美国处于启蒙、理想、秩序的时代。)

Ⅱ. Multiple Choice

1. D　富兰克林是第一个自力更生、白手起家的美国人的标志。
2. C　欧洲的启蒙运动对美国理性和独立革命时期产生了深远影响。
3. B　启蒙运动通常是指在18世纪初至1789年法国大革命间的一个新思维不断涌现的时代，与理性主义等一起构成一个较长的文化运动时期，所以法国启蒙运动时期被称为"理性时代"。18世纪的美国同样受到启蒙思想而影响，因而理性主义是这个时期美国文学的主导思想。
4. B　美国神学家乔纳森·爱德华兹最具代表性的布道是《愤怒的上帝手中之罪人》(*Sinners in the Hands of an Angry God*)。

5. B 作为美国财富和智慧的象征，美国人民把富兰克林的头像印在 100 美元纸钞的正面。200 多年来，这位智者的思想一直被那些希望拥有美德并过上富足生活的人们所遵循和实践着。他的个人生活和职业生涯代表了美国启蒙运动中世俗化的理想。

6. B 《穷理查历书》(*Poor Richard's Almanac*)它是由美国资本主义精神最完美的代表——本杰明·富兰克林所写。该出版物从 1732 年至 1758 年不断出现。它幽默、睿智、形式奇特，通篇贯彻着人类的智慧精华，书中的名言警句与人生箴言即使在现在看来也具有很积极的作用。

Ⅲ. Explain the following term.

1. the literary form of autobiography: An autobiography is a person's description of his or her life. It is usually written in narrative form. An autobiography presents life events from the author's point of view and offers insights into the author's own ideas and beliefs. Benjamin Franklin and his work *Autobiography* is the representative of autobiography.

Ⅳ. Essay questions

1. The book is probably the first of its kind in literature. It is the simple yet immensely fascinating record of a man rising to wealth and fame from a state of poverty and obscurity in which he was born, the faithful account of the colorful career of America's first self-made man. The book contains four parts, written at different times.

   It is, first of all, a Puritan document. It is Puritan because it is a record of self-examination and self-improvement. It is also a convincing illustration of the Puritan ethic that in order to get on in the world, one has to be industrial, frugal, and prudent.

   It is also an eloquent elucidation of the fact that Franklin was spokesman for the new order of the eighteenth-century enlightenment, and that he represented in America all its ideas, that man is basically good and free by nature, endowed by God with certain inalienable rights of liberty and the pursuit of happiness. Through telling a success story of self-reliance, the book celebrates, in fact, the fulfillment of the American dream.

   The style of the book is the pattern of Puritan simplicity, directness, and concision. The lucidity of the narrative, the absence of ornaments in wording and complex, involved structures in syntax, and the Puritan abhorrence of paradox are all well graphically demonstrated here and in the whole of the book. Taken as a whole, it is safe to say that the book is an exemplary illustration of the American style of writing.

2. Benjamin Franklin created a character, Poor Richard, in whose name the work appeared, and whose real existence was debated humorously and seriously. For almost a quarter of a century, he kept publishing Poor Richard's Almanac, expanding its literary part to the intense delight of its readers.

   Apart from poems and essays, he managed to put in a good many adages, and commonsense witticisms which became household words and many mottos of the most typical kind. He did not always write the maxims himself. He borrowed from others and made good use of his own wit and wisdom to simplify and enrich their axiom. There are many similar statements filling almanac, and taught as much as amused. The practical wisdom of Franklin shone forth rays of grandeur from its pages.

第3章 美国浪漫主义·欧文·库柏

3.1 复习笔记

I. Overview of American Romanticism	I. 美国浪漫主义简介
The Romantic period in American literature began in the late 18th century and was an important stage in the history of American literature until the outbreak of the Civil War.	美国文学中的浪漫主义时期开始于18世纪末，到南北战争爆发为止，是美国文学史上的重要阶段。
1. Background	**1. 背景**
(1) A vibrant, new America was hungry for new forms of literary expression. The rising state of the country and the upward spirit of the times contributed to the outbreak of romantic feelings. The literary environment has provided a wide space for literary creation. Various magazines have sprung up, contributing to a great extent to the long development of literature.	(1) 生机勃勃、开创新生活的美国渴望有新的文学表达形式。国家的上升状态、时代的上进精神促进了浪漫主义情感的爆发。文学环境为文学创作提供了广阔的空间。各种杂志如雨后春笋出现，在很大程度上促进了文学的长足发展。
(2) Foreign ideas and cultural influences inspired the spread of Romanticism in America. The Romantic movement that spread across England and Europe in the early 19th century played a significant role in the growth of American Romantic literature.	(2) 外国思想和文化影响激发了美国浪漫主义思潮的蔓延。19世纪初波及英国和欧洲的浪漫主义运动对美国浪漫主义文学的成长发挥了相当重要的作用。
(3) American Romanticism was influenced by the cultural heritage that is American Puritanism.	(3) 美国浪漫主义受到美国清教主义这一文化遗产的影响。
2. Characteristics	**2. 特点**
(1) From its inception, American Romantic literature has had its own unique attributes. It is the product of the fusion of several American factors. It expresses "a genuinely new experience" and contains "a strange quality".	(1) 美国浪漫主义文学自一开始便具有其独特的属性。它是美国因素融为一体的产物。它所表达的是"一种真正的新的经历"，包含着"一种陌生的特质"。
(2) Due to domestic and foreign factors, American Romanticism has both imitative and independently creative characteristics.	(2) 由于国内外因素的影响，美国浪漫主义既有模仿，也有独立创造的特性。
II. Washington Irving (1783–1859)	**II. 华盛顿·欧文**
1. Life	**1. 生平**
Born in New York to a wealthy merchant family, Irving was a keen reader from an early age and began writing poetry, prose and plays as a teenager. His first novel, *A History of*	欧文生于纽约一个富商的家庭，自幼酷爱读书，少年时代便开始写诗歌、散文和戏剧。他的第一

New York, was a great success. *The Sketch Book*, has brought him international fame. In 1826 Irving was sent to Spain as a diplomatic attaché, and from 1829 to 1832 he served as secretary of the U. S. Embassy in London. He lived most of his later years at his residence on the Hudson River. He was unmarried for life and died in 1859.

2. His literary contribution

Irving made a unique contribution to American literature, pioneering many of the precedents in the history of American literature.

(1) He was the first American writer to achieve international fame.

(2) He is known as the "father of American literature". The short story as a genre of American literature originated from Irving's *The Sketch Book*, which symbolizes the beginning of American Romantic literature. The book also symbolizes the beginning of American Romantic literature.

3. Literary career

Irving's literary career can be roughly divided into two important periods. The first period spanned from the publication of his debut work to 1832. The second period was the rest of his life.

(1) The first period Irving mainly depicted English or European themes. He sought values in the past and in the traditions of the old world.

(2) The second period saw Irving discovering a new democratic spirit in American sentiment and literature.

4. Writing style

Owen was a masterful stylist. His elegance, elegance, literary quality, and harmony are all fully reflected in his style of writing.

(1) First of all, he tries to avoid being preachy. His aim is to create something that is pleasing to the eye.

(2) He is good at setting the mood, which largely makes up for the lack of a thin plot.

(3) His characters are so well drawn that reading them is like hearing their voices and seeing their people.

(4) Humor is part of his literary style.

部小说《纽约外史》获得很大成功。《见闻札记》使他获得国际声誉。1826 年欧文作为外交随员被派往西班牙。1829 年至 1832 年他任美国驻伦敦大使馆秘书。他晚年大部分时间生活在哈德逊河畔的住所。他终身未婚，死于 1859 年。

2. 文学贡献

欧文对美国文学有着独特的贡献，他开创了美国文学史上的许多先河。

（1）他是第一个获得国际声誉的美国作家。

（2）他被称为“美国文学之父”。短篇小说作为美国文学的一种类型源于欧文的《见闻札记》。该书也象征着美国浪漫主义文学的开始。

3. 文学生涯

欧文的文学生涯大致可分为两个重要的时期。第一个时期从其处女作的发表到 1832 年。第二个时期跨越他的余生。

（1）第一个时期欧文主要描写英国或欧洲主题。他在过去和旧世界里的传统中寻求价值。

（2）第二个时期欧文在美国人情感和文艺中发掘新的民主主义精神。

4. 写作风格

欧文是一位精湛的文体家。他的雅人深致、文质彬彬及和颜悦色在他的文风里都能找到充分的反映。

（1）首先，他尽量避免说教。他创作的目的在于让人赏心悦目。

（2）他擅长烘托气氛，这很大程度上弥补了情节单薄这一不足。

（3）他的人物刻画得惟妙惟肖，读后如闻其声，如见其人。

（4）幽默是他文风的有机组成部分。

(5) His deep, rounded, musical and skillful works have been the focus of critical attention. **5. Major works** *A History of New York* *The Sketch Book* "The Authors Account of Himself" "Rip Van Winkle" "The Legend of Sleepy Hollow" *The history of Life and Voyages of Christopher Columbus* *A Chronicle of the Conquest of Granada* *Life of Goldsmith* *Life of Washington* *The Crayon Miscellany* "A Tour on the Prairies" "Astoria" *Adventures of Captain Bonneville* **6. Analysis of major works** ◆"Rip Van Winkle" The story reflects the author's conservative attitude. Before the war life was leisurely and peaceful. After the war, however, there were political party battles and the pace of life increased. This story demonstrates Irving's position that change and revolution disrupt the natural order of life and shows his reservations about a modern democratic America. ◆"The Legend of Sleepy Hollow" The creation of prototypes is one of Irving's high attainments. Ichabod is the representative of the New Englander who is through with power, the city slicker of the village, a destructive force that wants to commit fraud. He was finally driven out of the village where he did not belong, so the small village returned to peace and quiet. Brom Bones, on the other hand, is a Huckleberry-esque village boy, rude, energetic and self-supporting on the frontier. The battle between Ichabod and Brom's love affairs can again be seen as a competition between two moral groups under specific historical conditions. The writing style of the story also represents the highest level of Irving.	(5)其作品精深圆熟，富有音乐性且技艺娴熟，这些都成为评论界关注的焦点。 **5. 主要作品** 《纽约外史》 《见闻札记》 《作者自述》 《瑞普·凡·温克尔》 《睡谷的传说》 《哥伦布传》 《征服格拉纳达》 《哥尔斯密传》 《华盛顿传》 《克瑞恩文集》 《大草原之旅》 《阿斯托里亚》 《博纳维尔船长历险记》 **6. 主要作品分析** ◆《瑞普·凡·温克尔》 故事反映了作者保守的态度。战前生活悠闲、平和。战后却出现政党之争，生活节奏加快。这个故事表明了欧文的立场，即变革和革命打乱了生活的自然秩序，表明他对现代民主的美国持有保留的态度。 ◆《睡谷的传说》 原型的创造是欧文高超的造诣之一。伊卡包德是通权达变的新英格兰人的代表，他是村子里的城市滑头，一种欲行欺诈的破坏性力量。他最后被赶出本不属于他的村庄，于是小村子又恢复平静祥和。布鲁姆则是哈克·贝恩式村野之夫，粗鲁、精力充沛，在边疆自食其力。由此可看出，伊卡包德和布鲁姆的情场之争又可以看作是特定历史条件下两个道德群体之间的竞争。 该故事的写作风格也代表了欧文的最高水准。

III. James Fenimore Cooper (1789 –1851)	**III. 詹姆斯·费尼莫·库柏**
1. Life	**1. 生平**
Cooper was born in New Jersey to a wealthy family that owned large tracts of land. Cooper entered Yale University at the age of 14 and was later expelled for misconduct. He then went to sea as a sailor for five years. At the age of 20 he inherited a large inheritance from his father and later began writing. His second novel, *The Spy*, was a huge success. Over the next 30 years, he produced more than 30 more works, including 11 nautical novels. *Leatherstocking Tales* made him famous during his lifetime and still has a large readership today.	库柏出生于新泽西州一个富有家庭，家里拥有大片土地。库柏 14 岁进入耶鲁大学学习，后来因行为不端被开除。于是他出海做水手长达 5 年之久。20 岁时他继承了父亲的巨额遗产，后来开始写作。他的第二本小说《间谍》获得巨大成功。接下来的 30 年，他又创作了 30 余部作品，其中包括 11 部航海小说。《皮裹腿故事集》使他生前闻名遐迩，至今仍拥有大量读者。
2. Literary contribution	**2. 文学贡献**
Cooper was one of the first writers to depict the Westward Movement.	库柏是首批描写西进运动的作家之一。
Cooper's importance in American literature is reflected in the fact that he created a myth about the stages of American growth. In his novels, Cooper comes to realize that on the western frontier, social activity is governed by two conflicting principles, and Cooper's greatness lies in the fact that he points out that one is morally right and the other is practically imperative. This is where the contradiction in Cooper's thinking lies. He both promotes social order and the ideal of closeness to nature and freedom.	库柏在美国文坛的重要地位体现在他创造了一个关于美国成长阶段的神话。在其小说中，库柏逐渐意识到在西部边疆，社会活动受到两种相互矛盾的原则的制约，库柏的伟大之处在于，他指出其中一种在道义上是正确的，另外一种则在实际上是势在必行的。这也是库柏思想上的矛盾所在。他既推崇社会秩序，又崇尚亲近自然、无拘无束的理想境界。
3. Writing style	**3. 写作风格**
(1) Cooper specializes in fictional plots. His plots are sometimes too bizarre, but his stories are fascinating.	(1) 库柏擅长虚构情节。其情节虽有时过于离奇，但是他的故事十分引人入胜。
(2) The landscape under his pen is magnificent, quite like the style of Walter Scott's novels.	(2) 其笔下风景波澜壮阔，颇有司各特小说之风。
(3) He is very focused on connecting different scenes. He had never been to the frontier or lived with the Indians, yet he produced five epic masterpieces about them, which is a testament to Cooper's extremely fertile imagination. His Indians were among the first Indians to appear in American fiction, and they were perhaps the first "noble savages".	(3) 他很注重联系不同的场景。他从未去过边疆，也没有跟印第安人生活在一起过，但是他却创作了五部关于他们的史诗般巨作。这充分证明了库柏想象力极其丰富。他笔下的印第安人是美国小说中最早出现的印第安人之一，他们或许也是首批"高贵的野蛮人"。
(4) His style of writing is also flawed. His characterization is dull and lacks credibility, and the use of language, especially dialect, is not authentic.	(4) 他的文体也有缺陷。他的人物刻画呆板，缺乏可信度，语言尤其是方言的使用并不纯正。

4. Major works *The Spy* *Leatherstocking Tales* *The Pioneers* (1823) *The Last of the Mohicans* (1826) *The Prairie* (1827) *The Pathfinder* (1840) *The Deerslayer* (1841)	**4. 主要作品** 《间谍》 《皮裹腿故事集》 《拓荒者》 《最后的莫西干人》 《草原》 《探路者》 《猎鹿人》
5. Analysis of major work ◆*Leatherstocking Tales* (1) *Leatherstocking Tales* is a series of five tales about the life of American settlers. The protagonist Natty Bumppo is a mythic figure. When he first appears, we see a real frontiersman, a man of flesh and blood in the virgin forests of North America. But as the story moves on, he does so gathering more and more of the halo of a legendary and mythic nature around him. He becomes a type, a representation of a nation struggling to be born, progressing from old age to rebirth and youth. The protagonist in *Leatherstocking Tales* goes from the old to the golden age of youth. This is the true American myth. (2) *The Pioneers* is the first being published of *Leatherstocking Tales*. The novel is historically significant in that it is the first true frontier novel in the history of American literature. The story revolves around the conflict between Leatherstocking and Judge Temple. Leatherstocking advocates free and unrestrained jungle life, while Judge Temple believes that without law and order, man would be reduced to a savage. Bambo stands for the ideals of fraternity, closeness to nature, and freedom, and is the morally right side. While Judge Temple symbolizes law and civilization, and is the side of the unstoppable. Together, they built the Wild West into a civilized place, hence plural form is used in the title *The Pioneers*.	**5. 主要作品分析** ◆《皮裹腿故事集》 (1)《皮裹腿故事集》由五部描写美国西部移民生活的系列小说组成。主人公纳蒂·班波的形象颇具神话色彩。刚出场时，他是一位有血有肉、实实在在的活跃在北美丛林里的拓荒者形象。随着故事的不断深入，他的神话和传说成分愈渐增强。他成为一个典型，代表着整个国家努力从暮年走向重生、走向青春。皮裹腿系列小说主人公从暮年到青年黄金时代。这是真正的美国神话。 (2)《拓荒者》是《皮裹腿故事集》中最早发表的一部。该小说的重大历史意义在于，它是美国文学史上首部真正意义上的边疆小说。故事围绕皮裹腿和坦普尔法官之间的矛盾展开，皮裹腿崇尚自由自在、无拘无束的丛林生活，而坦普尔法官则认为没有法律和秩序人就会沦为野蛮人。班波代表了博爱、亲近自然、无拘无束的理想，是道义上正确的一方。坦普尔法官象征着法律和文明，是势不可挡的一方。他们一起把西部荒野建成了文明的地方，因而标题《拓荒者》使用了复数形式。

3.2 考研真题与典型题详解

I. Fill in the blanks.

1. "The Legend of Sleepy Hollow" was written by __________. (大连外国语学院 2008 研)
2. Ichabod Crane, the schoolmaster, is a character in the short story __________ collected in *The*

Sketch Book. （首师大2008研）

3. The Romantic period in the American literary history covers the time between the end of the __________ century to the outbreak of the __________. It started with the publication of Irving's __________ and ended with Whitman's __________. This period is also called __________.
4. In the early nineteenth century, Washington Irving wrote __________ which became the first work by an American writer to win financial success on both sides of the Atlantic.
5. __________ was regarded as the first great prose stylist of American romanticism.
6. __________ was regarded as Father of the American short stories.
7. In Washington Irving's work __________ appeared the first modern short stories and the first great American juvenile literature.
8. Washington Irving also wrote two biographies, one is *The Life of Oliver Goldsmith*, and the other is __________.
9. James Fenimore Cooper's novel __________ was a rousing tale about espionage against the British during the Revolutionary War.
10. The central figure in the *Leatherstocking Tales* is __________, who goes by the various names of Leatherstocking, Deerslayer, Pathfinder and Hawkeye.
11. In *The Pioneers*, __________ represents the ideal American, living a virtuous and free life in God's world.
12. In 1823 James Fenimore Cooper wrote *The Pioneers*, the first of the five novels that make up __________. The remaining four books: *The last of Mohicans* (1826), *The Prairie* (1827), *The Pathfinder* (1840), and *The Deerslayer* (1841), continue the story of Natty Bumppo, one of the most famous characters in American fiction.

Ⅱ. Multiple Choice

1. Which is NOT a main focus of the American Romantic Movement in general?（大连外国语学院2008研）

   A. A return to eastern philosophy.

   B. A deep and spiritual respect for nature and natural laws.

   C. The introduction of self-salvation as opposed to salvation through Christ.

   D. A demand for progress and productivity.

2. Which ONE of the following concepts is related to the understanding of American Romanticism?（四川大学2007研）

   A. Survival of the fittest　　B. indifference of the universe

   C. exaltation of emotion over reason　　D. the human beast

3. Which of the following words does not describe the features of Irving's writings?（天津外国语学院2009研）

   A. decorum　　B. humor　　C. musicality　　D. imagination

4. The following selection is taken from __________. （大连外国语学院2007研）

   A. *The Cask of Amontillado*　　B. *The Legend of Sleepy Hollow*

   C. *A Rose for Emily*　　D. *Babylon Revisited*

In the bosom of one of those spacious coves which indent the eastern shore of the Hudson, at that broad expansion of the river denominated by the ancient Dutch navigators the Tappan Zee, and where they always prudently shortened sail and implored the protection of St. Nicholas when they crossed, there lies a small market town or rural port, which by some is called Greensburgh, but which is more generally and properly known by the name of Tarry Town.

5. Which ONE of the following is the author of *The Leather-Stocking Tales*?（四川大学 2008 研）

A. Henry David Thoreau　　B. Washington Irving

C. Edgar Allan Poe　　D. James Fennimore Cooper

6. James Fennimore Cooper's novel ________ is the first to reveal the west and Native Americans' life in a passionate way.（北二外 2007 研）

A. *Go Down, Moses*　　B. *The Last of the Mohicans*

C. *Winesburg, Ohio*　　D. *O, Pioneers!*

7. Washington Irving's social conservation and literary for the past is revealed, to some extent, in his famous story, ________.

A. "The Legend of Sleepy Hollow"　　B. "Rip Van Winkle"

C. "The Custom-House"　　D. "The Birthmark"

8. It is on his ________ that Washington Irving's fame mainly rested.

A. tales about America　　B. early poetry

C. childhood recollections　　D. sketches about his European tours

Ⅲ. Explain the following term.

1. American Romanticism（四川大学 2007 研；北航 2008 研）

Ⅳ. Read the following quotations and answer the questions.

Passage 1

"There was, as usual, a crowd of folk about the door, but none that Rip recollected. The very character of the people seemed changed. There was a busy, bustling, disputatious tome about it, instead of the accustomed phlegm and drowsy tranquility. He looked in vain for the sage Nicholoas Vedder…"

Questions:

(1) From which work is this passage taken?

(2) How do you understand this selection?

Passage 2

"From the listless repose of the place, and the peculiar character of it sin habitants, who are descendants from the original Dutch settlers, this sequestered glen has long been known by the name of SLEEPY HOLLOW, and its rustic lads are called the Sleepy Hollow Boys throughout all the neighboring country. Drowsy, dreamy influence seems to hang over the land, and to pervade the very atmosphere. Some say that the place was bewitched by a high German doctor, during the early days of the settlement; others, that an old Indian chief, the product or wizard of his tribe, held his powwows there before the country was discovered by Master Hendrick Hudson."

Questions:

(1) Who is the writer of this short story from which the passage is taken?

(2) What is the title of this short story?
(3) Give a definition of "short story".

Passage 3

"Arms and the clarion for the battle, but the song of thanksgiving to the victory!" answered the liberated David. "Friend," he added, thrusting forth his lean, delicate hand forwards Hawkeye, in kindness, while his eyes twinkled and grew moist, "I thank thee the hairs of my head still grow where they were first rooted by Providence for, though those of other men may be more glossy and curling, I have ever found mine own well suited to the brain they shelter. That I did not join myself to the battle, was less owing to disinclination, than to the bonds of the heathen. Valiant and skilful hast thou proved thyself in the conflict, and I hereby thank thee, before proceeding to discharge other and more important duties, because thou hast proved thyself well worthy of a Christian's praise."…

Questions:

(1) This novel was written by the first American novelist. What is his name?
(2) What is the name of the novel?
(3) The central figure in this novel appeared in this passage. It is __________.

V. Short answer questions

1. Make an introductory comment on James Fenimore Cooper's frontier saga *The Leather Stocking Tales*. (四川大学 2009 研)
2. In American literature history, the Romantic Period, during which many famous writers and their masterpieces came into being, played an important role. Washington Irving, Nathaniel Hawthorne and Walt Whitman, etc, all of whom are not ignored by us. According to their writings, discuss the features of American literature in this period.

VI. Essay questions

1. Discuss the fiction written by American High Romantics with specific reference to one work. (大连外国语学院 2007 研)
2. What is the relationship between American Romanticism and European Romanticism?
3. What's Washington Irving's main contribution to American Literature?
4. Analyze *The Legend of Sleepy Hollow*.

参考答案及解析

I. Fill in the blanks.

1. Washington Irving
   (短篇小说《睡谷的传说》("The Legend of Sleepy Hollow"), 是华盛顿·欧文的代表作《见闻札记》(*The Sketch Book*) 中最著名的两篇故事中的一篇。另一篇是《瑞普·凡·温克尔》("Rip Van Winkle"。)
2. "The Legend of Sleepy Hollow".
   (Ichabod Crane 是一个小学校长，欧文的《睡谷的传说》中的人物。)
3. 18th, Civil War; *The Sketch Book*; *Leaves of Grass*; the American Renaissance
   (美国浪漫主义时期开始于十八世纪末，到内战爆发为止，是美国文学史上最重要的时期。华盛顿·欧文出版的《见闻札记》标志着美国浪漫主义文学的开端，惠特曼的《草叶集》是浪漫主义时期文学的压卷之作。浪漫主义时期的文学是美国文学的繁荣时期，所以也称为"美国的文艺复兴"。）

4. *The Sketch Book*

（美国作家华盛顿·欧文被英国作家萨克雷称为"新世界文坛送往旧世界的第一使节"。《见闻札记》被当时的英国评论界誉为"美国富有想象力的第一部真正杰作"，它"组成了它所属的那个民族文学的新时代"。）

5. Washington Irving

（华盛顿·欧文是美国著名作家，他被誉为美国第一位浪漫主义散文文体作家。）

6. Washington Irving

（华盛顿·欧文被誉为"美国短篇小说之父"。）

7. *The Sketch Book*

（华盛顿·欧文的作品《见闻札记》（*The Sketch Book*）是现代文学史上第一部短篇小说集和美国第一部伟大的青少年文学读物。）

8. *Life of Washington*

（华盛顿·欧文撰写了两部传记：《哥德史密斯传》（*The Life of Oliver Goldsmith*）和《华盛顿传》（*Life of Washington*）。）

9. *The Spy*

（詹姆斯·费尼莫尔·库柏（James Fenimore Cooper）认为他的小说《间谍》（*The Spy*）"应当是一部纯粹美国式的以爱国为主题的书"。）

10. Natty Bumppo

（《皮裹腿故事集》是美国作家詹姆斯·费尼莫尔·库柏的系列小说。该故事集中的主要人物是 Natty Bumppo。在不同的故事中他有皮裹腿、杀鹿者、探路人及鹰眼等别名。）

11. Natty Bumppo

（在詹姆斯·费尼莫尔·库柏的小说《拓荒者》（*The Pioneers*）中，主人公 Natty Bumppo 正直善良，向往无拘无束的生活，是理想美国人的化身。）

12. *The Leatherstocking Tales*

（《皮裹腿故事集》包括《拓荒者》《最后的莫西干人》《草原》《探路者》和《猎鹿人》五部小说。）

Ⅱ. Multiple Choice

1. D 美国的浪漫主义运动崇尚大自然的力量，提倡自我拯救。其中以爱默生为代表的一批作家，吸收了东方哲学的智慧，融合了欧洲神秘先验论思想，形成了超验主义。

2. C 浪漫主义把情感置于理性之上。其余三个选项都是达尔文主义的观点。

3. C 华盛顿·欧文的作品具有幽默风趣的笔调，活跃而优雅的写作风格，富于幻想的浪漫色彩。

4. B 题中片段选自美国著名小说家 Washington Irving《睡谷的传说》（"The Legend of Sleepy Hollow"）。此段文章交代了故事的背景。文章大意为：哈德逊河东岸有很多宽阔的小河湾，在一个河湾的深处，很久之前荷兰航海家们曾占领水域，并在那里小心地靠岸，寻求圣尼古拉斯的保护。现在，那里有个小镇，或者农村的港口，有些人叫它格林斯堡，而更多人叫它泰瑞镇。

5. D James Fenimore Cooper(库柏)，美国早期作家，*The Leather-Stocking Tales*(《皮裹腿故事集》)是他的经典之作。

6. B 《最后的莫西干人》是库柏《皮裹腿故事集》五部曲之一，描写的是美国西部边疆和美洲土著印第安人的生活。选项A《去吧，摩西》的作者是 William Faulkner(威廉·福克纳)；选项C《小城畸人》的作者是 Sherwood Anderson(舍伍德·安德森)；选项D的作者是女作家 Willa Cather(薇拉·凯瑟)。

7. B 《瑞普·凡·温克尔》在一定程度上反映了欧文的保守思想。

8. A 欧文的声望主要体现在关于美国的小说上。

Ⅲ. Explain the following term.

1. American Romanticism: American Romanticism is the name sometimes given to a flourishing of distinctively American literature in the period form the end of the 18th century throngh the outbreak of the Civil War. American Romanticism is represented by works of Ralph Waldo Emerson, H. D. Thoreau, Nathaniel Hawthorne, Herman Melville, and Walt Whitman. They share certain general characteristics: moral enthusiasm, faith in individualism and intuition.

Ⅳ. Read the following quotations and answer the questions.

Passage 1

(1) This passage is taken from Washington Irving's "Rip Van Winkle".

(2) It shows the change that Rip sees as he enters the village after the 20-year sleep and the destructive effect of the change. It also reveals, to some extent, the conservative attitude of its author.

Passage 2

(1) Washington Irving

(2) "The Legend of Sleepy Hollow"

(3) The short story in a short prose novel can usually be read in one sitting. It generally contains the six elements of a novel: characterization, setting, theme, plot, point of view, and style.

Passage 3

(1) James Fenimore Cooper

(2) *The Last of the Mohicans*

(3) Hawkeye

V. Short answer questions

1. *The Leather Stocking Tales* is a series of novels by American writer James Fenimore Cooper. Natty Bumppo is the protagonist of the series. Although his parents were white, he grew up with the Indians and became an almost fearless warrior, proficient with many weapons, one of which was the long gun. Out of respect for his forest home and its inhabitants, he hunts only what he needs to survive. He lives by the rule, "One shot, one kill." when he has to fire. He and his Mohican "brother" Chingachgook championed goodness and tried to stop the constant conflict between the Mohicans and Hurons. He is known as "Deerslayer" in *The Deerslayer*, "Hawkeye" and "La Longue Carabine" in *The Last of the Mohicans*, "Pathfinder" in *The Pathfinder*, "Leatherstocking" in *The Pioneers*, and "the trapper" in *The Prairie*. These novels tell the major events in the life of Natty Bumppo (1740 – 1806).

2. The whole nation had a strong sense of optimism and the mood of "feeling good", giving birth to the spectacular outburst of romantic feelings. The English counterpart, especially the cultural heritage, exerted a stimulating impact on the writings of the young nation. Taking foreign influence into consideration, the great works of American writers still carried typically American romanticist color. The young nation had brought forth its own Philosophy, Transcendentalism, stressing man's capacity of knowing truth intuitively, and of attaining knowledge transcending the reach of the senses.

Ⅵ. Essay questions

1. American Romanticism was influenced by its English and European counterparts since it was originated from those places. But when it came to the high romanticism, American Romanticism exhibited from the outset distinct features of its own.

The first was its puritan heritage and rejection of Puritanism. It was more moralizing, edifying more than mere entertainment. Sex and love, for example, are subjects American authors were particularly carefully approaching. The way in which Hawthorne wrote *The Scarlet Letter* suggests that American Romanticism adapted itself to American Puritanism. It takes eloquently about the effect of the adultery on the people rather than the sin itself. Hester Prynne uses her whole life to get out of the shadow of the sin while Dimmesdale dies at last under the pressure of puritan. Hawthorne criticizes the Puritanism, keeping skeptical of religion authority.

The second feature of fiction of High Romantics is its emphasis on psychological description. *The Scarlet Letter* employs many psychological activities to reveal directly the thoughts of characters and the psychological conflicts to develop the theme.

The third feature is that it explores the dark side of society and human nature. At that time, the society was under the control of Puritanism and human nature was tortured. Whereas Hester is able to reconstruct her life and win a moral victory, Dimmesdale undergoes the tragic experience of physical and spiritual disintegration. Though the scarlet letter refers to Adultery, Angel, Able, A may also represent Adamic, or prehistoric, an archetypal vice suggestive of "original sin". This reveals another feature of this period fiction, which is symbolism. Besides, there are other symbols like the Meteor, Pearl, and the Rosebush Next to the Prison Door.

2. American Romanticism had much in common with European Romanticism: In response to the Enlightenment and its emphasis on reason, Romanticism emphasized the emotional, imaginative, and subjective approaches.

European, and especially British, literary masters inspired the emergence of New World writers. American Romanticism also arose from a common cultural heritage, and was to some extent a continuation and development of English Romanticism.

Despite the great European influence, the typical works of American Romanticism have a strong American character. American writers illustrate their unique personalities in their works, growing up in the land of their homeland. The content of the American Romantic period was original and diverse. American writers also developed a number of new forms of fiction or poetry.

They also placed an increasing emphasis on the free expression of emotions and displayed an increasing attention to the psychic states of their characters. The strong tendency to exalt the individual and common man was another focus of the movement.

3. Washington Irving's contribution to American literature is unique in more ways than one. He did a number of things which have been regarded as the first of their kind in America.

   He was the first American writer of imaginative literature to gain international fame. When he returned home in 1832, he was acclaimed as the one American author whom people in Europe knew about, and the Americans took as a sign that American literature was emerging as an independent entity. To say that he was father of American literature is not much exaggeration.

   The short story as a genre in American literature probably began with Irving's *The Sketch Book*, a collection of essays, sketches, and tales, of which the most famous and frequently anthologized are "Rip Van Winkle" and "The Legend of Sleepy Hollow". The book touched the American imagination and foreshadowed the coming of Hawthorne, Melville, and Poe, in whose hands the short story attained a degree of perfection as a literary tradition. It also marked the beginning of American Romanticism. The Gothic, the supernatural, and the longing for the good old days which some of its pieces clearly exhibit, are Romantic enough in subject if not exactly in style, for Irving wrote in the neoclassical tradition of Joseph Addison and Oliver Goldsmith. Looking at a picture of Irving surrounded by his nieces, one does sometimes think of the old man, benign and pleasant and refined, as the uncle of American authors.

4. Washington Irving's short story *The Legend of Sleepy Hollow* is about the memorable event of an apparently headless horseman throwing his head at his rival in love, and the memorable character of Ichabod Crane with his mixture of shrewdness, credulity, self-assertiveness and cowardice.

   The creation of archetypes is a particularly subtle feat of Irving's consummate craftsmanship. We may see in Ichabod Crane a precocious, effete New Englander, shrewd, commercial, a city-slicker, who is rather an interloper, a somewhat destructive force, and who comes along to swindle the villagers. His book learning turns on him, and he is driven away from where he does not belong, so that the serene village remains permanently good and happy. Brom Bones, on the other hand, is of a Huck Finn-type of country bumpkin, rough, vigorous, boisterous but inwardly very good, a frontier type put out there to shift for himself. Thus the rivalry in love between Ichabod and Brom, viewed in this way, suddenly assumes the dimensions of two ethical groups locked in a kind of historic contest.

   As to the style of the piece, it represents Irving at his best. The association between a certain local and the inward movement of a character, the emotional loading of almost every line of the story, their effect on the five senses of the reader whose attention is so fully engaged and who feels so much involved in what is happening—all these have placed this and other Irving stories among the best of American short stories.

第4章 新英格兰超验主义·爱默生·梭罗

4.1 复习笔记

In 1836, Emerson's *Nature* came out, which shocked the American cultural and intellectual circles like thunder on the ground. *Nature* pushed American Romanticism into a new stage, its climax-the stage of New England Transcendentalism.	1836年爱默生的《论自然》问世，它如平地惊雷，震撼了美国文化思想界。《论自然》把美国浪漫主义推向了一个新的阶段，即它的高潮阶段——英格兰超验主义阶段。
I. New England Transcendentalism	**I. 新英格兰超验主义**
In the 1830s and 1840s, some New Englanders were extremely dissatisfied with the prevailing materialism at the time, so they gathered together to form an informal Transcendentalist Club to discuss literature, philosophy, trends in national life and so on. They published the journal, *the Dial*, to express and promote their ideas to the world. There are about thirty men and a few women in the club, including Emerson, Thoreau, Bronson Alcott and Margaret Fuller, most of whom are teachers or priests, who criticized the creed of Boston businessmen and the coldness and rigidity of monotheistic rationalism. The term "Transcendentalism" is not a native American word; it is a Kantian philosophical vocabulary. As Emerson said, it means "any thought that belongs to the category of intuitive consciousness."	19世纪三、四十年代一些新英格兰人对当时盛行的物质主义极其不满，他们聚集在一起组成非正式的"超验主义俱乐部"，讨论文学、哲学及国家生活的形势趋向。他们出版专刊《日晷》向世人宣传他们的主张。俱乐部成员约有三十几个男性和几个女性。其中包括爱默生、梭罗、阿尔科特及富勒等人。他们多为教师或牧师。他们针砭波士顿商人的信条，抨击唯一神论理性主义的冷酷、古板。"超验主义"一词并非美国本土词汇，它是个康德哲学词汇。它如爱默生所说，表示"任何属于直觉意识范畴的思想"。
1. Major features	**1. 主要特征**
(1) Transcendentalists emphasized the spirit, or the Oversoul, and believed that this was the most important factor of existence in the universe. The Oversoul was an omnipresent, omnipresent force that promoted good and suppressed evil, and was the foundation of all things and the belonging of all things. This is a totally new worldview. It opposed the 18th century mechanical concept of the universe, the development of America in the direction of mechanization and capitalism, and the trend of Americans indulging in getting rich and neglecting their spiritual life.	(1) 超验主义者强调精神，或超灵，认为这是宇宙间至为重要的存在因素。超灵是一种无所不容、无所不在、扬善抑恶的力量，是万物之本、万物之所属。这是一种新的世界观。它反对18世纪的机械宇宙观，反对美国朝着机械化、资本主义化的方向发展，反对美国人沉湎于发财致富而忽略精神生活的世风
(2) Transcendentalists emphasize the importance of the individual. They believed that the individual was the most important	(2) 超验主义者强调个人的重要性。他们认为个人是社会的最重

component of society. The ideal person was a self-reliant man. The individual soul communicated with the Oversoul and thus possessed divinity. This new view of individuals and their importance reflected new evaluations of people. It opposed the complete degeneration of Calvinism and the dehumanization of the rising stage of capitalism.

(3) Transcendentalists looked at nature from a new perspective, believing that the natural world was a symbol of the Oversoul or God. Everything in nature was symbolic, and the external world was the embodiment of the spiritual world. This in turn strengthened the tradition of symbolism in American literature.

2. Sources

New England Transcendentalism was the product of the fusion of various foreign and domestic elements.

(1) Idealistic philosophy of Germany and France.

(2) Oriental mysticism.

(3) American Puritanism.

Ⅱ. Ralph Waldo Emerson (1803 –1882)

1. Life

Emerson was born in the home of a prominent pastor in New England. The family was in decline when he was young. He used to study at Harvard University. Later, he accepted the doctrine of Unitarianism and became a Unitarian minister in the Second Church of Boston. But soon, he resigned because he disagrees with some of the traditional rituals of Unitarianism. He was influenced by European Romanticism when travelling to Europe. After returning to America, he formed an informal "Transcendentalism Club" with friends and edited the Transcendentalist journal, *the Dial*, to spread Transcendentalism. He was the most outstanding spokesperson of New England Transcendentalism. He was considered to be one of the top two to three writers in the United States during his lifetime, and the most influential philosopher and writer of his time. He was the prophet of that era, and had different degrees of influence on writers such as Thoreau, Whitman, and Hawthorne.

2. Analysis of major works

◆*Nature*

(1) Published in 1836, Nature is usually considered as the Bible of New England Transcendentalism.

要的组成因素。理想的人是自立自强的人。个人灵魂与上帝交流，因而具有神性。这种关于人及其重要性的新观点反映出对人的新评价。它反对加尔文教义中的彻底的堕落，反对资本主义上升阶段的非人性化现象。

(3) 超验主义者以全新的目光看待自然，认为自然界是超灵或上帝的象征。自然界万物皆具有象征性，外部世界是精神世界的体现。这又加强了美国文学中象征主义的传统。

2. 理论来源

新英格兰超验主义是国外和国内各种因素融合的产物。

(1) 法国和德国的唯心主义。

(2) 东方神秘主义。

(3) 美国清教主义。

Ⅱ. 拉尔夫·瓦尔多·爱默生

1. 生平

爱默生生于新英格兰一个显赫牧师之家。幼年时家道中落。他曾在哈佛大学就读。后接受唯一教教义，并成为波士顿第二礼拜堂唯一教牧师。不久，因对该教一些古板仪式持异议而辞职。赴欧洲旅行时受到欧洲浪漫主义的影响。回国后跟朋友结成非正式的"超验主义俱乐部"，编辑超验主义专刊《日晷》，传播超验主义思想。他是新英格兰超验主义最杰出的代言人。他生前被认为是美国最顶尖的两到三个作家之一，是同时代最富影响力的哲学家和文豪。他是那个时代的先知，对梭罗、惠特曼、霍桑等作家产生了不同程度的影响。

2. 主要作品分析

◆《论自然》

(1)《论自然》发表于 1836 年，它通常被认为是新英格兰超验主义的圣经。

(2) In this book, Emerson emphasizes that the Oversoul is everywhere. He believes that the universe consists of nature and human souls, and nature is the purest and most innocent, which can sanctify people's morality. He also advocates that people should directly experience the ubiquitous God in nature.	(2) 在这本书中，爱默生强调超灵无处不在。他认为宇宙由自然和人类灵魂组成。自然是最纯洁无瑕的。能够圣化人的心灵。倡导人们直接体验自然界无处不在的上帝。
(3) The divine God exists in the soul of man, so man is also divine. The divinity of man became a favorite topic of Emerson's speech and writing. Everyone should think that the world belongs to him, and that the world exists only for him. The idea Emerson wanted to convey was self-reliance, which, at a deeper level, was a reflection of the rising spirit of that times.	(3) 神圣的上帝存在于人的灵魂之中，因而人也是神圣的。人的神性成为爱默生演讲和写作挚爱的话题。每个人都应认为世界是属于他的，世界只为他而存在。爱默生要传达的思想是“自助”。在深层次上讲，“自助”是时代上升精神的反映。
(4) Nature is a symbol of God, and it coordinates the relationship between man and God. Emerson's view of nature implicates that the world around man is symbolic.	(4) 自然是上帝的象征，他协调人和上帝的关系。爱默生关于自然的观点表明，人类周遭的世界具有象征意义。
◆"*The American Scholar*"	◆《美国学者》
The American Scholar has been hailed as "America's Declaration of Intellectual Independence." Emerson believed that Americans should stop imitating and importing foreign literature, and instead portray the United States here and now. He called on American writers to create and portray the American land in a way unique to Americans. The importance of Emerson in the history of American cultural thought is that he embodies the ascendant America's desire to have its own unique identity and is willing to work hard for it.	《美国学者》被誉为“美国思想文化领域的独立宣言”。 爱默生认为美国人应停止模仿和引进外国文学，转而描绘此时此地的美国。他号召美国作家以美国人独有的方式进行创作、描绘美国大地。爱默生在美国文化思想史上的重要性在于他体现了处于上升阶段的美国渴望拥有自己独有的身份并愿为之努力奋斗。
Ⅲ. Henry David Thoreau (1817 –1862)	**Ⅲ. 亨利·大卫·梭罗**
1. Life	**1. 生平**
Thoreau was a famous New England Transcendentalist. He was a good friend of Emerson, 14 years younger than Emerson. He was born in Concord, Massachusetts, entering Harvard University at the age of 17. After graduating from Harvard, he became friends with Emerson and began to accept Emerson's ideas. In 1845 he moved into a small wooden house on the shore of Walden Pond and lived a simple and reclusive life for more than two years. During this period, he went to nearby villages from time to time, and once he was detained overnight for refusing to pay taxes. This inspired him to write the famous political essay, "Civil Disobedience". After returning to Concord, Thoreau wrote the famous *Walden* based on the more than two years of life experience in Walden Pond.	梭罗是著名的新英格兰超验主义者。他是爱默生的好友，比爱默生小14岁。他出生于马萨诸塞州的康科德镇。17岁时进入哈佛大学学习。大学毕业后跟爱默生成为好友并开始接受了爱默生的思想。1845年他搬进瓦尔登湖畔的一座小木屋，过了两年多简朴的隐居生活。这期间他不时去附近的村子，一次他因拒绝交税而被拘留了一夜。这激发他写成了著名的政论文《论公民的不服从权利》。回到康科德后，梭罗根据两年多在瓦尔登湖的生活经历写成了著名的《瓦尔登湖》。

In the history of American literature, there were three great 19th-century writers who were left out in the cold and only won fame in the 20th century, namely Thoreau, Herman Melville and Emily Dickinson. Thoreau is now considered an important writer in the 19th century. Literary critics believe that his literary achievements are even higher than Emerson. His influence extends beyond America. In 1969, Thoreau's statue was placed in the Hall of Fame in New York.

在美国文学史上生前备受冷落、在20世纪才赢得盛名的19世纪伟大作家有三位，即梭罗、梅尔维尔和艾米丽·迪金森。现在梭罗被认为是19世纪重要的作家。文学评论家认为他的文学成就高于爱默生。他的影响力超出了美国。1969年，梭罗的塑像被放进了纽约的“名人馆”。

2. Major Works

A Week On the Concord and Merrimack Rivers

Walden

Civil Disobedience

A Plea for John Brown

2. 主要作品

《康科德和梅里马科河上的一周》

《瓦尔登湖》

《论公民的不服从权利》

《为约翰·布朗请命》

3. Analysis of major works

◆*Walden*

Thoreau's work *Walden* is a masterpiece of Transcendentalism. It faithfully recorded Thoreau's reflections when he communicated with nature alone. It shows that Thoreau not only accepted Emerson's Transcendentalism philosophy, but also further clarified the pantheistic characteristics of nature. Walden is all-encompassing and can be interpreted from many angles.

(1) It is a book about man, explaining what he is, what he should and must be. Thoreau believes that the most important thing in life is to be self-sufficient and strive to achieve spiritual perfection. Thoreau is hailed as the forerunner of individualism in the history of American literature.

(2) Thoreau lashed out at modern civilization in the book. He believes that modern civilized life makes people lose their humanity and put people in a spiritual predicament.

(3) In addition, the book shows that Thoreau wants the people of his country to get rid of complacency. He records how he reduce his personal needs as much as possible on Walden Pond. He believes that spiritual wealth is true wealth. Human spirit may not help people to become prosperous, but it helps people to make real progress in the process of self-improvement.

(4) Thoreau went to live in the forest to experiment with a new way of life for himself and his compatriots. He was reborn when he came out of the forest, and his whole appearance was completely renewed. Regeneration is one of the important themes in *Walden* and determines the structure of the book.

3. 主要作品分析

◆《瓦尔登湖》

梭罗的代表作《瓦尔登湖》是一部超验主义巨作。它忠实地记录了梭罗独自与自然界交流时的反思。它表明梭罗不仅接受了爱默生的超验主义哲学，而且进一步亲身实践阐明自然界的泛神特性。《瓦尔登湖》包罗万象，可以从多种角度去解读。

（1）它是一本关于人的书，阐述人应该而且必须成为什么样的人。梭罗认为生活中最重要的事情是自给自足，努力实现精神上的完美。梭罗被誉为美国文学史上个人主义的先导。

（2）该书中梭罗猛烈抨击了现代文明。他认为现代文明生活使人失去了人性，将人置于精神上的困境。

（3）此外，该书表明梭罗希望国人摆脱自鸣得意、沾沾自喜的情绪。他记录了自己在瓦尔登湖上尽量将个人需求降到最低的情况。他认为精神上的富有才是真正的富有。人的精神或许不能帮助人飞黄腾达，却有助于人在自我完善的过程中取得真正的进步。

（4）梭罗去森林居住目的是为自己和同胞们实验一种新的生活方式。他从林中出来时获得了重生，整个人面貌焕然一新。重生成为《瓦尔登湖》中重要的主题之一，并且决定了该书的结构框架。

4.2 考研真题与典型题详解

I. Fill in the blanks.

1. Ralph W. Emerson believes in the concept of the ________. It is the ________ within which every man's particular being is contained and made one with all other. (国际关系学院 2009 研)
2. Ralph Waldo Emerson wrote ________, which has been called "the Manifesto of American Transcendentalism," and ________, which has been regarded as America's "Declaration of Intellectual Independence." (南开大学 2007 研)
3. In 1836, a little book came out which made a tremendous impact on the intellectual life of America. It was entitled *Nature* by ________.
4. The great work ________ not only demonstrates Emersonian ideas of self-reliance but also develops and tests Emerson's own transcendental philosophy.
5. Ralph Waldo Emerson's truest disciple, the man who put into practice many of Emerson's theories, was ________.
6. A superb book entitled ________ came out of Henry David Thoreau's two year experiment at Walden Pond.
7. From Henry David Thoreau's Concord jail experience came his famous essay ________.

Ⅱ. Multiple Choice

1. American renaissance started from ________. (北二外 2009 研)

   A. Pragmatism　　B. utilitarian
   C. New England transcendentalism　　D. the age of Realism

2. Which one of the following statements is applicable to the understanding of Transcendentalism? (四川大学 2008 研)

   A. It is strongly influenced by social Darwinism.
   B. Belief in individualism, independence of mind, and self-reliance.
   C. Man has no free-will.
   D. It holds that determinism governs everything.

3. Ralph Waldo Emerson's ________ is regarded as the "Declaration of Intellectual Independence". (北二外 2008 研; 首师大 2009 研)

   A. *Nature*　　B. *The Conduct of Life*
   C. *Representative Men*　　D. "The American Scholar"

4. Point out the work that was written by Henry David Thoreau. ________ (四川大学 2009 研)

   A. *The Fall of the House of Usher*　　B. *The Rise of Silas Lapham*
   C. *Walden*　　D. "The Legend of Sleepy Hollow"

5. "The universe is composed of Nature and the soul... Spirit is present every where". This is the voice of the book *Nature* written by Emerson, which pushed American Romanticism into a new phase, the phase of New England ________.

   A. Romanticism　　B. Transcendentalism
   C. Naturalism　　D. Symbolism

6. There is a good reason to state that New England Transcendentalism was actually __________ on the Puritan soil.

   A. Romanticism B. Puritanism C. Mysticism D. Unitarianism

7. Transcendentalists recognized __________ as the "highest power of the soul".

   A. intuition B. logic

   C. data of the senses D. thinking

8. Transcendentalist doctrines found their greatest literary advocates in __________ and Henry David Thoreau.

   A. Thomas Jefferson B. Ralph Waldo Emerson

   C. Philip Freneau D. Oversoul

Ⅲ. Explain the following terms.

1. Transcendentalism（北二外 2010 研；北航 2010 研；南开大学 2008 研）
2. Ralph Waldo Emerson（北航 2007 研）
3. Oversoul（武汉大学 2008 年）
4. self-reliance（北二外 2009 研）

Ⅳ. Read the following quotations and answer the questions.

Passage 1

To go into solitude, a man needs to retire as much from his chamber as from society. I am not solitary whilst I read and write, though nobody is with me. But if a man would be alone, let him look at the stars. The rays that come from those heavenly worlds, will separate between him and vulgar things. One might think the atmosphere was made transparent with this design, to give man, in the heavenly bodies, the perpetual presence of the sublime. Seen in the streets of cities, how great they are! If the stars should appear one night in a thousand years, how would men believe and adore; and preserve for many generations the remembrance of the city of God which had been shown! But every night come out these preachers of beauty, and light the universe with their admonishing smile.

Questions:

(1) This paragraph is taken from a famous essay. What is the name of the essay?

(2) Who is the author?

(3) What does the author say would happen if the stars appeared one night in a thousand years?

(4) Give a peculiar term to cover the author's belief.

Passage 2

Standing on the bare ground—my head bathed by the blithe air and uplifted in to infinite space—all mean egotism vanishes. I become a transparent eyeball; I am nothing; I see all; the currents of the Universal Being circulate through me; I am part or particle of God.

Questions:

(1) Which work is this selection taken from?

(2) How do you understand the philosophical ideas in these words?

Passage 3

There's a time in every man's education when he arrives at the conviction that envy is ignorance; that imitation is suicide; that he must take himself for better, for worse, as his portion... Trust thyself; every heart vibrates to that iron string.

Whoso would be a man must be a nonconformist.

Questions:

(1) This selection is selected from an essay. What is the title of that?

(2) Who is the author of the essay?

(3) According to the selection, what do you think the author believes in?

V. Short answer questions

1. Which of Emerson's works is called "America's intellectual Declaration of independence"?(国际关系学院 2007 研)
2. Emerson states: "Let a man then know his worth, and keep things under his feet." This indicates the author's belief in real virtue. Please make comments on this line.(南京大学 2009 研)
3. What is the major thematic concern of *Walden*?(国际关系学院 2007 研)

Ⅵ. Essay question

1. Analyze Ralph Waldo Emerson's theory of Transcendentalism with the analysis of Nature.

参考答案及解析

I. Fill in the blanks.

1. Transcendentalism; Oversoul

(爱默生信奉超验主义，在他看来，超灵为人所有共有，每个人的思想存在于超灵之中，人能以直觉官能与之交融。)

2. *Nature*; "The American Scholar"

(爱默生的《论自然》被称为"美国超验主义的宣言"，其《美国学者》则被誉为美国知识分子的独立宣言。)

3. Ralph Waldo Emerson

(拉尔夫·沃尔多·爱默生(Ralph Waldo Emerson, 1803 - 1882)美国散文作家、思想家、诗人。1836 年出版处女作《论自然》(*Nature*)。《论自然》的发表为美国思想界吹来一股清风，一扫机械主义自然观的乌烟瘴气。)

4. *Walden*

(梭罗的代表作《瓦尔登湖》表明梭罗不仅接受了爱默生的超然主义哲学，而且进一步亲身实践阐明自然界的泛神特性。)

5. Henry David Thoreau

(亨利·戴维·梭罗(Henry David Thoreau)是美国作家、哲学家，他最著名的作品为著名散文集《瓦尔登湖》和论文《论公民的不服从权利》。梭罗是爱默生最忠实的追随者并且将爱默生的许多理论付诸了实践。)

6. *Walden*

(《瓦尔登湖》(*Walden*)出版于 1854 年，梭罗在书中详尽地描述了他在瓦尔登湖湖畔一片再生林中度过两年零两月的生活以及期间他的许多思考。)

7. *Civil Disobedience*

(在瓦尔登湖生活期间，梭罗因为反对黑奴制拒交“人头税”而被捕入狱。友人替他代交了税款保其出狱，但这一亲身体验却激发他写成了著名的政论《抵制国民政府》(*Resistance to Civil Government*，后改名为《论公民的不服从权利》(*Civil Disobedience*)。)

Ⅱ. Multiple Choice

1. C　美国的文艺复兴，又称为新英格兰文艺复兴，源于新英格兰超验主义。
2. B　超验主义肯定人的神圣性，主张人能超越感觉和理性而直接认识真理，“相信你自己”，是超验主义者的座右铭。
3. D　“The American Scholar”(《论美国学者》)是爱默生在哈佛大学的一篇演讲词，爱默生在演说中主张建立独立的民族文化与文学，吹起了美国文化独立的号角。
4. C　梭罗是美国超验主义作家之一，其代表作是 *Walden*(《瓦尔登湖》)。选项 A《厄舍古屋的倒塌》是 Edgar Allan Poe(爱伦·坡)的作品；选项 B《塞拉斯·拉帕姆的发迹》是 William Dean Howells(豪威尔斯)的小说；选项 D《睡谷的传说》的作者是 Washington Irving(华盛顿·欧文)。
5. B　《论自然》(*Nature*)是爱默生的第 1 部重要哲学著作，最初发表于 1836 年。它集超验主义思想之大成，有新英格兰超验主义宣言的美称。《论自然》中强调精神，或超灵，认为这是宇宙至为重要的存在因素。超灵是一种无所不容、无所不在、扬善抑恶的力量，是万物之本、万物之所属，它存在于人和自然界内。
6. A　新英格兰超验主义深受清教思想的影响，由于清教主义自身积极性与消极性共存的复杂性，超验主义者对清教的态度也是复杂的。认同、接受与怀疑、超越共存，他们一方面肯定了清教思想与价值，另一方面又批判了清教社会对人的精神的负面影响。
7. A　超验主义者将直觉作为“心灵最伟大的力量”。
8. B　美国超验主义(American Transcendentalism)是美国的一个重要思潮，它兴起于十九世纪三十年代的新英格兰地区。它是与拉尔夫·沃尔多·爱默生以及梭罗相关的一种文学和哲学运动，宣称存在一种理想的精神实体，超越于经验和科学之处，通过直觉得以把握。

Ⅲ. Explain the following terms.

1. Transcendentalism: Transcendentalism is a New England movement, which flourished from about 1835 to 1860. It had its roots in romanticism and in post-Kantian idealism by which Coleridge was influenced. It had a considerable influence on American art and literature. Basically religious, it emphasized the role and importance of the individual conscience, and the value of intuition in matters of moral guidance and inspiration. The actual term was coined by opponents of the movement, but accepted by its members. The group of people was also social reformers. Some of the members, besides Emerson, were famous, including Bronson Alcott, Henry David Thoreau and Nathaniel Hawthorne.

2. Ralph Waldo Emerson: Ralph Waldo Emerson (1803 – 1882) was an American essayist, philosopher, and poet, best remembered for leading the Transcendentalist movement of the mid 19th century. He gradually moved away from the religious and social beliefs of his contemporaries, formulating and expressing the philosophy of Transcendentalism in his 1836 essay, *Nature*. As a result of this ground breaking work, he gave a speech entitled “The American Scholar” in 1837, which Oliver Wendell Holmes, Sr. considered to be America's “Intellectual Declaration of Inde-

pendence".

3. Oversoul: "The Oversoul" is an essay by Ralph Waldo Emerson, first published in 1841. For Emerson, the term denotes a supreme underlying unity which transcends duality or plurality, much in keeping with the philosophy of Advaita Vedanta. Over-soul has more recently come to be used by Eastern philosophers such as Meher Baba and others as the closest English language equivalent of the Vedic concept of Paramatman. The term is used frequently in discussion of Eastern metaphysics and has also entered western vernacular. In this context, the term "Over-soul" is understood as the collective indivisible Soul, of which all individual souls or identities are included.
4. self-reliance: "Self-Reliance" is an essay written by American Transcendentalist philosopher and essayist, Ralph Waldo Emerson. It contains the most solid statement of one of Emerson's repeating themes, the need for each individual to avoid conformity and false consistency, and follow his or her own instincts and ideas. Emerson's ideas are considered a reaction as a commercial identity; he calls for a return to individual identity.

Ⅳ. Read the following quotations and answer the questions.

Passage 1

(1) *Nature*

(2) Ralph Waldo Emerson

(3) Then, the men cannot believe and adore the God, cannot preserve the remembrance of the city of God which had been shown.

(4) Transcendentalism

Passage 2

(1) *Nature*

(2) He regards nature as the purest, and the most sanctifying moral influence on man, and advocates a direct intuition of a spiritual and immanent God in nature. In this connection, Emerson's emotional experiences are exemplary in more than one ways. Now this is a moment of "conversation" when one feels completely merged with the outside world, when one has completely sunk into nature and become one with it, and when the soul has gone beyond the physical limits of the body to share the omniscience of the Oversoul. In a word, the soul has completely transcended the limits of individuality and become part of the Oversoul. Emerson sees spirit pervading everywhere, not only in the soul of man, but behind nature, throughout nature.

Passage 3

(1) "Self-Reliance"

(2) Ralph Waldo Emerson

(3) He believed above all the individualism, independence of mind, and self-reliance.

V. Short answer questions

1. "The American Scholar" is called "America's intellectual Declaration of independence". It was a speech given by Ralph Waldo Emerson on August 31, 1837 to the Phi Beta Kappa Society in Harvard. He was invited to speak in recognition of his groundbreaking work *Nature*, published a

year earlier, in which he established a new way for America's fledgling society to regard the world. Sixty years after declaring independence, American culture was still heavily influenced by Europe, and Emerson, for possibly the first time in the country's history, provided a visionary philosophical framework for escaping "from under its iron lids" and building a new, distinctly American cultural identity.

2. This line is a representation of Emerson's transcendental ideas that the individual is the most important of all and an individual should know about his own worth and give full play to his worth. If man relies upon himself, cultivates himself and brings about the divine in himself, he can hopefully become better and more perfect. He tries to convince people that doing things based on their knowledge of their worth is a perfect way to develop and improve themselves. Each man should determine his own existence. Men should and could be self-reliant. Self-reliance is also an expression of the hope that man can become the best person he could hope to be.
3. *Walden* is informed by American Transcendentalism, a philosophy developed by Thoreau's friend and spiritual mentor Ralph Waldo Emerson. It emphasizes the importance of solitude, contemplation, and closeness to nature in transcending the "desperate" existence that, he argues, is the lot of most people. Thoreau was putting into practice the Transcendentalist belief that one can best transcend normality and experience the Ideal, or the Divine, through nature.

Ⅵ. Essay question

1. Emerson was the leading New England Transcendentalist. His *Nature* is usually regarded as the Bible of New England Transcendentalism. In *Nature* Emerson affected a most articulate synthesis of the Transcendentalist views.

    One major element of his philosophy is his firm belief in the transcendence of the "Over-soul". He states in *Nature* "the universe is composed of Nature and the Soul." He sees the world as phenomenal, and emphasizes the need for idealism, for idealism sees the world in God. He regards nature as the purest, and the most sanctifying moral influence on man, and advocates a direct intuition of a spiritual and immanent God in nature. In this connection, Emerson's emotional experiences are exemplary in more than one way.

    Emerson holds that the individual, not the crowd, is the most important of all. If man depends upon himself, cultivates himself, and brings out the divine in himself, he can hope to become better and even perfect. He tries to convince people that the possibilities for man to develop and improve himself are infinite. Men should and could be self-reliant.

    In Emerson's Transcendentalist eyes, nature was, to him as to his Puritan forebears, emblematic of God. It mediates between man and God, and its voice leads to higher truth. In a word, "Nature is the symbol of spirit." That is probably why he called his first philosophical work *Nature* rather than anything else. To him nature is a wholesome moral influence on man and his character. A natural implication of Emerson's view on nature is that the world around is symbolic.

第5章 霍桑·麦尔维尔

5.1 复习笔记

I. Nathaniel Hawthorne (1804－1864)

1. Life

Hawthorne was born in Salem, Massachusetts. Some of his ancestors were men of prominence in the Puritan theocracy. One of his ancestors was a colonial magistrate, notorious for his part in the persecution of the Quakers, and another was a judge at the Salem Witchcraft Trial in 1692. As his family fortune declined, Hawthorn was intensely conscious of the wrongdoing of his ancestors and this evil nature of humanity.

2. Ideas

(1) Hawthorne is seen as "a black romantic" writing the irrational, the demonic and the gothic. Viewing evil as the inherent human nature, he was haunted by a sense of sin and evil in life. In almost every book he wrote, Hawthorne discussed sin, evil and guilt.

(2) He rejected the Transcendentalists' transparent optimism about human nature and science. He holds a complicate attitude towards Puritanism.

(3) Tragedies occur as sin or evil can be passed from generation to generation. Hawthorne believed people can be educated when sin gets its punishment.

(4) He believed that romance was the predestined form of American narrative. He took a great interest in history and antiquity, which nourished his mind.

3. Writing style

(1) His literary style features ambiguity and romanticism in the American literature history. Hawthorne's ambiguity is a noticeable feature of his art. It can be seen in the narrative technique of multiple views employed in the last part of his masterpiece *The Scarlet Letter*.

I. 纳撒尼尔·霍桑

1. 生平

霍桑出生于马萨诸塞州的萨勒姆镇，他的一些祖先是17世纪新英格兰清教神权统治中的显赫人物。他的一位祖先是殖民地行政官，因参与迫害贵格党人而臭名昭著。另一位祖先则是1692年萨勒姆审巫案的法官。随着家族渐渐走向没落，霍桑强烈地意识到他的祖先曾犯下的错误和人性的邪恶。

2. 思想

(1)霍桑被视为"黑色浪漫主义"的代表，他的作品常触及非理性的和邪恶的力量，并带有哥特式风格。他认为罪恶是人性的一部分，一生被罪恶感萦绕。几乎他的每一部作品都涉及到了罪行、邪恶与悔恨。

(2)他反对超验主义者对人性和科学抱着纯粹乐观的态度，对清教持有两面性的复杂态度。

(3)原罪与恶行会代代相传并导致悲剧。但霍桑相信惩罚罪恶能对人们起到教化作用。

(4)他认为传奇是美国小说叙事的注定形式。他对历史和文物古迹有浓郁的兴趣，认为它们可以滋养思想的成长。

3. 写作风格

(1)霍桑的是一位思想矛盾、写作手法娴熟的美国浪漫主义作家。矛盾性是霍桑写作艺术的一个显著特征，在他的代表作《红字》的最后一部分作家运用了多重视角的写作技巧。

(2) Anatomist of "the interior of the heart", Hawthorne is an expert at psychoanalysis and exploration of human nature. His works are full of mental activities.	(2)他善于探究人的复杂心理，是人物内心的剖析师。他的作品有着丰富的心理活动描写。
(3) Hawthorne is a master of symbolism and allegory to reveal and attack the crushing blows of reality, which he took from the Puritan tradition and bequeathed to American literature in a revivified form. The symbol can be found everywhere in his writing, and especially in his masterpiece, *The Scarlet Letter*.	(3)寓言是对现实沉重的打击，象征主义则是揭露和抨击的武器。霍桑是象征主义和寓言大师，他继承了清教的传统并将此文学遗产传给美国文学界的后人。象征在他的作品中随处可见，尤其在他的代表作《红字》中找到确证。
4. Influence	**4. 影响**
Hawthorne exerts great influence on his successors. He was accorded due recognition by his contemporary James Russell Lowell in the latter's *A Fable for Critics*. He changed Herman Melville's original scheme for his *Moby Dick*. Hawthorne's fiction set examples for novel-writing practice of writers like William Dean Howells. In 20th century, William Faulkner and some Gothic novelists clearly show their indebtedness to him.	霍桑的影响可谓深远。詹姆斯·拉塞尔·洛威尔在《写给批评家的寓言》的末了给予他以应有的认可。他改变了赫尔曼·麦尔维尔《白鲸》中最初的创作意图。威廉·迪安·豪威尔斯学着用霍桑的作品作为他们小说创作的基准。在20世纪，威廉姆·福克纳和一些哥特式小说家对他也怀感恩之情。
5. Major works	**5. 主要作品**
The Scarlet Letter	《红字》
Twice-told Tales	《重讲一遍的故事》
Mosses from an Old Manse	《古屋青苔》
The House of the Seven Gables	《带有七个尖角阁的房子》
The Blithedale Romance	《福谷传奇》
The Marble Faun	《玉石雕像》
"Young Goodman Brown"	《年轻的小伙子布朗》
"The Minister's Black Veil"	《牧师的黑面纱》
"Rappacini's Daughter"	《拉普奇尼博士的女儿》
6. Analysis of his major works	**6. 主要作品分析**
◆*The Scarlet Letter*	◆《红字》
(1) Theme-Centering on the universality of guilt, the novel explores the complexities and ambiguities of man's choices. Hawthorne does not simply describe a story of love or sin, instead he focuses on the ethical and psychological effects or consequences of the sin on common people and main characters in particular. In this way, he presented to readers the tension between society and individuals. To Hawthorne, everybody is potentially a sinner, and great moral courage is necessary for the improvement of human nature. Meanwhile, Hawthorne reveals the double sides of Puritanism in portray of the priest Mr. Wilson. His accusation of Dimmesdale and Hester shows the persecution of Puritanism on people betraying its doctrine,	(1)主题——这部小说展现了罪恶的普遍性并探究了人们面临选择时的复杂与矛盾心理。霍桑无意去讲述一个关于爱情或罪恶的故事，而是关注于罪恶感带给普通人或一些主要角色在道德和心理方面的影响，从而展示了社会与个人之间的紧张状况。对于霍桑来讲，每个人都是潜在的罪人，道义上的勇气对人性的改善是必不可少的。同时，霍桑通过塑造牧师威尔森的形象揭示了清教的两面性。威尔森对丁梅斯戴尔和海斯特通奸的指责表现了清教对违反其教规的人的压迫，

while his charitable admonition on Pearl's behalf shows the benevolence of Puritanism.

(2) Symbolism-Hawthorne describes Hester as an aristocratic and sensitive young woman who faces her execution with dignity and courage. When she is released, she does not flee the community but supports herself and her child by doing fancy needlework, taking care of her child and helping the sick and the poor. She wins the admiration and love of her fellow villagers again. So, The Scarlet Letter is a hymn on the moral growth of the woman. The scarlet letter at first indicates Adultery, a token of shame. Then it changes to Able, symbolizing genuine sympathy and help she offers to her fellow villagers. In the end, A appearing in the sky signifies Angel.

而他的劝诫又是为了珠儿的未来考虑，体现出清教仁爱的一面。

(2)象征主义——霍桑将海斯特描绘成一位仪态高贵并善感的年轻女子，从容勇敢地面对判决。当她获释后，她并没有逃离社区。她带着孩子靠做精美的针线活自力更生，将爱奉献给自己的孩子并帮助老弱病残，重新赢得了同乡人的赞美和爱戴。因此，《红字》就是一曲歌颂海斯特道德成长的赞歌。红字最初是羞耻的象征，是"通奸"；然后因为她对同乡人真诚的同情和帮助使得红字的意义变为"能干"；最后，红字A出现在天空中，意味着"天使"。

Ⅱ. Herman Melville (1819 – 1891)

1. Life

Melville is an American novelist, short story writer, and poet of the American Renaissance period. He had a humble educational background and began to work after dropping school. There are three things that influenced his life: being a sailor, his marriage and his friendship with Hawthorne. His experiences and adventures on the sea furnished him with abundant material for fiction. Melville had to do hackwork for the money so that he could keep his wife's extravagant style. Melville saw from Hawthorne's works an unusual understanding of evil and blackness at the core of American life. Melville revised the original design of his masterpiece *Moby Dick* after the two great minds met, and the novel was rewritten into a world classic today.

2. Major works

Redburn
Typee
Omoo
Moby Dick
Mardi
White Jacket
Pierre
Billy Budd
The Confidence Man
Clarel

Ⅱ. 赫尔曼·麦尔维尔

1. 生平

麦尔维尔是美国文艺复兴时期著名的小说家和诗人。他接受的教育有限，辍学之后即开始工作。影响他一生的事件有三：出海，他的婚姻及其与霍桑的友谊。他在海上的经历和冒险为他的小说创作提供了丰富的素材。在婚姻生活上，麦尔维尔不得不创作劣质作品以满足妻子的奢华生活。麦尔维尔认为霍桑理解美国社会之恶与黑暗的视角不同寻常。当两个人相会后，麦尔维尔的代表作《白鲸》的创作意图发生了重大改变。改写后的作品成为当今世界的文学经典。

2. 主要作品

《莱德伯恩》
《泰比》
《奥姆》
《白鲸》
《玛地》
《白外套》
《皮埃尔》
《比利巴德》
《骗子》
《克拉勒尔》

3. Analysis of major work	3. 主要作品分析
◆*Moby Dick* (1) *Moby Dick* embodied Melville's bleak view of the American world in which he lived. For characters in the novel, they have no god or and purpose. The loss of faith and the sense of futility and meaninglessness which feature western modern life were expressed in Melville's *Moby Dick* so well that the twentieth century has found it both fascinating and great. (2) One of the major themes of this novel is isolation, which exists between man and man, man and society, and man and nature in the time where Melville lived. Melville also criticizes New England Transcendentalism of its emphasis on individualism and Oversoul. Another theme of this novel is "rejection and quest". (3) Symbolism is another feature of the novel. The voyage itself is a metaphor for "search and discovery" and indicates the desire for the ultimate truth of experience. Moby Dick is the most conspicuous symbol in the novel and scholars have many interpretations of him. It is viewed as a symbol of evil, goodness, or both. Its whiteness is a paradoxical color, signifying death and corruption as well as purity, innocence, and youth. It represents the unfathomable final mystery of the universe. (4) Melville manages to achieve the effect of ambiguity through employing the narrative technique of multiple view of his narratives. He tends to write periodic sentences. He has been praised for his rich rhythmical prose and poetic power.	◆《白鲸》 (1)《白鲸》代表了麦尔维尔对他所生活的时代悲凉的世界观。这里没有上帝也毫无意义可言。西方现代生活中信仰的丢失、无用感及无意义等淋漓尽致地表现在梅尔维尔的这部作品中，因此20世纪读者认为这部作品伟大且引人入胜。 (2) 该小说的主题是疏离。疏离存在于麦尔维尔生活时代的不同层面，如人与人之间，人与社会之间，以及人与自然之间。麦尔维尔同时对新英格兰超验主义过度强调个人主义和超灵进行了批判。该小说的另外一个主题是拒绝与追寻。 (3) 该小说富有象征意义。航行本身是探索和发现，寻求最终真相的隐喻。莫比·迪克是全书中最明显的象征，它可以有多种解释。有人认为它代表邪恶，有人认为它代表了善良，也有人认为它二者兼有。它的白色是自相矛盾的颜色，既代表了死亡和腐朽，又代表了纯洁、天真和青春。它代表宇宙深不可测的最终奥秘。 (4) 麦尔维尔通过运用多重视角的叙事技巧以实现文本的模糊性。他倾向于写掉尾句。他富有韵律的散文和文笔的诗意得到了大众的赞美。

5.2 考研真题与典型题详解

I. Fill in the blanks.

1. Pearl is a character in __________ written by __________.（大连外国语学院2007研）
2. As a reflection of Hester Prynne's moral development, the __________ symbolically undergoes a gradual and imperceptible change from "__________" to "able" and last to "angel".（天津外国语学院2008研）
3. Tashtego, Daggoo and Queequeg are the three main harpooners in the novel __________.（首师大2008研）
4. The way in which __________ wrote *The Scarlet Letter* suggests that American Romanticism adapted itself to American puritan moralism.

5. Hester Prynne is the heroine in Hawthorne's novel ________.
6. ________ is famous for writing stories about the sea and the islands of the Southern Pacific. In his masterpiece ________, he tells a story of a whaling voyage which is set a symbolic account of the conflict between man and his fate.
7. ________ is the narrator in *Moby Dick*.

Ⅱ. Multiple Choice

1. The most influential novelist in Romantic period is ________. (北二外 2009 研)
   A. Nathaniel Hawthorne B. Edgar Allan Poe
   C. Emily Dickinson D. Fennimore Cooper
2. In ________, Captain Ahab is obsessed with the revenge on a whale which sheared off his leg on a previous voyage, and his crazy chasing of it eventually brings death to all on board the whaler except Ishmael, who survives to tell the tale. (天津外国语学院 2007 研)
   A. *Typee* B. *White Jacket* C. *Moby Dick* D. *Billy Budd*
3. ________ is the most ambivalent writer in the American literary history.
   A. Nathaniel Hawthorne B. Walt Whitman
   C. Ralph Waldo Emerson D. Mark Twain
4. The finest example of Nathaniel Hawthorne's symbolism is the recreation of Puritan Boston in ________.
   A. *The Scarlet Letter* B. *Young Goodman Brown*
   C. *The Marble Faun* D. *The Ambitious Guest*
5. "There is evil in every human heart, which may remain latent, perhaps, through the whole life; but circumstances may rouse it to activity." The thought is reflected in ________.
   A. Nathaniel Hawthorne's *Young Goodman Brown*
   B. Mark Twain's *The Adventures of Huckleberry Finn*
   C. Walt Whitman's *Leaves of Grass*
   D. Herman Melville's *Moby Dick*
6. ________ is an appalling fictional version of Nathaniel Hawthorne's belief that "the wrong doing of one generation lives into the successive ones" and that evil will come out of evil though it may take many generations to happen.
   A. *The Marble Faun* B. *The House of Seven Gables*
   C. *The Blithedale Romance* D. *Young Goodman Brown*
7. Which is not Nathaniel Hawthorne's long novel?
   A. *The Marble Faun* B. *The Blithedale Romance*
   C. *The House of Seven Gables* D. *Dr. Heidegger's Experiment*
8. In *Moby Dick*, the voyage symbolizes ________.
   A. the microcosm of human society B. a search for truth
   C. the unknown world D. nature

Ⅲ. Read the following quotations and answer the questions.

Passage 1 (北航 2009 研)

Young Goodman Brown came forth at sunset into the street at Salem village; but put his head back after crossing threshold, to exchange a parting kiss with his wife. And Faith, as the wife was aptly named, thrust her own pretty head into the street, letting the wind play with the pink ribbons on her cap while she called to Goodman Brown.

Questions:

(1) This passage is taken from "Young Goodman Brown", who is the author?

(2) What is the symbolic meaning of "pink ribbons"?

(3) What is a symbol in literature?

Passage 2 (北航 2007 研)

"Who is that man, Hester?" gasped Mr. Dimmesdale, overcome with terror. "I shiver at him! Dost thou know the man? I hate him, Hester!"

She remembered her oath, and was silent.

"I tell thee, my soul shivers at him," muttered the minister again. "Who is he? Who is he? Canst thou do nothing for me? I have a nameless horror of the man."

"Minister," said little Pearl. "I can tell thee who he is!"

"Quickly, then, child!" said the minister, bending his ear close to her lips. "Quickly! —and as low as thou canst whisper."

Pearl mumbled something into his ear, that sounded, indeed, like human language, but was only such gibberish as children may be heard amusing themselves with, by the hour together At all events, if it involved any secret information in regard to old Roger Chillingworth, it was in a tongue unknown to the erudite clergyman, and did but increase the bewilderment of his mind. The elvish child then laughed aloud.

"Dost thou mock me now?" said the minister.

"Thou wast not bold! —thou wast not true!" answered the child.

"Thou wouldst not promise to lake my hand, and mother's hand, tomorrow noontide!"

Questions:

(1) Which fiction is this excerpt from?

(2) Who is the author? What are the major artistic features of the author?

(3) Try to comment on the irony in this excerpt.

Passage 3

Hester Prynne's term of confinement was now at an end. Her prison-door was thrown open, and she came forth into sunshine which falling on all alike, seemed, to her sick and morbid heart, as if meant for no other purpose than to reveal the scarlet letter on her breast. Perhaps there was a more real torture in her first unattended footsteps from the threshold of the prison, than even in the procession and spectacle that have been described, where she was made the common infamy, at which all mankind was summoned to point its finger. Then, she was supported by an unnatural tension of the nerves, and by all the combative energy of her character, which enabled her to convert the scene into a kind of lurid triumph.

Questions:

(1) Which novel is this selection taken from?

(2) What is the name of the novelist?

(3) What do you think is the symbolic meaning of the scarlet letter on Hester's breast?

Ⅳ. Short answer questions

1. Give some different explanations of the symbolic meaning of "A" in *The Scarlet Letter* by Hawthorne. (人大2006研；南京大学2008研)
2. What does the white whale in *Moby Dick* symbolize? Why do you think so? (国际关系学院2007研)
3. *Moby-Dick* features several seemingly insane characters. How does insanity relate to this story? How do these characters contrast with one another? (北航2009研)
4. Discuss the allegory and symbolism in *Young Goodman Brown*.

Ⅴ. Essay questions

1. Due to his family background and his understanding of human nature, Nathaniel Hawthorne seems to be haunted by a sense of sin and evil in life. Explain his "black" vision in *The Scarlet Letter*. (天津外国语学院2007研)
2. Make a comment on Herman Melville's novel *Moby Dick*. (四川大学2008研)
3. *Moby Dick* by Herman Melville is one of the few books in American literature that has produced an exciting effect upon readers. Try to discuss the symbolism in the book.

参考答案及解析

Ⅰ. Fill in the blanks.

1. *The Scarlet Letter*, Nathaniel Hawthorne
   (Pearl是美国作家Nathaniel Hawthorne小说《红字》中的人物。)
2. scarlet letter A, adultery
   (霍桑的小说《红字》中海斯特·白兰经历了道德的洗礼，红字A的含义也逐渐由"通奸"转变为"能干"以至后来的"天使")
3. *Moby Dick*
   (这三个人是《莫比·狄克》里的捕鲸手。)
4. Nathaniel Hawthorne
   (纳撒尼尔·霍桑的小说《红字》暗示了美国浪漫主义遵循美国清教伦理道德。)
5. *The Scarlet Letter*
   (海斯特·白兰是霍桑小说《红字》中的女主人公。)
6. Herman Melville; *Moby Dick*
   (赫尔曼·麦尔维尔因写南太平洋的大海和岛屿的故事而著名。他的代表作《白鲸》讲述了以人与他自己命运的冲突作为象征的捕鲸航程。)
7. Ishmael
   (以实玛利是小说《白鲸》的叙述者。)

Ⅱ. Multiple Choice

1. A　美国十九世纪最有影响的浪漫主义小说家是霍桑。
2. C　Captain Ahab(亚哈船长)是梅尔维尔的小说*Moby Dick*(《白鲸》)里的主人公。
3. A　纳撒尼尔·霍桑是美国文学历史上最为矛盾的作家。
4. A　《红字》(*The Scarlet Letter*)是美国19世纪影响最大的浪漫主义小说家和心理小说家纳

撒尼尔·霍桑(Nathaniel Hawthorne)的代表作。该小说是成功运用象征手法的典范。

5. A　霍桑认为罪恶是人生来所带的标记。几乎他的每一部作品都涉及到了罪与恶。

6. B　《红字》(*The Scarlet Letter*)发表后获得巨大成功，霍桑继而创作了不少作品。其中《带有七个尖角阁的房子》(*The House of Seven Gables*)描写品钦家族的祖先(Colonel Pyncheon)谋财害命而使后代遭到报应的故事，说明财富是祸患，“一代人的罪孽要殃及子孙”；这部小说也反映了资本主义发展初期的血腥掠夺。

7. D　《黑德格医生的实验》(*Dr. Heidegger's Experiment*)是霍桑的中短篇小说。其余三项《玉石雕像》(*The Marble Faun*)，《福谷传奇》(*The Blithedale Romance*)，《带有七个尖角阁的房子》(*The House of Seven Gables*)都是霍桑的长篇小说。

8. B　小说《白鲸》中航程象征了对真理的探寻。

Ⅲ. Read the following quotations and answer the questions.

Passage 1

(1) Nathaniel Hawthorne

(2) In this story, “pink ribbons” appear three times. They symbolize the faith Brown holds toward God and human that religion and human are pure and upright.

(3) A symbol is a sign which suggests more than its literal meaning. In other words, a symbol is both literal and figurative. A symbol is a way of organizing the narrative and conveying thematic meanings. The best symbols are those that are believable in the lives of the characters and also fascinating as they allow readers to go beyond the literal level of the story. If the symbol is obscure or ambiguous, then the very obscurity and the ambiguity may also be part of the meaning of the story.

Passage 2

(1) This excerpt is from *The Scarlet Letter.*

(2) The author is Nathaniel Hawthorne. Much of Hawthorne's writing centers on New England, with many works featuring moral allegories with Puritan doctrines. His fiction works are considered part of the Romanticism and, more specifically, dark romanticism. His themes often center on the inherent evil and sin of humanity, and his works often have ethical messages and deep psychological complexity.

(3) When Pearl asked Mr. Dimmesdale to stand with her and her mother on the platform the next day, the minister refused. He only promised to stand together with them before the judgment-seat at the great judgment day, and thus “the daylight of this world shall not see our meeting”. In fact, he did not want to announce his relationship with Hester and Pearl. So, Pearl's words “Thou wast not bold! —thou wast not true!” are ironic.

Passage 3

(1) *The Scarlet Letter*

(2) Nathaniel Hawthorne

(3) Symbolism is traditionally a sign or token of something. In the matter of literature, the definition of the literary device, symbolism is more complicated. Symbols of literature are usually metaphysical. In this novel, the scarlet letter “A” changes its meaning in many different times. This change is significant. It shows growth in the characters, and the community in

which they live. The letter "A" begins as a symbol of sin. It then becomes a symbol of alone and alienation, and finally it becomes a symbol of able, angel and admirable.

Ⅳ. Short answer questions

1. The letter "A" begins as a symbol of adultery, which is worn on Hester's chest. This is the puritan way of punishing her for the crime of adultery. It then becomes a symbol of alone and alienation. Hester's social life is virtually eliminated as a result of her shameful past. And little Pearl is the only companion of her lonely life. Finally it becomes a symbol of able, angel and admirable. The villagers who condemn her now believe the scarlet letter stands for her ability to make beautiful needlework and for her unselfish assistance to the poor and sick. Hester is a strong admirable woman who goes through more emotional torture than most people go through in a lifetime. "A" may also represent Adamic, or prehistoric, an archetypal vice suggestive of "original sin".
2. For Captain Ahab, the white whale represents evil. After the loss of his leg in his encounter with the white whale, Ahab begins to hate Moby Dick and goes into lengths to kill the whale. It seems that Ahab consigned all of the evil to the white whale. For other members on the whaling ship, the white whale symbolizes the unknown, mysterious natural force of the universe. For the readers, the white whale is capable of many interpretations, for it is "paradoxically benign and malevolent, nourishing and destructive," "massive, brutal, monolithic, but at the same time protean, erotically beautiful, infinitely variable."
3. In *Moby-Dick*, Ishmael describes Ahab as mad in his narration as he intends to rebel against the forces of nature or God. However, some of the other characters in the novel whom Ishmael labels insane—notably Pip and Gabriel—might be otherwise viewed as wise, thus prompting readers to think about the possibility of making a clear distinction between sanity and insanity. Gabriel, the prophet figure aboard the *Jeroboam*, behaves irrationally and makes a number of ridiculous-sounding predictions. Gabriel's prophecies are aimed at earning fair treatment for the crew from the ship's officers and at avoiding the danger that will come from trying to hunt Moby Dick. Like Ahab, he manipulates the crew's superstitions and religious beliefs in order to gather support. But whereas Ahab's obsession is monomaniacal and selfish, Gabriel's "madness" is a response to irrational and unjust behavior on the part of those who control his ship. The ship ironically represents the American society with fixed social status and power relationship.
4. Young Goodman Brown, essentially an allegory, which is included in Hawthorne's *Mosses from an Old Manse*, is one of his most profound tales. Through the story, Hawthorne sought to bring about the moral that, "There is evil in every human heart, which may arouse latent, perhaps, through the whole life; but circumstances may arouse it to activity."

   While using allegory to hold fast against the crushing blows of reality, the symbol serves as a weapon to attack and penetrate it. Hawthorne took his symbolism from Puritan tradition and bequeathed it to American literature in a revivified form. His view of man and history originates, to a great extent, in Puritanism. Hawthorne was burdened with a sense of guilt due to his ancestor's notorious role in Salem Witch Trials. This sensibility led to his understanding of evil being at the very core of human life, which is typical of the Calvinistic belief that human beings are basically depraved and corrupted, hence, they should obey god to atone for their sins.

V. Essay questions

1. All his life, Hawthorne seems to be haunted by his sense of sin and evil in life. Reading his tales and romances, one cannot but be overwhelmed by the "black" vision which these works reveal. The blackness of vision which comes as a natural corollary has become his trade mark. It illustrates to some extent the influence that the Calvinist doctrine of "original sin" and total depravity had upon his mind. One source of evil in Hawthorne is overweening intellect. Hawthorne's intellectual characters are usually villains, dreadful because devoid of fellow feeling.

   In *The Scarlet Letter*, the experience of Hester and Dimmesdale recalls the story of Adam and Eve because, in both cases, sin results in expulsion and suffering. But it also results in knowledge—specifically, in knowledge of what it means to be human. The real villain in *The Scarlet Letter* is Roger Chillingworth, the scholar, the embodiment of pure intellect, who commits "the Unpardonable Sin"—the violation of the human heart. He keeps preying on Dimmesdale's conscience until the poor wretch is tormented to death. The end of Chillingworth, when it comes, is also tragic enough. Dimmesdale declares God's judgment on him before he breathes his last: "Thou, too, hast deeply sinned!" And Chillingworth simply shrivels. The last time we see him, he is kneeling down beside Dimmesdale "with a blank, dull countenance, out of which the life seemed to have departed." Chillingworth's misshapen body reflects (or symbolizes) the evil in his soul, which builds as the novel progresses, similar to the way Dimmesdale's illness reveals his inner turmoil.

2. *Moby-Dick* is often referred to as "the Great American Novel" and is considered one of the treasures of world literature.

   In the novel, Melville employs stylized language, symbolism, and metaphor to explore numerous complex themes. Through the main character's journey, readers can explore the concepts of class and social status, good and evil, and the existence of gods from the perspective of Ishmael as he contemplates upon his personal beliefs and his place in the universe.

   Moby-Dick is a symbolic work, but also includes chapters on natural history. Major themes include obsession, religion, and idealism versus pragmatism, revenge, racism, sanity, hierarchical relationships, and politics. All of the members of the crew have biblical-sounding, improbable, or descriptive names, and the narrator deliberately avoids specifying the exact time of the events and some other similar details. These together suggest that the narrator is deliberately casting his tale in an epic and allegorical mode. The white whale has also been seen as a symbol for many things, including nature and those elements of life that are out of human control.

3. It is a mixture of fantasy and realism based on the South Pacific whaling industry. It might be read as an initiation story about Ishmael, the outcast, finding himself in a real world of hard work and danger and an unreal world of speculation and mystery.

   It is a fabulous dramatization of Ahab's obsessed determination to revenge himself in the pursuit of one particular whale who previously destroyed his boat and humiliated him by ripping off one of his legs. The book has so often been interpreted in so many ways, allegorically and symbolically.

Melville is a master of allegory and symbolism. Instead of putting the battle between Ahab and the big whale into simple statements, he used symbols to indicate their confrontation. Different people on board the ship are representations of and different social, ethnic groups, facts become symbols and incidents acquire universal meanings; the Pequod is the microcosm of human society with certain power relationship and the voyage becomes a search for truth. The white whale, Moby Dick, symbolizes nature for Melville, for it is complex, unfathomable, malignant, and beautiful as well.

For the character Ahab, however, the whale only represents evil. Moby Dick is like a wall, hiding some unknown, mysterious things behind. Moby Dick is a mystery, an ultimate mystery of the universe, and the voyage of the mind will forever remain a search, not a discovery, of the truth. The whole story turns out to be a symbolic voyage of the mind quest of the truth and knowledge of the universe, a spiritual exploration into man's deep reality and psychology.

第6章 惠特曼·狄金森

6.1 复习笔记

I. Walt Whitman (1819 –1892) **1. Life** Whitman grew up in a working-class family, on Long Island, New York. He didn't have much schooling but took on a good deal of "loafing" and reading. Hungry for experience and companiable in habit, Whitman experienced plenty of jobs and obtained a direct knowledge of life and people in the new world. The life with the people and the country laid a basis as both the material and the guiding spirit for his epic, *Leaves of Grass*. When the Civil War started, he worked as a "wound dresser" in a military hospital. In 1873, paralysis condemned him to a good care of friends in New Jersey where he continued to revise his *Leaves of Grass*. **2. Literary point of view** (1) Affected by the leading New Englander Emerson, Whitman claims that the greatest poet should breathe into the world the grandeur and life of the universe. (2) Art should be based organically on nature and the poet's work grows out of nature and derives its form from within. (3) Whitman embraces idealism. He relies on insight and intuition very much. **3. Themes** (1) He shows great concern for the whole diligent people and the flourishing life of cities. (2) He advocates the realization of the individual value. Most of the poems in *Leaves of Grass* celebrate not only the "en-masse" but also the self in word. (3) Pursuit of love and happiness is endorsed constantly and affectionately in his lines. It's important to respect the individual person and his desires. (4) Some of Whitman's poems are politically committed.	**I. 沃尔特·惠特曼** **1. 生平** 惠特曼成长于纽约州长岛一个工人阶级家庭。他上学时间不长，大量地游荡并广泛地阅读书籍。由于渴望经验和喜爱社交的习性，他尝试了多种多样的工作并获得了新世界的生活和在这里生活的人们的第一手材料。惠特曼与人们的交往及游览美国大好山河的经历，为他的史诗《草叶集》提供了素材和导向精神。内战开始后，他在战地医院做看护员。1873 年患半身不遂迁至新泽西，在那儿受到朋友的照顾，修订《草叶集》直至去世。 **2. 文学观点** (1)受新英格兰领军人物爱默生的影响，惠特曼认为最伟大的诗人给世界注入了宇宙的壮观和生机。 (2)艺术以自然为基础。诗人的作品来源于自然。 (3)惠特曼信奉理想主义。他依赖于自己的内心与直觉。 **3. 主题** (1)他关注辛勤劳动的人民和迅速发展的城市生活。 (2)他提倡个体价值的实现。《草叶集》中大部分的诗作不仅歌颂了全体，还有个体。 (3)他的诗行中不断深情地赞颂对爱和幸福的追求。作为个体的人和他的欲望应受尊重。 (4)惠特曼的一些诗有坚定的政治立场。诗中他向战场上丧失了年轻的生命表达哀思，并展示了坚

Before and during the Civil War, Whitman expressed much lamentation for the pains of the young lives in the battlefield and demonstrated a strength of will to carry on the fighting fearlessly until the ultimate victory. Later, he wrote down plenty of poems to express his grief due to the loss of Lincoln, and one of the famous is "When Lilacs Last in the Dooryard Bloom'd."

持无畏战斗直至最后胜利的决心。之后，他写下了很多诗表达对林肯遇刺的悲痛，其中著名的一首为《当紫丁香最近在庭院开放》。

4. Writing style

(1) Instead of the traditional iambic pentameter, Whitman wrote "free verse", that is, poetry without a fixed beat or regular rhyme scheme.

(2) There is a strong sense of the poems being rhythmical. Parallelism and phonetic recurrence at the beginning of the lines contribute a lot to the musicality of his poems.

(3) Most of the scenes he painted with words are honest, undistorted images of various aspects of America at that time.

(4) Whitman's language is relatively simple and even rather unsubtle. Another characteristic in Whitman's language is his great usage of oral English. Whitman's vocabulary is astonishing. He would use tough, vivid, as well as rarely-used words.

4. 写作风格

（1）惠特曼打破了五步抑扬格的传统，并创作“自由体”诗歌，也就是没有固定韵律的诗歌。

（2）惠特曼的诗歌有很强的节奏感，诗行前几句排比和语音重复使他的诗歌颇具音乐美感。

（3）他用语言描述的大部分画面都是反映美国社会当时各个方面的真实景象。

（4）惠特曼语言相对简单朴实，甚至十分粗犷，另一个特点是口语化。惠特曼词汇惊人，他总能用有力的、生动的、别人不常用的语言。

5. Whitman's influence

Whitman's influence over modern poetry is great in the world as well as in America. Whitman has been compared to great mountain in American literary history. For his innovations in diction and versification, his frankness about sex, his inclusion of the commonplace and the ugly and his censure of the weakness of the American democratic practice—these have led to his achievement of immortality in American literature.

5. 惠特曼的影响

惠特曼对当代诗歌的影响在美国以致在世界范围内都同样深远。惠特曼被比作美国文学历史上的高山，因他在措辞和诗律方面的创新，对性这一话题的坦率，诗作中反映有平凡和丑陋的题材，以及他对美国民主弊端的指责，这些都为他在美国文学上的不朽地位奠定了基础。

6. Major works

Leaves of Grass
"Song of Myself"
"The Poet"
"When Lilacs Last in the Dooryard Bloom'd"
"O Captain, My Captain"
"I Hear America Singing"
"There was a Child Went Forth"
"Out of Cradle Endlessly Rocking"
Two Riverlets
Drum Traps

6. 主要作品

《草叶集》
《自我之歌》
《诗人》
《当紫丁香最近在庭院开放》
《哦，船长，我的船长》
《我听到美国在唱歌》
《有一个孩子向前走去》
《从永久摇荡的摇篮里》
《两条小河》
《桴鼓集》

7. Analysis of major works

◆*Leaves of Grass*

(1) Grass, the most common thing with the greatest energy, is not only an image of the poet himself, but also a symbol of the then rising American nation and an manifestation of his ideals about democracy and freedom.

(2) In this giant work, he pays much attention to openness, freedom, especially individualism which advocates that the rights and freedom of individual people are of most significance.

(3) He expresses warm approval of nature, democracy, labor and creation, and sings of man's dignity and equality, and of the brightest future of human beings. Most of the poems in *Leaves of Grass* sing of not only the "en-masse" but also the self.

◆"Song of Myself"

Whitman praises the perfect concept of equality and democracy and celebrates the dignity, the self-reliant spirit, and the pleasure of the common man enthusiastically, "Song of Myself" reveals a world of equality, in which there is not rank and hierarchy at all.

◆"When Lilacs Last in the Dooryard Bloom'd"

It is concerned about the typical Whitmansque love-and-death motif. It was written for President Lincoln. In the poem, when the poet looks up, he spots the western fallen star, and then when he looks around, he notices the lilac bush blossoming in the dooryard. Here the fallen star signifies death, the lilac with a representation of life for the dead. Instead of the end, death is the beginning of life.

Ⅱ. Emily Dickinson (1830 – 1886)

1. Life

Dickinson grew up in a Calvinist family. Her father, an old Puritan, with a heart "pure and terrible", had a great affect on his daughter. She was timid, sensitive, but rebellious from time to time. Emily had became a recluse since she was twenty-year-old. She wanted to live simply as a completely independent person.

2. Themes

(1) Inspired by her own life experiences, joys or sorrows, she writes about doubt and belief about religious subjects, suffering and frustration due to love, success and failure.

7. 主要作品分析

◆《草叶集》

（1）草叶，最为平凡却也最有生机，是诗人自己的形象，也是崛起中美国的象征和诗人关于民主自由理想的体现。

（2）在这部巨作中，开放，自由，尤其是个体主义（主张个人的权利和自由最为重要）是他最为关注的。

（3）这部作品中他也赞美了自然，民主，劳动和创新，也歌颂了人的尊严和平等，憧憬了人类最美好的未来。《草叶集》中大部分诗歌赞颂了大众和自我。

◆《自我之歌》

惠特曼赞美了平等和民主的理想，赞美了人的高尚，自力更生的精神，和普通人的快乐。《自我之歌》呈现了一个没有阶层和等级的平等世界。

◆《当紫丁香最近在庭院开放》

这首诗体现了典型的惠特曼作品中的爱与死的主题。他为纪念林肯总统而作。在这首诗中，当诗人仰望天空，他看到西天星星陨落；当他环望四周，他发现了紫丁香花在庭院的开放。这里陨落的星星是死亡的象征，丁香花丛是死者生命的象征。死亡不是终点，而是新生的开始。

Ⅱ. 艾米莉·狄金森

1. 生平

狄金森生于一个信奉加尔文教的家庭。她的父亲，是有着"纯洁而可怕的心"的一位虔诚清教徒，对女儿产生了很大的影响。她害羞，思想敏感，有时具有反叛精神。在她二十多岁时她成为一名隐士。她希望完全独立，简单生活。

2. 主题

（1）基于她个人的经历，喜与悲，她的诗歌是关于宗教主题的疑惑和信仰，爱情中的痛苦和挫折，成功与失败。

(2) Dickinson's poetry attaches great attention to death and immortality. In Dickinson's perspective, death brings about immortality.

(3) Nature is considered as both gaily benevolent and cruel.

(4) Ethically Dickinson believes that beauty, truth and goodness are not separated from each other.

(5) She gives special importance to free-will and responsibility belonging to human.

3. Writing styles

(1) Her poetry is filled with telling images. In the best of her poems, every word constitutes a picture. As a result, she is considered as the precursor of Imagism poetry.

(2) Her poetic idiom is well-known for its conciseness, directness and great usage of the plainest words.

(3) Dickinson's poems are usually short, and the first line of Dickinson's poems tend to be the title at the same time.

(4) The capital letters in her poems are used for prominence.

4. Comparison: Whitman VS. Dickinson

Similarities:

(1) On the level of theme, they both sing the praise of an emergent America, its expansion, its individualism and its Americanness, whose poetry constitute "American Renaissance" from different perspectives.

(2) On the level of writing technics, they both added to the literary independence of the new nation by breaking free of the tradition of the iambic pentameter and displaying a freedom in form unprecedented in history; they were pioneers in American poetry.

Differences:

(1) Whitman seems to keep his eye on society from a large scale; Dickinson explores the inner life from the individual perspective.

(2) Whereas Whitman is "national" in his interpretation, Dickinson is "regional".

(3) Dickinson prefers to the "catalogue technique" (direct, simple style) which Whitman doesn't approve.

(2) 狄金森的大部分诗歌是关于死亡与永生的。对狄金森来说，死亡导向永生。

(3)狄金森视自然为仁慈并冷酷残忍的。

(4) 在伦理的层面上，狄金森认为真善美是合而为一的。

(5) 她强调自由意志和人类责任。

3. 写作风格

(1) 她的诗歌描绘有各种意象。在她创作的最好的诗歌中，每一个词都是一幅画。所以她被视作意象派诗歌的先驱。

(2) 她诗歌的风格简明，直接，善用最平易的词。

(3) 狄金森的诗歌通常篇幅较短，第一句往往是诗歌的题目。

(4) 诗歌中用做强调的词均大写。

4. 比较：惠特曼 VS. 狄金森

相同点：

(1) 主题选择上，他们都用不同的方式歌颂了一个新兴的美国，辽阔，个人主义和自身特色，他们的诗歌是"美国文艺复兴"的组成部分。

(2) 写作技巧上，他们打破了传统诗歌创作的五步抑扬格，给诗歌创作形式上以很大的自由，在新兴的国家独立地创作，这是史无前例的。他们是美国诗歌的先驱。

不同点：

(1)惠特曼更细致地关注社会生活，而狄金森更倾向于探索人的内心世界。

(2) 惠特曼的视野放眼"全国"，而狄金森关注"地方"。

(3) 狄金森创作风格直接简洁，而惠特曼并非如此。

5. Influence Dickinson's poetry is filled with telling images. Her poetic idiom is well-known for its laconic brevity, directness and great usage of the plainest words. All these features of her poetry were to become well-liked by Stephen Crane with the Imagists such as Ezra Pound and Amy Lowell in the twentieth century. She was considered as the precursor of the Imagist movement.	**5. 影响** 她的诗歌意象丰富，诗歌风格简洁，直接，用词平易。这些特点很受斯蒂芬·克莱恩和20世纪意象派诗人艾兹拉·庞德和艾米·洛威尔的欢迎。她被视作意象派诗歌的先驱。
6. Major works "The Soul selects her own Society" "My life closed twice before its close" "Because I could not stop for Death" "I heard a fly buzz when I died" "Mine—by the Right of the White Election" "Wild Nights—Wild Nights" "Death is a Dialogue between" "I died for Beauty—but was scarce"	**6. 主要作品** 《心灵选择了自己的友伴》 《我的生命在结束之前已结束了两次》 《因为我不能停步等待死神》 《我死时听到了苍蝇的嗡嗡声》 《我的——根据白色选举的权利》 《狂风夜——狂风夜!》 《死是一场对话》 《我为美而死》

6.2 考研真题与典型题详解

I. Fill in the blanks.

1. Author ________ Title ________（南京大学2008研）

   Not one of all the purple host
   Who took the flag today
   Can tell the definition,
   So clearly, of victory.

2. *Leaves of Grass*, either in content or form, is an epoch-making work in American literature; its democratic content marked the shift from ________ to ________, and its ________ form broke from old poetic conventions to open a new road for American poetry.
3. In ________, Whitman's own early experience may well be identified with the childhood of a young growing America.
4. The poetic style Walt Whitman devised is now called ________, that is poetry without a fixed beat or regular rhyme scheme.
5. In his cluster of poems called *Leaves of Grass*, ________ gave America its first genuine epic poem.

II. Multiple Choice

1. Which ONE of the following is the author of the poem *Song of Myself*?（四川大学2008研）

   A. Walt Whitman　　B. Stephen Crane
   C. Edgar Allan Poe　　D. Henry Wadsworth Longfellow

2. "By day her meals untouch'd, then at night fitfully sleeping, often waking" is taken from "I Hear America Singing". The female described here is the ________ of the dead person.（首

师大 2009 研）

A. mother　B. wife　C. sister　D. daughter

3. "I celebrate myself, and sing myself, /And what I assume you shall assume, /For every atom belonging to me as good belongs to you."

In the above quoted verse lines taken from Walt Whitman's poem "Song of Myself", what does the central image "myself" refer to?（四川大学 2009 研）

A. Merely the poet himself.　B. The common people of America.

C. Masculine sublime ego.　D. American puritans.

4. Which ONE of the following is an influential poet whose poems often express a thematic concern about the issue of death and eternity?（四川大学 2009 研）

A. Walt Whitman　B. Ralph Waldo Emerson

C. Henry Wadsworth Longfellow　D. Emily Dickinson

5. The following poems were all composed by Emily Dickinson EXCEPT ________.（四川大学 2007 研）

A. "Because I Could Not Stop for Death"　B. "A Psalm of Life"

C. "I Died for Beauty—but Was Scarce"　D. "I Heard a Fly Buzz—When I Died"

6. Which of the following features cannot characterize poems by Walt Whitman?

A. Lyrical and well-structured.　B. Free-flowing.

C. Simple and rather crude.　D. Conversational and casual.

7. In Walt Whitman's "There was a Child Went Forth." the child refers to ________.

A. the poet himself as a child　B. any American child

C. the young America　D. one of the poet's neighbor

8. American literature produced only one female poet during the 19th century. She was ________.

A. Anne Bradstreet　B. Jane Austen

C. Emily Dickenson　D. Harriet Beecher

9. The main theme of Emily Dickinson is the following except ________.

A. religion　B. love and marriage

C. life and death　D. war and peace

10. Emily Dickinson's poetic idiom is noted for the following except ________.

A. brevity　B. directness　C. plainest words　D. obscure

Ⅲ. Explain the following term.

1. free verse（首师大 2009 研）

Ⅳ. Read the following quotations and answer the questions.

Passage 1（北航 2008 研）

I Heard a Fly Buzz—when I died—
The Stillness in the Room
Was like the Stillness in the Air—
Between the Heaves of Storm—
The Eyes around—had wrung them dry—
And Breaths were gathering firm

For that last Onset—when the King
Be witnessed—in the Room—
I willed my Keepsakes—Signed away
What portion of me be
Assignable—and then it was
There interposed a Fly—
With Blue—uncertain stumbling Buzz—
Between the light—and me—
And then the Windows failed—and then
I could not see to see—

Questions:

(1) Identify the author of the passage.

(2) What are the effect and the meaning of "I heard a Fly buzz—when I died—"?

(3) What is the meaning of the last two lines?

Passage 2

"I celebrate myself, and sing myself.
And what I assume you shall assume,
For every atom belonging to me as good belongs to you."

Questions:

(1) Who wrote these lines? What is the poet celebrating?

(2) Whom does "you" refer to?

(3) What are the two principle beliefs that the poet set forth on this poem?

Passage 3

Because I could not stop for Death—
He kindly stopped for me—
The Carriage held but just Ourselves—
And Immortality.

Questions:

(1) Who is the writer of these lines?

(2) In which category would you place this poem?

(3) Emily Dickinson is noted for her use of ___________ to achieve special effects.

V. Short answer question

1. Why *Leaves of Grass* is considered a milestone in American literature?

VI. Essay question

1. Discuss the themes and artistic features of Emily Dickinson's poems. （山东大学 2016 研）

参考答案及解析

I. Fill in the blanks.

1. Emily Dickinson; *Success is Counted Sweetest*

（题目节选自狄金森的 *Success is Counted the Sweetest*《成功最甜美》。艾米莉·狄金森，美国最富传奇性的抒情诗人。生前只发表了7首诗，诗作几乎全部在她死后才发表。她被视为20世纪现代主义诗歌的先驱之一，和美国文学之父欧文、诗人惠特曼比肩。)

2. Romanticism; Realism; free verse

(《草叶集》无论是从内容上还是形式上都是美国文学划时代的作品，它有关民主的内容标志着浪漫主义到现实主义的转变，它采用自由体，从而打破了旧时诗歌的传统，为美国诗歌独辟蹊径。)

3. *Song of Myself*

(在惠特曼的《自我之歌》中他将自己早期的经历同一个正在成长中的美国等同起来。)

4. free verse

(沃尔特·惠特曼(Walt Whitman, 1810 – 1892)是美国著名诗人、人文主义者，他创造性地运用了诗歌的自由体(Free Verse)，其代表作品是诗集《草叶集》(*Leaves of Grass*)。自由诗是诗体的一种，其结构自由，段数、行数、字数没有一定规格；语言有自然节奏而不用韵。)

5. Walt Whitman

(《草叶集》(*Leaves of Grass*)是十九世纪美国作家沃尔特·惠特曼(Walt Whitman)浪漫主义诗集。《草叶集》是惠特曼一生创作的总汇，也是美国诗歌史上一座灿烂的里程碑。作品包含了丰富而深刻的思想内容，充分反映了十九世纪中期美国的时代精神。)

Ⅱ. Multiple Choice

1. A　Walt Whitman(沃尔特·惠特曼)，美国著名诗人，*Song of Myself*(《自我之歌》)代表其创作的最高峰，后来收录在他的*Leaves of Grass*(《草叶集》)中。
2. A　这首诗是惠特曼"Come Up From The Fields, Father"里的几句，描写的是母亲接到儿子的死讯以后痛苦的心情。节译：白天她茶饭不思，晚上她无法安睡。
3. B　惠特曼在《自我之歌》里歌颂的是伟大的美国劳动人民。
4. D　艾米丽·狄金森的诗歌表达了一种对于死亡和永恒的关注，如"因为我不能停下来等待死亡""我死前听见一只苍蝇在嗡嗡"等。
5. B　《人生礼赞》的作者是美国诗人Henry Wadsworth Longfellow(朗费罗)，其余选项都是狄金森的诗作。
6. A　沃尔特·惠特曼创造性地运用了诗歌的自由体(Free Verse)自由诗是诗体的一种，其结构自由，段数、行数、字数没有一定规格；语言有自然节奏而不用韵。
7. C　惠特曼的诗歌《有一个孩子向前走去》中孩子是指成长中的美国。
8. C　Emily Dickenson是19世纪美国浪漫主义时期的唯一的女诗人，Anne Bradstreet是17世纪的女诗人，Jane Austen是英国18世纪末的小说家，Harriet Beecher是美国19世纪的小说家。
9. D　艾米丽·狄金森诗歌的主题不涉及战争与和平。
10. D　艾米丽·狄金森的用词简洁、直率、平易，而非晦涩。

Ⅲ. Explain the following term.

1. Free verse is a term describing various styles of poetry that are written without using a strict rhyme scheme, but still recognizable as poetry by virtue of complex patterns of one sort or another that readers will perceive to be part of a coherent whole. Walt Whitman is a representative who employed free verse successfully.

Ⅳ. Read the following quotations and answer the questions.

Passage 1

(1) The author is Emily Dickenson.

(2) In this poem, the speaker is waiting for her last moment. The room is still, and the eyes of her relatives have been dry. All these together create a solemn and woeful atmosphere. The speaker is going to see the "King", but at this time, she hears a fly buzz. Fly is generally regarded as a disgusting creature, and sometimes it gathers around the corpse. Its appearance disconcerts us and makes the "immortality" doubtful.

(3) The fly's wings cut the speaker off from the light, and then the speaker closes her eyes and dies. Here, the light that she sees is from the Heaven. The speaker imagines that she is on the way to the Heaven. Just at this moment, the fly appears, between the speaker and the heaven. Thus, her hope of immortality becomes doubtful. The speaker is not sure whether she can really go to the heaven with "the King".

Passage 2

(1) These lines are taken from Walt Whitman's *Songs of Myself*. The poet is celebrating individualism and nationalism in this poem. Here "I" does not necessarily mean the poet or a particular person, because the poet mingles the first person with the second person by the word "assume".

(2) Here "you" refers to the democratic "en-masse" of America.

(3) The two beliefs are the theory of universality and the belief in the singularity and equality.

Passage 3

(1) Emily Dickinson

(2) dramatic

(3) slant rhyme

V. Short answer question

1. Whitman's *Leaves of Grass* has always been considered a monumental work because of its uniquely poetic embodiment of American democratic ideal.

   In this work, the abundance of themes voices freshness. Whitman shows concern for the whole hardworking people and the burgeoning life of the cities. The realization of the individual value also found a tough position in Whitman's poems in a particular way. In celebrating the self, Whitman gives emphasis to the physical dimension of the self and openly celebrates sexuality. And some of Whitman's poems are politically committed.

   Stylistically, Whitman experiments with a mixture of the colloquial diction and prose rhythm of journalism. The direct address is another salient feature of his poetry. He constructs a democratic "I", a voice that sets out to celebrate itself and the rapture of its sense experiencing the world. In addition, Whitman initiated the form of free verse in America that endows his poems with a flow of musicality and a sense of rhythm.

Ⅵ. Essay question

1. (1) themes:

①Love, death, pain and nature are subjects Dickinson dwells on and Dickinson's poems are usually based on her own experiences, her sorrows and joys. Among these themes, death is the most important one.

②Emily Dickinson was a pessimistic poet, Dickinson had a tragic message. Dickinson seems to have accepted death as an inevitable conclusion of life. Her greatest lyrics are on the theme of death, personified as a monarch, a lord, or a kind but irresistible lover, yet her moods varied widely from melancholy to exuberance, grief to joy, leaden despair to spiritual intoxication. She sensed the inherent beauty and the frightening coldness of the world. She perceived beauty in the wholeness and harmonious relationships of nature, and her works reflected a spiritual unrest and an awareness of the human predicament that defied all easy categories.

③She wrote of God, man, and nature with a knowledge that seemed impossible for a person so limitedly experienced. She knew love and death as few would have known them.

(2) artistic features:

①Her poem is short, condensed and often based on a single image or symbol, it is remarkable for its variety, subtlety, and richness. Dickinson's poetry is unique and unconventional in its own way. Her poems have no titles, hence are always quoted by their first lines.

②Influence of Christian tradition: She used the Biblical language and allusions and strikingly illuminated hidden recesses in the human soul. She was religiously oriented. She wrote poems that could be sung, as a matter of fact, just like a Christian hymn.

③Use of the persona "I." She would pretend to be a small girl and write cute little poems with which she examined personal emotion.

④Use of paradox and irony, unorthodox syntax and punctuation. For example, she used the subjunctive where the indicative should be used. She often did not inflect the third person singular form of the verb. She just left it uninflected. Her capitalization and dashes were often used willfully.

⑤Counter-poetic style. Her counter-poetic style is characterized by lexical surprises, frequent use of oxymoron and synaesthesia, which creates a world of resonant possibility.

⑥Innovation in rhyme. She was not restricted by full rhyme. "Moon, soon, coon, swoon" are full rhymes with the same vowel and the same consonant. But she used "consonance" which means similarity of final consonants, but not vowels such as "reach—touch." And the other kind of rhyme she used is assonance. For assonance, the final vowel sounds correspond, but the consonants are different. Consonance and assonance break the rules of poetry.

⑦On the whole, her poetry is irregular in rhyme and rhythm. Dickinson's style is characteristic of frequent use of dashes, sporadic capitalization of nouns, convoluted and ungrammatical phrasing, off-rhymes, broken meters, bold and unconventional and often startling metaphors, and aphoristic wit.

第 7 章　埃德加·爱伦·坡

7.1　复习笔记

I. Edgar Allan Poe

1. Life

Poe's childhood was a miserable one. His parents passed away when he was young, and he was taken care of by a wealthy merchant of Virginia, John Allan. But Poe enjoyed nothing but an unhappy relationship with the Allans. At 17 Poe entered the University of Virginia but did not finish. He went to West Point as a cadet but was expelled from the school for misconduct. Throughout his short life, Poe spent much time writing and editing. He was poor all his life. At 27 he married his thirteen-year-old cousin, whose death in 1847 was a great grief to him. In October, 1849, he died mysteriously. For a long time after his death Poe remained probably the most controversial and most misunderstood literary figure in the history of American literature. But today Poe is recognized as a great novelist, a first-rate poet, and a critic of great insight. His works are widely read around the world, which are understood and appreciated.

2. Literary point of view

(1) Theories for short story

①The length of the short story should be brief and concise to ensure the reader's impression of the story as a whole.

②he first sentence ought to help to bring out the "single effect" of the story. Do not use words which do not fit the "pre-established" design of the work (compression).

③The novel should reveal some logical inspiration, and should end with the last sentence, which can leave a sense of finality with the reader.

(2) Theories for Poetry

①Poems should be short and concise, so that readers can read them all at once.

I. 埃德加·艾伦·坡

1. 生平

坡有着悲惨的童年。他年幼时父母双亡，他被弗吉尼亚富商约翰·爱伦收养，但他与养父家之间的关系并不好。17 岁时坡进入弗吉尼亚大学学习，但是没能完成学业。后来去了西点军校，却又因为行为不端而被校方开除。他短暂的一生中大部分时间都在从事写作和编辑工作。他终身贫困潦倒。27 岁时，他和 13 岁的表妹结婚，1847 年妻子的离世使他悲痛万分。1849 年 10 月，他离奇地去世。坡死后相当长的时间里仍是美国文学史上最具争议性、被误解最深的文学家。而现在坡被认为是一位伟大的小说家、一流的诗人和具有敏锐洞察力的评论家。他的作品在世界范围内被广泛阅读，并获得了赞赏和理解。

2. 文学批评观

(1) 短篇小说理论

①短篇小说的篇幅应简洁，这样可以确保读者对故事的整体印象。

②第一句话应当帮助引出故事的"单一效果"。不使用不符合"预先制定"情节的词(紧凑)。

③小说应当具备一些符合逻辑的启发，最后一句应给人一种"完结感"。

(2) 诗歌理论

①诗歌应该简短，使读者可以一口气读完。

②The aim of poem writing is to express beauty; the most beautiful thing described by a poem is the death of a beautiful woman; the best tone of a poem is melancholy.

②诗歌创作的目的是表现美；最富诗意的美莫过于美丽女子的死亡；诗的最佳基调应是忧郁。

③He dislikes poems which are designed to teach people a moral lesson.

③他反感说教性的诗歌。

④He emphasized the form of poem, especially the beautiful and neat rhyme. He defined poetry as "the rhythmic creation of beauty".

④他强调诗歌的形式，尤其强调韵律的美感。他认为"诗是美的节奏性创作"。

3. Theme and style

3. 主题及写作风格

He is a romantic poet, preoccupied with the theme of the death of one's beloved lover, who is a combination of intelligence and beauty. He also writes about horror (Gothic) novels, murder, and insanity.

他是浪漫主义诗人，专注于深爱的情人之死这样的主题，通常她们集智慧与美丽于一身。他也写恐怖小说（即哥特式小说），谋杀及精神错乱。

Poe's style is traditional and very rational, too ordinary to reflect the peculiarity of his theme. Somehow he fails to incorporate the newness of his idea into his style, so it is difficult to make his central theme understood. He is not easy to read. Poe's choice of words and his syntax are the reasons why his works are difficult to understand.

坡的写作风格很传统，很重理性，让人觉得太过平常而不易发掘他写作主题的特性。他不能将他想法的新意揉进他的风格，从而他难以使他作品的主题思想被人看透。他的作品不好理解，作品的选词和句法是他散文难以理解的原因。

4. Influence

4. 影响

His influence on modern literature is worldwide. His aesthetic views and superb writing skills attack on the didactic function of literature, and his call for "the rhythmical creation of beauty" have an impact on French symbolists and the devotees of "art for art's sake". Poe is the father of psychoanalytic criticism and the father of detective fiction.

坡对现代文学的影响是世界性的。他的美学观点和精湛的写作技艺，对文学说教功能的抨击，以及他倡导的"诗是美的节奏性创作"对法国象征主义者和"为艺术而艺术"的信徒产生影响。坡是精神分析之父和侦探小说之父。

5. Major works

5. 主要作品

Tales of the Grotesque and the Arabesque	《奇异怪诞故事集》
"MS. Found in a Bottle"	《瓶子里发现的手稿》
"The Murders in the Rue Morgue"	《毛格街杀人案》
"The Fall of the House of Usher"	《厄舍古屋的倒塌》
"The Masque of the Red Death"	《红色死亡的化妆舞会》
"The Cask of Amontillado"	《一桶酒的故事》
"The Raven"	《乌鸦》
"Israfel"	《伊斯拉菲尔》
"Annabel Lee"	《安娜贝尔李》
"To Helen"	《致海伦》
The Philosophy of Composition	《创作哲学》
The Poetic Principle	《诗歌原理》

6. Analysis of major works	6. 主要作品分析
◆"To Helen" "To Helen" is one of Poe's most famous lyric poems It was inspired by the beauty of a classmate's mother when Poe was at school in Richmond, Virginia. The poem is famous for a number of things, for example, its rhythm, varied line lengths, the metaphor of a travel on the sea, and the frequently quoted lines, "To the Glory that was Greece / And the grandeur that was Rome."	◆《致海伦》 《致海伦》是坡最著名的抒情诗之一。这首诗的灵感来源于坡在弗吉尼亚州里士满上学时一位同学母亲的美貌。该诗以其韵律、多变的句子长度、海上旅行这一比喻及经常被引用的诗行"光荣属于希腊，伟大属于罗马"而著称。
◆"The Raven" "The Raven" embodies Poe's theory of poetry creation. It has about 100 lines (108 in fact), perfectly readable at one sitting. A sense of melancholy over the death of a beloved beautiful young woman pervades the poem: a young man mourning the passing of Lenore. The bird that appears at the beginning of the poem repeats a word, which turns the man's grief into madness. On the verge of a mental collapse the young man outpours his sorrow to the bird when he is half asleep and half awake. The phantom of the bird is a poetic imagination, enhancing the effect of the tragedy of the bereavement. Poe's poems are heavily tinted in a dreamy, hallucinatory color. And the narrator is in a semi-conscious state.	◆《乌鸦》 《乌鸦》体现了坡的诗歌创作理论。这首诗大概有一百行(实际上是108行)，读者可以一气呵成，读完全诗。整首诗弥漫着因心爱的年轻美人逝去而忧郁的气氛。诗歌描写了一位年轻人哀悼逝去的丽诺，诗歌开篇出现的鸟儿反复重复一个词，在此影响下，他的悲伤继而转化为疯狂。 这位年轻人的精神濒临崩溃的边缘，在半梦半醒之间，面对鸟儿倾吐自己的悲伤。鸟儿的幻影是一种诗意的想象，增强了失去爱人的悲剧性。坡的诗歌中梦幻的色调较重，叙述者处于一种半昏迷的状态。

7.2 考研真题与典型题详解

I. Fill in the blanks.

1. In consideration of the beauty of poems, ________ concludes that "the death of a beautiful woman is unquestionably the most poetical topic in the world." (天津外国语学院2007研)
2. ________ is regarded as the father of psychoanalytic criticism and the detective story. (首师大2008研)
3. ________ is generally thought of as the true beginner of the short stories because he was the first writer who formulated poetics of the short stories.
4. ________ is usually acknowledged as the originator of detective stories. He is also credited with developing many of the standard features of detective fiction. His detective M August Dupin of *The Murders in the Rue Morgue* and *The Purloined letter* is the forerunner of a long line of fictional detectives who are eccentric and brilliant.
5. ________'s poems have the musical quality and romantic beauty. *The Raven* is his best-known poem.

Ⅱ. Multiple Choice

1. Mark the novelist whose major works are characterized by the elements of the "grotesque"?（四川大学2008研）

   A. Philip Freneau　　B. Edgar Allan Poe

   C. Washington Irving　　D. Emily Dickson

2. Edgar Allan Poe's first collection of short stories is ________.

   A. *Tales of a Traveller*　　B. *Leatherstocking Tales*

   C. *Canterbury Tales*　　D. *Tales of the Grotesque and Arabesque*

Ⅲ. Read the following quotations and answer the questions.

Passage 1（人大2007研）

"Prophet!" said I, "thing of evil! —prophet still, if bird or devil! —
Whether tempter sent, or whether tempest tossed thee here ashore,
Desolate yet all undaunted, on this desert land enchanted—
On this home by horror haunted—tell me truly, I implore—
Is there—is there balm in Gilead? —tell me—tell me, I implore!"

Questions:

(1) Give the title of the work and the full name of the author.

(2) Explain the implications of the underlined parts.

Passage 2（北航2007研）

Although, as boys, we had been even intimate associates, yet I really knew little of my friend. His reserve had been always excessive and habitual. I was aware, however, that this very ancient family had been noted, time out of mind, for a peculiar sensibility of temperament, displaying itself through long ages, in many works of exalted art, and manifested, of late, in repeated deeds of munificent yet unobtrusive charity, as well as in a passionate devotion to the intricacies, perhaps even more than to the orthodox and easily recognizable beauties, of musical science. I had learned, too, the very remarkable fact, that the stem of the Usher race, all time-honored as it was, had put forth, at no period, any enduring branch; in other words, that the entire family lay in the direct line of descent, and had always, with very trifling and very temporary variation, so lain. It was this deficiency, I considered, while running over in thought the perfect keeping of the character of the premises with the accredited character of the people, and while speculating upon the possible influence which the one, in the long lapse of centuries, might have exercised upon the other—it was this deficiency, perhaps, of collateral issue, and the consequent undeviating transmission, from sire to son, of the patrimony with the name, which had, at length, so identified the two as to merge the original title of the estate in the quaint and equivocal appellation of the "House of Usher"—an appellation which seemed to include, in the minds of the peasantry who used it, both the family and the family mansion.

Questions:

(1) Which fiction is this excerpt from?

(2) Who is the author? What are the artistic features of the author?

(3) What literary technique is the fiction famous for, as embodied in this excerpt?

Ⅳ. **Short answer question**

1. How does Edgar Allan Poe anticipate the 20th-century literature?（国际关系学院 2007 研）

Ⅴ. **Essay question**

1. What are the artistic achievements of Edgar Allan Poe?

参考答案及解析

I. Fill in the blanks.

1. Edgar Allan Poe

（爱伦·坡认为，美的效应在于使灵魂激动而变得高尚；无论哪种美，其最高形式必然使敏感的灵魂悲泣。因此，诗的基调应该是"忧郁"。人最感到忧郁的事莫过于死，而最富于诗意的死莫过于心爱的年轻女子离世。）

2. Edgar Allan Poe

（爱伦·坡被认为是精神分析批评之父和侦探小说的鼻祖。）

3. Edgar Allan Poe

（爱伦·坡被视作短篇小说的真正始祖因为他是第一个在小说中赋予了诗意的作家。）

4. Edgar Allan Poe

（爱伦·坡被视作侦探小说的鼻祖。）

5. Edgar Allan Poe

（爱伦·坡的诗歌富有音乐感和浪漫主义色彩，《乌鸦》是最知名的一首。）

Ⅱ. **Multiple Choice**

1. B　Edgar Allan Poe（爱伦·坡），美国著名诗人、短篇小说家、文学评论家。他的短篇小说着意描写人的内心世界，对表现人的思想病态尤其感兴趣。其后期的短篇小说，经常充满一种恐怖气氛，情节阴森古怪，令人毛骨悚然。

2. D　埃德加·爱伦·坡（Edgar Allan Poe）（1809～1849）十九世纪美国诗人、小说家和文学评论家，在世时长期担任报刊编辑工作。《怪异故事集》（*Tales of the Grotesque and Arabesque*）是爱伦·坡的第一部短篇小说集。

Ⅲ. **Read the following quotations and answer the questions.**

Passage 1

(1) *The Raven* by Edgar Allan Poe

(2) Prophet: The narrator here calls the raven as a prophet, who can give him some clues to his puzzle of his beloved one.

implore: This word means that the narrator anxiously asks the raven to tell him whether there are ways to cure his pain.

balm in Gilead: This sentence is quoted from the Bible, which means that whether there are some medicines to ease the narrator's pain.

Passage 2

(1) This excerpt is from "The Fall of the House of Usher."

(2) The author is Edgar Allan Poe. As a remarkable poet and critic, Poe emphasizes rhythm, considers true poetry as "the rhythmical creation of beauty," and advocates that "music is the perfection of the soul, or idea, of poetry." Poe is a short-story writer of the imagination. In his

psychological fiction, he puts the subconscious mental state under investigation and explores beneath the surface of normal existence. He was the first author in American literature to make the neurotic the heroic figure, the protagonist, in his stories. He is the father of many things including psychoanalytic criticism and the detective novel.

(3) *The Fall of the House of Usher* possesses the essential features of the Gothic novel. It is a literary genre that combines elements of both horror and romance. The outstanding features of Gothic fiction include terror (both psychological and physical), mystery, the supernatural, ghosts, haunted houses and Gothic architectures, castles, darkness, death, decay, doubles, madness, secrets, and hereditary curses.

Ⅳ. Short answer question

1. Allan Poe anticipates the 20th century literature and his influence is world-wide in modern literature. He was one of the earliest American practitioners of the short story and is considered the father of psychoanalytic criticism and the detective novel. Poe is further credited with contributing to the emerging genre of science fiction. His aesthetic views and superb writing skills attack on the didactic function of literature, and his call for "the rhythmical creation of beauty" have an impact on French symbolists and the advocates of "art for art's sake."

Ⅴ. Essay question

1. Edgar Allan Poe has been recognized as a great writer of fiction, a first-rate poet, and a critic with deep insight. Poe is the father of many things, one of which is psychoanalytic criticism, the other being the detective novel.

   Poe was good at generalizing. He tried to cash in on his literary practice to rationalize about literary creation. His poetic theories are clear, which are best reflected in his "The Philosophy of Composition" and "The Poetic Principle." He believes that the poem should be short and its aims are to produce a sense of beauty and melancholy. Moreover, he insists on a metrical flow in versification.

   His theories for the short story are equally remarkable. In his opinion, the short story should be short and reveal some logical truth. Poe is a short-story writer of the imagination. In terms of the theme, Poe anticipates the twentieth-century literature in his treatment of the division of the self. He puts the subconscious mental state under investigation and explores beneath the surface of normal existence.

第 8 章　现实主义时期 · 豪威尔 · 詹姆斯

8.1　复习笔记

I. American Realism Realism as a literary movement aiming to reflect reality itself reacts against romanticism and paved the way to modernism. During this period a new generation of writers, dissatisfied with the Romantic ideas in the older generation, came up with a new inspiration. This new attitude was characterized by a great interest in the realities of life. It aimed at the interpretation of the realities of any aspect of life, free from subjective prejudice, idealism, or romantic color. Instead of thinking about the mysteries of life and death and heroic individualism, people's attention was now directed to the interesting features of everyday existence, to what was brutal or sordid, and to the open portrayal of class struggle. So writers began to describe the integrity of human characters reacting under various circumstances and picture the pioneers of the Far West, the new immigrants and the struggles of the working classes. Mark Twain, Howells and Henry James are three leading figures of the American Realism. **II. William Dean Howells** **1. Life** Although he came from a small and humble town (Martins Ferry) in Ohio, he made a remarkably successful life by his magnificent letters. He had little formal education but read widely. He was the first president of the American Academy of Arts and Letters, once the editor-in-chief of the country's most influential journal, *The Atlantic Monthly*. As a prolific writer, he produced volumes of drama, poetry, and novels as well as criticism, travelogues, and autobiography. **2. Literary point of view** (1) He defines realism as "fidelity to experience and probability of motive". Realism should mirror commonness rather than uniqueness.	**I. 美国现实主义** 现实主义是对浪漫主义的一种反抗，并为现代主义做了铺垫。 在这一时期，新一代的作家对浪漫主义观点颇为不满，于是提出了新的思想。新的理念对现实生活产生极大的关注，目的在于真实地反映现实生活的各个方面，摒弃主观的偏见，理想主义或是浪漫主义色彩。人们不再考虑生与死的神秘和个人英雄主义，而是直接关注日常生活的特点，写生活的残忍和卑贱，坦率地描述阶级斗争。 作家开始描述各种各样环境下人性格当中的正直，并描写在遥远西部的拓荒者，新移民和工人阶级的斗争。 马克吐温，豪威尔斯，和亨利 · 詹姆斯是美国现实主义的代表作家。 **II. 威廉姆 · 迪恩 · 豪威尔斯** **1. 生平** 尽管豪威尔斯出生在俄亥俄州一个小城镇，在一个卑微的环境中成长，但是他凭借精湛的文字艺术最终功成名就。他没有受过多少正规的教育，但阅读涉猎广泛。他曾是美国艺术文学院的院长，并曾担任过国内最有影响力的期刊——《大西洋月刊》的主编。他是一位多产的作家。他写了大量的戏剧、诗歌和小说，另外还有评论文、旅行见闻及自传。 **2. 文学批评观** （1）他指出，“现实主义忠实于生活，反映动机的可能性”，寻求表现一般性和习惯性，而不是特殊性或独特的高尚或卑微现象。

(2) Howell's fictions are devoted to displaying human in his natural and honest stupidity.

(3) The core principle of realism is to grasp characters' "motives" and inward conflicts rather than simply to reflect the appearance strictly.

(4) The American spirit was best expressed through realism's sympathetic analysis of the "common feelings of commonplace people".

(5) Howells thinks that literary criticism should not contain subjective and unreasonable judgements but should analyze a book objectively and reasonably as doing scientific description, interpretation, and classification.

3. Major works

The Rise of Silas Lapham

A Modern Instance

A Hazard of New Fortunes

Criticism and Fiction

4. Analysis of major work

◆*The Rise of Silas Lapham*

Howell's novelist qualities are illustrated thoroughly by this novel. It tells the story of a Boston new upstart in the mid-19th century. It sets a classic example for American realism. This novel is loyal to the realistic principle of mirroring commonness rather than uniqueness.

In this novel the author emphasizes ethics, the need for sympathy and moral integrity, and the need for a harmonious interaction between different social classes. The author criticizes the rise of materialism in American life.

Ⅲ. Henry James

He is considered the founder of psychological realism. He was the first American writer to conceive his artistic work in international themes.

1. Life

Henry James came from a rich New England cultured family. His brother, William James, was a renowned philosopher and psychologist. To some extent, his family background decides his theme: he wrote about the wealthy, deep-rooted leisure class. The European culture influenced him since he was a baby. The French culture may stamp on him most as he called Balzac his "greatest master". In 1876, he settled down in London, and almost spent the rest of his life there.

(2) 他表现的主体是自然、不矫揉造作而愚笨无聊的人。

(3) 现实主义的中心原则是把握人物的"动机"及其心理矛盾，而不是简简单单一丝不苟地反应事物的表面。

(4) 现实主义饱含同情地分析了"普通人的日常情感"，由此，美国精神得到了最好的诠释。

(5) 关于文学批评，豪威尔主张文学批评家不应随意地主观地去评价作品，应该中立地去做准确精练的描述，阐释和分类。

3. 主要作品

《塞拉斯·拉帕姆的发迹》

《现代婚姻》

《新财富的危害》

《批评与小说》

4. 主要作品分析

◆《塞拉斯·拉帕姆的发迹》

该小说充分体现了豪威尔斯这位小说家的素养。它讲述了 19 世纪中期波士顿一个暴发户的故事。它是美国现实主义文学的典范。这里没有英雄主义，没有戏剧化或非同寻常的情节。豪威尔斯专注于描写渺小、琐碎及平常的事务。

在这部小说中作者强调道德，强调同情心、道德高尚以及不同社会阶层互相适应、和谐相处的必要性。作者批判了美国生活中的物质主义。

Ⅲ. 亨利·詹姆斯

他是心理现实主义的先驱。他是美国第一个致力于国际题材的作家。

1. 生平

亨利·詹姆斯生于新英格兰一个家境富裕的书香门第。他的哥哥威廉·詹姆斯是著名的哲学家和心理学家。在一定程度上，他的家庭背景决定了他写作的主题：他的作品主要是叙述富有悠闲的上流社会的生活。他早年深受欧洲文化的影响。也许法国文化对他影响最深，正如他称巴尔扎克是他的"最出色的老师"。1876 年他定居伦敦，几乎在那里度过余生。

2. James' literary point of view (1) As a realist, he holds that life is bound with art and representing life is the goal of a novel. He advocates novel-writing must get rid of numerous limitations and welcome vulgar and mediocre items. (2) James's psychological analysis of his topic characterize his realism. His characters' inner awareness and inner conflicts against reality are the focus in his works rather than the details of their surroundings. (3) His aesthetic of the novel centers on "point of view". James endeavors to refrain from the artificial omniscience and attempts to make his characters reveal themselves.	**2. 詹姆斯的文学批评观** （1）作为一个现实主义作家，他认为艺术与生活息息相关，小说存在的理由就是表现生活。他主张应予小说写作极大的自由，作品应包括所有不愉快、丑陋的现象。现实的气氛是小说最大的优点。 （2）詹姆斯作品的题材有明显的心理分析的特点，他不仅细致地描述外部环境，更多的是强调人物的内心活动。 （3）詹姆斯关心叙事角度，这是他小说美感的关键。他避免用全知视角，他让角色表现他们自己而尽量不加干涉。
3. Theme James established himself as a legendary writer with "the international theme": the meeting of America and Europe, American innocence in contact and contrast with European decadence, and its moral and psychological complications. The meeting symbolizes America grows from innocence to maturity.	**3. 主题** 詹姆斯的名声主要是建立在他的小说主题"国际主题"上的，即美国和欧洲的相会。美国的天真和欧洲的堕落、道德和心理上的复杂性相对照。对美国人而言，这是一个从积累经验、增长知识、走向成熟的过程。
4. Style It is hard to understand James. He is often highly refined and insightful. His large vocabulary enables his word selection to be exact and appropriate for his literary imagination. Therefore Henry James is not only one of the most important realists of the period before the First World War, but also the most expert stylist of his time.	**4. 写作风格** 詹姆斯的作品不易理解。他语言优美，眼光独到。他词汇量丰富，选词准确，力求寻找能够表达他所想的最佳表达方式。因此詹姆斯不仅是一战前的这段时期最重要的现实主义作家之一，也是最老练的文体家。
5. Major works *The American* *Daisy Miller* *The Portrait of a Lady* *The Bostonians* *The Princess Casamassima* *The Turn of the Screw* *What Maisie Knew* *The Ambassadors* *The Wings of the Dove* *The Golden Bowl*	**5. 主要作品** 《美国人》 《黛西·米勒》 《贵妇人的画像》 《波士顿人》 《卡萨玛西玛公主》 《拧螺丝》 《梅西见闻》 《专使》 《鸽翼》 《金碗》

6. **Analysis of major works**	6. **主要作品分析**
◆*The Portrait of a Lady* An optimistic and innocent Jamesian American girl, Isabel Archer, arrives in Europe to live a free and noble life, only to be the victim of two vulgar and corrupt expatriates, Madame Merle and Gilbert Osmond. Her ignorance of evil around her and her wealth destroy her dreams and hope.	◆《贵妇人的画像》 小说讲述了典型的詹姆斯式的美国姑娘伊莎贝尔·阿切尔，来到欧洲，满怀希望过一种自由和高贵的生活，却不幸沦为两个粗野且不择手段的美国侨民——默尔太太和吉尔伯特·奥斯蒙德——的受害者。伊莎贝拉的美梦和期望破碎了：她对周围人对她及她的财富的虎视眈眈毫无察觉，这导致了她的毁灭。
◆*The Ambassador* James considered *The Ambassadors* as his "most perfect" artistic work, which parodies American and European manners. Although Strether, a middle-aged commonplace American, is expected to bring back his wealthy fiancée's son Chad, who is crazy about the European culture, to inherit the Newsome family business in New England, he is turned to believe that Paris should be home to Chad and himself. Mutual understanding and sympathy are stressed.	◆《专使》 《专使》是詹姆斯自认为最完美的著作。它是一部关于美国和欧洲举止方式的喜剧。它讲述了平庸的中年美国男子斯特雷瑟赴巴黎接一位迷恋欧洲的年轻人回新英格兰继承家业，但是最终却相信巴黎才是这个年轻人和他自己应该生活的地方。詹姆斯强调了相互理解和同情。

8.2 考研真题与典型题详解

I. Fill in the blanks.

1. The American novelist ________ probed deeply at the individual psychology of his characters, writing in a rich and intricate style that supported his intense scrutiny of complex human experience.（人大 2006 研）
2. *Daisy Miller* was written by ________.（大连外国语学院 2007 研）
3. The name of the heroine in *The Portrait of a Lady* is ________.（人大 2006 研）
4. The Age of Realism is also what Mark Twain referred to as "________".
5. By 1875, American writers were moving toward ________ in literature. We can see this in the true-to-life descriptions of Bret Harte, William Dean Howells, Hamlin Garland.
6. The most straightforward definition of realism is probably the one given by the American realist ________: that is, "nothing more and nothing less than the truthful treatment of material."
7. Howells' ________ is a fine specimen of American realistic writing.

Ⅱ. Multiple Choice

1. ________ divides the 19th century into the age of romanticism and realism in American literature.（北二外 2009 研）
   A. The Spanish-American war　　B. The Civil War
   C. WWI　　D. WWII
2. Realism in American literature stretches from ________ to the end of 19th. C.（北二外 2007 研）

A. early 17th. C
B. early 18th. C
C. American Civil War
D. Spanish-American War

3. William Dean Howells explores the life of ________ Americans. (北二外 2009 研)

A. lower-class B. upper-class C. working-class D. middle-class

4. Which of the following works by Henry James does not deal with "the international theme"? ________ (天津外国语学院 2009 研)

A. *Daisy Miller*
B. *The Turn of the Screw*
C. *The Portrait of a Lady*
D. *The Ambassadors*

5. Which of the following novels is not written by Henry James? (天津外国语学院 2007 研)

A. *Daisy Miller*
B. *The Golden Bowl*
C. *What Maisie Knew*
D. *The Rise of Silas Lapham*

6. Which ONE of the following concepts is related to the understanding of literary realism? (四川大学 2010 研)

A. spontaneous outflow of feelings
B. faith in individualism, independence of mind and self-reliance
C. representation of characters, human nature and social actualities in a non-idealized way
D. survival of the fittest

7. With William Dean Howells, James, and Mark Twain active on the scene, ________ became the major trend in the seventies and eighties of the nineteenth century.

A. sentimentalism B. romanticism C. realism D. naturalism

8. Where Mark Twain and William Dean Howells satirized European manners at times, ________ was an admirer.

A. O. Henry B. Henry James C. Walt Whitman D. Jack London

9. Choose the novel which is not written by Henry James.

A. *The Ambassadors*
B. *The Wings of the Dove*
C. *The Bostonians*
D. *The Mysterious Stranger*

10. The main theme of ________ *The Art of Fiction* reveals his literary credo that representation of life should be the main object of the novel.

A. Henry James'
B. William Dean Howells'
C. Mark Twain's
D. O. Henry's

Ⅲ. Explain the following terms.

1. The Age of Realism in American Literature(四川大学 2010 研)
2. Realism
3. Psychological realism

Ⅳ. Read the following quotations and answer the questions.

Passage 1 (人大 2006 研)

Isabel always felt an impulse to pull out the pins; not that she imagined they inflicted any damage on the tough old <u>parchment</u>, but because it seemed to her aunt might make better use of her sharpness. She was very critical herself—it was <u>incidental to her sex, and her nationality</u>; but she was very sentimental as well, and there was something in Mrs. Touchett's dryness that set her own moral fountains flowing.

Questions:

(1) Give the title of the work and the full name of the author.

(2) Explain the implications of the underlined parts of the passage.

Passage 2

Isabel always felt an impulse to pull out the pins; not that she imagined they inflicted any damage on the tough old parchment, but because it seemed to her her aunt might make better use of her sharpness. She was very critical herself—it was incidental to her sex, and her nationality but she was very sentimental as well, and there was something in Mrs. Touchett's dryness that set her own moral fountains flowing.

"Now what's your point of view?" she asked of her aunt. "When you criticize everything here you should have a point of view. Yours doesn't seem to be American you thought everything over there so disagreeable. When I have mine; it's thoroughly American!"

"My dear young lady", said Mrs. Touchett, "there are as many points of view in the world as there are people of sense to take them. You may say that doesn't make them very numerous. American? Never in the world; that's shockingly narrow. My point of view, thank God, is personal!"

Isabel thought this a better answer than she admitted; it was a tolerable description of her own manner of judging, but it would not have sounded well for her to say so.

Questions:

(1) This passage is taken from a well-known novel. What is the name of the novel?

(2) Who is the author of this novel?

(3) Make a brief comment on the heroine Isabel Archer.

(4) What is Jamesian theme?

Passage 3

Under certain circumstances there are few hours in life more agreeable than the hour dedicated to the ceremony known as afternoon tea. There are circumstances in which, whether you partake of the tea or not—some people of course never do—the situation is in itself delightful. Those that I have in mind in beginning to unfold this simple history offered an admirable setting to an innocent pastime. The implements of the little feast had been disposed upon the lawn of an old English country-house, in what I should call the perfect middle of a splendid summer afternoon. Part of the afternoon had waned, but much of it was left, and what was left was of the finest and rarest quality. Real dusk would not arrive for many hours; but the flood of summer light had begun to ebb, the air had grown mellow, the shadows were long upon the smooth, dense turf. They lengthened slowly, however, and the scene expressed that sense of leisure still to come which is perhaps the chief source of one's enjoyment of such a scene at such an hour. From five o'clock to eight is on certain occasions a little eternity; but on such an occasion as this the interval could be only an eternity of pleasure.

Questions:

(1) From which novel is this paragraph taken from?

(2) Who is the author of this novel?

(3) What is conveyed in this opening paragraph about English convention?

V. Short answer questions

1. How does Henry James describe the Americans in his novels? (国际关系学院 2007 研)
2. Who are the three dominant figures of the American Realistic Period and what are their literary differences?

VI. Essay questions

1. What literary movements dominated the periods immediately before and after the American Civil War? What factors mainly caused the shift? Please name two representative authors respectively. (西安交大 2008 研)
2. What led to the rise of American Realism? (北航 2007 研)
3. According to Henry James's viewpoint, what is the conflict between the American personalities and European personalities?
4. What is the most famous theme in Henry James' fiction? What is his favorite approach in characterization, which makes him different from Mark Twain and W. D. Howells as realists? Please take *The Portrait of a Lady* as an example to give sound ground for your points.

参考答案及解析

I. Fill in the blanks.

1. Henry James
   (美国小说家亨利·詹姆斯的作品善于挖掘人物心理。)
2. Henry James
   (《黛西·米勒》是美国作家 Henry James 的国际主题小说。)
3. Isabel Archer
   (《一位贵妇的画像》(*The Portrait of a Lady*)是亨利·詹姆斯的早期代表作，也是他的杰作之一。该小说的女主人公是伊莎贝尔·阿切尔。)
4. The Gilded Age
   (现实主义时期被马克·吐温看作"镀金时代"。)
5. realism
   (到 1875 年后美国文学过渡到了现实主义时期，我们可以在布勒特·哈特，威廉姆·迪恩·豪威尔斯和哈姆林·加兰的作品中找到对生活逼真的描述。)
6. William Dean Howell
   (现实主义最明确的定义是威廉姆·迪恩·豪威尔斯提出来的，"对材料的处理很真实，恰到好处。")
7. *The Rise of Silas Lapham*
   (豪威尔的《塞拉斯·拉帕姆的发迹》是美国现实主义的优秀作品。)

II. Multiple Choice

1. B 内战是美国浪漫主义文学和现实主义文学的分水岭。
2. C 美国的现实主义阶段是从南北战争到 19 世纪。
3. D 豪威尔斯擅长描写上升中的美国中产阶级，其代表作是《塞拉斯·拉帕姆的发迹》。
4. B *The Turn of the Screw*(《螺丝在拧紧》)是亨利·詹姆斯的一部哥特式心理小说，描写的是一位年轻女教师应聘到乡下一家富户照看两个失去双亲的孩子，在其家中见到死去的前任女教师及这家男仆的幽影，气氛越来越紧张，最后一个孩子死去，另一个精神错乱。其余三个选项都是詹姆斯关于“国际题材”的作品。

5. D *The Rise of Silas Lapham*(《塞拉斯·拉帕姆的发迹》是 William Dean Howell(豪威尔斯)的作品，其余都是亨利·詹姆斯的作品。

6. C 现实主义的核心观念为客观再现当代社会现实，展现人物性格、人类本质和社会现实。选项 A 是浪漫主义的核心观念，选项 B 是个人主义的观念，选项 D 是达尔文的“适者生存”观念。

7. C 19 世纪七、八十年代现实主义成为美国文学的主流。威廉·豪威尔斯、亨利·詹姆斯和马克·吐温是这一时期的代表作家，他们在理论和实践上都对美国现实主义文学的发展做出了重大贡献。

8. B 马克·吐温、亨利·詹姆斯和威廉·豪威尔斯并驾齐驱，被誉为是 19 世纪美国现实主义文学的三大倡导者。欧洲风情受到亨利·詹姆斯的赞美，却不时成为马克·吐温和威廉·豪威尔斯讽刺的对象。

9. D 《神秘的陌生人》(*The Mysterious Stranger*)是马克·吐温的作品，其余三项《大使》(*The Ambassadors*)，《鸽翼》(*The Wings of the Dove*)，《波士顿人》(*The Bostonians*)都是亨利·詹姆斯的作品。

10. A 除小说以外，亨利·詹姆斯(Henry James)对文学贡献的另一部分是他的文学批评。在《小说的艺术》(*The Art of Fiction*)中詹姆斯明确指出，小说的目的是反映现实生活。

Ⅲ. Explain the following terms.

1. In American literature, the Civil War brought the Romantic Period to an end. The Age of Realism came into existence. It came as a reaction against the lie of romanticism and sentimentalism. Realism turned from an emphasis on the strange toward a faithful rendering of the ordinary, a slice of life as it is really lived. It expresses the concern for commonplace and the low, and it offers an objective rather than an idealistic view of human nature and human experience.
2. Realism: It's a mode of writing that gives the impression of recording or reflecting faithfully an actual way of life. Realism in literature attempts to describe life without idealization or romantic subjectivity. The representatives of American Realism are Henry James, William Dean Howells and Mark Twain.
3. Psychological realism: It is the realistic writing that probes deeply into the complexities of characters' thoughts and motivation. Henry James' novel *The Ambassadors* is considered to be a masterpiece of psychological realism.

Ⅳ. Read the following quotations and answer the questions.

Passage 1

(1) *The Portrait of a Lady*, Henry James

(2) parchment: This word implies the old European culture with a long history.
incidental to her sex, and her nationally: This phrase implies it's her aunt's nature to be sharp because sharpness is the nature of a woman and an English person.

Passage 2

(1) *The Portrait of a Lady*

(2) Henry James

(3) An optimistic and innocent Jamesian American girl, Isabel Archer, arrives in Europe to live a free and noble life, only to be the victim of two vulgar and corrupt expatriates, Madame Merle and Gilbert Osmond. Her ignorance of evil around her and her wealth destroy her dreams and hope.

(4) Jamesian theme refers to Henry James's handling of his major fictional theme, "the international theme": the meeting of America and Europe, American innocence in contact and contrast with European decadence and its moral and psychological complications.

Passage 3

(1) *The Portrait of a Lady*

(2) Henry James

(3) In English society, it seems that everything goes according to convention. Afternoon tea is almost a routine ritual in English society and English men's seriousness about this process is a reflection of their conservative character.

V. Short answer questions

1. The novels of Henry James largely dealt with "the international theme": the meeting of America and Europe. James enjoyed juxtaposing American moral innocence with the somber decadence of Europe. In his novels, the Americans are usually innocent, fresh, full of energy and curiosity, open and assertive. When confronting European sophistication, some of them triumph over it and some others are overwhelmed.
2. The three dominant figures of the period were William Dean Howells, Mark Twain, and Henry James. Though the three prominent writers all worked for realism, they had different understandings of "truth". While Mark Twain and Howells seem to have paid more attention to the "life" of the Americans, Henry James has apparently laid a greater emphasis on the "inner world" of man. He is a realist of the inner life. Though Twain and Howells both share the same concern in presenting the truth of the American society, they have each of them different emphasis. Howells focuses his discussion on the rising middle class and the way they live, while Twain deals with his own region and people of the lower class of society at the forefront of his stories. James writes mostly of the upper reaches of American society.

VI. Essay questions

1. Transcendentalism dominated the periods immediately before the American Civil War and realism dominated after the American Civil War.

   Literary theme and technique are influenced by and switch in accord with political and social events. The sweeping factory, which beat the farm boosted the American capitalism. The Civil War from 1861 to 1865 not only changed the American social structure but also altered the nature of American morality.

   Since the end of the Civil War, the national economy is dominated by commerce. In the east, urbanization rate reached 50% till 1880, and meanwhile the trend toward towns and cities was obvious. Although the tremendous and rapid industrialization and mechanization produced abundant wealth, the gap between wealth and poverty was enlarged to extreme degrees.

What makes the gap worse was the disappearing frontier. The ideals of the New World are less attractive to people. For example, people began to doubt whether pursuing an American dream was worthwhile or whether the charm of the New World is true. Suffering and unhappiness began to surface in the prosperous phenomenon. Feelings of disenchantment and frustration swept the country from coast to coast. The "Golden Age" was indeed a "Gilded" one as nicknamed by Mark Twain.

The literary movement, realism, developed as an opposite posture against romanticism and sentimentalism. It was concerned with and was devoted to displaying reality itself no matter whether it was beautiful or not. It tried to represent commonness rather than uniqueness. William Dean Howells, Henry James, and Mark Twain pushed realism into the central literary movement through the 1870s and the 1880s.

2. Literary theme and technique are influenced by and switch in accord with political and social events. The sweeping factory, which beat the farm boosted the American capitalism. The Civil War from 1861 to 1865 not only changed the American social structure but also altered the nature of American morality.

Since the end of the Civil War, the national economy is dominated by commerce. In the east, urbanization rate reached 50% till 1880, and meanwhile the trend toward towns and cities was obvious. Although the tremendous and rapid industrialization and mechanization produced abundant wealth, the gap between wealth and poverty was enlarged to extreme degrees.

What makes the gap worse was the disappearing frontier. The ideals of the New World are less attractive to people. For example, people began to doubt whether pursuing an American dream was worthwhile or whether the charm of the New World is true. Suffering and unhappiness began to surface in the prosperous phenomenon. Feelings of disenchantment and frustration swept the country from coast to coast. The "Golden Age" was indeed a "Gilded" one as nicknamed by Mark Twain.

The literary movement, realism, developed as an opposite posture against romanticism and sentimentalism. It was concerned with and was devoted to displaying reality itself no matter whether it was beautiful or not. It tried to represent commonness rather than uniqueness. William Dean Howells, Henry James, and Mark Twain pushed realism into the central literary movement through the 1870s and the 1880s.

3. H James established himself as a legendary writer with "the international theme": the meeting of America and Europe, American innocence in contact and contrast with European decadence, and its moral and psychological complications. American heroes and heroines tackling European sophistication are always the focus among Henry James' novels. His novels represent these characters' ruin or success.

He saw that Americans often regarded Europeans as over-refined, degenerate, and artificial, and that many Europeans considered Americans naive, vulgar, and ignorant. The misunderstanding caused personality conflicts. The national differences provided an opportunity for contrasts of characters. The typical American in a James novel is fresh, enthusiastic, not perhaps as cultured as he might be, but eager to learn, and basically "good" in spite of his disregard of the outworn conventions and social graces of Europe. The European, on the other hand, is highly cultivated, urban, sometimes boring, but always correct. He was, however, sometimes unprincipled. In James, the Americans often appeared to stand for morality, the Europeans for manners. This is true even the case of characters like Daisy Miller.

4. His main theme is the innocence of the New World (America) in conflict with the corruption and wisdom of the Old (Britain).

His favorite approach in characterization is psychological approach, and unlike W. D. Howells and other realists, his realism is called psychological realism.

The Portrait of a Lady explores the conflict between the individual independence and the British society's convention. Isabel Archer is a young American woman who must choose between her independent spirit and the demands of social convention. After professing and longing to be an independent woman, autonomous and answerable only to herself, Isabel falls in love with and marries the sinister Gilbert Osmond, who wants her only for her money and who treats her as an object, almost as part of his art Collection. Isabel must then decide whether to honor her marriage vows and preserve social propriety or to leave her miserable marriage and escape to a happier, more independent life, possibly with her American suitor Caspar Goodwood.

The most important part of the book is where she realizes her mistake. She sits all alone, late at night, in her "house of darkness". James shows her inner consciousness in this quiet moment. There is a great drama in his description of her "motionlessly seeing" the mistake she has made. The drama is not created by her actions but by the thoughts in her mind.

James is one of America's great psychological realists, and he uses all his creative powers to ensure that Isabel's conflict is the natural product of a believable mind, and not merely an abstract philosophical consideration.

第9章 地方色彩小说·马克·吐温

9.1 复习笔记

I. Local Colorism	I. 地方色彩主义
Local colorism as a trend became dominant in America literature in the late 1860s and early 1870s. As a variation of American literary realism, it shows the cohesion of historical and aesthetic energy.	19世纪60年代末70年代初，地方色彩主义成为美国文学的主流。作为美国现实主义文学的一个分支，它体现了历史与艺术力量的凝聚。
The development of local colorism was influenced by the social and cultural climate of the country. Socially, the country was expanding westward, and the psychological need of seeking for cultural identity motivated people to show their local characters. Culturally, the frontier humorists prospered "talk tales" and provided conditions for the development of local colorism.	地方色彩主义的发展受到当时社会文化环境的影响。从社会层面来说，国家向西扩张，寻求文化认同的心理需求促使人们展现自己的地方特色。文化上，边疆幽默作家发展了话本故事，为地方色彩主义的发展提供了条件。
Local colorists concentrated on the elements which characterize a local culture, such as speech, customs, and more peculiar to one particular place. They emphasize the physical settings and those distinctive qualities of landscape which condition human thought and behavior. Major local colorists are Bret Harte, Hanlin Garland, Harriet Beecher Stowe, Kate Chopin and Mark Twain.	地方色彩主义作家关注的是当地文化的特征要素，如语言、习俗，以及一个特定的地方的独特之处。他们强调自然环境和那些影响人类思想和行为的独特的景观品质。主要的地方色彩主义作家包括布莱特·哈特、汉林·加兰德、哈里耶特·比彻·斯托、凯特·肖邦及马克·吐温等。
II. Mark Twain (1835 –1910)	**II. 马克·吐温**
1. Life	**1. 生平**
Mark Twain, pen name of Samuel Langhorne Clemens, is a great literary giant of America. He grew up in the river town of Hannibal, Missouri. After his father died, he left school and began to seek his own fortune. He once worked as a printer's apprentice, a tramp printer, a silver miner, a steamboat pilot and a frontier journalist. Twain's writing took the form of humorous journalism of the time, and it enabled him to master the technique of narration. The short story *The Celebrated Jumping Frog of Calaveras County* brought him international attention. Two of the best books during his period are The Adventure of Tom Sawyer and *The Adventures of Huckleberry Finn*.	马克·吐温，原名萨缪尔·朗赫恩·克莱门斯，是一位美国文学巨匠。他在密苏里州的河畔小镇汉尼拔长大。他父亲去世后，他离开了学校，开始自谋出路。他当过印刷所学徒、排字工、银矿矿工、舵手还有记者。马克·吐温的写作采用了当时的幽默新闻的形式，这使他掌握了叙述的技巧。短篇小说《卡拉维拉斯县著名的跳蛙》使他获得了国际关注。在他的时代，最好的两本书是《汤姆·索亚历险记》和《哈克贝利·费恩历险记》。

The former was regarded as a classic book written for boys, while the latter is Twain's most representative work. His early works show his optimistic attitude towards life. But later in his work, he changed writing styles and turned into a despairing and cynical determinist. His tragic experience led to this change, but more importantly, he saw the dark side of social life.	前者被认为是为男孩写的经典著作，而后者是马克·吐温的代表作。他的早期作品表现了他乐观的人生态度。但后来在他的作品中，他改变了写作风格，变成了一个绝望和讽刺的宿命论者。他的悲惨经历造成了这一改变，但更重要的是，他看到了社会生活的阴暗面。
2. Comparisons among Howells, Henry James and Mark Twain	**2. 豪威尔斯、亨利·詹姆斯和马克·吐温的比较**
Although Howells, James and Mark Twain all worked for realism, there were obvious differences between them.	尽管豪威尔斯、亨利·詹姆斯和马克·吐温都是美国现实主义作家，但是三者之间具有明显的不同。
(1) In terms of the theme, James focused on the upper class of American society. Howells paid more attention to the daily life of middle class, while Twain concentrated on the life of the udder class.	(1)就主题而论，亨利·詹姆斯主要写美国的上层社会，豪威尔斯侧重写社会中层，而马克·吐温则写社会下层人民的生活。
(2) Technically, Howells wrote in a gentle way, and James worked on a kind of imaginative or psychological realism. But Mark Twain made remarkable contributions to the development of American literature in terms of realistic novel theory and novel language style.	(2)从技巧上讲，豪威尔斯运用的是温文尔雅的现实主义风格，亨利·詹姆斯致力于一种“想象”处理或者心理现实主义。但是马克·吐温在现实主义小说理论和小说语言风格方面，为美国文学的发展做出了卓越贡献。
3. Comments on Mark Twain	**3. 对马克·吐温的评价**
(1) Mark Twain was a famous American literary giant. He was a humorist and acclaimed as “the true father of our national literature” by Mencken.	(1)马克·吐温是美国一位著名的文学巨匠。他是一位幽默大师，被门肯评价为“我们真正的民族文学之父”。
(2) Descriptions of familiar local regions are being used in Mark Twain's novel to represent American social life. His works are based on his abundant knowledge about people and events.	(2)马克·吐温的小说用了人们熟悉的地方来描述美国的社会生活。他的作品是基于他对人和事的丰富了解。
(3) Mark Twain's extensive use of the colloquial speech has made it a highly regarded form of American literature. His style of language influenced many later writers like Sherwood Anderson, Hemingway, etc.	(3)马克·吐温对口语的大量运用使其成为美国文学中备受推崇的一种文学形式。他的语言风格还影响了舍伍德·安德森和海明威等很多后世作家。
(4) Mark Twain was also a social critic. He loved life and people, advocated freedom and justice, and respected fraternity and mutual assistance among people. He hated hegemonism and despised injustice and cruelty.	(4)马克·吐温同时也是一位社会批评家。他热爱生活和人民，主张自由和正义，推崇人与人之间的友爱互助。他厌恶霸权主义，蔑视不公和残暴。

(5) Mark Twain was a friend of the Chinese. He cared about the Chinese people who were oppressed in the United States and the Chinese people who were humiliated by the great powers.

(5)马克·吐温是中国人民的朋友。他关心在美国饱受压迫的华侨，关心备受列强凌辱的中华民族。

4. Major works

Innocents Abroad
Roughing it
The Gilded Age
The Adventures of Tom Sawyer
The Prince and the Pauper
Life on the Mississippi
The Adventures of Huckleberry Finn
A Connecticut Yankee in King Arthur's Court
The Man That Corrupted Hadleyburg
The Mysterious Stranger
Autobiography

4. 主要作品：

《傻子出国记》
《艰难时代》
《镀金时代》
《汤姆·索亚历险记》
《王子与贫儿》
《密西西比河上的生活》
《哈克贝利·费恩历险记》
《亚瑟王宫廷中的美国佬》
《败坏哈德莱堡的人》
《神秘的陌生人》
《自传》

5. Analysis of major work

◆*The Adventures of Huckleberry Finn*

(1) It is a sequel to *The Adventures of Tom Sawyer*, but much deeper and more mature in theme and technique. It is generally considered to be one of the most excellent works of western literature and western civilization. Hemingway described it as the book from which "all modern American literature comes".

(2) It tells a story of a teenager Huck who finds himself floating on a raft down the Mississippi River with an escaping slave, Jim. In the course of their adventurous journey, Huck and Jim meet with danger and finally Huck abandons his discrimination against the black people, realizing that Jim is his close friend.

(3) This novel is a portrayal of real life. It discusses some social and cultural issues from the perspective of a child, showing the collision between wilderness and civilization. It is a classic local colorism novel, but by describing the experience of Huck's adventure, the novel tells us a universal value that humanity will prevail.

(4) Another notable feature of the novel is its language. Using the informal language of uneducated Americans, Mark Twain makes the colloquial style a highly respected literary form in the history of American literature.

5. 主要作品分析

◆《哈克贝利·费恩历险记》

(1) 这部小说是《汤姆·索亚历险记》的续篇，但是其主题更深刻，写作技巧更成熟。它通常被认为是西方文学和西方文明最伟大的著作之一。海明威曾评价其为"现代美国文学之源"。

(2) 它讲述了一个少年哈克发现自己和一个逃跑的奴隶吉姆一起在密西西比河上漂流的故事。在冒险的旅程中，哈克和吉姆遇到了危险，最终哈克放弃了对黑人的歧视，意识到吉姆是他的好朋友。

(3) 这部小说是对现实生活的真实写照。它从一个孩童的角度讨论了一些社会文化问题，展现了野蛮与文明的碰撞。这是一部经典的地方色彩小说，但通过描述哈克的冒险经历，小说告诉我们一个普遍的价值观，即人性将战胜一切。

(4) 小说的另一个特点就是其语言。马克·吐温使用未受过教育的美国人的非正式语言，使口语体成为美国文学史上一种备受推崇的文学形式。

9.2　考研真题与典型题详解

I. Fill in the blanks.

1. Mark Twain, pseudonym of Samuel Langhome ________, started off as a ________ colorist. His novel ________ is the one book from which, as Hemingway noted, "all ________ American literature comes".（国际关系学院2010研）
2. Harriet Beecher Stowe's masterpiece is ________.
3. One of Samuel Langhorne Clemens' best books ________ is built around his experiences as a steamboat pilot.
4. The result of Mark Twain's European trip was a series of newspaper articles, later published as a book called ________.
5. William Sidney Porter, whose pen name was ________, was the author of *The Cop and the Anthem.*
6. Many of O. Henry's stories tell about the life of poor people in ________.

II. Multiple Choice

1. West Humor is best represented in ________'s short story writing. （北二外2007研）

A. O Henry　　B. Flannery O'Connor

C. Henry James　　D. Mark Twain

2. ________'s stories still had many unrealistic qualities: "tall tales" and unlikely coincidences. He is never a pure realist.

A. Henry James　　B. Mark Twain

C. Nathaniel Hawthorne　　D. Henry David Thoreau

3. Mark Twain wrote most of his literary works with a ________ language.

A. grand　　B. pompous　　C. simple　　D. vernacular

4. Mark Twain was a great social critic and a friend of the Chinese. His *Disgraceful Persecution of a Boy* is a scathing piece of criticism directed against the persecution of the ________ immigrants in California.

A. Quakers　　B. Chinese　　C. French　　D. Japanese

III. Explain the following term.

1. Local Colorism（山东大学2016研；北二外2008研；四川大学2009研）

IV. Read the following quotations and answer the questions.

Passage 1

I took the sack of corn meal and took it to where the canoe was hid, and shoved the vines and branches apart and put it in; then I done the same with the side of bacon; then the whisky-jug. I took all the coffee and sugar there was, and all the ammunition; I took the wadding; I took the bucket and gourd; took a dipper and a tin cup, and my old saw and two blankets, and the skillet and the coffee-pot. I took fish-lines and matches and other things—everything that was worth a cent. I cleaned out the place. I wanted an ax, but there wasn't any, only the one out at the woodpile, and I knew why I was going to leave that. I fetched out the gun, and now I was done.

Questions:

(1) Which novel is this passage taken from?

(2) Analyze the language style of this passage.

V. Short answer questions

1. Why is Mark Twain considered a social critic?(国际关系学院2007研)
2. In *The Adventures of Huckleberry Finn*, Huck Finn is a thirteen-year-old boy. Why does Mark Twain use a child as the center of consciousness in this book?
3. What is special about Mark Twain's realism?
4. How do you understand Mark Twain's use of Local Color in his writing?

Ⅵ. Essay questions

1. Charles Dickens and Mark Twain are both well-known literary realists. Name one of the masterpieces by each of them and make a brief comparison and/or contrast so as to tell the similarities and/or differences between British and American realism.(武汉大学2007研)
2. What's the difference between Henry James's realism and Mark Twain's realism?

参考答案及解析

I. Fill in the blanks.

1. Clemens; local; *The Adventures of Huckleberry Finn*; modern

(马克·吐温(Mark Twain),原名萨缪尔·兰亨·克莱门(Samuel Langhorne Clemens)是美国的作家,19世纪后期美国现实主义文学的杰出代表。开始时他是个乡土作家,《哈克贝利·芬恩历险记》被海明威称为"现代美国文学之源"。)

2. *Uncle Tom's Cabin*

(比彻·斯托夫人(Harriet Beecher Stowe 1811-1896)的名作长篇小说《汤姆叔叔的小屋》(*Uncle Tom's Cabin*)是19世纪最畅销的小说(以及第二畅销的书,仅次于最畅销的书《圣经》)并被认为是刺激1850年代废奴主义兴起的一大原因。)

3. *Life on the Mississippi*

(马克·吐温凭着年轻时驾驶河船的经验,写成了脍炙人口的自传《密西西比河上的生活》(*Life on the Mississippi*)。以密西西比河及沿岸的城镇为舞台背景,生动地写下作者的生活体验、童年岁月以及他所热爱的乡土。)

4. *Innocents Abroad*

(马克·吐温游历欧洲时写了一系列文章,讽刺而幽默地记录他的所见所闻,这些文章后来整理出版成书,名为《傻子旅行》(*Innocents Abroad*)。)

5. O. Henry

(欧·亨利(O. Henry),原名为威廉·西德尼·波特(William Sydney Porter),他是美国著名批判现实主义作家,世界三大短篇小说大师之一。《警察与赞美诗》是其著名的短篇小说。)

6. New York

(欧·亨利(O. Henry)善于描写美国社会尤其是纽约(New York)百姓的生活。他的作品构思新颖,语言诙谐,结局总使人"感到在情理之中,又在意料之外";又因描写了众多的人物,富于生活情趣,被誉为"美国生活的幽默百科全书"。)

II. Multiple Choice

1. D　美国西部幽默的代表人物是马克·吐温。
2. B　马克·吐温的小说中有很多不现实的特质，荒诞不经的故事和不大可能发生的巧合。
3. D　马克·吐温大多数的作品都是用口语化的语言写的。
4. B　美国作家马克·吐温是伟大的社会批评家、中国人民的朋友。对于迫害加利福尼亚州华人的行为，马克·吐温在 *Disgraceful Persecution of a Boy* 中给予了辛辣的抨击。

III. Explain the following term.

1. Local Colorism: Local Colorism is an unique variation of American literature realism. Generally, the works by localism are concerned with the life of a small region or province. This kind of fiction depicts the characters from a specific settings or an era, which are marked by its customs, dialects, landscape, or other peculiarities that have escaped standardizing cultural influence. Task of local colorism is to write or present local characters of their regions in truthful depiction distinguished from others. Mark Twain's *The Adventures of Huckleberry Finn* is the most representative one.

IV. Read the following quotations and answer the questions.

Passage 1

(1) *The Adventures of Huckleberry Finn*

(2) In addition to several words, most of the words are simple colloquial words. These words are short, concrete and easy to understand.

Most of the sentence structures are simple or compound sentences, with connective words such as "and" and "then" being used.

In the article, repeated verbs are widely used, and the concrete picture is presented through the description of specific characters and actions.

One other specific peculiarity is that the style of the book does approximate the actual speech habit of an uneducated American boy at that time.

V. Short answer questions

1. Mark Twain is a satirist for he criticized many aspects of the American society. He dealt largely with the lower strata of society and preferred to represent social life through portraits of local places which he knew best. Mark Twain is also a strong supporter of anti-imperialism, abolition, emancipation, anti-racism and women's rights.
2. In using a child protagonist, Twain is able to imply a comparison between the powerlessness and vulnerability of a child and those of a black man in pre-Civil War America.

   Huck and Jim frequently find themselves in the same predicaments: each is abused, each faces the threat of losing his freedom, and each is constantly at the mercy of adult white men. As we see in Huck's moral dilemmas, however, Jim is also vulnerable to Huck, who, although he occupies the lowest rung of the white social ladder, is white nonetheless.

   Twain also uses his child protagonist to dramatize the conflict between socialized or received morality on the one hand and a different kind of morality based on intuition and experience on the other. As a boy, Huck is a character who can develop morally, whose mind is still open and being formed, who does not take his principles and values for granted.

By tracing the education and experiences of a boy, Twain shows that conclusions about right and wrong that are based on logic and experience often stand at odds with the society's rules and morals, which are often hypocritical rather than logical.

3. Mark Twain's contribution to the development of realism and to American literature as a whole was partly through his theories of Local Colorism in American fiction, and partly through his colloquial style.

   Mark Twain drew heavily from his own rich fund of knowledge of people and places. He confined himself to the life with which he was familiar. By quoting from his own experience, Mark Twain managed to transform art into the freedom and humor, in short, the finest elements of Western culture.

   Another feature of Mark Twain's realism is its language. He reproduced actual daily speech with a degree of accuracy and made colloquial speech an accepted, respectable literary medium in the literary history of America.

4. Mark Twain's narratives are distinguished for his use of local color. This may be defined as the careful attention to details of the physical scene and to those mannerisms in speech, dress, or behavior peculiar to a geographical locality.

   Twain emphatically insisted that the job of the native novelists was not to generalize the nation but to depict each of the country's regions and peoples accurately. Only in this way, the peculiarity of American experience, the polyglot tongues of its people, and the vastness of the continent could be captured.

   After the civil war a number of American writers exploited the possibilities of local color in various parts of America.

VI. Essay questions

1. In the nineteenth century, many progressive writers wrote excellent works to unveil the dark society. Charles Dickens (1812 ~ 1870) and Mark Twain (1835 ~ 1910) were the most outstanding representatives of them. *Oliver Twist* is the masterpiece of Charles Dickens and Mark Twain's masterpiece is *The Adventures of Huckleberry Finn*. The two books share the theme of a corrupt adult society, and the irony in both works is often centered on racism and religion. Both novels are adventures of children.

   Oliver Twist is based on real life materials such as the New Poor Law of 1834 and the current trial of a notorious fence and thief-trainer. By following the most unfortunate experience of a poor orphan boy, Oliver, the author means to give a vivid picture of the underworld with all kinds of thieves, prostitutes and murderers as well as the horrible cruelty of the workhouse system of the time. Oliver is the first of that brilliant group of child characters who are the very images of innocence, love and honesty. The novel leads to a happy ending. Dickens lives and writes in the Victorian age when English society began to feel the impact of change but still managed to keep the old values intact. Industrialization and capitalism had begun to bring wretchedness into the country, but life had not become totally impossible. So, English realist writers like Dickens were basically optimistic. They were aware of modern ills which they lost no time to castigate, but still wrote with the notion that the world was basically good and could become better.

The Adventures of Huckleberry Finn tells a story about the United States before the Civil War, around 1850, when the great Mississippi Valley was still being settled. Here lies an America, with its great national faults, full of violence and even cruelty, yet still retaining the virtues of "some simplicity, some innocence, some peace." Here is a "hymn" to that ante bellum America, the moral values of which vanished with the war. The machine and the worship of money were on their way in, but the river-god, with its "sunlight, space, uncrowded time, stillness, and danger," has not been forgotten. Similar to English realists, American realist novelists took the side of the defenseless or oppressed, and fought corruption, privilege and abuse of the society, but the Civil War and the American Dream played important roles in their writing.

2. Although Henry James and Mark Twain were both American realistic writers, there were obvious differences between them. In terms of the theme, James focused on the upper class of American society, while Twain concentrated on the life of the udder class. Technically, James worked on a kind of imaginative or psychological realism, but Mark Twain made remarkable contributions to the development of American literature in terms of realistic novel theory and novel language style.

   Henry James believed that the only reason for the existence of a novel is that it does attempt to represent life. Such realism is therefore merely the obligation that the artist assumes to represent life as he sees it, which may not be the same life as it "really" is. James shifted the ground of realistic art from the outer to the inner world.

   Mark Twain preferred to represent social life through portraits of local places that he knew best. He drew heavily from his own rich fund of knowledge of people and places. He confined himself to the life with which he was familiar. By quoting from his own experience, Mark Twain managed to transform art into the freedom and humor, in short, the finest elements of western culture.

第10章 美国自然主义·克兰·诺里斯·德莱赛·罗宾逊

10.1 复习笔记

I. American Naturalism	**Ⅰ. 美国自然主义**
1. Historical Background	**1. 历史背景**
(1) In the decades after the Civil War, "Modern America" has risen. The promotion of industrialization caused polarization between rich and poor. The number of slums increased drastically, and the urban poor were homeless, suffering from torture and violence.	(1)内战以后的年代见证了现代美国的崛起。工业化的推广造成贫富两极分化。贫民窟的数量急剧增加，城市的贫民生活没有着落、饱受折磨和暴力的侵袭。
(2) The westward expansion continued, and the frontier extended to the Pacific coast. People were ruthlessly manipulated by various forces, including railways. The high freight rates of railway goods forced farmers to go bankrupt.	(2)西进扩张继续推进，边疆推至太平洋沿岸。人们被各种力量无情地操纵着，这其中包括铁路，高昂的铁路货物运费逼得农民破产。
(3) People who lived in a cold, indifferent, and Godless world no longer had free will. People began to be pessimistic. Darwinian evolutionary thoughts such as "survival of the fittest" or "human beasts" became popular terms and moral standards in this morally degraded world.	(3)生活在冷酷、淡漠、没有上帝的世界里的人早已没有自由意志可言。人们开始悲观，"适者生存"或"人类畜类"这一类的达尔文进化思想在这个道德沦丧的世界成为流行用语、道德标准。
2. Features of Naturalist writings	**2. 自然主义作品的特点**
(1) American naturalism was a new and harsher realism. Naturalism is derived from realism, but it is a step forward than realism in describing social reality.	(1) 美国自然主义是一种新的更为严苛的现实主义。自然主义源于现实主义，但在描述社会现实方面比现实主义更向前一步。
(2) American naturalist writers no longer portray social reality gently. They describe the weakness and helplessness of human beings in the cruel world, as well as their lack of dignity in the face of crushing forces such as the environment and genetic factors.	(2)美国自然主义作家不再温和地描绘社会现实，他们描写在冷酷的世上人类无助及微不足道，以及其在面临环境、遗传因素等粉碎性力量面前缺乏尊严。
(3) The works of naturalism reveal a miserable world. People live in a cold, harsh, and indifferent environment to fight hopelessly against overwhelming forces. The power that human beings cannot manipulate determines people's life. The style of the work is gloomy, and the overall tone is hopeless or even desperate.	(3)自然主义的作品揭示了一个悲惨的世界，在这样的世界里人类在冷酷、恶劣又无动于衷的环境下与压倒一切的力量做无望的斗争，他们的人生由自身无法决定的力量操控。作品中整个画面阴郁而黑暗，总体基调是无望甚至是绝望。

3. Major American Naturalists

Stephen Crane
Frank Norris
Theodore Dreiser
Edwin Arlington Robinson
Jack London
Upton Sinclair

3. 美国自然主义主要作家

斯蒂芬·克兰
弗兰克·诺里斯
西奥多·德莱赛
埃德温·阿灵顿·罗宾森
杰克·伦敦
厄普顿·辛克莱尔

II. Stephen Crane (1871 –1900)

1. Life

Stephen Crane was born in a Methodist family in New Jersey. He had been in a military preparatory school for less than a year. Then he moved to New York and became a freelance writer. His first-hand knowledge of the New York slums provided the writing material for his *Maggie: a Girl of the Streets*. *The Red Badge of Courage* published in 1895 and his first collection of poems *The Black Riders* made him a famous writer. He reported the Spanish-American War as a war correspondent in Cuba. He left the United States and settled in the United Kingdom for his marriage. He became good friends with Conrad and James there.

II. 史蒂芬·克兰(1871 –1900)

1. 生平

史蒂芬·克兰出生在新泽西的一个卫理公会教派的家庭。他曾在一所军事预备学校待了不到一年。然后他移居到了纽约，成为了一名自由撰稿人。他对纽约贫民窟的第一手了解为他的《街头女郎玛吉》提供了写作素材。1895 年出版的《红色英勇勋章》和他的第一部诗集《黑衣骑士》使他成为著名的作家。他曾在古巴做战地记者报道美西战争。由于其婚姻关系，他离开美国定居英国，并与康拉德和詹姆斯成为好朋友。

2. Literary contributions

(1) Crane was a pioneer of American naturalism. His writings provided "a sudden direction and a fresh impulse" for the entire aesthetic movement in the 1990s.

(2) Crane is also a pioneer of modern poetry. His early poems were concise and catchy without rhyme. His poetry broke the orthodoxy with impressive imagination, which had a huge impact on modern poetry.

2. 文学贡献

(1) 克兰是美国自然主义的先驱。他的作品为 90 年代整个美学运动提供了“一个突然的方向和新鲜的动力。”

(2) 他也是现代诗歌的先驱。他早期的诗歌语言简练，朗朗上口，没有韵脚，打破正统地简洁，想象力令人印象深刻，这些都对现代诗歌产生了巨大的影响。

3. Major works

Maggie: a Girl of the Streets
The Black Riders
The Red Badge of Courage
"The Open Boat"
"The Blue Hotel"
"An Experiment in Misery"

3. 主要作品

《街头女郎玛吉》
《黑衣骑士》
《红色英勇勋章》
《海上扁舟》
《蓝色宾馆》
《悲苦中的实验》

4. Analysis of major work

◆ *The Red Badge of Courage*

(1) The story is set in the American Civil War. The basic theme is human life in a cold, manipulating world. In this work, Crane explores the primeval emotions of man and tries to tell the basic facts of human life.

(2) Crane's exposure of the war shows the feature of modernism. In this novel, war is nothing more than a slaughterhouse. There is no heroism on the battlefield. There is only fear of death, timidity, and the human instinct to run away from the dangerous situations. Crane's non-romantic and non-heroic treatment of the war started the modernist tradition of telling the truth about the basic human condition by all means and describing the war according to real human experience.

4. 主要作品分析

◆《红色英勇勋章》

（1）故事以美国内战为背景。基本主题是在冰冷且操纵一切的世界中的人类。在这部作品里，克兰探究了人的原始情感并试图讲述人类生活的基本事实。

（2）克兰对战争的揭露具有现代派独有的特点。在这部小说中战争只不过是个屠宰场。战场上没有英勇或英雄主义，有的只是对死亡的恐惧、胆怯，以及人想要逃离险境的本能。克兰这种对战争非浪漫主义和英雄主义的处理，开创了现代派的传统，即不计一切代价讲述人类基本生存状况的真相，将战争描写成人真实的经历。

III. Frank Norris (1870 – 1902)

1. Life

Frank Norris was born in Chicago and his family moved to San Francisco in 1884. During the year at Harvard, he wrote *McTeague*. He had planned to write a trilogy on the production, sale and consumption of wheat. The first, *The Octopus*, was his best work, the second, *The Pit*, and the third, *The Wolf*, was unfinished. Frank Norris was a literary critic as well. His essays were collected in *The Responsibility of the Novelist*. He died of meningitis in 1902. Norris had a great influence on the writers of the 1920s and 1930s including William Faulkner and John Steinbeck.

III. 弗兰克·诺里斯

1. 生平

弗兰克·诺里斯生于芝加哥，1884年举家搬到了旧金山。在哈佛逗留的那一年他写了《麦克提格》。他生前计划写关于小麦生产、销售和消费的三部曲。第一部《章鱼》是他的最佳作品，第二部是《粮食交易所》，第三部《狼》未完成。诺里斯也是一位文学批评家。他的文学评论文章收集在他的《小说家的责任》一书内。他于1902年死于脑膜炎。诺里斯对威廉·福克纳和约翰·斯坦贝克等20世纪二三十年代的作家产生了巨大的影响。

2. Writing style

Mr Norris's works are sometimes loose and thrilling, but the language is simple and catchy, like poetry. His fresh images are also one of the precious treasures of literature in that period.

2. 写作风格

诺里斯的作品有时结构松散，情节过于惊险，但是语言简洁，朗朗上口，宛如诗歌。他那清新的意象也是这一时期文学的宝贵财富之一。

3. Major works

Mcteague

The Octopus

The Pit

The Responsibility of the Novelist

3. 主要作品

《麦克提格》

《章鱼》

《粮食交易所》

《小说家的责任》

4. Analysis of major work	**4. 主要作品分析**
◆*McTeague*	◆《麦克提格》
(1) It is "the first full-bodied naturalist American novel" and "a consciously naturalistic manifesto." It is a classic about the inevitable impact of environment and genetics on human life.	(1)《麦克提格》被誉为"第一部全面的美国自然主义小说"及"美国自然主义的宣言"。它是关于环境及遗传对人类生活产生不可避免影响的经典之作。
(2) McTeague is a typical "human beast". His behavior is primitive and ancestral with wild desires. His tragedy is reflected in his inability to get rid of the wild power which is destined to destroy him.	(2) 主人公麦克提格是"人形兽类"的典型，他的行为原始且具有返祖性，他还有着野性的欲望。他的悲剧性在于无法摆脱注定要毁灭他的野性力量。
(3) This novel added vitality to the naturalism that has just begun to rise in the United States.	(3) 这部小说给刚刚开始影响美国的自然主义增添了力量。
Ⅳ. Theodore Dreiser (1871 – 1945)	**Ⅳ. 西奥多·德莱赛**
Dreiser was the most accomplished American literary naturalist.	德莱赛是美国最伟大的自然主义作家。
1. Life	**1. 生平**
Dreiser was born in Indiana as the ninth child. His parents were German immigrants, and the family was extremely poor. His first novel, *Sister Carrie*, was rejected because of its ruthless revealing of the essence of American life. *Sister Carrie* was published in 1900, and his other works were also published later. Dreiser's thoughts are left-sided. He visited Russia with great sympathy for socialism. With his *Dreiser Looks at Russia* and *Tragic America*, he conveyed his new belief. He then joined the American Communist Party.	德莱赛出生在印第安纳州，是家中第九个孩子，父母是德国移民，童年极度贫困。其第一部小说《嘉莉妹妹》因其无情地揭示美国生活的本质而被拒绝出版。1900年《嘉莉妹妹》出版，其他作品也相继出版。德莱赛思想偏左，他访问过俄国并对社会主义产生了极大的同情，写下《德莱塞访苏印象记》和《悲惨的美国》表达其新信仰。他在去世前加入了共产党。
2. Dreiser's points of view	**2. 德莱赛的观点**
(1) Dresser believes in social Darwinism. He believes that man is just an animal driven by greed for survival. Only the fittest can survive in the struggle for survival. Life is fixed, and people have no right to express their wishes.	(1)德莱赛信奉社会达尔文主义。他认为人只是为了生存而被贪婪驱使的动物，在生存斗争中只有适者才能生存。人生既定，人无权表达自己的意愿。
(2) He severely criticized his country because he believed that the American social moral model distorted human nature.	(2)他严厉批判他的国家，因为在他的眼里美国的社会道德模式歪曲了人的本性。
3. Major works	**3. 主要作品**
Sister Carrie *Jennie Gerhardt* *The Financier*	《嘉莉妹妹》 《珍妮姑娘》 《金融家》

The Titan 《巨头》

The Stoic 《斯多噶》

The Genius 《天才》

An American Tragedy 《悲惨的美国》

Dreiser Looks at Russia 《德莱塞访苏印象记》

Tragic America 《美国悲剧》

The Bulwark 《堡垒》

4. Analysis of major work

◆*Sister Carrie*

(1) *Sister Carrie* is a story about a country girl who went to Chicago to seek a better life and realize the American dream.

(2) *Sister Carrie* embodies Dreiser's naturalistic idea that human inheritance, instinct, and coincidence will control and restrict people.

(3) In a cruel and indifferent world, the lonely and helpless Sister Carrie is mechanically driven by desire and blindly seizes opportunities to survive better. She can only be manipulated by forces that she cannot understand and control.

(4) As the most noteworthy symbol in the novel, the rocking chair represents the uncertainty of life.

4. 主要作品分析

◆《嘉莉妹妹》

(1)《嘉莉妹妹》是一个乡村女孩到芝加哥寻求更好生活和实现"美国梦"的故事。

(2)《嘉莉妹妹》体现了德莱赛的自然主义的观点，即人总是被遗传、本能和机缘巧合操控及限制。

(3) 在残酷冷漠的世界，孤独无助的嘉莉妹妹机械地被欲望驱使，盲目的抓取机会以能更好地生存。她只能受自己不能理解和控制的力量所摆布。

(4) 小说中最明显的象征是那把摇椅，它代表了人生的不确定性。

V. Other authors of the period

1. Edwin Arlington Robinson (1860 – 1935)

Robinson was the most accomplished poet in America in the 1920s.

◆Major works

"Man Against the Sky"

"Richard Cory"

"Miniver Cheevy"

"Flammonde"

2. Jack London (1876 – 1916)

Jack London was very popular in the early 20th century. He moved from the lower class to the upper class through hard work. After he became a millionaire, he found that life in mainstream society was empty and dull. So he was frustrated and committed suicide.

V. 同时期其他作家

1. 埃德温·阿灵顿·罗宾逊

罗宾逊被认为是20世纪20年代美国最伟大的诗人。

◆主要作品

《天边人影》

《理查德·科里》

《米尼弗·契维》

《弗拉蒙德》

(2) 杰克·伦敦

杰克·伦敦是20世纪初美国著名的作家。他来自社会的底层，努力的工作并跻身于社会的上流阶层。但是当他成为百万富翁后，他发现主流社会的生活是空虚、索然无味的。他在绝望中自杀。

◆**Major works** *The Call of the Wild* *White Fang* *The Sea Wolf* *Martin Eden*	◆**主要作品** 《野性的呼唤》 《白獠牙》 《海狼》 《马丁·伊登》
3. O. Henry (1862 –1910) O. Henry is the pen name of William Sidney Porter. He has many popular works as a famous short story writer in the world.	**(3) 欧·亨利** 欧·亨利是威廉·西德尼·波特的笔名。他十分多产，是世界著名的短篇小说家。
◆**Major works** "The Gift of the Magi" "The Cop and the Anthem" "The Last Leaf"	◆**主要作品** 《麦琪的礼物》 《警察与赞美诗》 《最后一片叶子》

10.2 考研真题与典型题详解

I. Fill in the blanks.

1. Dreiser's novel __________, a commercial and critical failure when first published in 1900, was reissued in 1907 and won high praise for its grim, naturalistic portrayal of American society. (人大 2006 研)
2. Naturalism stresses the determinism of __________ and __________ . (国际关系学院 2009 研)
3. __________ is the novel into which Jack London put most of himself. (人大 2006 研)
4. The impact of Darwin's evolutionary theory on the American thought and the influence of the nineteenth century French literature on the American men of letters gave rise to another school of realism: American __________ .
5. In 1859, Darwin published __________, which exerted great influence on American Naturalism.
6. __________ is the pioneer who wrote in the naturalistic tradition.
7. War in Crane's novel __________ is a plain slaughterhouse. There is nothing like valor or heroism on the battlefield, and if there is anything, it is the fear of death, cowardice, the natural instinct of man to run from danger.
8. __________ had an evident influence on naturalism. It seemed to stress the animality of man, to suggest that he was dominated by the irresistible forces of evolution.
9. The identification of potency with money is at the heart of Theodore Dreiser's masterpiece __________.
10. The protagonist of Theodore Dreiser's *Trilogy of Desire* is __________ .
11. Theodore Dreiser's novel __________, a commercial and critical failure when first published in 1900, was reissued in 1907 and won high praise for its grim, naturalistic portrayal of American society.

12. __________ is the pioneer who wrote in the naturalistic tradition.

13. Stephen Crane's novel __________ relates the story of a good woman's down fall and destruction in a slum environment.

14. Benjamin Frank Norris's novel __________ has been called "the first full-bodied naturalistic American novel" and "a consciously naturalistic manifesto".

15. O. Henry's __________ is a very moving story of a young couple who sell their best possessions in order to get money for a Christmas present for each other.

16. In __________, a novel about American Civil War, the protagonist keeps asking himself the question, "Will I run from a battle?" and at last he does run away from the battle field. (天津外国语学院 2009 研)

17. In *The Octopus* written by __________, wheat farmers struggle to grow crops and send them to market for a profit, while being beleaguered by the inflated prices of the giant railroad conglomeration. (大连外国语学院 2008 研)

18. As a literary movement, __________ came in the latter half of the 19th century as a reaction against the "lie" of romanticism and sentimentalism. (天津外国语学院 2007 研)

II. Multiple Choice

1. Which of the following books deals with American Civil War? (天津外国语学院 2008 研)

A. *The Red Badge of Courage*　　B. *For Whom the Bell Tolls*

C. *Slaughterhouse-Five*　　D. *Catch 22*

2. __________ does not belong to Theodore Dreiser's *Trilogy of Desire*. (首师大 2009 研)

A. *The Financier*　　B. *The Titan*

C. *The Stoic*　　D. *An American Tragedy*

3. All the following concepts can be found in American naturalistic fiction EXCEPT __________. (四川大学 2008 研)

A. determinism

B. survival of the fittest

C. effects of hereditary and environmental forces

D. search for identity

4. "The Lure of the Spirit: The Flesh in Pursuit" is the title of one chapter in Dreiser's novel __________.

A. *An American Tragedy*　　B. *Sister Carrie*

C. *Dreiser Looks at Russia*　　D. *Jannie Gerhardt*

5. "__________" was a term created by the French novelist, Emile Zola.

A. realism　　B. transcendentalism

C. naturalism　　D. veritism

6. Jack London was at his height of his powers when he wrote __________, which is deeply influenced by Darwinism.

A. *The Sea Wolf*　　B. *To Build a Fire*

C. *The Call of the Wild*　　D. *Martin Eton*

Ⅲ. Explain the following term.

1. American Naturalism(北二外 2007 研；南开大学 2008 研)

Ⅳ. Read the following quotations and answer the questions.

Passage 1 (西安交大 2008 研)

When Carolin Meeber boarded the afternoon train for Chicago, her total outfit consisted of a small truck, a cheap imitation alligator-skin satchel, a small lunch in a paper box, and a yellow leather snap purse, containing her ticket, a scrap of paper with her sister' s address in Van Buren Street, and four dollars in money. It was in August, 1889. She was eighteen years of age, bright, timid, and full of the illusions of ignorance and youth... When a girl leaves her home at eighteen, she does one of two things. Either she falls into saving hands and becomes better, or she rapidly assumes the cosmopolitan standard of virtue and becomes worse. Of an intermediate balance, under the circumstances, there is no possibility. The city has its cunning wiles, no less than the infinitely smaller and more human tempter. There are large forces which allure with all the soulfulness of expression possible in the most cultured human. The gleam of a thousand lights is often as effective as the persuasive light in a wooing and fascinating eye. Half the undoing of the unsophisticated and natural mind is accomplished by forces wholly superhuman. A blare of sound, a roar of life, a vast array of human hives appeal to the astonished senses in equivocal terms. Without a counselor at hand to whisper cautious interpretations, what falsehoods may not these things breathe into the unguarded ear! Unrecognized for what they are, their beauty, like music, too often relaxes, then weakens, then perverts the simpler human perceptions.

Questions:

(1) What novel is the above passage taken from? Who is the author?

(2) How many types of tempters exist? What are they?

(3) Please identify all the instances of "large forces". What can these large forces do?

(4) What is suggested as a solution to an eighteen-year-old girl' s falling into folly?

(5) What realistic features are revealed in the passage? Please expound your argument in detail.

(6) What naturalistic ideas are revealed in the passage? Please explain your argument in detail.

Passage 2 (国际关系学院 2007 研)

When a girl leaves her home at eighteen, she does one of two things. Either she falls into saving hands and becomes better, or she rapidly assumes the cosmopolitan standard of virtue and becomes worse. Of an intermediate balance, under the circumstances, there is no possibility. The city has its cunning wiles, no less than the infinitely smaller and more human tempter. There are large forces which allure with all the soulfulness of expression possible in the most cultured human. The gleam of a thousand lights is often as effective as the persuasive light in a wooing and fascinating eye. Half the undoing of the unsophisticated and natural mind is accomplished by forces wholly superhuman. A blare of sound, a roar of life, a vast array of human hives, appeal to the astonished senses in equivocal terms. Without a counselor hand to whisper cautious interpretations, what falsehoods may not these things breathe into the unguarded ear? Unrecognized for what they are, their beauty, like music, too often relaxes, then weakens, the perverts the simpler human perceptions.

Questions:

(1) Who is the author of the novel from which this paragraph is taken? What is the title of the novel?

(2) With which literary school is the author usually identified?

(3) How does the paragraph express the main points of that school?

(4) What do you think about the author's way of writing as reflected in the paragraph?

V. Short answer question

1. What are the characteristics of O. Henry's writing?

Ⅵ. Essay questions

1. In what ways does *Sister Carrie* or some other major works by Theodore Dreiser reveal his perception of the "American Dream"? What do you know and think of the controversy about Dreiser as a man and as a writer? (人大2007研)
2. Please briefly comment on Theodore Dreiser's novel *Sister Carrie*. (四川大学2007研)
3. Discuss Jack London's writing style and theme.
4. Discuss Theodore Dreiser's style.
5. Discuss the reflection of realistic and naturalistic tendencies on the American 19th-century novels.

参考答案及解析

I. Fill in the blanks.

1. *Sister Carrie*

   (德莱赛的《嘉莉妹妹》在1900年首次出版时在商业上和文学批评界是失败的，在1907年重新被发现，因其对美国社会的自然描写赢得了很高的评价。)
2. heredity; social environment

   (自然主义强调遗传和社会环境决定论。)
3. *Martin Eden*

   (杰克·伦敦名作《马丁·伊登》(*Martin Eden*)是一部带有自传色彩的长篇小说。)
4. naturalism

   (达尔文的进化论对美国思想和19世纪法国文学产生深远影响，从而产生了美国自然主义这一新的学派。)
5. *Origin of the Species*

   (1859年达尔文发表的《物种起源》对美国自然主义产生了很大的影响。)
6. Stephen Crane

   (史蒂芬·克兰是美国文学自然主义传统的先锋人物。)
7. *The Red Badge of Courage*

   (克兰的小说《红色英勇勋章》中战争是就一个屠场，战争中并没有展示战士的勇猛和英雄主义，只是对死亡的恐惧，懦弱和人性中逃离危险的自然本能。)
8. Darwinism

   (达尔文主义(Darwinism)对自然主义(Naturalism)影响深远。达尔文主义强调人的"动物本性"，认为人是由遗传和不可抗拒的外部力量共同支配的。)
9. *An American Tragedy*

（德莱塞代表作长篇小说《美国的悲剧》（*An American Tragedy*）（1925）通过一个穷教士儿子克莱特·格里菲斯为追逐金钱财势堕落为蓄意杀人犯的故事，揭示了利己主义恶性膨胀的严重后果，同时更揭露了金钱至上的美国生活方式对人的普遍的罪恶性腐蚀毒害作用。）

10. Frank Cowperwood

（西奥多·德莱塞的《欲望三部曲》（*Trilogy of Desire*）包括《金融家》（*The Financier*），《巨人》（*The Titan*），《斯多葛》（*The Stoic*）。《欲望三部曲》的主人公是法兰克·柯帕乌（Frank Cowperwood）。）

11. *Sister Carrie*

（《嘉莉妹妹》）（*Sister Carrie*）是美国伟大的自然主义作家德莱塞的处女作。该小说 1900 第一次出版时广受非议，但是 1907 年再发行时却因娴熟地运用自然主义的创作手法、极强的社会表现力而赢得较高的赞扬。）

12. *Stephen Crane*

（斯蒂芬·克莱恩（Stephen Crane，1871～1900），是美国著名作家，他是美国自然主义文学的先驱者，其代表作有《街头女郎玛吉》（*Maggie*：*A Girl of the Streets*）和《红色英勇勋章》（*The Red Badge of Courage*）。）

13. *Maggi*：*A Girl of the Streets*

（美国自然主义作家斯蒂芬·克莱恩第一部小说《街头女郎玛吉》（*Maggie*：*A Girl of the Streets*）是美国文学史上重要的自然主义作品。他通过小说的主人公玛吉的成长历程来探索主体的社会化过程，最终寻找促使玛吉走向毁灭的"现实"。本文旨在从社会心理学的角度探讨该部作品，进而挖掘其小说的社会心理表征。）

14. *McTeague*

（美国自然主义作家弗兰克·诺里斯（Frank Norris 1870－1902）的小说《麦克提格》（*McTeague*）是美国文学史上第一部真正意义上的自然主义作品，被称为美国自然主义流派小说的宣言。）

15. *The Gift of the Magi*

（《麦琪的礼物》（*The Gift of the Magi*）是美国著名文学家欧·亨利的一篇短篇小说，它描写了一个感人的故事：在圣诞节前一天，一对小夫妻互赠礼物，结果阴差阳错，两人珍贵的礼物都变成了无用的东西，而他们却得到了比任何实物都宝贵的东西——爱。）

16. *The Red Badge of Courage*

（《红色英勇勋章》是以美国内战为背景，讲的是名叫亨利的青年怀着对战争的美妙幻想，不顾母亲的反对，参加了北方军。虽然战争很刺激，但是面对死亡的威胁，他动摇了。他一直问自己："我会从战场上逃跑吗?"后来，他还是从阵地上逃跑了。后来，他为此十分内疚，重上战场，获得显赫战功，但是无论他逃跑时的怯弱还是冲锋时的英勇都不过是一种歇斯底里的表现。）

17. Frank Norris

（弗兰克·诺里斯，美国小说家，《章鱼》是其代表作。）

18. Realism

（作为一场文学运动，现实主义作为对浪漫主义和感伤主义的"谎言"的对抗出现在 19 世纪后半期。）

II. Multiple Choice

1. A 《红色英勇勋章》是美国作家 Stephen Crane 的小说，描绘了美国内战的残酷。《丧钟为谁而鸣》是美国作家 Ernest Miller Hemingway 以西班牙内战为背景的小说。《第五屠宰场》是美国小说家 Kurt Vonnegut 关于第二次世界大战的反战科幻小说。《第二十二条军规》是美国作家 Joseph Heller 以第二次世界大战为背景的小说。
2. D 德莱塞的欲望三部曲包括《金融家》《巨人》和《斯多葛》。
3. D 自然主义小说家们推崇生物决定论和适者生存，认为生理遗传和社会环境都是人类社会发展的决定性因素。
4. B 《嘉莉妹妹》(*Sister Carrie*)是德莱塞创作的第一部小说。该小说体现了作者的自然主义观点。德莱塞认为人是由遗传、本能和机遇控制与操纵的。其中"灵的诱惑：肉的追求"("The Lure of the Spirit: The Flesh in Pursuit")是《嘉莉妹妹》20 章和 21 章的标题。
5. C 自然主义是由法国小说家左拉提出的。这一术语对美国自然主义产生了深远影响。
6. C《野性的呼唤》是杰克伦敦在其鼎盛时期写的一部深受达尔文主义影响的小说。

III. Explain the following term.

1. American Naturalism appeared in the late 19th to early 20th century. The movement was inspired by the principles and methods of natural science, especially Darwinism, Naturalism is derived from realism, but it is a step forward than realism in describing social reality. The works of naturalism reveal a miserable world. People live in a cold, harsh, and indifferent environment to fight hopelessly against overwhelming forces. The power that human beings cannot manipulate determines people's life. The style of the work is gloomy, and the overall tone is hopeless or even desperate. Typical American Naturalism is represented by Stephen Crane's *The Red Badge of Courage*, Frank Norris's *McTeague* and Theodore Dreiser's *Sister Carrie*.

IV. Read the following quotations and answer the questions.

Passage 1

(1) The above passage is taken from Theodore Dreiser's *Sister Carrie*.

(2) There are two types of tempters. One is the luxury life in the city; another is the tempter from human.

(3) "Large forces" include the gleam of a thousand lights, the persuasive light in a wooing and fascinating eye, a blare of sound, a roar of life and a vast array of human hives. The forces will relax, then waken, then pervert the simpler human perceptions.

(4) A counselor who can recognize the tempters tells them all the time and teaches them to recognize the tempters.

(5) Firstly, realism emphasizes a faithful rendering of the ordinary, the slice of life as it really lives. In this paragraph, the life of Carrie, a girl from countryside to Chicago to realize her American Dream, is described in detail. What she is bringing, even very tidy items, are listed faithfully. Secondly, realism is objective rather than idealized with close observation of life. In the first description of Carrie, the author doesn't make a judge of her, but tells her situation in an objective way by words like board, consist, outfit. Thirdly, realism is concerned with social problems, revealing the frustrations of characters in an environment of depravity. In the second half of this paragraph, the author uses many sentences to depict the tempters of city and the

depravity.

(6) American naturalist writers no longer portray social reality gently. They describe the weakness and helplessness of human beings in the cruel world, as well as their lack of dignity in the face of crushing forces such as the environment and genetic factors. The works of naturalism reveal a miserable world. People live in a cold, harsh, and indifferent environment to fight hopelessly against overwhelming forces. The power that human beings cannot manipulate determines people's life. The style of the work is gloomy, and the overall tone is hopeless or even desperate. In this paragraph, there are only two ways for a young girl in such condition—if she has others' help, she will be better; if she assumes the social standard, she will be worse. She can't make a change by her struggle for there are so many strong forces. Man is negative to act. What's more, the cruel realities of capitalism are revealed, which is one respect of naturalism.

Passage 2

(1) The author is Theodore Dreiser. The title of the novel is *Sister Carrie*.

(2) Theodore Dreiser belongs to American Naturalism. American Naturalism reported truthfully and objectively, with a passion for scientific accuracy and an overwhelming accumulation of factual detail. They painted life as it was lived in the slums, and were accused of telling just the hideous side of it and making "a god of the dull commonplace."

(3) American naturalist writers no longer portray social reality gently. They describe the weakness and helplessness of human beings in the cruel world, as well as their lack of dignity in the face of crushing forces such as the environment and genetic factors. The works of naturalism reveal a miserable world. People live in a cold, harsh, and indifferent environment to fight hopelessly against overwhelming forces. The power that human beings cannot manipulate determines people's life. In this paragraph, there are only two ways for a young girl in such condition—if she has others' help, she will be better; If she assumes the social standard, she will be worse. She can't make a change by her struggle for there are so many strong forces. Man is negative to act.

(4) ①As a naturalist, Theodore Dreiser attempted to achieve extreme objectivity and frankness. For example, in this paragraph, "When a girl leaves her home at eighteen, she does one of two things... Of an intermediate balance, under the circumstances, there is no possibility." This sentence is very objective in tone. This is also an evidence to show that he also mixed philosophical speculations with scenes of the harsh society in this novel. ②Dreiser is good at using the journalistic repetitive methods to leave a deep impression on readers. He showed his interest in painting through the text and pictures, the sharp contrast, the authenticity of colors and the dynamic sense of outline. For instance, "The city has its cunning wiles, no less than the infinitely smaller and more human tempter. There are large forces which allure with all the soulfulness of expression possible in the most cultured human. The gleam of a thousand lights is often as effective as the persuasive light in a wooing and fascinating eye."

V. Short answer question

1. His stories are usually short. The plots are exceedingly clever and interesting, humor abounds with the surprising ending. A story usually has two endings, the first is an unexpected ending,

and the other is a completely different ending and contains a better surprise. Many of his stories contain a lot of spoken and local expressions, which makes them difficult to understand by outsiders. This form of language is used to show partial color, so that the story matches the characters and scenes described. O. Henry's style, whether spoken or written, is always pure and clear.

VI. Essay questions

1. Each of Dreiser's characters in *Sister Carrie* search for their own "American Dreams"— the ones offered by a growing and prosperous democratic country. Carrie, a poor country girl, arrives in Chicago, filled with the expectations of acquiring the better things in life. She imagines the elegant clothes she will wear, the exciting places to which she will go, and the fashionable people with whom she will associate, thinking that everyone who lives beyond the boundaries of her Midwestern state has achieved that higher status. Drouet seeks his own version of the American Dream. He has achieved a certain station in life and wears the clothes to prove it. He frequents the important establishments in town and has befriended many of the right people. Yet, he pursues the other appointments that represent his dream, such as a beautiful woman to adorn his arm and his own home. Hurstwood has the woman, the established home and family, and a good position. He, though, wants more. He knows that his employers leave him out of important decision making, and he knows his friends like him for his position. He seeks love, appreciation, and more prestige. However, at the end of the story, each of them ends up disillusioned.

   Dreiser was controversial throughout his life. He was accused of immoral behavior, improper thinking as a political activist. People criticized him for his heavy style and weak narrative consciousness. As a man who grew up in a harsh environment and a low class, Dreiser had an American dream. He wanted to be rich and respected. But he also saw the cruel reality of American society and the tragedy of chasing the American dream. As a writer, he has the responsibility to reveal reality and awaken people. Among all contemporary writers, he is the bravest man willing to show the true face of society. Over time, Dreiser was recognized as a foresight critic of American values and an influential novelist.

2. *Sister Carrie* is a story about a country girl who went to Chicago to seek a better life and realize the American dream. *Sister Carrie* embodies Dreiser's naturalistic idea that human inheritance, instinct, and coincidence will control and restrict people. Dreiser described the three different worlds in which Sister Carrie lived in detailed records. These scenes present a rough and barbaric panorama of social life in the early 20th century. The details of the novel reflect surprising completeness and precision. In a cruel and indifferent world, the lonely and helpless Sister Carrie is mechanically driven by desire and blindly seizes opportunities to survive better. She can only be manipulated by forces that she cannot understand and control.

3. Jack London was very popular in the early 20th century. His writing style is full of vitality and color. Instead of words, he tells his story through actions and rarely stops to communicate with the readers. His early magazine experience is very helpful to him. Every sentence in his prose can arouse readers' interest. His shortcomings are that his character is usually very rigid and his dialogue is stereotyped. London's themes focus on primitive violence, biological evolution, class warfare, and mechanism determinism. He believes that human beings are victims of forces be-

yond people's control. Human beings have been manipulated by the animal instincts of lower animals. Survival is a non-stop war. The strong and the weak are often engaged in cruel struggles.

4. Theodore Dreiser's style has always attracted attention. So far, people have realized that Dreiser's novels have obvious shortcomings and advantages. His writing is sometimes formless and clumsy, and the characters in the story are relatively simple. But Dreiser's stories are always fascinating and interesting with the clear plot and dynamic characters. Dreiser is good at using the journalistic repetitive methods to leave a deep impression on readers. He showed his interest in painting through the text and pictures, the sharp contrast, the authenticity of colors and the dynamic sense of outline. This is the key for Dreiser to become one of the most important American novelists.
5. Since William Dean Howells first proposed realism in American literature, many realist works with personal characteristics have emerged in the United States. American realists uphold the principle of being honest with life and focus on the faithful reflection of human society.

   The Rise of Silas Lapham, Howell's best-known novel, is the study of a self-made businessman who is ultimately ruined financially by his determination not to compromise his integrity; Mark Twain successfully used local color and historical settings to illustrate and shed light on the contemporary society. The employment of the local dialects and the colloquial language gives impetus to his works. Henry James, however, explored the literary possibility of the inner life in the characters.

   As to the naturalist writers, Stephen Crane's *The Red Badge of Courage*, Frank Norris's best-known works *McTeague* and *The Octopus* reflect the concern with social and economical forces and their effect on human lives. And Dreiser's naturalist idea found expression in almost every book he wrote.

第 11 章　20 世纪 20 年代·意象派·庞德

11.1　复习笔记

I. Overview of the 1920s	**I. 20 世纪 20 年代概况**
1. Background	**1. 背景**
(1) The 1920s was in between two important historical events: WWI and the Great Depression.	(1) 20 世纪 20 年代被夹在第一次世界大战和经济危机两大重大历史事件之间。
(2) In the years after the war, the country's development became increasingly urbanized, and a new industrial economy began to develop. Large-scale production, large-scale consumption, and entertainment became essential parts of economic and cultural life, and quickly became the dominant culture and customs of the nation.	(2) 战后这些年国家发展日趋城市化，一种新的工业经济开始发展。大规模生产、大规模消费和娱乐成为经济文化生活的要素，并迅速成为国家文化和习俗的主导。
(3) After the war, the heroism, patriotism, and enthusiasm for democracy that a generation had believed in, the romantic feelings for war, proved to be false and meaningless.	(3) 战后，一代人曾信仰的英雄主义、爱国主义及对民主的热情这些对战争的浪漫情怀被证明是虚假毫无意义的。
(4) At the social level, the entire American society is in a state of low tolerance. All radical forms and all claims of social and religious rights are considered intolerable.	(4) 在社会层面上，整个美国社会处于一种高度的不容异说的状态。所有的激进形式和所有对社会和宗教权利的主张都被认为是无可容忍的。
(5) Darwin's theory of evolution had made people lose their faith, and this crisis of faith was severely intensified in the 20th century. Without faith, life was fragmented and chaotic. People found themselves living in a spiritual wasteland.	(5) 达尔文进化论使人们丧失了信仰，这种信仰危机在 20 世纪严重加剧。失去信仰，生活支离破碎、混乱不堪。人们发现自己生活在精神的荒原之中。
2. New expressions in the field of art and literature	**2. 文学艺术领域的新表达形式**
Impressionism Dadaism Expressionism Symbolism Surrealism	印象主义 达达主义 表现主义 象征主义 超现实主义
II. The coming of the image	**II. 意象主义的兴起**
The Imagist poem was a movement initiated by some English and American poets in the early 20th century to seek new ways of writing poetry. This movement went through three stages.	意象派诗歌运动是 20 世纪初由一些英美诗人发起的寻求诗歌新的写作方式的运动。这个运动经历了三个发展阶段。

1. Phase Ⅰ (1908 – 1909) The British poet T. E. Hulme founded a Poets' Club in 1908, where poets met and discussed poetry in Soho, London every Wednesday. Hulme favored absolutely accurate expression and no verbiage.	**1. 第一阶段** 英国诗人 T. E. 休姆于 1908 年创立了一个"诗人俱乐部"，每周三在伦敦索豪区一处会餐和讨论诗歌问题。休姆强调绝对准确表达和不讲空话。
2. Phase Ⅱ (1912 – 1914) Ezra Pound was the leading figure of this phase. He and Flint created the Poetic Principle's as follows: (1) Direct description of the "thing", either subjective or objective thing; (2) To avoid words that does not contribute to the presentation; (3) In terms of rhythm, to compose in accordance with the musical phrase, instead of a metronome.	**2. 第二阶段** 埃兹拉·庞德是这一阶段的领军人物。庞德和弗林特制定的诗歌原则为： (1) 直接主观或客观地描绘"事物"； (2) 不使用任何与表达该事物无关的词语； (3) 至于诗歌的韵律，应按音乐的小节而不是按节拍器来组织。
3. Phase Ⅲ (1914 – 1917) After Pound, Amy Lowell took the movement into the "Amygism" period. Disagreements emerged among the Imagist poets and the Imagist movement gradually lost its momentum.	**3. 第三阶段** 艾米·洛威尔代替庞德把运动推向"艾米主义"时期。意象派诗人之间出现分歧，意象派诗歌运动逐渐失去发展动力。
4. Conception of image T. E. Hulme: The image must enable one "to dwell and linger upon a point of excitement, to achieve the impossible and convert a point into a line". Ezra Pound: An image is "that which presents an intellectual and emotional complex in an instant of time". Richard Aldington: Accurate choice of words can make the image produced by the reader consistent with the image when the author is writing.	**4. 意象的概念** T. E. 休姆：意象必须能使人留恋某个令人兴奋的时刻，使不可能变为现实，能使一个点变成一条线。 埃兹拉·庞德：意象描绘瞬间出现在脑际的复杂的思想与情感。 理查德·奥尔丁顿：精准的选词能让读者眼前产生的意象与作者写作时的意象一致。
5. American Imagists Ezra Pound Amy Lowell William Carlos Williams Wallace Stevens T. S. Eliot Carl Sandburg	**5. 美国意象派诗人** 埃兹拉·庞德 艾米·洛厄尔 威廉·卡洛斯·威廉斯 华莱士·史蒂文森 T. S. 艾略特 卡尔·桑德堡
Ⅲ. Ezra Pound (1885 – 1972) Ezra Pound is known as the father of modern American poetry and the most influential leader of the Imagist Movement.	**Ⅲ. 埃兹拉·庞德** 埃兹拉·庞德被称为"美国现代诗歌之父"，他也是意象派诗歌运动最具影响力的领军人物。

1. Life Pound was born in Hailey, Idaho in 1885 and grew up in Pennsylvania. He studied Roman language at Hamilton College and the University of Pennsylvania. Pond arrived in Europe in 1908 and published his first collection of poetry, *A Lume Spento* in Venice. After arriving in London, he met T. E. Hulme and participated in his Poets' Club, and later launched Imagism with H. D. and Richard Aldington. In 1914 he parted ways with Amy Lowell and turned to Vorticism; the aesthetics of both movements left an indelible mark on his works. Pound is also the most controversial figure in the history of American literature. After the outbreak of WWII, he began to deliver some pro-Fascist speeches against Britain and America. He was arrested and charged with treason after the War. He was detained in an American prison near Pisa, and was later then declared insane and interned at St. Elizabeths Hospital. In 1958, with the efforts of celebrities such as T. S. Eliot, Frost and Hemingway, Pound was released in 1958 and returned to Italy, where he worked until his death in 1972.	**1. 生平** 庞德1885年出生于美国爱达荷州的海利镇，在宾夕法尼亚长大。他在汉密尔顿大学和宾夕法尼亚大学学习，主修罗马语。1908年庞德到达欧洲并在威尼斯出版了他的第一部诗集《灯光熄灭之时》。到达伦敦后他结识了休姆并参加了"诗人俱乐部"，后来与H. D. 和理查德·奥尔丁顿发起意象新诗运动。1914年他与艾米·洛厄尔分道扬镳，转向"漩涡主义"，这两个运动的美学思想在他的作品中留下了不可磨灭的印记。庞德也是美国文学史上一位饱受争议的作家。二战爆发后，他发表了一些亲法西斯反对英美的演说。战后，他以叛国罪被捕。他被关押在比萨附近的一所美国监狱，后来被宣布精神失常，被拘禁圣伊丽莎白医院。经过T. S. 艾略特、弗罗斯特和海明威等名人的努力，1958年庞德获释回到意大利，在那里工作直到1972年去世。
2. Comments on Ezra Pound (1) Pound is one of the poetic giants of English and American Modern poetry. (2) What Pound saw in the West in the early years of the 20th century was a chaotic, broken, and barbaric world. He believes that he has an obligation to protect the crumbling civilization. He tries to discover the standards of the past culture and resurrect the lost principles of order. (3) We can find easily in his poetry the traits of Greek, Provencal, Latin, Anglo-Saxon poetic traditions. (4) Pound was also deeply influenced by Chinese culture, especially Confucius. The pictographic features and colorful images in Chinese poetry also have a profound impact on Pound's poetry. (5) He had a huge impact on the modernist writers in Britain and America after WWⅡ.	**2. 对埃兹拉·庞德的评价** (1) 庞德是英美现代派诗歌的一位巨匠。 (2) 庞德看到20世纪初的西方是一个混乱、破碎、野蛮的世界。他认为有义务保护摇摇欲坠的文明，他试着发掘过去文化的标准、复活失去的秩序。 (3) 在他的诗作中不难发现古希腊、意大利、古英语以及普罗旺斯诗歌传统的痕迹。 (4) 庞德也深受中国文化的影响，特别是孔子的影响。中国诗歌中语言象形表意的特点以及多姿多彩的意象也对庞德的诗歌创作产生了深刻的影响。 (5) 庞德对二战后英美的现代作家产生颇多影响。

3. Major works *A Lume Spento* *Personae* *The Spirit of Romance* *Cathay* *Homage to Sextus Propertivs* *Hugh Selwyn Mauberley* *Cantos* "In a Station of the Metro"	**3. 主要作品** 《灯火熄灭之时》 《人物》 《罗曼斯精神》 《华夏》 《向塞克斯特斯普罗波蒂斯致敬》 《休·赛尔温·毛伯利》 《诗章》 《在地铁车站》
4. Analysis of major works ◆"In a Station of the Metro" One of the most representative and classical pieces of work of Pound. Pound was once in a subway station in Paris and was struck by the faces of some pretty women and children hustling out of the damp and somber station. This scene left an extremely deep impression on him, so he decided to describe this picture in poetic language. That was where this poem came from. "The object" is those faces in that dim station. The impression is represented vividly by the simple image of flower petals on a wet, black bough, which serves as the most concise, direct, and accurate representation of the "faces in the crowd".	**4. 主要作品分析** ◆《在地铁车站》 这是意象派诗歌的一首经典佳作。庞德有次在巴黎地铁站被眼前的景象所打动。在人群中，他看到几个漂亮的女人和孩子的面孔。他们正匆匆忙忙地走出潮湿幽暗的地铁站。这场景给他留下了极其深刻的印象，于是他决定以诗歌的语言来展现这幅画面。最后写成了这首诗。诗中描写的对象是潮湿幽暗环境中的面孔。诗人用一枝湿漉漉的黑色粗枝上的花瓣这一简单的主导意象来形象地表达出这种印象。花瓣简洁、直接、确切地代表了"人群中的面孔"。
◆*The Cantos* (1) *The Cantos* is called Pound's "intellectual diary since 1915". There are in total 117 poems included in this collection. It is a social history, integrating heterogeneous cultures and languages. The world in *The Cantos* is depressive and somber. The poet attempts to give order and meaning to the chaotic and meaningless world through art. (2) An important theme of The cantos is usury which, in Pound's eyes, is like a beast with a hundred legs that destroys light, life, and love. (3) Pound found strength and wisdom in Chinese history and Confucianism, which is in contrast to the gloom and chaos of the West. The ideals of harmony and order could be found shining in many chapters of *The cantos*.	◆《诗章》 (1)《诗章》被称为庞德"1915年后的思想日记"，共117首。它是社会历史，是多种语言文化的混合凝练。诗人企图通过艺术赋予杂乱无章、毫无意义的世界以秩序和意义。《诗章》描写了一个沉闷阴郁的世界。 (2)《诗章》的一个重要主题就是高利贷的思考。在庞德的眼中，高利贷就像多脚猛兽摧毁了光明、生活和爱。 (3) 庞德在中国历史和儒家思想中找到了力量和智慧的源泉，这与西方的阴郁与混乱是相对的。许多章节闪耀着和谐与秩序理想的光芒。

11.2 考研真题与典型题详解

I. Fill in the blanks.

1. "In a Station of the Metro" by Ezra Pound goes like this: The apparition of these faces in the crowd; ________ .(首师大 2008 研)
2. ________, by Ezra Pound, employs the complex association of scholarly lore, anthropology, modern history and personages, private history and Witticism, and obscure literary interpolations in various languages. (人大 2006 研)
3. Author ________ Title ________(南京大学 2007 研)
   The apparition of these faces in the crowd;
   Petals on a wet, black bough.
4. Ezra Pound's lifelong endeavor had been devoted to the writing of ________, which contains ________ poems.(国际关系学院 2007 研)
5. Pound was the leader of a new movement in poetry which he called the "________" movement.

II. Multiple Choice

1. Imagist poems are mainly composed in the form of ________ .(北二外 2008 研)
   A. blank verse　B. free verse　C. sonnet　D. Quatrain
2. The Imagist writers followed three principles. They respectively are direct treatment, economy of expression and ________ .
   A. local color　B. irony　C. clear rhythm　D. blank verse
3. ________ showed great interest in Chinese literature and translated the poetry of Li Po (Li Bai) into English, and was influenced by Confucian ideas.
   A. Ezra Pound　B. Robert Frost
   C. T. S. Eliot　D. E. E. Cummings
4. ________ championed the imagist movement from 1912 to 1914, setting down the imagist principles. Then Amy Lowell led the movement into the period of "Amygism," as Pound called it, from 1914 to 1917.
   A. T. S. Eliot　B. H. D.　C. Ezra Pound　D. Carl Sandburg

III. Explain the following terms.

1. Imagism(北外 2009 研; 南开大学 2009 研; 北京邮电大学 2010 研)
2. Avant-Garde(上海交大 2007 研)

IV. Read the following quotation and answer the questions.

Passage 1 (北航 2009 研)

The apparition of these faces in the crowd;
Petals on a wet, black bough.

Questions:

(1) What is the title of this short poem?
(2) Who is the author?
(3) What two images are juxtaposed or placed next to each other in this poem?

V. Short answer questions

1. Why the decade of the 1920s can be termed the second renaissance in the history of American literature?（厦门大学 2007 研）
2. Comment on the artistic features of the poem"In a Station of the Metro" by Ezra Pound.（南京大学 2008 研）

参考答案及解析

I. Fill in the blanks.

1. Petals on a wet, black bough.
（这是意象派诗人庞德的名作，意为：人群中这些面孔幽灵一般显现，湿漉漉的黑色枝条上许多花瓣。）
2. *The Cantos*
（庞德的《诗章》包罗万象，是庞德的代表作。）
3. Author: Ezra Pound Title: "In a Station of the Metro"
（题目节选自庞德的《在一个地铁车站》，该诗是以一个意象作为叙述语言的典型范例。）
4. *The Cantos*; 117
（庞德把毕生精力都投入到写作《诗章》当中，《诗章》共包括 117 首诗。）
5. Imagist
（庞德是意象主义运动的领军人物。）

II. Multiple Choice

1. B 意象派诗人主张诗歌创作在韵律上突破英诗传统格律五音步抑扬格的限制，追求一种更加灵活的自由体。
2. C 意象主义在其宣言中提出了三大原则，分别是：(1) 直接主观或客观地描绘"事物"；(2) 不使用任何与表达该事物无关的词语；(3) 至于诗歌的韵律，应按音乐的小节而不是按节拍器来组织。
3. A 庞德对中国文学很感兴趣，他将李白的诗歌翻译成英文，并且深受儒家思想的影响。
4. C 庞德是意象主义第二阶段的领导者，而艾米·洛威尔是第三个阶段的领导者。

III. Explain the following terms.

1. Imagism is a literary movement that took shape in Britain and U. S. in about 1910. It is a reaction to traditional English poetry and aims to express the sense of fragmentation and dislocation. The imagists, with Ezra Pound as the leading figure, believe that the best means to express momentary impressions is to use one dominant image. Three poetic principles of Imaginism are as follows: i) direct treatment of subject matter; ii) economy of expression; iii) in terms of rhythm, to compose in the sequence of the musical phrase, instead of a metronome. Ezra Pound's "In a Station of the Metro" is a well-known imagist poem.
2. Avant-garde, a French word referring to the vanguard of an army or political movement. Its definition was extended since the late 19th century to those artists and writers who are dedicated to making art as an experiment and revolt against tradition. Ezra Pound's view that 'Artists are the antennae of the race, is a distinctly modern one, implying a duty to stand ahead of one's time by

constantly innovating in terms of forms and subjects.

Ⅳ. Read the following quotation and answer the questions.

Passage 1

(1) *In a Station of the Metro*

(2) Ezra Pound

(3) The writer uses the image of "petals" on another image, that is, "wet, black bough". The poem is considered one of the most significant poems of the Imagist. It is written in a Japanese haiku style. There are only fourteen words in this poem, manifesting that Imagism focuses on the concision of language, the precision of imagery and that it experiments with non-traditional verse forms. Pound contrasts the actual, mundane image that he saw with a metaphor from nature and thus incorporates this "apparition" with visual beauty. The word "apparition" is regarded as crucial since it creates an uncanny and supernatural sense of imprecision which is then enhanced by the metaphor of the second line. The poem reflects the moment of revelation and intense emotion Pound felt at the Metro in Paris. Due to its treating subject's appearance by way of the poem's own vision, it is regarded as a typical Imagist text.

V. Short answer questions

1. The 1920s was in between the two most significant historic events, WWI and the Great Depression. There were at least two important reasons that made the decade different from the periods other periods: WWI, and the sense of life being dislocated and fragmented which was more strongly felt in the first years of the twentieth century. The 1920s was a peculiar period, in which the economic boom after the war and the sense of spiritual disorder were mixed. The greatness of the literature in this period is that it tried to capture that mood and record that for future generations. Just as Emerson and his contemporaries showcase the spirit of their age in their works, T. S. Eliot and Hemingway, and other writers also constituted a lot in terms of recording the spirit of their times.

2. ①It is identified as one of the most significant poems of the Imagist. There are only fourteen words in this poem, manifesting that Imagism focuses on the concision of language, the precision of imagery and that it experiments with non-traditional verse forms. ②It is written in a Japanese haiku style. ③It is a work produced at the early stage of Modernist poetry. It attempts to "break from the pentameter", incorporates the use of visual spacing as a poetic instrument, and contains not a single verb. ④Eight words were arranged in the first line and six in the second, mirroring the octet-sestet, mirroring octet-sestet of the Italian sonnet form .

第 12 章 艾略特·史蒂文斯·威廉斯

12.1 复习笔记

I. T. S. Eliot (1888 –1965) T. S. Eliot is a great modern American poet, playwright and literary critic.	**I. T. S. 艾略特** T. S. 艾略特是一位伟大的美国现代诗人，剧作家和文学评论家。
1. Life Elliott was born in St. Louis, Missouri, where his grandfather organized University of Washington. Both of his parents were cultured and educated, so Eliot received a good education from an early age, especially in classical literature. In 1906 Eliot entered Harvard University, where he studied under Santayana, Barrett Wendell and Irving Babbitt, and was deeply influenced by their neo-humanist ideas. After receiving his master's degree from Harvard, Eliot went on to study in Paris and Oxford. He settled in England in 1915, where he worked as a teacher and bank clerk, and wrote book reviews for publishers. He became a British citizen in 1927 and was awarded the Nobel Prize for Literature in 1948 for his work on *Four Quartets*.	**1. 生平** 艾略特出生在密苏里州的圣路易斯，他的祖父在那儿筹办了华盛顿大学。他的父母都是有文化教养的人，因此艾略特自幼就受到良好的教育，特别是在古典文学方面。1906 年艾略特进入哈佛大学学习，师从桑特亚那、巴雷特·温德尔和欧文·巴比特，并深受他们新人文主义思想的影响。艾略特在哈佛获得硕士后，又在巴黎和牛津学习过。1915 年他定居英国，先后做过教师和银行职员，并为出版商撰写书评。他 1927 年成为英国公民。1948 年因创作《四个四重奏》而获诺贝尔文学奖。
2. Literary criticism (1) The basic themes of Eliot's literary criticism are the relationship between tradition and individual talent, and the relationship between the past, present and future, etc. (2) Eliot's most famous theory is the "impersonal theory" or the theory of impersonality and objectivity. He also proposed that the focus of literary criticism should be the poem itself rather than the poet, and that the literary work itself is a separate entity. These ideas drove the emergence of the New Criticism. (3) Eliot also contributed greatly to the re-evaluation and popularization of the 17th century "Metaphysical Poets" and late 19th century French symbolism.	**2. 文学批评观** (1)艾略特文艺评论的基本主题是传统与个人才能间的关系，以及过去、现在和未来之间的关系等。 (2)艾略特最著名的理论是"非个人化理论"或非个人化和客观性理论。他还提出文学评论的焦点应该是诗歌本身而不是诗人，文学作品本身是独立的实体。这些观点推动了新批评的产生。 (3)艾略特也为重新评价、普及 17 世纪的"玄学派诗人"和 19 世纪晚期的法国象征主义做出了巨大的贡献。

3. Artistic features of Eliot's poetry	**3. 艾略特诗歌的艺术特点**
(1) Eliot's poetry mainly reveals the barrenness and uselessness of Western culture, expresses people's frustration and despair, and pursues the reconstruction of the spiritual world.	(1)艾略特的诗歌主要揭示西方文化的贫瘠与无用，表达人们的沮丧与绝望，追寻精神世界的重建。
(2) In his poetry, Eliot was adept at using symbolism, juxtaposition and complex literary allusions.	(2)在其诗歌创作中，艾略特善于运用象征主义、并列和复杂的文学典故。
(3) Eliot's poetry has no fixed poetic style or rhyme. But people are able to find rules in irregularities and taste rhymes in irregular rhythms.	(3)艾略特的诗歌没有固定的诗体或诗韵，但是人们能够在不规则中找到规则，在不固定的韵律中品出韵律。
4. Major works	**4. 主要作品**
The Love Song of J. Alfred Prufrock	《普鲁弗洛克的情歌》
"Gerontion"	《小老头》
The Waste Land	《荒原》
"Hollow Man"	《空心人》
Ash Wednesday	《圣灰节》
Four Quartets	《四个四重奏》
Murder in the Cathedral	《大教堂的凶杀案》
Cocktail Party	《鸡尾酒会》
The Confidential Clerk	《机要秘书》
"Tradition and the Individual Talent"	《传统与个人才能》
5. Analysis of major works	**5. 主要作品分析**
◆*The Love Song of J. Alfred Prufrock*	◆《普鲁弗洛克的情歌》
(1) This poem is about a timid and timid middle-aged man who wants to propose to a young woman and is apprehensive all the way.	(1) 这首诗歌讲述的是一个胆小怯懦的中年男人欲向一位年轻女人求婚而又一路忐忑忧虑。
(2) The poem uses an inner monologue like Browning's poetry, and the themes of the poem are frustration and emotional conflict.	(2) 这首诗采用了像勃朗宁诗歌一样的内心独白。诗的主题是沮丧和情感冲突。
(3) Prufrock is a depressed, unhappy and tragic figure of a 20th century Western intellectual, who is divided by passion and cowardice, desire and incompetence.	(3) 普鲁弗洛克是一位抑郁不乐、颇具悲剧性的20世纪西方知识分子的形象，是一个被激情与怯懦、欲望与无能分割的现代知识分子。
(4) The title of the poem is very ironic. In fact, the "love song" is a song without love.	(4) 该诗的题目极具讽刺意味。事实上"情歌"竟是"没有情感之歌"。
◆*The Waste Land*	◆《荒原》
(1) *The Waste Land* is a landmark epic. It depicts the spiritual crisis in post-war Europe and reads like a manifesto for the "lost generation". It also established Eliot's position in the literary world.	(1)《荒原》是具有划时代意义的史诗。描绘了战后欧洲的精神危机，读起来像是"迷惘的一代"的宣言书。它也奠定了艾略特的在英美文坛的地位。

(2) The poem's inscription is quoted from the first-century Roman satirist Petronius' *Satyricon*. The title of the poem is based on the Fisher King Legend.	(2)该诗的题记引自一世纪古罗马讽刺家佩特罗尼斯的《风流韵事记》。诗的题目引自"渔王"传说。
(3) An important feature of the poem is that the failure of sexuality implies spiritual emptiness.	(3)该诗的一个重要特点就是性爱的失败意味着精神的虚空。
(4) The poem is a bold innovation in rhyme and style. It not only presents the full picture of the chaos of the modern Western material world and the desolation of the spiritual world, but also reflects the general mood of frustration and despair of the entire post-war generation.	(4)该诗在韵律和文体上进行了大胆的创新。它不仅展现了现代西方物质世界混乱、精神世界荒凉的全貌，也反映了整个战后一代普遍的沮丧与绝望情绪。
(5) The poem is divided into five separate sections: "The Burial of the Dead," "A Game of Chess," "The Fire Sermon." "Death by Water" and "What the Thunder Said". Through the absence of intervals, connectives and dissonance, the poet wants the reader to see and feel the fragmentation of life.	(5)该诗共分为五个独立的部分：《死者葬礼》《对弈》《火诫》《水里的死亡》《雷霆的话》。通过间隔、连接词的缺省及不和谐的缺省，诗人想要读者看到和感受生活的支离破碎。
II. Wallace Stevens (1879 – 1955)	**II. 华莱士·史蒂文斯**
1. Life	**1. 生平**
Wallace Stevens was an unusual poet in modern American literary history. He began his literary work relatively late, publishing his first collection of poetry at the age of 44. He was both a successful businessman and a famous poet. He won the Pulitzer Prize and the National Book Award in the year of his death.	华莱士·史蒂文斯是美国文学史上一位与众不同的诗人。他开始文学创作比较晚，44 岁时才出版了第一部诗集。他既是一位成功的商人，也是一位著名的诗人。他在去世的那一年获得了普利策奖和国家图书奖。
2. Literary point of view	**2. 文学观点**
(1) Wallace Stevens insists that poets live in two worlds, the real and the imaginary, and strives to build a bridge between them. He believed that poets should find beauty, joy and meaning in the filthy reality.	(1)华莱士·史蒂文斯坚持认为诗人生活在现实和想象两个世界，并努力搭建它们之间的桥梁。他认为诗人应从污秽的现实中发现美、快乐和意义。
(2) For Stevens, poetry creates an aesthetic order that also transforms stressful, ominous and destructive environments into explainable, submissive ones. Stevens brought imagination and art to the pinnacle of success in American literary history.	(2)对史蒂文斯来说，诗歌创造了一种美学秩序，也把充满压力，带有恶兆和毁灭性的环境转变为可解释的、顺从的环境。史蒂文斯使想象和艺术在美国文学史上的成功达到顶峰。

3. Features of Stevens' poems

(1) Stevens sought the artistic beauty of poetry, and he often used musical and pictorial techniques to add to the artistic appeal of his poetry.

(2) Stevens's poetry exudes a spirit of optimism rarely found in modern Western poetry.

(3) Stevens, like Keats, is a poet of the senses. He likes to depict the world that can be felt by the senses, hoping to relieve the dull and dreary feeling of daily life by discovering the pleasure of the senses.

(4) Later in his poetic career, Stevens's style became contemplative, even puzzling, and more difficult to appreciate.

3. 诗歌的特点

(1)史蒂文斯追求诗歌的艺术美，他经常运用音乐和绘画技术来增加诗歌的艺术魅力。

(2)史蒂文斯的诗歌流露着现代西方诗歌少有的乐观精神。

(3)史蒂文斯和济慈一样是一位感官诗人。他喜欢描绘感官可以感受到的世界，希望通过发掘感官的快乐来缓解每日生活的枯燥沉闷感。

(4)在他的诗歌创作后期，史蒂文斯的诗风变得富于沉思甚至是令人费解并且更加难以欣赏。

4. Major works

Harmonium

Ideals of Order

The Man with the Blue Guitar

Parts of a World

Transport to Summer

The Auroras of Autumn

The Necessary Angel

4. 主要作品

《风琴》

《关于秩序的思想》

《携蓝色吉他的人》

《世界的某些部分》

《转入夏季》

《秋天的晨曦》

《必不可少的天使》

5. Analysis of major work

◆"Anecdote of the Jar"

(1) In a way, the poem is rather odd and not easy to explain. Wallace Stevens was rather opposed to telling people what his poems mean. Therefore, we can only get the meaning of this poem by placing them in the larger context of his aesthetic tenets and related themes.

(2) The "I" in the poem may be a symbol of the art world and, by extension, of the imagination, as the poem seems to be discussing the relationship between art and nature. Art and imagination give form and meaning to nature and the real world. A society without art is a society without order. Man creates order according to his own perceptions, and half of the world he lives in is of his own making.

5. 主要作品分析

◆《坛子的故事》

(1) 在某种程度上，这首诗比较怪异，不容易解释。华莱士·史蒂文斯相当反对告诉人们他的诗的意思。因此，我们只能把诗歌置于他的美学信条和相关主题的大环境中，以此来得到其诗歌的意思。

(2) 诗中的"我"可能是艺术世界的象征，推而广之是想象的象征。这首诗歌似是讨论艺术和自然之间的关系。艺术和想象力赋予自然和现实世界以形式和意义。没有艺术的社会是没有秩序的社会，人按自己的认知创造秩序，人所生活的世界有一半是他自己创造的。

Ⅲ. William Carlos Williams (1883 – 1963)	**Ⅲ. 威廉·卡洛斯·威廉斯**
1. Life	**1. 生平**
William Carlos Williams was friends with Bond. He received the National Book Award in 1950. Williams had his own independent view of literary creation. He had his own unique views on the nature of poetry, the role of the poet, and the creation of poetry, which differed greatly from Eliot's views. He did not write poetry because he had to, but because he wanted to. He did not think he had to be recognized by the giants of the poetry world, such as Eliot, Pound and Yeats.	威廉·卡洛斯·威廉斯跟庞德是朋友。他于1950年获得国家图书奖。威廉斯对文学创作有自己的独立见解。在诗歌的性质、诗人的作用，以及诗歌的创作方面他有自己独到的见解，与艾略特的观点大相径庭。他之所以进行诗歌创作并不是他不得不写而是因为他想写诗。他认为自己不必非得得到当时诗坛的巨擘如艾略特、庞德以及叶芝等人的承认。
2. Literary points of view	**2. 文学观点**
(1) Williams strongly disapproves of Pound Eliot's "international", literate poetry. He asserts that American poetry must be rooted in American soil, which is the source of the poet's creative inspiration, material and creative subject.	(1)威廉斯极不赞同庞德-艾略特式的"国际的"、文人味十足的诗歌。他主张美国诗歌必须根植于美国本土，这是诗人创作灵感、素材和创作主体的来源。
(2) Williams firmly asserts that poetry must be based on everyday life, using the language of ordinary people and the rhythms of this living language.	(2)威廉斯坚决主张诗歌必须以日常生活为基础，使用普通人的语言以及这种生活语言的韵律。诗歌必须摒弃一切的虚华粉饰。
(3) He argued that poets should not write about arcane and vague things. The poet should start from the concrete and the particular, find the universal in the particular, discover the relationship between the real world and the spiritual world, the relationship between the ancient and the modern. Creative ideas should be expressed in their own unique way.	(3)他主张，诗人不应写玄妙模糊的东西，应当从具体和特殊出发，在特殊中发现普遍，发现现实世界与精神世界的关系、古和今的关系，用自己独特的方法表达有创见的思想。
(4) For Williams, life is the beginning and the end of the poet's creation. Life with all its details and rhythms, carefully observed and fully understood by the poet, is itself simple and pure poetry.	(4)对威廉斯来说，生活是诗人创作的起点和终点。经过诗人仔细观察和充分理解的具有各种细节和节奏的生活本身就是简单纯粹的诗歌。
3. Major works	**3. 主要作品**
"The Red Wheelbarrow"	《红色手推车》
The Tempers	《气质》
"Spring and All"	《春天及一切》
In the American Grain	《美国性格》
Paterson	《佩特森》

4. Analysis of major works	4. 主要作品解析
◆"The Red Wheelbarrow" (1) This poem embodies the poetic theory of the Imagist poet Williams and is often regarded as his masterpiece. (2) The poem fully expresses Williams' fidelity to life through the use of simple words and imagery from everyday life. (3) The poem's style uses the traditional British rereading form to create the typical "American" image.	◆《红色手推车》 (1) 这首诗体现了意象派诗人威廉斯的诗学理论，常被认为是他的代表作。 (2) 这首诗通过日常生活中的简洁词汇和意象的运用充分表现了威廉斯对生活的忠实。 (3) 这首诗的文体摒弃传统的英国重读形式来创作典型的"美国"形象。
◆*Paterson* ①This work of Williams' poetry is in five volumes. He initially planned to write four volumes: the first to introduce "the natural features of the native land", the second to depict modern landscapes, the third to seek a language that would give voice to them, and the fourth to write about "the river below the falls". ②This poem reflects Williams' aesthetic view. By writing this long poem, he wanted to find an imagery that could embody the intelligible world around him. ③This long poem is innovative in terms of writing technique. It naturally uses poetry at times and prose at others, naturally adding confessions, dialogues and letters, faithfully reproducing the quiet rhythm of life itself with its fresh and airy style. It also includes, in its extremely flexible form, many of the themes he presents.	◆《佩特森》 ①威廉斯的这部诗作共5卷。他最初计划写四卷：第一卷介绍"本土的自然特点"，第二卷描绘现代风景，第三卷寻求一种使之发出声音的语言，第四卷写"瀑布下的河流"。 ②这首诗体现了威廉斯的美学观点。他通过写这首长诗，希冀寻觅一种可以体现他周围的可知世界的意象。 ③这首长诗在写作技法上具有创新性。它自然而然地时而运用诗歌，时而运用散文，自然地加进自白、对话和书信，以其清新、飘逸的风格忠实再现出生活自身恬静的节奏。这首诗也以其极为灵活的形式包括了他所表现的诸多主题。

12.2 考研真题与典型题详解

I. Fill in the blanks.

1. In 1927, T. S. Eliot announced that he was a royalist in ________, a classicist in ________, and an Anglo-Catholic in ________.（国际关系学院 2007 研；首师大 2008 研）
2. Eliot's ________ is a morality play in verse dealing with the assassination of Archbishop Thomas Becket by knights of Henry II.（人大 2006 研）
3. ________ was successful in two fields of activity which did not seem compatible with one another: he was a very successful businessman and a very remarkable contemporary poet at the same time.（人大 2006 研）
4. *The Waste Land* was written by ________.（大连外国语学院 2008 研）
5. Taking the form of soliloquy, ________ by T. S. Eliot depicts a timid middle-aged man going

(or thinking of going) to propose marriage to a lady but hesitating all the time. (天津外国语学院 2007 研)

6. T. S. Eliot's poem *The Waste Land* is divided into __________ sections. The waste land here stands for __________. (国际关系学院 2009 研)
7. Winner of the National Book Award in 1950 and the Pulitzer Prize in 1963, __________ is the author of the five-volume epic *Paterson* which is a lucid statement of the author's aesthetics.
8. At the age of 44, Wallace Stevens was finally persuaded to publish a book of poems, entitled __________.
9. After his death, Wallace Stevens's previously uncollected works appeared under the title __________.
10. In 1920, Thomas Stearns Eliot published his __________, containing, among other essays, "Tradition and the Individual Talent", the earliest statement of his aesthetics.
11. As Thomas Steams Eliot declared, he followed strictly the advice of his close friend __________ in cutting and concentrating *The Waste Land.*
12. Thomas Steams Eliot's later poetry took a positive turn toward faith in life. This was demonstrated by __________, a poem of mystical conflict between faith and doubt.
13. In his work __________, Thomas Steams Eliot satirized the straw men, the Guy Fawkes men, whose world would end "not with a bang, but a whimper".
14. Few men of letters have been more fully honored in their own day than __________, and even those who strongly disagree with him seemed content with his selection for the Nobel Prize in 1948.
15. Thomas Stearns Eliot's last important work was __________, a profound meditation on time and timelessness, written in four parts.

II. Multiple Choice

1. __________ once declared himself a "classicist in literature, royalist in politics, and Anglo-Catholic in religion". (首师大 2008 研)

   A. Walt Whitman　　B. Emily Dickinson

   C. Wallace Stevens　　D. T. S. Eliot

2. __________ are not only poets but also literary critics. (北二外 2007 研)

   ① Edgar Allan Poe ② Carl Sandburg ③ T. S. Eliot ④ Ezra Pound

   A. ①③④　　B. ①②③　　C. ①②④　　D. ①②③④

3. The central character J. Alfred Prufrock in T. S. Eliot's famous poem "The Love Song of J. Alfred Prufrock" is __________. (天津外国语学院 2009 研)

   A. an old man　　B. a godlike figure

   C. a restless young man　　D. a muse

III. Read the following quotations and answer the questions.

Passage 1 (首师大 2009 研)

And I have known the arms already, known them all—
Arms that are braceleted and white and bare
(But in the lamplight, downed with light brown hair!)

Is it perfume from a dress
That makes me so digress?
Arms that lie along a table, or wrap about a shawl.
And should I then presume?
And how should I begin?

Questions:

(1) What is the name of the narrator?

(2) What is he going to do and why does he fail to achieve his goal?

Passage 2（南开大学 2008 研）

Anecdote of the Jar

I placed a jar in Tennessee,
And round it was, upon a hill.
It made the slovenly wilderness
Surround that hill.
The wilderness rose up to it,
And sprawled around, no longer wild.
The jar was round upon the ground
And tall and of a port in air.
It took dominion every where.
The jar was gray and bare.
It did not give of bird or bush
Like nothing else in Tennessee.

Questions:

(1) What shape is the jar? Where does the speaker place it?

(2) According to the second stanza, what happens to the wilderness around the jar?

(3) What does the jar "take" everywhere? Of what does it "not give"?

(4) Explain in your own words the effect of the jar on the Tennessee wilderness. Does its effect seem positive in the first two stanzas? In the third? Why is jar an appropriate word?

(5) How is a jar different from the wilderness? What might the jar represent?

(6) Do you think ambiguity makes a poem more memorable? More effective?

Passage 3

Let us go then, you and I,
When the evening is spread out against the sky
Like a patient etherized upon a table;
Let us go, through certain half-deserted streets,
The muttering retreats
Of restless nights in one-night cheap hotels
And sawdust restaurants with oyster-shells:
Streets that follow like a tedious argument
Of insidious intent

To lead you to an overwhelming question...
Oh, do not ask, "What is it?"
Let us go and make our visit.
In the room the women come and go
Talking of Michelangelo.

Questions:

(1) This is the first 14 lines of a famous poem "The love Song of J. Alfred Prufrock." What is the name of the poet who wrote it?

(2) What image is created in this passage?

(3) Do you think Prufrock is a tragic figure? Why?

(4) Is this poem a dramatic monologue? Why?

Passage 4

The Burial of the Dead

April is the cruellest month, breeding
Lilacs out of the dead land, mixing
Memory and desire stirring
Duil roots with spring rain.
Winter kept us warm, covering
Earth in forgetful snow, feeding
A little life with dried tubers.

Questions:

(1) This is the first seven lines of a masterpiece poem. What is the name of this masterpiece?

(2) Who is the author of this masterpiece?

(3) What theme can you get from these lines?

Ⅳ. Short answer questions

1. How many parts are there in *The Waste Land*?(国际关系学院2007研)
2. Discuss the concept of Wasteland in relation to the works of those writers in the 20th century American literature.

V. Essay questions

1. Analysis of Wallace Stevens *Anecdote of the Jar*.
2. Brief summary of Thomas Sterns Eliot's *The Waste Land*.
3. What is the subject of T. S. Eliot's masterpiece *The Waste Land*? What is the significance of the poem? Point out some of the features and innovations that you particularly appreciate in it. Who was T. S. Eliot probably influenced by in creating the poem?(人大2006研)
4. Analyze "The Love Song of J. Alfred Prufrock".(北航2008研)

参考答案及解析

I. Fill in the blanks

1. politics; literature; religion
(艾略特宣称自己在政治上是个保皇派，文学上是古典主义者，宗教上是英国天主教徒。)

2. *Murder in the Cathedral*

(艾略特的《大教堂的谋杀案》是一部道德剧，讲述了亨利二世的骑士暗杀托马斯·贝克特大主教的故事。)

3. Wallace Stevens

(华莱士·史蒂文斯(Wallace Stevens)是美国20世纪的著名诗人。他集企业家和诗人于一身。)

4. T. S. Eliot

(艾略特，美国著名现代派诗人和文艺评论家，《荒原》是其代表作。)

5. *The Love Song of J. Alfred Prufrock*

(艾略特在《J·阿尔弗雷德·普鲁弗洛克的情歌》中，采用独白的方式，讲述了一个中年男人去(或者想去)向一位女士求婚，但一直犹豫不决的故事。)

6. five; the spiritual ruins in Europe

(艾略特最著名的长诗《荒原》分为五部分：《死者葬礼》《对弈》《火诫》《水里的死亡》和《雷霆的话》，将一战后的欧洲描写为一片人欲横流、精神堕落的荒原，折射出现代西方人的幻灭感和精神危机。)

7. William Carlos Williams

(威廉·卡洛斯·威廉斯的代表作是《佩特森》，它清晰地表达了诗人的美学观点。)

8. *Harmonium*

(1923年，44岁的华莱士·史蒂文斯出版了他的第一部诗集《风琴》(*Harmonium*)。)

9. *Opus Posthumous*

(华莱士·史蒂文斯死后，其之前未收集的诗作集合成册于1957年发表，名为《遗作》(*Opus Posthumous*)。)

10. *The Sacred Wood*

(1920年，T. S. 艾略特的批评文集《圣林》(*The Sacred Wood*)的出版奠定了他在20世纪文学理论和批评界的重要地位。其中《传统与个人才能》("Tradition and the Individual Talent")这篇论文最早阐释了他的美学观点。)

11. Ezra Pound

(埃兹拉·庞德(Ezra Pound)，帮助T. S. 艾略特整理删节了《荒原》(*The Waste Land*)的初稿，并向出版社推荐出版。

12. *Ash Wednesday*

(T. S. 艾略特在1930年出版的《圣灰节》(*Ash Wednesday*)鼓吹服从上帝旨意和悔罪的基督教教义，是艾略特创作中对文学和宗教认识发生转变的标志。)

13. *The Hollow Men*

(艾略特其他重要诗作如《空心人》(*The Hollow Men*)(1925)，绝望情绪更明显：人只是死亡国土上的一个空架子，一个填满了稻草的人。)

14. Thomas Stearns Eliot

(T·S·艾略特(Thomas Stearns Eliot)作为诗人、评论家、剧作家，其作品在二十世纪乃至今日的文学史上影响极为深远。1948年，60岁的艾略特迎来了他一生中最大的荣誉——诺贝尔文学奖。)

15. *Four Quartets*

(《四个四重奏》(*Four Quartets*))是一组由四部分组成的宗教冥想诗，它探索了超越时间的宗教启示，充满了《圣经》以及宗教仪式方面的典故，与早期的作品迥然不同。

II. Multiple Choice

1. D 艾略特曾宣称自己是文学上的古典主义者，政治上的保皇派，宗教上的国教徒。

2. A 爱伦·坡、艾略特和庞德都既是诗人，又是文学评论家，只有桑德堡只是诗人。

3. C 艾略特在《普鲁弗洛克的情诗》中描写了一位焦躁不安的上层社会年轻人求爱的矛盾心理。模仿了法国象征派诗人儒尔·拉夫格的风格，具有很浓的讽刺意味，刻画了当时社会背景下的人对于爱情对于生活的复杂心理。

III. Read the following quotations and answer the questions.

Passage 1

(1) The name of the narrator is J. Alfred Prufrock.

(2) He is going to propose marriage to a lady. Prufrock is a kind of tragic figure caught in a sense of defeated idealism and tortured by unsatisfied desire. His tragic flaw is timidity; his "curse" is his idealism. Knowing everything, but not being able to do everything, he lives in an area of life and death; and caught between the two worlds, so he belongs to neither. He craves love but has no courage to declare him.

Passage 2

(1) The jar is round. The speaker places it in Tennessee, upon a hill.

(2) The wilderness rose up to the jar, and sprawled around, no longer wild.

(3) The jar takes dominion everywhere. It does not give of bird and bush.

(4) In the first two stanzas, the effect seems positive. When "I" put the jar in the wilderness, it controls the whole disorderly landscape. The world of nature, shapeless and slovenly, takes shape and order from the presence of the jar. The world of art and imagination gives form and meaning to that of nature and reality. But in the third stanza, it seems that the world of reality exists to determine the limits of art, and that imagination can construct only on the basis of the world of nature.

"Jar" is an appropriate word because a jar is a man-made object, and, similar to the urn in the "Ode on a Grecian Urn", it is the fruit of human art and imagination.

(5) The jar differs from the wilderness in that it is an artificial thing. "It did not give of bird or bush /Like nothing else in Tennessee". The Tennessee wilderness is a symbol of the chaos and formlessness of nature. The jar suggests a world of art and imagination.

(6) Yes, I do think ambiguity can be effective in increasing the memorability of a poem. Great poems such as "The Waste Land" and "Anecdotes from the Altar" are usually not very explicable. Stevens has said that what comes from the imagination, or emotion, is usually vague and uncertain, so it is difficult to understand the rational implications without destroying the inherent vagueness and uncertainty of the imagination and emotion. I agree with Eliot's view that poetry is an autonomous structure that can be interpreted in many ways.

Passage 3

(1) Thomas Stearns Eliot

(2) A patient etherized upon a table

(3) Yes, Prufrock is the image of an ineffectual, sorrowful, tragic twentieth-century Western man divided between passion and timidity, between desire and impotence. His tragic flaw is timidity; his curse is his idealism. Knowing everything, but able to do nothing, he lives in an area of life and death. He despairs of life. He discovers its emptiness and yet finds nothing to replace it. Thus the poem develops a theme of frustration and emotional conflict.

(4) Yes, it is a dramatic monologue. He is a character created by Eliot, and he speaks directly to us. He tells us his thoughts in leaps and bounds, jumping from one image to another, just as a human mind does.

Passage 4

(1) *The Waste Land*

(2) Thomas Stearns Eliot

(3) The theme of the poem is the barrenness of the modern spirit, a reaction to the despair and depression of people after the First World War, the sterility and turmoil of the modern world. It also reflects the regret that in the face of the decline and collapse of Western culture, modern people are powerless to do anything about it.

IV. Short answer questions

1. *The Waste Land* is a great long poem written by T. S. Eliot. It consists of five parts, which are entitled as "The Burial of the Dead", "A Game of Chess", "The Fire Sermon", "Death by Water" and "What the Thunder Said".
2. *The Waste Land* is a poem written by T. S. Eliot on the theme of the sterility and chaos of the contemporary world. This most widely known expression of the despair in the postwar era has appeared over and over again in the works of those writers in the 20th century American literature. Faulkner exemplified T. S. Eliot's concept of modern society as a wasteland in a dramatic way he condemned the mechanized, industrialized society that has dehumanized man by forcing him to cultivate false values and decrease those essential human values such as courage, fortitude, honesty and goodness. Fitzgerald sought to portray a spiritual wasteland of the Jazz Age. Beneath the masks of relaxation and joviality, there was only sterility, meaninglessness and futility amid the grandeur and extravagance, and there was a hint of decadence and moral decay. Hemingway, the leading spokesman of the Lost Generation, though disillusioned in the post war period, strove to bring about man's "grace under pressure". He tried to bring out the idea that man can be physically destroyed but never defeated spiritually.

V. Essay questions

1. "Anecdote of the Jar" is a strange poem in some ways and not very easy to interpret. Wallace Stevens seems to agree with T. S. Eliot's notion of poetry as an autonomous construction capable of more than one interpretation.

   We can only decipher the meaning of "Anecdote of the Jar" by placing it in the larger context of his aesthetic credo and thematic concerns. Here lies the wildand chaotic and formless-rural Tennessee, which let us assume is a symbol of the world of nature. Then the "I" of the poem places in it a tall, round jar, a manmade object, which is suggestive of the world of art, and by extension, the world of imagination. What happens when the jar is standing there is almost a miracle: it controls the whole disorderly landscape, so that "The wilderness rose up to it, /And sprawled around, no longer wild."

The poem seems to be talking about the relationship between art and nature. The natural world, though formless and massless, takes shape and order by the presence of the jar. The world of art and imagination gives meaning to the natural and real world, so the author may be suggesting that any society without art would be disorderly. Stevens is convinced that the poet is the archetype of human understanding of some creative force. His poets are the "necessary angels of the earth" in whose sight mankind re-examines the world. In other words, the poet is the instrument that helps mankind see life in its entirety again.

2. *The Waste Land* is 433 lines long. The whole poem is divided into five parts: I. "The Burial of the Dead", II. "The Game of Chess", III. "The Fire Sermon", IV. "Death by Water", V. "What the Thunder Said". There is no sufficient formal connection between them. Things stop and begin without explicate shift. This radical disconnectedness is true even of the transition between the different sections within any one part of the poem, and between the different ideas within any one section. Through gap, absence of connective tissues, and discordance juxtaposition, the poet intends the reader to see and feel the fragmentary nature of life.

   The Waste Land reveals its author's strong historical sense. To T. S. Eliot the past is of great significance to writers. The past should be altered by the present as much as the present is directed by the past. In *The Waste Land* Eliot uses the past as a yardstick to measure the present and underscore what is missing from the present. In a word, he is trying to throw into relief the negative qualities of the present by contrasting them with the positive ones of the past, and shock the reader into a recognition of the dismal truth about modern life.

   The theme of the poem is the barrenness of the modern spirit, the despair and depression after the First World War, the turmoil of the modern world, and the decline and collapse of Western culture. The poem is notable for its varying lengths and rhythms. The poem conveys the author's central ideas in coordinated thematic variations, rhyme-free lines, and borrows heavily from various writers, employing material from Grail legends, Fraser's anthropological work The Golden Bough, and popular songs; as a result, the poem is obscure and logically lacking in continuity. T. S. Eliot's *The Waste Land*, however, is widely regarded as one of the most well-known landmarks of modernism.

3. (1) The subject: *The Waste Land*, Eliot's most important single poem, has been hailed as a landmark and a model of the 20th-century English poetry, comparable to Wordsworth's *Lyrical Ballads*. With bold technical innovations in versification and style, the poem not only presents a panorama of physical disorder and spiritual desolation in the modern Western world, but also reflects the prevalent mood of disillusionment and despair of a whole post-war generation.

   (2) A poem concerned with the spiritual rupture of modern civilization and the loss of meaning in human life, *The Waste Land* has developed a set of historical, cultural and religious themes. However, it is often thought of as primarily a reflection of the disillusionment and frustration of people in society in the 20th century. The horror and menace, the pain and disillusion-

ment expressed in his poetry have been tormenting all sensitive people in the post-war generation. More importantly, his poetry used new styles, such as drawing extensively from other cultures and classics, that inspired many later writers. This poem is considered a landmark of modern poetry.

(3) Feature Appreciation: The style of the work in part grows out of Eliot's interest in exploring the possibilities of dramatic monologue. Eliot also enjoyed the music hall, and something of the flavor of this popular form of entertainment gets into the poem. It follows the pattern of the musical fugue, in which many voices enter throughout the piece re-stating the themes. Above all perhaps it is the disjointed nature of the poem, the way it jumps from one adopted manner to another, the way it moves between different voices and makes use of phrases in foreign languages, that is the most distinctive feature of the poem's style.

(4) Maybe Eliot was influenced by Homer, Sophocles, Petronius, Virgil, Dante Alighieri, William Shakespeare, Edmund Spenser, Geoffrey Chaucer, Thomas Middleton, John Milton, Andrew Marvell, and Walt Whitman for pieces of their works are frequently seen from this poem.

4. "The Love Song of J. Alfred Prufrock" is Eliot's most striking early achievement. The poem is a sort of dramatic monologue, suggesting an ironic contrast between a pretended "love song" and a confession of his incapability of facing up to love and to life in a sterile upper-class world. The poem presents the meditation of an aging young man over the business of proposing marriage. Prufrock, the protagonist of the poem, is mentally ill, neurotic, self-important, illogical and incapable of action. He is a figure representative of frustrations in modern bourgeois society.

Human predicament is the theme. Prufrock is a kind of tragic figure caught in a sense of defeated idealism and tortured by unsatisfied desire. The action of the poem consists of the interplay of impressions in the protagonist's mind.

The poem is extremely anti-romantic, with visual images of hard, rough and elusive hellish atmosphere. The surface appears to be anxiety about over-civilization, but the underlying mood is one of fear and malice. Individual words and phrases are borrowed from past works, bringing a richness of meaning to this poem. Within traditional English poetry, the rhyme scheme is varied and rhymes superbly.

第13章　弗罗斯特·桑德堡·卡明斯·哈特·克兰·穆尔

13.1　复习笔记

I. Robert Frost (1874–1963)	I. 罗伯特·弗罗斯特
1. Life	**1. 生平**
Robert Frost was born in San Francisco and spent his early childhood in the western United States. His father died when Frost was eleven, and the family moved to New Hampshire. After graduating from high school, he entered Dartmouth College. In 1913 his first collection of poems *A boy's Will* came out in London. His second volume *North of Boston* was published in 1914. The next year, Frost came back to the United States. At that time, he was already recognized as a great poet. He won the Pulitzer Prize four times and received awards from the American Academy of Arts and Letters and the Poetry Society of America respectively in 1938 and 1941. He received honorary titles from forty-four institutions. He became the nation's unofficial Poet Laureate when invited to read his poem at President Kennedy's inauguration in 1961.	罗伯特·弗罗斯特出生于旧金山，在美国西部度过了童年。他11岁时父亲去世，全家迁往新罕布什尔。中学毕业后，他进入达特茅斯学院。1913年他的第一部诗集《少年的意志》在伦敦出版。1914年第二部诗集《波士顿以北》发表。第二年弗罗斯特返回美国时，他已经被公认为大诗人。他曾四次获得普利策诗歌奖，并于1938年和1941年分别获得美国艺术与文学院和美国诗歌协会的嘉奖。他一生获得44个机构授予的荣誉称号。1961年他应邀出席约翰·肯尼迪总统的就职典礼，从此成为美国非官方的“桂冠诗人”。
2. Features of Frost's poems	**2. 诗歌特点**
(1) His poems are full of tact and wisdom, calmness and harmony, serenity and pleasure, making people temporarily away from confusion.	(1) 他的诗歌中充满着机敏与智慧，平静与和谐，祥和与愉悦，使人暂时地远离困惑。
(2) Frost's poems have something to do with nature. Nature has the role of interpretation and regulation, which can be used as a standard for human behavior.	(2) 弗罗斯特的诗歌很多都与自然有关。自然具有解释和调节的作用，它可作为人类行为的参考标准。
(3) Most of his poems are set in New England, and are based on ordinary people's daily life.	(3) 他的很多诗歌多以新英格兰为背景，取材于普通人的日常生活。
(4) Frost's poems are written in the traditional form. He shows little interest in experimentation in form.	(4)弗罗斯特的诗歌一般都遵从传统诗歌的形式。他并不热衷于实验新的诗歌形式。
(5) Frost's works demonstrate dark and terrifying facts. He is deeply aware of the fragmentation of modern life. His poems focus on the experiences of abnormal people.	(5) 弗罗斯特的诗歌也描绘了一些黑暗、恐怖的事实。他深切地意识到现代生活的支离破碎。他的诗歌描绘了很多畸形人的经历。

3. Major works *A Boy's Will* *North of Boston* "The Road Not Taken" "Mending Wall" "After Apple-Picking" "Birches" "Stopping by Woods on a Snowy Evening" "The Wood Piles" "Design" "Desert Places" "Home Burial" "A Servant to Servants" "The Black Cottage"	**3. 主要作品** 《少年的意志》 《波士顿以北》 《未选择的路》 《补墙》 《摘苹果之后》 《白桦树》 《雪夜驻足在林边》 《木堆》 《意图》 《沙漠地方》 《家里的埋葬》 《仆人之仆》 《黑屋》
4. Analysis of major poems ◆"The Road Not Taken" The poem presents a common and typical life situation, where man is faced with the dilemma of making choices. What the speaker seems to express is that ultimately life would end in a cycle and the roads taken lead to the similar results. In addition, the poem contains a kind of complaint that life offers people limited choices. ◆"Mending Wall" One possible interpretation of the poem could be that the poem talks about the inherent alienation of life and human nature. The "I" in the poem feels that he is wiser as he no longer lives in the darkness while his neighbor is still groping. But actually, the neighbor is the wiser because his experience taught him the paradox of life and human nature: distance makes people more intimate, which echoes Benjamin Franklin's famous saying that "Fish and visitors stink in three days."	**4. 主要诗歌分析** ◆《未选择的路》 该诗呈现了一个典型的人生境遇，即作抉择所面临的难处。诗人似乎在说人生在世诸事皆归于循环，任何选择的结果大概都相去不远。此外，诗中也包含关于人生供人选择的余地太少的感叹与抱怨。 ◆《补墙》 关于这首诗的解读之一是，它描写了生活和人性内在的疏远特性。诗中的"我"自我感觉良好，认为他的邻人仍在黑暗中摸索。但细想，恐怕还是邻人对人性和人生内在的自相矛盾：距离使人更为亲密，了解得更为深刻。它令人记起富兰克林"朋友与鱼三日腥"的至理名言。
II. Carl Sandburg (1878 – 1967) Carl Sandburg was one of the Mid-western poets that became known in the Chicago Renaissance (1912 – 1925). Other famous Chicago poets include Vachel Lindsay and Edgar Lee Masters.	**II. 卡尔·桑德堡** 卡尔·桑德堡是在"芝加哥文艺复兴"运动中闻名的美国中西部诗人之一。其他著名的芝加哥文艺复兴诗人是林赛和马斯特斯。

1. Features of Sandburg's poems

(1) Sandburg's ideal was to express "the voice of the people." He realized the importance of the people. There are the thoughts, feelings and wishes of ordinary people in his poems.

(2) Sandburg was an optimist. He saw an America in the future. He held a positive attitude toward American industrial civilization.

(3) He was involved in the poetic revolution. His long poems showed the influence of Imagist poetry. He wrote in free verse and his works are full of spontaneous slang. He made outstanding contributions to the colloquial style in American literature.

2. Major works

In Reckless Ecstasy
Chicago Poems
Cornhuskers
Smoke and Steel
Good Morning, *America*
The People, *Yes*.
Collected Poems
"Fog"
"Lost—"
"The Harbor"
"Cool Tombs"
"I am the People, the Mob"
The American Songbag
The Prairie Years
The War Years

Ⅲ. E. E. Cummings (1894 – 1963)

E. E. Cummings was a representative of modern pioneering spirit in the history of modern American literature.

1. Features of Cummings' poems

(1) He disliked science and technology, believing they were inhumane and made it dehumanizing.

(2) The prevailing rebellious spirit in the art and literature of the time inspired Cummings, who has a dynamic personality, to challenge the tradition and fully express his unique style in his daring experiments.

(3) He attaches great importance to vitality, celebrates individualism and opposes collectivism. The usual themes on love and lust recur; an increasing number of nature poems reveal the poet's love for the world, especially a child's world. The simplicity, innocence and spontaneous happiness of this world are vividly shown in his poems.

1. 诗歌的特点

(1) 桑德堡的理想是成为"人民之声"，在同代人中，他最了解人民大众的重要性。他的诗歌表现了普通人的思想、情感和理想抱负。

(2) 桑德堡是乐观主义者，他洞察美国未来的状况。他对美国工业机械文明持肯定的态度。

(3) 他参与了诗歌改革运动。他的长诗体现了意象主义诗歌的影响。他运用自由体写诗，作品中充满着活力充沛的俚语。他对美国文学中口语风格的发展做出了卓越的贡献。

2. 主要作品

《心醉神迷》
《芝加哥诗集》
《剥玉米机》
《烟与钢》
《早安，美国》
《人民，是的》
《诗集》
《雾》
《失落—》
《港口》
《清冷的墓》
《我是人民群众》
《美国歌集》
《草原年代》
《战争年代》

Ⅲ. 卡明斯

卡明斯是美国现代文学史上开拓精神的代表。

1. 诗歌的特点

(1) 他对科学技术十分反感，认为其极不人道并使人失去人性。

(2) 当时弥漫在文学艺术界的时代叛逆精神激励了卡明斯在诗歌创作上大胆尝试，向传统挑战，打破传统形式的束缚，充分表现自己的独特风格。

(3) 他珍视活力，歌咏个性反对"集体"，反对因袭传统。他描写爱情和性欲；他的自然诗表明他对世界、特别是对儿童天真世界的热爱；这个世界的朴实、纯真和快乐在他的诗歌中表现得淋漓尽致。

2. **Major works**

The Enormous Room

"Chanson Innocenter"

"O sweet spontaneous"

Ⅳ. Hart Crane (1899 – 1932)

1. Life

Hart Crane was born in Ohio. He began writing poetry when he was a teenager, and published his first poem at 17. His early work, published in *Little Review*, showed the characteristics of Elizabethan literature and French symbolism and recorded his nervous state of mind and homosexual orientation. His first collection of poems , *White Buildings* came out in 1926, and was received with mixed comments. His major work, The Bridge, was published in 1930, which was not unanimously appreciated. His unstable life, his father's death, the estrangement from his mother and later from many friends, and the Depression of the 1930s—all these bring great pressure on his increasingly fragile nerves. In 1930 he traveled to Mexico. In 1932, he jumped into sea on his way back to New York.

2. Major works

White Buildings

The Bridge

"For the Marriage of Faustus and Helen"

"Voyages"

"At Melville's Tomb"

Collected Poems

Complete poems and Selected Letters and Prose

3. Analysis of major work

◆*The Bridge*

The Bridge consists of "To Brooklyn Bridge" as a preface and eight sections, a total of 15 poems.

The Bridge is one of the long poems with the twentieth-century American modern epic tradition. The poem is the most majestic since *The Waste Land*. What Crane tried to accomplish was to create a modern and mythological synthesis of the American experience, in order to make sense of the experience, point out the close relationship between the present and the past and show the hope for the future. He considers the Brooklyn Bridge as a symbol of America's future and its unique identity. He sees hope in the mechanical civilization which was criticized by his contemporary writers. Obviously, Crane was writing about the American myth in "an epic of modern consciousness".

2. **主要作品**

《巨大的房间》

《单纯之歌》

《啊甜蜜的自发的》

Ⅳ. 哈特·克兰

1. 生平

哈特·克兰出生于俄亥俄州。十几岁时就开始写诗，17 岁时发表了第一首诗。他发表在《小杂志》上的早期诗歌，表现出伊丽莎白文学和法国象征主义的特点，记录了他紧张的精神状态和同性恋倾向。1926 年他的第一部诗集《白色的楼房》问世，评论界贬褒不一。他的主要作品《桥》于 1930 年出版，同样未获得一致赞赏。不稳定的生活，父亲的去世，他与母亲及后来与许多朋友的疏远，20 世纪 30 年代的大萧条，都给他渐趋脆弱的神经带来压力。1930 年克兰赴墨西哥旅行。1932 年他在返回纽约的途中投海自尽。

2. 主要作品

《白色的楼房》

《桥》

《为浮士德和海伦的婚姻而作》

《旅行》

《凭吊梅尔维尔墓》

《诗集》

《哈特·克兰诗作全集及书信与散文选》

3. 主要作品分析

◆《桥》

《桥》由一首序诗和八部分，共 15 首诗组成。

《桥》是 20 世纪美国诗坛出现的著名长诗之一。这首诗可以说是《荒原》问世以来用意最雄壮的诗作。克兰希望通过此诗对美国经历进行一种现代性、神话性的综合，以期彻底了解这种经历，指出现在与过去的紧密关系以及对未来的希望。他把布鲁克林桥视为美国的未来和独特身份的象征。他从同时代作家所抨击的机械文明中看到了希望。显然，克兰写的是一首关于美国神话的"现代意识的史诗"。

V. Marianne Moore (1887 – 1972)

1. Life

Marianne Moore was born in Missouri and graduated from Bryn Mawr where she met her classmate H. D. She began to publish poems in the *Poetry* magazine around 1915 and became known for novelty and liveliness of her poems. For some time she was editor of the literary magazine, *the Dial*, and published poems by many of the best poets at that time. In 1951 her *Collected Poems* came out and won a Pulitzer Prize, the Bollingen Prize, and a National Book Award. Her *Completed Poems* came out in print in 1967. Late in life Marianne Moore was also known for her love of baseball.

2. Literary contributions

Moore was a very original poet born and raised in the United States, She did a couple of things worth remembering for future generations.

(1) First, she was one of the first "new" poets in the early 20th century along with William Carlos Williams and Wallace Stevens.

(2) Another thing for which Moore is remembered as an influence over the following generations is her careful observation and description of minute details.

3. Major works

Collected Poems

Complete Poems

"Poetry"

"The Fish"

"Silence"

"The Students"

V. 玛利安·穆尔

1. 生平

玛利安·穆尔生于密苏里州，毕业于布林茅尔学院，大学时和诗人希尔达·杜利特尔是同窗。她在1915年左右开始在《诗歌》杂志上发表的诗作，以其新颖和活泼见长。后来她担任《日晷》杂志的主编，刊出了不少优秀新人的诗作。1951年她的《诗歌选集》问世，获得普利策奖、伯林根诗歌奖及全国图书奖。1967年她的《诗歌全集》出版，晚年她还以对棒球的喜好而闻名。

2. 文学贡献

穆尔是美国土生土长的颇富独创力的诗人。她有几件事值得后人铭记。

(1) 一是她和威廉姆斯及史蒂文斯在20世纪初叶成为新时代的新诗人。

(2) 穆尔让后人铭记的第二件事是她对大小事务的细腻观察和描绘，她的这个特点影响了年轻的一代。

3. 主要作品

《诗歌选集》

《诗歌全集》

《诗歌》

《鱼》

《沉静》

《学生》

13.2 考研真题与典型题详解

I. Fill in the blanks.

1. Author __________ Title __________(南京大学2009研)

I shall be telling this with a sigh
Somewhere ages and ages hence:
Tow roads diverged in a wood, and I—
I took the one less traveled by,
And that has made all the difference.

2. "After Apple-Picking" is a well-known poem written by __________.

3. __________ combined traditional verse forms with a clear American local speech rhythm, forming his own characteristic.
4. At one time, Sandburg's reputation mainly rested on a multi-volume biography of __________ including *The Prairie Years* and *The War Years*.

II. Multiple Choice

1. __________ was regarded as America's poet laureate and invited to read his poem at the inauguration of President kennedy. (首师大 2009 研)
   A. T. S. Eliot　　B. E. E. Cummings
   C. Robert Frost　　D. Ezra Pound
2. Which of the following was not written by Robert Frost?
   A. "Tilbury Town"　　B. "A Witness Tree"
   C. "Steeple Bush"　　D. "In the Clearing"
3. Robert Frost is famous for his lyric poems. Which of the following lyric poems was not written by Robert Frost?
   A. "Richard Cory"　　B. "Stopping by Woods on a Snowy Evening"
   C. "After Apple-Picking"　　D. "The Road Not Taken"
4. "Two roads diverged in a yellow wood and sorry I could not travel both" In the above two lines of Robert Frost's "The Road Not Taken", the poet, by implication, was referring to __________.
   A. a travel experience　　B. a marriage decision
   C. a middle-age crisis　　D. one's course of life
5. To many who read "Fog" (1916), "I Am the People, the Mob" (1916), *Grass* (1918), and the 21 sections of *Good Morning*, *America*, __________ was successor to 19th-century poet Walt Whitman as the proclaimer of the American spirit.
   A. T. S. Eliot　　B. Ezra Pound
   C. Robert Frost　　D. Carl Sandburg
6. Carl Sandburg had also taken interest in folk songs which he tried to collect and sing during his travels. These folk songs appeared eventually in print in his well-known __________.
   A. *Good Morning*, *America*　　B. *The People*, *Yes*
   C. *In Reckless Ecstasy*　　D. *The American Songbag*
7. The three poets Ezra Pound, T. S. Eliot and __________ opened the way to Modern poetry.
   A. O. Henry　　B. Henry David thoreau
   C. E. E. Cummings　　D. Robert Frost

III. Read the following quotations and answer the questions.

Passage 1 (北外 2009 研)

"Stopping by Woods on a Snowy Evening"

Robert Frost

Whose woods these are I think I know.
His house is in the village, though;
He will not see me stopping here

To watch his woods fill up with snow.
My little horse must think it queer
To stop without a farmhouse near
Between the woods and frozen lake
The darkest evening of the year.
He gives his harness bells a shake
To ask if there is some mistake.
The only other sound's the sweep
Of easy wind and downy flake.
The woods are lovely, dark, and deep.
But I have promise to keep,
And miles to go before I sleep.
And miles to go before I sleep.

Question:

Try to analyze the poem.

Passage 2（北师大 2008 研）

The Road Not Taken

Two roads diverged in a yellow wood,
And sorry I could not travel both
And be one traveler, long I stood
And looked down one as far as I could
To where it bent in the undergrowth;
Then took the other, as just as fair,
And having perhaps the better claim,
Because it was grassy and wanted wear;
Though as for that the passing there
Had worn them really about the same.
And both that morning equally lay
In leaves no step had trodden black.
Oh, I kept the first for another day!
Yet knowing how way leads to way,
I doubted if I should ever come back.
I shall be telling this with a sigh
Somewhere ages and ages hence:
Two roads diverged in a wood, and I –
I took the one less traveled by,
And that has made all the difference.

Questions:

(1) Please analyze the symbolic meanings of this poem with your understanding of the theme implied in it;

(2) Please point out one or two artistic features of the poem with the examples in the text.

Passage 3

Some say the world will end in fire,
Some say in ice.
From what I've tasted of fire.
I hold with those who favor fire.
But if it had to perish twice,
I think I know enough of hate
To say that for destruction ice
Is also great and would suffice.

Questions:

(1) What is the title of the poem?

(2) What is the name of the poet?

(3) What do fire and ice respectively symbolize?

(4) What does the poet think the world will end in?

Ⅳ. Essay questions

1. Discuss Robert Frost's poetic style.
2. Analysis of Robert Frost's "The Road Not Taken".

参考答案及解析

I. Fill in the blanks.

1. Robert Frost; "The Road Not Taken"

(题目节选自罗伯特·弗罗斯特的"The Road Not Taken"(《未选择的路》)中的最后一节。《未选择的路》是美国著名诗人罗伯特·弗罗斯特的著名诗篇。罗伯特·弗罗斯特堪称美国20世纪最受欢迎的诗人之一,是美国非官方的桂冠诗人。)

2. Robert Frost

(《摘苹果之后》是罗伯特·弗罗斯特(Robert Frost)的名诗。)

3. Robert Frost

(弗罗斯特将传统诗歌形式与美国本土口语体结合起来,形成了独特的诗歌特点。)

4. Abraham Lincoln

(卡尔·桑德堡(Carl Sandburg)美国现代诗人及传记作家。20世纪20和30年代,他创作并出版了林肯的传记《草原年代》(*The Prairie Years*)和《战争年代》(*The War Years*)。)

II. Multiple Choice

1. C　罗伯特·弗罗斯特是美国的桂冠诗人,多次获普利策奖,1961年87岁高龄的弗罗斯特应邀在约翰·肯尼迪总统(John . F. Kennedy)的就职典礼上朗诵自己的诗作。

2. A　选项A "Tilbury Town"是埃德温·阿灵顿·罗宾逊的诗。其余三个选项"A Witness Tree","Steeple Bush","In the Clearing"都是罗伯特·弗罗斯特的作品。

3. A　罗伯特·弗罗斯特以抒情诗著称,《雪夜林边小驻》("Stopping by Woods on a Snowy Evening"),《摘苹果之后》("After Apple-Picking"),和《未选择的路》("The Road Not Taken")都是弗罗斯特著名的抒情诗。而选项A "Richard Cory"的作者是埃德温·阿灵

顿·罗宾逊。

4. D　在《未选择的路》一诗中，作者想要表达的实际是人生的境遇。

5. D　桑德堡的理想是成为“人民之声”，在同代人中，他最了解人民大众的重要性。他的诗歌表现了普通人的思想、情感和理想抱负。

6. D　美国诗人及传记作家卡尔·桑德堡 Carl Sandburg）对民歌很感兴趣，他在旅途中收集和吟唱民歌。这些民歌后来出版名为《美国歌袋》(*The American Songbag*)。

7. C　庞德、艾略特和卡明斯在诗歌方面都具有创新精神，他们开启了现代派诗歌之门。

III. Read the following quotations and answer the questions.

Passage 1

"Stopping by Woods on a Snowy Evening" is a poem written in 1922 by Robert Frost, and came out in 1923 in his New Hampshire volume.

The poem is written in iambic tetrameter in the Rubaiyat stanza created by Edward Fitzgerald. Each verse (save the last) follows an a-a-b-a rhyming scheme, with the following verse's a rhyming with that verse's b, which is a chain rhyme. Overall, the rhyme scheme is AABA-BBCB-CCDC-DDDD.

The poet expresses a mixed feeling about mingling with the beautiful and quite nature and the responsibility which the speaker bears in the real world.

In the poem, the speaker is impressed by the snowy woods on a winter evening. Although the woods may have owner,, now it is part of the nature and it only belongs to the speaker. The little horse shows its puzzle when the speaker is indulging in the beautiful snowy woods, so "He gave his harness bells a shake to ask if there is any mistake". Here, the personification is used. Although the woods are lovely and quiet, the speaker has to continue his journey. "Sleep" also indicates "death". It is not the time for him to "sleep" for he has to fulfill his responsibility.

The poem shows the typical features of Robert Frost's poems. The language of his poems is co-oncise, but he always tries to express some sensitive feeling toward the life and people's innermind. He attaches importance to the natural scene and ordinary thing. Imagery and personification are used skillfully in the poem.

Passage 2

(1) The poem seems to be about the poet, who is walking in the woods in autumn, and choosing which road he should follow on his way. In the poem, the poet hesitates for a long time, wondering which road to take, because they look both good. In the end, he follows the one which seems to have fewer travelers on it. Symbolically, he chooses to follow an unusual, solitary life; perhaps he is talking about his choice to become a poet rather than some ordinary profession. But he always remembers the road which he might have taken, and which would have given him a differentlife.

In reality, it is about the important decisions which one must make in life, when one must give up a desirable thing in order to pursue another. Then, whatever the outcome, one must accept the consequences of one's choice for it is not possible to go back or have another chance to make a different choice. The different road one takes, the different kind of life one will have.

(2) In addition to the symbols used in this poem, other artistic features are employed in the rhythm

aspects. This poem is written in classic five-line stanzas, with the rhyme scheme a-b-a-a-b and conversational rhythm. Alliteration is also employed in this poem. For example, "wanted wear" in the third line of the second stanza.

Passage 3

(1) The title of the poem is "Fire and Ice".

(2) The poet is Robert Frost.

(3) Fire symbolizes human desires while ice symbolizes hatred between people.

(4) The poet think desires are more dangerous than hatred because he says "I hold with those who favor fire." though he admits that hatred is also very destructive.

Ⅳ. Essay questions

1. Frost used concise language, a graceful style and traditional poetic form. He achieved an internal dynamics in his poetry by applying the rhythms of everyday language instead of the formal pattern of line and stanza. He often used regular iambic meter. Sometimes he used blank verse. He tends to be simple, but he explores complexity through triviality. He used symbols from everyday life to imply profound ideas. He made his poems seem effortless by using colloquial and direct expression and conversational rhythms. His success mainly includes two aspects: he combined traditional poetic forms with American vocabulary and language rhythms; he composed individual poems into a larger whole by presenting in them a recurrent "persona" in the image of a wise country man.

2. This poem is written in classic five-line stanzas, with an a-b-a-a-b rhyme and dialogue rhythm. The poem seems to be about the poet, who is walking in the woods in autumn, and choosing which road he should follow on his way. In reality, it is related to the important decisions which a person must make in life, when a person must give up one desirable thing in order to have another. Then, regardless of the outcome, one must accept the consequences of his choice, because it is not possible to go back and have another chance to make a different choice.

   In the poem, the poet hesitates for a long time, not knowing which way to go, because they are both good. In the end, he follows the one which seems to have fewer travelers on it. Symbolically, he chose to follow an unusual and lonely life; perhaps he was talking about his choice to become a poet rather than some ordinary profession. But he always remembers the road which he might have taken, and which would have given him a differentlife.

第14章　菲茨杰拉德·海明威

14.1　复习笔记

I. F. Scott Fitzgerald (1896 – 1940) Fitzgerald was essentially a 1920s American novelist. His *Tales of the Jazz* portrays this crucial period in the cultural history of America. He was best known for his works depicting the flamboyance and excess of the Jazz Age.	**I. 弗·司各特·菲茨杰拉德** 菲茨杰拉德是20世纪20年代最具代表性的美国作家。他的短篇小说集《爵士乐时代的故事》描绘了20年代的美国，他的许多作品都刻画了“爵士乐时代”的浮华社会与奢侈物欲。
1. Life Fitzgerald was born into a middle-class family in St. Paul, Minnesota. He had education first in private schools and then at Princeton. He dropped out university in 1917 to join the Army. But he never went to the war. During the period of 15 months of service in the army, while stationed in Alabama, he fell in love with Zelda Sayre, the daughter of a judge. Zelda promised that she would marry him only if he could get up in the literary world. In 1920 Fitzgerald's *This Side of Paradise* was published and became immensely popular, which earns Zelda for him. In the 1920s, Fitzgerald frequented Europe, where he was influenced by the modernist writers and artists of the "Lost Generation". Fitzgerald suffered from an unhappy marriage. They were also fighting each other all the time. Zelda began to have breakdowns and had to be put in a mental institution. Loneliness, alcohol and the awareness that he was dissipating his talent eventually combined to break the talent down. In the last year of his life, he began to write one very interesting novel, *The Last Tycoon*, which he never finished. In 1940, he died at the age of 44.	**1. 生平** 菲茨杰拉德出生于明尼苏达州首府圣保罗的一个中产阶级家庭。他被送进私立学校学习。后进入普林斯顿大学。1917年他离校入伍，但未出国参战。在部队服役的15个月期间，他在驻扎阿拉巴马爱上了一位法官的女儿，泽尔达·赛尔。泽尔达告诉菲茨杰拉德只有他飞黄腾达才能娶到她。1920年菲茨杰拉德的第一部小说《人间天堂》一经出版即大获成功。这部小说的成功还使得他赢得了泽尔达。随后菲茨杰拉德常到访欧洲，并结识了被称为“迷惘的一代”的现代主义作家，他的写作也受到了“迷惘的一代”的影响。菲茨杰拉德夫妇婚后生活并不幸福，他们之间的争吵愈演愈烈，后来泽尔达精神崩溃，被送进了精神病院。孤独寂寞，常借酒消愁，再加上感到自己在浪费才华，这些最终断送了这位英才。在其生命的最后一年，他开始写一部很有意义的小说《最后的大亨》，可惜未完成便在1940年与世长辞，年仅44岁。
2. Major works *This Side of Paradise* *Flappers and Philosophers* *Tales of the Jazz Age* *The Beautiful and the Damned.* *The Great Gatsby*	**2. 主要作品** 《人间天堂》 《轻佻女郎与哲学家》 《爵士乐时代的故事》 《美丽与诅咒》 《了不起的盖茨比》

Tender is the Night

All the Sad Young Men

"The Rich Boy"

Taps at Reveille

The Last Tycoon

The Crack-Up

《夜色温柔》

《一代悲哀的年轻人》

《富家子弟》

《清晨起床号》

《最后的大亨》

《崩溃》

3. Analysis of major work

◆*The Great Gatsby* (1925)

(1) Gatsby's personal experience reflects the predicament of the Americans in the first few decades of the twentieth century. Modern man lives in sterility and futility, and in excess of life, as best illustrated by Gatsby's essentially pointless parties. Thus Gatsby's personal life has assumed a magnitude as a "cultural-historical allegory" for the nation. The novel is widely considered to be a literary masterwork and nominated for the title of the Great American Novel.

(2) The very rich attracted and repelled Fitzgerald at the same time. But on the whole, Fitzgerald critiques the rich in that wealth emotionally weakens them. In *The Great Gatsby*, Tom and Daisy are completely dehumanized by wealth and corrupting others.

(3) Fitzgerald's craftsmanship is impeccable in this novel. The use of a dramatic narrator, through whose consciousness everything filters, ensures the integration of the work. Carraway's limited perspective determines the facts that he deals but information in such a manner that he seems to withhold it first, thus creating a mysterious effect of suspense.

(4) Fitzgerald was one of the great stylists in American literature. Fitzgerald's prose is smooth, penetrating, and completely original in its diction and metaphors. His language style features both simplicity and gracefulness, showing skill of manipulating the relationship between the general and the specific. Bold use of colors is a component of the novel's impressionism. The counter-realism in the novel can be seen is the uncertain boundaries between the animate and the inanimate. These techniques portray characters' personalities, convey the authorial vision, and reveal Fitzgerald's consummate artistry.

3. 主要作品分析

◆《了不起的盖茨比》

(1) 盖茨比的个人经历反映出20世纪前几十年美国整个国家所经历的困境。现代人生活在物欲横流的精神荒原之上，生活已失去目的和意义，看看盖茨比豪华但毫无意义的宴会便可略知一二。盖茨比的个人生活已成为整个国家文化历史上的伟大寓言。《了不起的盖茨比》被视为文学名著，且被提名为最伟大的美国小说。

(2) 菲茨杰拉德对富人和富贵的态度有羡慕，但更有鄙夷，鄙夷无疑多于羡慕。他试图解释财富对其笔下人物性格分裂的影响。在《了不起的盖茨比》中汤姆和黛西这两个人物象征了财富本身意味着堕落，也诱使他人堕落。

(3) 菲茨杰拉德的写作技巧无可挑剔。他选择了卡拉韦这一戏剧化的叙述者。通过卡拉韦的意识事件得以过滤，这保证了整个故事的结构统一、紧凑。卡拉韦的有限视角决定了他对信息似乎有所保留，这制造了一种神秘及悬念之感。

(4) 菲茨杰拉德是美国文学史上一位伟大的文体家。菲茨杰拉德的语言通顺流畅，观察细致入微，措辞和比喻极具独创性。他的文章质朴、雅致，较好地把握了整体与细节之间的关系。作者对色彩的大胆运用体现了小说的印象主义手法。而小说对动静态界限的模糊则体现了反现实主义的特色。这些技巧展现了人物的特质，传达了作者的观点，显示了菲茨杰拉德高超的艺术才能。

Ⅱ. Ernest Hemingway (1899 –1961)

1. Life

Born in Oak park, Illinois, Hemingway grew up in an nearly affluent family with his father being a physician and his mother a music teacher. At the age of 17, he tried to enlist in the army but was rejected because of his injured eye. He then became a reporter in the *Kansas City Star* and served as its reporter. Then he was recruited as an ambulance driver working with the Red Cross and went to Europe. His war experience was so shattering and horrifying that his life and writings were permanently affected. He was a world traveler. In 1920s, Hemingway lived in Europe as a crucial member of the expatriate artists of the "Lost Generation". After the end of the Spanish Civil War, from 1939 to 1960, he lived in Cuba where he wrote many important novels such as *The Old Man and the Sea* (1952).

The modernist writer Hemingway was a myth in American literature. He was publicly acclaimed and his style of writing probably influenced other writers. His public image was one of a tough guy. He won the Nobel Prize for literature in 1954. In his later years he often behaved in an odd manner and looked much older than his years. Possibly due to the loss of writing talent failure to act out his code, or his ill health, he shot himself to death on July 2, 1961. The world was shocked by his death because an era had come to an end.

2. The Hemingway Hero

Throughput his life, Hemingway explores one theme, which is summed up in the famous phrase "grace under pressure". He shapes a Hemingway hero to demonstrate the theme. Hemingway's world is essentially chaotic and meaningless, in which man fights a solitary struggle against a unfathomable force. A sense of despair arose from the awareness that he must end in defeat, no matter how hard he strives against i. But the Hemingway hero possesses the despairing courage. This courage is a code of honor that allows a man to keep humanity and behave like a man, to assert his dignity in face of adversity. Hemingway's characters,

Ⅱ. 欧内斯特·海明威

1. 生平

海明威出生于伊利诺州的奥克帕克。父亲是内科医生，母亲是音乐教师。他 17 岁时曾试图参军，但因眼疾而未能成行，就到《堪萨斯城星报》任见习记者。后志愿参加美国红十字会组织的战地救护队，在意大利前线当救护车司机。这对他的一生产生了深远的影响。这段如恶梦般的战争经历长期地影响了海明威的生活和写作。20 世纪 20 年代海明威作为“迷惘的一代”的作家代表旅居欧洲，而西班牙内战结束后他居住在古巴长达 30 年，并创作出《老人与海》等脍炙人口的作品。

现代主义作家海明威是美国文学的神话。他是星光闪耀的公众英雄，他的写作风格和生活方式受到很多人的模仿。在公众眼里，他是个十足的硬汉子。1954 年海明威获得了诺贝尔文学奖。晚年海明威行为古怪，看起来比实际年龄苍老许多。或许因为其文思枯竭，或许因为他不能实践自己的行为准则，又或许二者皆有之，再加上他疾病缠身，他于 1961 年 7 月 2 日开枪自杀，举世为之震惊，海明威的逝世标志着美国文学史上一个时代的结束。

2. 海明威式英雄

海明威的一生都在描写一个主题，即“重压下的风度”。他同时塑造了典型的海明威式英雄。海明威笔下的世界在本质上混乱不堪，毫无意义可言。在这样的世界里，人单枪匹马去抵抗他自己都无法理解的力量。人物最终意识到无论自己多么努力，最终还是会以失败告终，这必然招致失望的情绪。但是海明威式英雄表现出一种绝望中的勇气。这种勇气是一种荣誉准则，使他表现出大丈夫气概，在逆境中保持尊严。海明威小说中的人物，

Nick Adams, Jake Barnes, Frederic Henry, and Santiago are all typical Hemingway heroes.	尼克·亚当斯、杰克·巴恩斯、弗瑞德里克·亨利、圣地亚哥等都是典型的海明威式英雄。
3. Writing style In his declining years, Hemingway came to be known as "Papa Hemingway". This compliment refers in the main to his contribution to the development of the new colloquial style of writing in America. Hemingway's prose is simple and apparently natural. It has the effect of directness, clarity and freshness. His words always carry connotations.	**3. 写作风格** 海明威晚年被称作"爸爸海明威"，这一赞誉主要指他为美国文学史上的口语形式——这一新的写作风格做出了突出的贡献。海明威的文章简朴、自然，直截了当，清晰易懂，新颖活泼，而且意蕴丰富。
4. Major works *The Torrents of Spring* *Three Stories and Ten Poems* *In Our Times* *Men Without Women* *Winner Take Nothing* "Indian Camp" *The Sun Also Rises* *A Farewell to Arms* *Death in the Afternoon* *Green Hills of Africa* *To Have and Have not* *The Fifth Column* *For Whom the Bell Tolls* *Across the River and into the Trees* *The Old Man and the Sea*	**4. 主要作品** 《春潮》 《三篇短篇小说和十首诗》 《在我们的时代里》 《没有女人的男人》 《胜者无所获》 《印第安营寨》 《太阳照样升起》 《永别了，武器》 《午后之死》 《非洲青山》 《有钱人与没钱人》 《第五纵队》 《丧钟为谁而鸣》 《穿林过河》 《老人与海》
5. Analysis of major works ◆*The Sun Also Rises* *The Sun Also Rises* (1926) is Hemingway's first important novel, portraying the image of the Lost Generation. People were trapped in the war trauma and cut off from the old value. Yet they were unable to come to terms with the new era when civilization had gone mad. The characters in the novel are seen wandering pointlessly and restless and impotent. They are absorbed in the material enjoyment of fishing, swimming, bullfight and sightseeing but are fully aware all the while that the world is meaningless and futile. The sense of loss of the protagonist is a symbol for modern man's spiritual impotence.	**5. 主要作品分析** ◆《太阳照样升起》 《太阳照常升起》是海明威第一部重要的小说。该书描绘了"迷惘的一代"的形象。这一代人处于战后的尴尬年代，旧的价值观业已过时，而新的时代文明已经近乎疯狂。小说中的人物迷惘、无能为力，逃避现实，沉湎于垂钓、游泳、斗牛和欣赏自然美景中，但他们时刻意识到这个世界已变得疯狂和毫无意义。主人公的迷茫象征着现代人精神上的无能。

◆*A Farewell to Arms* *A Farewell to Arms* can be read as a footnote to *The Sun Also Rises*. Set in Spain during the Civil War, the novel shapes the character Frederic Henry who has been to the war field but found out but ironically found it like a horrible slaughterhouse without sacred and glorious. Henry fights single hand against overwhelming odds as a typical Hemingway hero of action and of few words. Hemingway depicts an individual, alone even when with other people, as somewhat an outsider, and keeping emotions under control. *A Farewell to Arms* reflects the despairing mood of the post-war generation who had lost hope and brings international fame to Hemingway.	◆《永别了，武器》 《永别了，武器》在某种意义上是《太阳照常升起》的注脚。弗瑞德里克·亨利亲历战争，却发现战争毫无神圣光荣可言，而是活生生的屠宰场。亨利孤军奋战，他是典型的海明威式英雄，少言寡语，行动果断。即使与他人在一起，通常表现的是个局外人，善于控制自己的感情。《永别了，武器》反映了一战后普遍存在于西方的失望情绪，为海明威带来了国际声誉。
◆*For Whom the Bell Tolls* The title of *For Whom the Bell Tolls* come from John Donne's Meditation (XVIII) "Any man's death diminishes me because I am involved in mankind, and therefore never send to know for whom the bell tolls; It tolls for Thee." In this novel, the protagonist Robert Jordan is no longer alone but having a respected career and a cooperating group. More importantly, he has someone to love and die for. The war he is fighting is, for him, a metaphor for a struggle for freedom. It is for democracy that he sacrifices himself for freedom and democracy. Nowhere else in Hemingway foregrounds the theme of human brotherhood in this novel.	◆《丧钟为谁而鸣》 《丧钟为谁而鸣》的标题来自约翰·多恩的《祈祷文集》第 18 章，"任何人的死亡都是对我的缩小，因为我是处于人类之中；因此不必去知道丧钟为谁而鸣，它就是为你而鸣。"在这部小说里，海明威塑造了一个崭新的艺术形象。主人公罗伯特已经不是孑然一身，有了愿为之奋斗的事业，有了可以并肩作战的团队，最重要的是有了他珍爱且愿为之牺牲的爱人。战争对他而言象征了为自由而战。为了民主事业他愿意牺牲自己。在这部小说里海明威突出地反映出人与人之间兄弟情义的主题。
◆*The Old Man and the Sea* *The Old Man and the Sea* is a novella about an old Cuban fisherman Santiago and his battle with a great marlin. Santiago represents the spirit of Hemingway type of individualism, contending with a force he knows it is futile to rebel against. He keeps on fighting because he believes that "a man is not made for defeat. A man can be destroyed but not defeated." However, the old man eventually realizes that he has met his doom because he goes far out alone "beyond all the people in the world." He starts to miss being one of the human group and being friend to the natural world. His love for his fellowmen and nature testifies that Hemingway's vision of the world has undergone a profound change.	◆《老人与海》 《老人与海》是海明威著名的短篇小说，它描写了古巴老渔翁圣地亚哥与一条马林鱼做斗争的故事。在圣地亚哥身上我们看到了海明威式个人的精神。他明知道徒劳无益，但是还是勇于斗争。他奋斗不懈因为他坚信"人不是为打败而生，人可以被毁灭，但不能被打败。"但是，老人最终意识到，独自一人出海，远离人群，才遇到厄运。他因自己是人类社会和自然界的一员而感到欣慰。他开始对人类及自然界的生物产生友爱之情，这充分表明了海明威的世界观发生了重大的变化。

14.2 考研真题与典型题详解

I. Fill in the blanks.

1. Set in Spain during the Civil War, the novel ______ stated again Hemingway's view of love found and lost, and described the indomitable spirit of the common people. (人大2006研)
2. F. Scott Fitzgerald's first novel ______, with its portrayal of casual dissipations of "flaming youth", was an immediate commercial success.
3. F. Scott Fitzgerald summarized the experiences and attitudes of the 1920s decade in his masterpiece novel ______.
4. F. Scott Fitzgerald's second novel ______ describes a handsome young man and his beautiful wife, undoubtedly modelled after himself and Zelda.
5. The hero in F. Scott Fitzgerald's novel ______ is a psychiatrist who marries a rich patient. The author condemns the wasted energy of misguided youth.
6. American writers of the first postwar era self-consciously acknowledged that they were a "______", devoid of faith and alienated from a civilization.
7. In the same way that F. Scott Fitzgerald's *Tales of the Jazz Age* became the symbol for an age, Ernest Hemingway's novel ______ painted the image of a whole generation, the Lost Generation.
8. Ernest Hemingway's stature as a writer was confirmed with the publication of his novel ______ in 1929. The novel portrayed a farewell both to war and to love.
9. In the story *The Old Man and the Sea*, Ernest Hemingway portrayed an old fisherman named ______, who is triumphant even in defeat.
10. In 1954, Ernest Hemingway was awarded a ______ for his "mastery of the art of modern narration".

II. Multiple Choice

1. Which of the following novels is a good illustration of the "Roaring 20s" and hence serves as a "cultural-history allegory" for the America? (首师大2007研)

   A. *A Farewell to Arms* B. *The Great Gatsby*
   C. *A Lost Lady* D. *The Portrait of a Young Lady*

2. In *The Great Gatsby*, Nick is the narrator who belongs to the type of ______. (首师大2008研)

   A. participant B. non-participant
   C. unreliable D. innocent eye

3. The following selection is taken from ______. (大连外国语学院2007研)

   A. *Sister Carrie* B. *Treasure Island*
   C. *The Great Gatsby* D. *Heart of Darkness*

   In my younger and more vulnerable years my father gave me some advice that I've been turning over in my mind ever since. "Whenever you feel like criticizing anyone," he told me, "just remember that all the people in this world haven't had the advantages that you've had."

4. "The lost generation" refers to the writers who relocated to Paris in the post WWI years to reject

the values of American materialism. All the following but ________ are involved in this group.（北二外 2007 研）

A. F. S. Fitzgerald　　B. Ernest Hemingway

C. Theodore Dreiser　　D. John Dos Passos

5. Ernest Hemingway is noted for the following EXCEPT ________.（首师大 2008 研）

A. Lost Generation　　B. iceberg theory

C. American Dream　　D. "grace under pressure"

6. Among the following writers, who is often acclaimed literary spokesman of the Jazz Age?

A. William Faulkner　　B. F. Scott Fitzgerald

C. Henry James　　D. Eugene O'Neill

7. "There was music from my neighbor's house through the summer nights. In his blue gardens men and girls came and went like moths among the whisperings and the champagne and the stars..." This quotation is taken from ________.

A. *Moby Dick* by Herman Melville　　B. *Daisy Miller* by Henry James

C. *Sister Carrie* by Theodore Dreiser　　D. *The Great Gatsby* by F. Scott Fitzgerald

8. Which of the following figures does not belong to "The Lost Generation"?

A. Ezra Pound　　B. William Carlos Williams

C. Robert Frost　　D. Theodore Dreiser

9. Nick's night trip to the Indian village and his experience inside the hut can be taken as ________.

A. an initiation to pain and suffering　　B. a confrontation with evil and sin

C. an essential lesson about Indian tribes　　D. a learning process of human connections

10. Ernest Hemingway was badly wounded in Italy and sent to a hospital where he fell in love with a nurse. These two persons later became the characters of his novel ________.

A. *The old Man and the Sea*　　B. *For Whom the Bell Tolls*

C. *The Sun Also Rises*　　D. *A Farewell to Arms*

Ⅲ. Explain the following terms.

1. the Jazz Age（北二外 2009 研；国际关系学院 2007 研；首师大 2009 研）
2. The Lost Generation（四川大学 2010 研；北航 2007 研）
3. "Hemingway Heroes"（武汉大学 2008 年）
4. Santiago（北航 2009 研）

Ⅳ. Read the following quotations and answer the questions.

Passage 1（北航 2007 研）

Most of the big shore places were closed now and there were hardly any lights except the shadowy, moving glow of a ferryboat across the Sound. And as the moon rose higher the inessential houses began to melt away until gradually I became aware of the old island here that flowered once for Dutch sailors' eyes-a fresh, green breast of the new world. Its vanished trees, the trees that had made way for Gatsby's house, had once pandered in whispers to the last and greatest of all human dreams; for a transitory enchanted moment man must have held his breath in the presence of this continent, compelled into all aesthetic contemplation he neither understood nor desired, face to face for the last time in history with something commensurate to his capacity for wonder.

And as I sat there brooding on the old, unknown world, I thought of Gatsby's wonder when he first picked out the green light at the end of Daisy's dock. He had come a long way to this blue lawn, and his dream must have seemed so close that he could hardly fail to grasp it. He did not know that it was already behind him, somewhere back in that vast obscurity beyond the city, where the dark fields of the republic rolled on under the night.

Gatsby believed in the green light, the orgiastic future that year by year recedes before us. It eluded us then, but that's no matter-tomorrow we will run faster, stretch out our arms farther And one fine morning—

So we beat on, boats against the current, borne back ceaselessly in to the past.

Questions:

(1) Which fiction is this excerpt from? Who is the author of the novel?

(2) What does "Daisy's dock" stand for?

(3) Why are the Dutch sailors mentioned here? In what way does it contribute to the novel?

Passage 2（北航 2008 研）

In the later summer of that year we lived in a house in a village that looked across the river and the plain to the mountains. In the bed of the river there were pebbles and boulders, dry and white in the sun, and the water was clear and swiftly moving and blue in the channels. Troops went by the house and down the road and the dust they raised powdered the leaves of the trees. The trunks of the trees too were dusty and the leaves fell early that year and we saw the troops marching along the road and the dust rising and leaves, stirred by the breeze, falling and the soldiers marching and afterward the road bare and white except for the leaves.

…

Poor, poor dear Cat. And this was the price you paid for sleeping together. This was the end of the trap. This was what people got for loving each other. Thank God for gas, anyway. What must it have been like before there were anesthetics? Once it started, they were in the mill-race. Catherine had a good time in the time of pregnancy. It wasn't bad. She was hardly ever sick. She was not awfully uncomfortable until toward the last. So now they got her in the end. You never got away with anything, Get away hell! It would have been the same if we had been married fifty times. And what if she should die? She won't die. People don't die in childbirth nowadays. That was what all husbands thought. Yes, but what if she should die? She won't die. She's just having a bad time. Afterward we'd say what a bad time and Catherine would say it wasn't really so bad. But what if she should die.

Questions:

(1) Identify the author and the work from which the passage is selected.

(2) What is the symbolic meaning of the title?

(3) How do you understand the features of heroes in the author's works?

(4) Comment on author's writing style and philosophy underlying all his works?

Passage 3（中山大学 2018 研）

That's my middle west—not the wheat or the prairies or the lost Swede towns but the thrilling, returning trains of my youth and the street lamps and sleigh bells in the frosty dark and, the shadows of holly wreaths thrown by lighted windows on the snow. I am part of that, a little solemn with the feel of those long winters, a little complacent from growing up in the Carraway house in a city where dwellings are still called through decades by a family's name. I see now that this has been a story of the West, after all—Tom and Gatsby, Daisy and Jordan and I, were all Westerners, and perhaps we possessed some deficiency in common which made us subtly unadaptable to Eastern life.

Questions:

(1) Identify the title and the author of the novel from which the above excerpt is taken. Who is the narrator? (3%)

(2) What do "west" and "east" refer to respectively in the excerpt? Explain their symbolic meaning with respect to the social and cultural context of 1920's America. (15%)

V. Short answer questions

1. Why did F. Scott Fitzgerald use "great" to modify the protagonist's name Gatsby in the title of his novel *The Great Gatsby*? (南京大学 2009 研；人大 2006 研)
2. What are the most striking features of Hemingway's writing style? (国际关系学院 2007 研)
3. Why was Fitzgerald regarded as spokesman of the "Jazz Age"?
4. What are the artistic characteristics in Hemingway's novels?

VI. Essay questions

1. The relationship between man and nature is a recurrent theme, and perhaps one of the most important themes, in American literature. Write a short essay on it by contrasting two or three American literary works, or two or three American literary movements, to tell what you know about their different views of nature. (武汉大学 2009 研)
2. Hemingway's war novel ends with a scene in a maternity hospital. How does this final topic, the death of a woman and a child in childbirth, force us to enlarge or reconsider what we took to be the central subject of the novel? In what sense is the novel a war novel? What is its subject if it is not war, battle, engagement with the enemy, strategy, etc.? Sufficient textual information is required to illustrate your viewpoints. (南京大学 2007 研)
3. Irving Howe considers *The Great Gatsby* as a prose version of *The Waste Land*. What do you think of this view? (天津外国语学院 2009 研)

参考答案及解析

I. Fill in the blanks.

1. *For Whom the Bell Tolls*

(海明威的小说《丧钟为谁而鸣》(*For Whom the Bell Tolls*)以西班牙内战为背景，该小说陈述了海明威对爱与失去的观点，描写了普通人不屈不挠的精神。)

2. *This Side of Paradise*

(1920 菲茨杰拉德发表第一部长篇小说《人间天堂》，一举成名。书中描写了一战后年轻一代的精神面貌和生活方式。)

3. *The Great Gatsby*

(《了不起的盖茨比》(*The Great Gatsby*)是美国作家弗朗西斯·司各特·菲茨杰拉德所写的

一部以20世纪20年代的纽约市及长岛为背景的小说，被视为美国文学“爵士时代”的象征。该书敏锐地抓住了当代社会生活的主题，并以象征手法展现了“美国梦”传奇之下的嘲讽及悲怅。）

4. *The Beautiful and the Damned*

（1922年菲茨杰拉德的第二部小说《美丽与诅咒》（*The Beautiful and the Damned*）出版。这部小说讲了一个年轻的有钱人，由于婚姻的不幸而导致感情和精神崩溃的故事。书中男女主角无疑是以菲茨杰拉德及其妻子泽尔达为原型而塑造的。）

5. *Tender is the Night*

（菲茨杰拉德的小说《夜色温柔》（*Tender is the Night*）讲述了一个美国精神病医生与一位美丽而又富有的病人结合终遭失败的故事。该小说反映了强烈的怀旧情绪、悔恨心理、失落的希望、破灭的幻想、人格的分裂。）

6. Lost Generation

（第一次世界大战后以海明威为代表的一些美国作家自称是“迷惘的一代”。所谓“迷惘”，是指他们共有的彷徨和失望情绪。这些作家中，大多数人亲身经历过第一次世界大战。在战场上，他们目睹了战争给人类带来的巨大灾难，经历了战争的折磨。）

7. *The Sun also Rises*

（菲茨杰拉德的短篇小说集《爵士乐时代的故事》（*Tales of the Jazz Age*）是爵士时代的标志，而海明威的小说《太阳照样升起》（*The Sun Also Rises*）则刻画了整个“迷惘的一代”的形象。）

8. *A Farewell to Arms*

（海明威的第二部力作是1929年出版的《永别了，武器》（*A Farewell to Arms*）。此书以爱情与战争两条主线，阐述了作者对战争及人生的看法和态度。）

9. Santiago

（《老人与海》（*The Old Man and the Sea*）是海明威最著名的作品之一，小说讲述了一位老年古巴渔夫圣地亚哥（Santiago），与一条巨大的马林鱼在离岸很远的湾流中搏斗的故事，表明了人可以被毁灭，但不能被打败的人生态度。）

10. Nobel Prize

（1954年海明威获诺贝尔文学奖。获奖理由：“因为他精通于叙事艺术，突出地表现在其近著《老人与海》之中；同时也因为他对当代文体风格之影响”。）

II. Multiple Choice

1. B 《了不起的盖茨比》既反映了20世纪20年代美国的精神面貌，也是关于美国的一种文化—历史性的寓言。
2. A 在《了不起的盖茨比》中，尼克既是一个叙述者，又是小说中的一个参与者。
3. C 题中片段选自美国著名小说家Francis Scott Fitzgerald的代表作《了不起的盖茨比》，是小说的开头部分，参考译文为：我年纪还轻，阅历不深的时候，我父亲教导过我一句话，我至今还念念不忘。“每逢你想要批评任何人的时候，”他对我说，“你就记住，这个世界上所有的人，并不是个个都有过你拥有的那些优越条件。”
4. C 菲茨杰拉德、海明威和帕索斯都属于“迷惘的一代”，选项C德莱塞则是一位自然主义作家。
5. C 海明威既是“迷惘的一代”的代表，也是“冰山理论”的提出者，其作品主题不少是关于

"压力之下的优雅"，但他并非"美国梦"的代表作家。

6. B　菲茨杰拉德是爵士乐时代的发言人。

7. D　这段话选自菲茨杰拉德的《了不起的盖茨比》，描写了盖茨比家举办晚会的情景。

8. D　西奥多·德莱赛是自然主义作家，他不属于"迷惘的一代"。

9. A　在《印第安营寨》中尼克开始了解到了人生的痛苦。

10. D　一战期间，海明威在意大利身受重伤，被送进医院。在那里他爱上了一个护士。海明威本人和这个护士日后成为小说《永别了，武器》(*A Farewell to Arms*)主人公人物的原型。

Ⅲ. Explain the following terms.

1. The Jazz Age refers to a period in American history following the end of World War I, continuing through the Roaring Twenties, and ending with the onset of the Great Depression. It marked a period of changing values alongside a soaring stock market. From the vantage point of historical and cultural studies it contrasts with the parallel Roaring Twenties descriptor with its greater emphasis on Modernism in its many forms. The age takes its name from jazz, which saw a tremendous surge in popularity among many segments of society. Among the prominent concerns and trends of the period are the public embrace of technological developments (typically seen as progress)—cars, air travel and the telephone—as well as new modernist trends in social behavior, the arts, and culture. One of the most representative literary works of the Jazz age is American writer F. Scott Fitzgerald's *The Great Gatsby* (1925).

2. The Lost Generation: The "Lost Generation" is a term used to characterize a general motif of disillusionment of American literary notables who lived in Europe, most notably Paris, after the First World War. Figures identified with the "Lost Generation" included authors and artists such as Ernest Hemingway, F. Scott Fitzgerald, Ezra Pound, Sherwood Anderson, Waldo Peirce, John Dos Passos, John Steinbeck, and Cole Porter.

3. "Hemingway Heroes": The works of Ernest Hemingway generally center on the concept of heroism. Each of his novels contains a "Hemingway hero"—a man of honor and integrity who expresses himself with actions rather than words. The Hemingway hero is a noble but tragic hero fighting alone with the overwhelming and unfathomable force; though he knows that he will be defeated at last, he decides to act like a hero.

   A Hemingway hero is not a Godlike figure, but an ordinary, often flawed mortal who must look to himself for strength. The Hemingway hero is actually a mirror image of the author himself. Frederic Henry in *A Farewell to Arms* and Santiago in *The Old Man and the Sea* are typical Hemingway heroes.

4. Santiago is the protagonist of *The Old Man and the Sea*, written by American novelist Ernest Hemingway. He is an old man who hasn't caught any fishes for eighty-four days. On the final journey he has a fight with shakes. This character depicted by Hemingway is a typical "tough guy". Santiago embodies Hemingway's definition of courage as "grace under pressure". He never loses dignity in the face of death. The glory and honor Santiago accrues comes not from his battle itself but from his pride and determination to fight. His famous words are "A man is not made for defeat... a man can be destroyed but not defeated."

Ⅳ. Read the following quotations and answer the questions.

Passage 1

(1) This excerpt is from *The Great Gatsby* by F. S. Fitzgerald.

(2) The green light at the end of Daisy's dock represents Gatsby's hopes and dreams about Daisy. Thus, "Daisy's dock" stands for Daisy and also the American Dream.

(3) The Dutch sailors are connected to the early settlement of the New York area. To the Dutch sailors, America is a place full of wonder and promise where they may fulfill their dreams. The same is for Gatsby who newly becomes a millionaire and wants to gain Daisy's love with his wealth. The Dutch sailors can be taken as an allegory in the novel.

Passage 2

(1) The passage is selected from *A Farewell to Arms* by Ernest Hemingway.

(2) The title has two symbolic meanings: First, it means Henry says goodbye to the war, for the word "arms" has the meaning of "weapon". The second meaning is that Henry says goodbye to his dear wife Catherine Berkley who dies in the hospital. The "arms" also symbolizes Catherine's arms.

(3) Hemingway's world is a world essentially chaotic and meaningless, in which man fights a solitary struggle against an unfathomable force. The Hemingway hero possesses "despairing courage." It is this courage that enables a man to behave like a man, to assert his dignity in face of adversity. The typical Hemingway hero is one who, wounded but strong, enjoys the pleasures of life in face of ruin and death and maintains, through some notion of a code, an ideal of himself. A Hemingway code hero can be destroyed but not defeated.

(4) Hemingway uses short sentences and paragraphs and vigorous and positive language. He always manages to choose words concrete, specific, more commonly found, more Anglo-Saxon, casual and conventional, and employ them often in syntax of short, simple sentences, which are orderly and patterned, conversational, and sometimes ungrammatical. The philosophy underlying his works is Iceberg Principle. Hemingway said: "If a writer of prose knows enough about what he is writing about he may omit things that will have a feeling of those things as strongly as though the writer had stated them. The dignity of movement of an iceberg is due to only one-eighth of it being above water. A good writer does not need to reveal every detail of a character or action."

Passage 3

(1) The title of this novel is *The Great Gatsby* and the author is Fitzgerald. The narrator is Nick.

(2) "East" represents a world of wealth and emptiness. "West" represents traditional ideas and values of American. Nick himself came from a wealthy family in the Midwest. After the war, he returned home from the battlefield. He felt that the Midwest was no longer like the west. So he went to the east to study bond business to make money. However, in less than a year in the east, after witnessing the tragedy of Gatsby and the hypocrisy and fraud of the rich in the east, he felt the east is a cold place. So he returned from the fashionable and corrupt eastern to the boring and chaotic but simple and natural west. This dislocation of ideals indicates the inevitability of the failure of the American dream. The ideal can only be realized in the west. It's im-

possible to realize it in the east. Then the so-called "American dream" has entered a dead end.

V. Short answer questions

1. Gatsby is great because he is able to create a new identity for himself when he needs to be someone else. His determination and audacity are amazing since he focuses on a goal of winning Daisy and he does whatever is necessary to attain it. He establishes that he needs wealth to keep Daisy in the manner she is accustomed to, and so he attains a "business" that gives him financial wealth. What is more, he studies mannerisms and expressions he thinks is what the social elite says and does.

   That Gatsby is great is also because of his unworldly love for Daily. He takes the blame for Daisy when she commits a crime and that takes a great man.

   Gatsby is great because he is a mythical figure whose personal experience approximates a state of mind that embodies America. Gatsby is the last of the romantic hero, whose energy and sense of commitment take him in search of his personal grail.

2. Hemingway once said, "The dignity of movement of an iceberg is due to only one-eighth of it being above water." He adopts "Iceberg" theory in his own writing. He always manages to choose words concrete, specific, more commonly found, more Anglo-Saxon, casual and conversational, and employ them often in syntax of short, simple sentences, which are orderly and patterned, conversational, and sometimes ungrammatical. But it is good to note that Hemingway's style is also deliberate and polished and is never natural as it seems to be, and its simplicity can be disastrously deceptive, as it is highly suggestive and connotative and capable of offering layers of undercurrents of meaning.

3. Fitzgerald was a representative figure of the 1920s. He never failed to remain detached and foresee the tragedy of the "Dollar Decade." His works mirror the exciting age in almost every way. Through the glittering world of his fiction run the themes of moral waste and decay and necessity of personal responsibility. *The Great Gatsby*, a book about the Jazz Age, is a case study in people's pursuit of an elusive American Dream. It is also a powerful criticism of American society. Thus he is often acclaimed literary spokesman of the Jazz Age.

4. Hemingway's characterization is typical of the "iceberg" analogy in psychoanalysis. According to Hemingway, good literary writing should be able to make readers feel the emotion of the characters directly and the best way to produce the effect is to observe every particular kind of feeling without any authorial comments or conventionally emotive language but with a bare minimum of adjectives and adverbs. Seemingly simply and natural, Hemingway's language style is actually polished and tightly controlled. The outward physical events and sensations express the meaning of the story and convey the complex emotions of his characters with a considerable range and astonishing intensity of feeling. Besides, Hemingway develops the style of colloquialism initiated by Mark Twain. The accents and mannerisms of human speech are so well presented that the characters are full of flesh and blood. The use of short, simple and conversational words and sentences has an effect of clearness, terseness and great care.

Ⅵ. Essay questions

1. American literature can be called a young literature, but American writers take the relationship between man and nature as an important theme with changing views of nature. We can see the subtle change from two literary works: Melville's *Moby Dick* and Hemingway's *The Old Man and the Sea.*

   In *Moby Dick*, the captain Ahab is driven by a monomaniacal desire to kill Moby Dick, the whale that maimed him on the previous whaling voyage. The white whale has also been seen as a symbol for nature and those elements of life that are out of human control. To Ahab, killing the whale becomes the ultimate goal in his life, and this observation can also be expanded allegorically so that the whale represents everyone's goals. Furthermore, his vengeance against the whale is analogous to man's struggle against nature.

   The Old Man and the Sea recounts a battle between an aging Cuban fisherman Santiago and a giant marlin, when he straps the marlin to the side of his skiff and heads home, he finds that sharks are attracted by the marlin's blood and he has to fight against the sharks. In this novel, although Santiago kills fishes to make money and survive, he is friendly and grateful to the creatures in the sea.

   The relationship between man and nature in American literature has changed from conquering nature to making proper use of nature, from taking nature as an enemy to regarding it as a friend. People are realizing that man needs to exist harmoniously with nature.

2. *A Farewell to Arms* is considered to be the greatest war novels of all time, because it reveals the nature of the war. In the novel, the war is not glamorized; instead, it is presented in a very real and horrifying fashion from the perspective of the ambulance driver. At some moments, war is derided as a game for the ruling classes in which the poor suffer. War is only rarely viewed in a patriotic fight and more often seen as tiresome.

   As a nurse, Catherine is able to transfer herself to the hospital where Frederic is recovering. Then, she flees with him to Switzerland where she dies from internal bleeding resulting from a difficult childbirth. In her death she is the picture of heroism and her statements are full of dark humor. "I am not afraid. I just hate it." Concerning this, we can conclude that this novel is also a tragic love story, in which man is doomed to be trapped in difficult situations and in misery.

   Besides the subject of war, the novel also explores the searching of identity. Frederick Henry represents the experience of a whole nation, who is wounded in war and disillusioned with the insanity and futility of the universe. This subject is important to the story because it expresses the general question of the individual in the postwar world. Frederic represents this questioning of what is the force that can cause such awful destruction and human suffering. Frederic's identity is displaced by the late introduction of his name to the reader, the fact of his being an American in an Italian army, and his constant play with words. He speaks Italian, but not well enough. All these examples try to show Frederic does not know who he is.

3. Both *The Great Gatsby* and *The Waste Land* both reflect the loss of an ideal and the disillusionment that people's incorruptible dream is smashed into pieces by the relentless reality. Both of them reflect a world in which desires are filled with, spirits fall down, moral is lost and life is

corrupt. Through the two works, the general disappointment toward reality, world and human civilization are shown. So *The Great Gatsby* interprets *The Waste Land*' s theme by the story of Gatsby.

But in another respect, the artistic feature of *The Great Gatsby* is that the language manifests the poetic quality. The style of F. Scott Fitzgerald, closely related to his themes, is explicit and chilly. His accurate dialogues and his sensitive styles provide the reader with a vivid sense of reality. He uses the scenic method in his chapters, each one of which consists of one or more dramatic scenes. Sometimes he intervenes passages of narration, leaving the tedious process of transition to the readers' imagination. He also skillfully chooses a dramatic narrator through whose "central consciousness" everything is delivered to organize the wholeness of the work. The accurate details, the completely original diction and metaphors, the bold impressionistic and colorful quality have all revealed his consummate artistry. His words are like pieces of poems, provoking reader' s imagination and placing them in the beauty of poetry. In this sense, *The Great Gatsby* is a prose version of *The Waste Land.*

第 15 章　南方文艺复兴·威廉姆·福克纳

15.1　复习笔记

I. The Southern Renaissance	**I. 南方文艺复兴**
1. Historical background	**1. 历史背景**
The American south has been a unique region all along. Different to the Hamiltonian north, the Jeffersonian south is of its own history and customs, which remind us of the conflict between the two regions in the national history The Civil War is a crucial historical point, after the war the agricultural south became more subordinate to the industrial north, and the long-existing glaring gap in culture and thinking mode between the two parts contributes even more to the intensity of the north-south relationship. Measures were taken to develop the south; economic improvements slowly came about. Although the south in many aspects remained conservative, in the field of literature, there glittered a visible spark of change, efforts were taking to reassess the past and the present and to carry out self-searching. Thus the blooming of southern literature in the 1920s and 1930s were given rise to.	美国南方一直是一个独特的地区。不同于杰斐逊式的北方，哈米尔顿式南方有着自己的历史和风俗，这也提醒我们在美国历史上两个地区间存在的冲突。美国内战是一个关键的历史节点，战后，农业式的南方越发地从属于工业化的北方。这两个地区之间在文化和思维方式上长期存在的显著差距使得南北关系更加紧张。国家采取措施以促进南方发展，其经济方面缓慢地取得了进展。尽管南方在许多方面仍旧保守，在文学上却闪现出了变革的火花，人们努力重新评估过去和现在，并且进行自我探索。这样就推动了 19 世纪二三十年代南方文学的繁荣。
2. Major writers of the South Renaissance	**2. 南方文艺复兴主要作家**
Ellen Glasgow, whose series of novels are characteristic of the Virginia setting, concentrated more on tomorrow rather than keeping casting eyes on the old times. In her novels, such as *Virginia* and *Barren Ground*, the builders of the future of Virginia are depicted in elaboration. Glasgow made her unique contribution to the emergence of William Faulkner.	埃伦·格拉斯高的一系列小说以弗吉尼亚为背景，她更多地关注明天而不是不停地回顾旧时光。在其小说如，《弗吉尼亚》和《不毛之地》中，弗吉尼亚未来的建设者们得到了细致的描绘。格拉斯高为威廉姆·福克纳的出现做出了独有的贡献。
As the most important figure among the Southern Renaissance writers, Faulkner, with altogether 19 novels and countless short stories elaborating on the American south, provided profound scrutiny of the problems deep-rooted in the south. Historically speaking, Faulkner contributed to the American renaissance cause of the 1920s and helped usher in a whole new group of southern authors of the 1930s such as Katherine Anne Porter, Eudora Welty, and Carson McCullers.	作为南方文艺复兴中最重要的作家，福克纳的 19 部长篇小说和众多短篇小说都与南方息息相关。这些作品详细考察了南方所面临的困境。福克纳竭力为 20 年代南方文艺复兴做出了贡献，并且引领了 30 年代一群新的南方作家。如凯瑟琳·安·波特，尤多拉·韦尔蒂和卡森·麦卡勒斯。

After the WWII, there were a number of younger writers continuing probing into the southern tradition, among whom Flannery O'Connor, William Styron, and Walker Percy are representatives. These writers have endeavored to write about the southern theme and made it evergreen in American literature.

二战后出现了许多继续探索南方文学传统的作家，如弗兰纳里·奥康纳，威廉姆·史泰伦，沃克·珀西等。这些作家保持了南方主题的连续性，使得南方主题在美国文学中常青。

Ⅱ. William Faulkner (1897 – 1962)

Ⅱ. 威廉姆·福克纳

1. Life

Faulkner was born the eldest of the four sons into a Southern family with a fairly long tradition . The town of Oxford where he was brought up became the model for his fictional Jefferson. His own family history was also written into his novels. Faulkner joined the Royal Flying Corps in Canada and still under training when the war was over. After the military service, he went back home and attended the University of Mississippi for a year, maintaining himself with several odd jobs. His first two novels were not very promising, but *Sartoris* (1929) showed Faulkner's growth and maturity as a promising writer. His next book, *The Sound and the Fury*, was definitely the mature work of a major work, especially for its technical sophistication. In the following years, his major works appeared one after another. In 1946, Malcoim Cowley edited *The Viking Portable Faulkner* with a generous introduction of his works. Faulkner was gradually seen as the center of critical attention. He won the Nobel Price for literature in 1949.

1. 生平

福克纳出生于一个历史悠久的南方家庭，是家中四个孩子中的长子。他在牛津镇长大，该镇后来成为其小说中虚构的杰斐逊镇的原型。他的家族史也被写进了他的小说中。一战早期他曾在加拿大参加英国陆军航空队，训练未完一战就已结束了。回国后他在密西西比大学就读一年，后做过多种杂工。他的前两部小说并未引起注意，而1929年出版的《沙特里斯》却表现出作为一名前途光明的作家其创作已渐臻成熟。他的下一部《喧哗与骚动》是一部较为成熟的作品，尤其是它复杂的技巧。尔后，他的主要作品陆续出版。1946年文学批评家马尔科姆·考利编辑了他的作品选集《福克纳读本》，并详细介绍他的著作。福克纳成为文学批评界的焦点。福克纳于1949年获得诺贝尔文学奖。

2. Subject matter

The Faulkner oeuvre includes altogether 19 novels and three volumes of short stories. In these works the Deep South is depicted in great detail. An important part of Faulkner's works have been termed the Yoknapatawpha saga, which tells the histories of a number of southern aristocratic families. In the very rise of these family fortunes, Faulkner already foresees their inevitable fall for the displacement of the Indians

2. 创作题材

福克纳共创作了19部长篇小说和3本短篇小说集。在这些作品里，福克纳极为细致地刻画了美国南方。福克纳作品中最重要的一部分被称为“约克纳帕特发世家小说”。在这些作品里福克纳描写了许多南方贵族的家族史。在这些家族发迹时福克纳就预示到他们必然的衰落。

and the enslavement of the black race, thus putting a curse upon the land as well as their own fate. When the same narration on the tragic ebb and flow of these families continues to occur novel after novel, it assumes symbolic proportion. Evidently, Faulkner talks about the American south as much as the universal human situation. He conveys the message that the typical spiritual deterioration in modern life derives directly from the loss of love and the unquenchable desire of emotional response.

因为他们剥夺了印第安人的土地，奴役了黑人，使得他们的土地和自己的命运都受到了诅咒。当悲壮的兴衰史在一部部小说中不断呈现时，它就具有了象征性的意义。很显然，福克纳想要表达的不仅仅涉及美国南方，也包括人类普遍的生活状况。福克纳传递了这样的信息：现代生活中典型的精神堕落直接源于爱的缺乏和无法得到满足的对情感回应的欲望。

3. Characteristics of Faulkner's writings

Faulkner was a daring formal experimentalist. He kept evolving his literary strategies so as to be better able to communicate his ideas.

(1) Characterization was, to Faulkner, an essential medium to reveal the multifaceted nature of man. His characterization allowed the characters a maximum degree of autonomy and independence. One of the most important devices to achieve such effect is authorial transcendence, which means the author makes himself invisible by employing a fallible narrator or multiple narrators.

(2) Faulkner is a demanding writer. His novels consist of a large bumber of interior monologues, many of which are composed through the stream of consciousness technique. Faulkner's words breaks the graphological rules, which are seen running together, lacking capitalization and proper punctuation. As for sentences, they are not always clearly indicated and many long ones are pushed together in peculiar ways. Besides, the pronouns are blurred in reference, causing the texts' perplexity.

(3) Faulkner's prose style ranges from colloquial, regional dialects to highly charged courtroom rhetoric, covering a variety of "registers" of the English language.

(4) Faulkner's power of imagination are extraordinary. Rooting his works in the Deep South, he manages to create a literary milieu of his own through which he tries to transcend the limits of particularity to reach universality. In his works, Faulkner manifests a tendency toward the rhetoric power and vitality of myth and succeeds eventually in elevating plain, down-to-earth stories of human life on to the plane of an elaborate mythology.

3. 写作特点

福克纳在形式上大胆地进行创新实验，他不断发展文学策略以更好地表达他的观点。

(1) 福克纳极重视人物的塑造，这是他表现人的多面性的关键所在。他给予角色最大程度的自主和独立。为达到这种效果，最重要的一种手段是借助于"作者的超脱"，即通过不可靠的叙事者和多位叙事者的手法使作者本人隐身。

(2) 要读懂福克纳是很吃力的事。他的作品里有很多的内心独白，且多用现代意识流技巧来呈现。福克纳的词语打破了语相规则，单词常挤到一块，没有大写和标点符号。在句子层面上，句子意义指代不明，长句子奇怪地堆积到一起。此外，代词的模糊指代加重了其文章的复杂性。

(3) 福克纳散文的语言风格包含日常口语，地方方言，又有规范的文学语言，涵盖了英语语言的多个语域。

(4) 福克纳的想象力异常丰富。他把作品植根于美国南部历史，创造出一种独特的文学氛围，最终超越具体的人或事的局限而触及普遍性的问题。在其作品中福克纳展现了逐步向神话的修辞力量和生命力运动的趋势，他成功地把人生的简单却真实的故事提高到神话的高度。

4. Major works

The Marble Faun
Soldier's Pay
Mosquitoes
Sartoris
Sound and Fury
Sanctuary
Light in August
Absalom, Absalom!
Go Down, Moses
"*A Rose for Emily*"
The Unvanquished
Knight's Gambit
As I Lay Dying
The Wild Palms
Requiem for a Nun
The Hamlet

5. Analysis of major work

◆*The Sound and the Fury*

The Sound and the Fury (1929) is Faulkner's fourth novel. The title is taken from Macbeth's lines in Shakespeare's *Macbeth* "It (life) is a tale / Told by an idiot, full of sound and fury, / Signifying nothing." The novels details the destruction and downfall of the aristocratic Compson family from four different points of view. There is enough despair and nihilism as conveyed from Macbeth but not much love and emotion in this sad story of the Compsons. The whole novel is divided into four sections. The first three are presented from the perspectives of the three Compson sons: Benjamin ("Benjy"), the "idiot"; Quentin, the suicidal student; and Jason, the failed businessman. The fourth section has a third-person omniscient narrator. All but the second section are set in fictional Yoknapatawpha County, Mississippi, in April 1928.

It is a story of deterioration from the past to the present. The past is idealized to form a striking contrast with the loveless present. There is in the book an acute feeling of nostalgia toward the happy past. Through Benjy' narration Faulkner highlights the theme of loss. Quentin's suicide could be regarded as an example of a thorough negation of the present. To some extent, Quentin's value system may reflect Faulkner's own view towards an ideal way of life, that of an antebellum society. Through the selfish and heartless individual Jason, the triumph of rationalism over feeling and compassion is best illustrated.

4. 主要作品

《玉石雕像》
《士兵的报酬》
《蚊群》
《沙特里斯》
《喧哗与骚动》
《圣殿》
《八月之光》
《押沙龙，押沙龙!》
《去吧，摩西》
《献给艾米丽的玫瑰花》
《不败者》
《马弃兵》
《我弥留之际》
《野棕榈》
《修女安魂曲》
《村子》

5. 主要作品分析

◆《喧哗与骚动》

《喧哗与骚动》(1929)是福克纳的第四本小说。标题选自莎士比亚的《麦克白》中麦克白的台词，“人生如痴人说梦，充满着喧哗与躁动，却没有任何意义。”小说从四个不同的视角详细讲述了贵族康普生家族的毁灭和衰落。在康普生一家悲剧性的故事里没有爱与情感，弥漫着绝望情绪和虚无主义。整部小说分为四个部分。前三部分是从康普生家族三个儿子的角度呈现的：本杰明(“班吉”)，“白痴”；昆汀，自杀的学生；杰森，失败的商人。第四部分出现了第三人称全知叙述者。除了第二部分之外，其余部分都以 1928 年 4 月密西西比的约克纳帕塔法县为背景。

故事讲述了从过去到现在的堕落。过去被人为地理想化了，与现在的冷酷无情形成了强烈的对比。书中充满了强烈的怀旧之情。通过班吉的叙述作者渲染了“失去”这一主题。昆丁的自杀可被视作对现在的完全否定的一个例证。在某种程度上，昆丁的价值体系折射了福克纳本人关于理想生活方式，即战前社会的看法。在自私自利的杰生的身上，我们看到理性战胜了情感与同情之心。

15.2 考研真题与典型题详解

I. Fill in the blanks.

1. ________ wrote about the disintegration of the old social system in the American Southern States and its effect on the lives of modern people, both black and white. (人大2006研)
2. In his novel, William Faulkner has invented a county named ________ and the seat of the county ________.(国际关系学院2009研)
3. The works written by ________ may be viewed as a culmination of the development of twentieth-century southern fiction.
4. Quentin is a character in William Faulkner's novel ________.
5. Joe Christmas is a character in William Faulkner's novel ________.

II. Multiple Choice

1. William Faulkner is NOT the writer of ________.(北二外2008研)

   A. *Herzog* B. *A Rose for Emily*
   C. *As I Lay Dying* D. *Go Down, Moses*

2. The author of *The Sound and the Fury* also wrote ________.(大连外国语学院2008研)

   A. *Billy Budd* B. *As I Lay Dying* C. *Sea Wolf* D. *Dangling Man*

3. Of the four Compson Children, ________'s life embodies all the vices of the modern world. (天津外国语学院2009研)

   A. Quentin B. Caddy C. Jason D. Benjy

4. Among the many novels written by William Faulkner, the title of ________ is associated with the Bible. (首师大2008研)

   A. *The Sound and the Fury* B. *Absalom, Absalom!*
   C. *As I Lay Dying* D. *Light in August*

5. Which of the following is not written by William Faulkner?(首师大2007研)

   A. *The Sound and the Fury* B. *For Whom the Bell Tolls*
   C. *Light in August* D. *Hamlet*

6. The fictional place that bears marked similarities to the town where ________ had been raised was called by himself his "little postage stamp of native soil".

   A. William Styron B. Mark Twain
   C. William Faulkner D. John Barth

7. Which of the following is not a theme of *The Sound and the Fury*?

   A. The decline of a family B. The South vs. the North
   C. The past vs. the present D. racial problems

8. Thomas Sutpen is a character in William Faulkner's novel ________.

   A. *Absalom, Absalom!* B. *Light in August*
   C. *Go Down, Moses* D. *The Sound and the Fury*

9. ________ is about Thomas Sutpen's attempt to found a Southern dynasty.

   A. *Soldier's Pay* B. *Absalom, Absalom!*
   C. *The Sound and the Fury* D. *Light in August*

10. __________ is said to be a "historical novel" by Faulkner.

A. *Go Down, Moses*　　B. *Light in August*

C. *The Sound and the Fun*　　D. *Absalom, Absalom*

Ⅲ. Explain the following terms.

1. Southern Renaissance (北二外 2010 研；北航 2008 研)
2. Yoknapatawpha (北航 2007 研)
3. Multiple point of view

Ⅳ. Read the following quotations and answer the questions.

Passage 1 (首师大 2009 研)

So she vanquished them, horse and foot, just as she had vanquished their fathers thirty years before about the smell. That was two years after her father's death and a short time after her sweetheart—the one we believed would marry her—had deserted her. After her father's death she went out very little; after her sweetheart went away, people hardly saw her at all. A few of the ladies had the temerity to call, but were not received, and the only sign of life about the place was the Negro man—a young man then—going in and out with a market basket.

Questions:

(1) What is the title of this work?

(2) What is the theme of the whole work?

Passage 2

Then we noticed that in the second pillow was the indentation of a head. One of us lifted something from it, and leaning forward, that faint and invisible dust dry and acrid in the nostrils, we saw a long strand of iron-gray hair.

Questions:

(1) Which short story is this passage taken from?

(2) What is the identity of the narrator "us"?

(3) Whose is the iron-gray hair?

(4) What causes the indentation in the pillow?

(5) Is the story a tragedy or a comedy?

Ⅴ. Short answer questions

1. Which of William Faulkner's works impresses you most? Why? (国际关系学院 2007 研)
2. Where did William Faulkner usually locate his stories? What does the place stand for?
3. In what way is William Faulkner called a Southern writer?
4. Discuss William Faulkner's style.

Ⅵ. Essay questions

1. In what way is Emily Grierson a monument of tradition? (天津外国语学院 2009 研)
2. William Faulkner once said, "she [Caddy Compson] was the beautiful one", "She was my heart's darling. That's what I wrote the book about and I used the tools which seemed to me the proper tools to try to tell, try to draw the picture of Caddy." How do you understand Faulkner's appraisal of Caddy? (天津外国语学院 2007 研)
3. Analysis of William Faulkner's *The Sound and the Fury*.

参考答案及解析

I. Fill in the blanks.

1. William Faulkner

（福克纳的作品主要是关于美国南方的沉浮。在这中间，黑人和白人，南方与北方，农业和工业之间发生剧烈的摩擦和冲动。结果是腐朽的古老传统被新兴的资本势力所击败，急剧的演变过程中形形色色的人物终不免成为客观势力和主观弱点的牺牲品。）

2. Yoknapatawpha ; the town of Jefferson

（福克纳在自己的一系列著作中虚构了位于密西西比州北部的约克纳帕塔法县，这个县的中心是杰斐逊镇。）

3. William Faulkner

（威廉·福克纳的作品可以看做是20世纪美国南方小说发展的巅峰之作。）

4. *The Sound and the Fury*

（昆丁（Quentin）是威廉·福克纳小说《喧哗与骚动》（*The Sound and the Fury*）中的人物，同时也是该小说第三部分的叙述者。）

5. *Light in August*

（《八月之光》（*Light in August*）是威廉·福克纳写的一部批判种族主义的小说。乔·克里斯默斯（Joe Christmas）是该小说的主人公。）

II. Multiple Choice

1. A　*Herzog*（《赫索格》）的作者是Saul Bellow（索尔·贝娄），其余选项都是福克纳的作品。

2. B　《喧嚣与骚动》的作者是美国作家威廉·福克纳，他其他的重要作品还有：*As I Lay Dying*（《我弥留之际》），*Light in August*（《八月之光》）、*Absalom*，*Absalom*！（《押沙龙！押沙龙》），*Go Down*，*Moses*（《去吧，摩西》）等。*Billy Budd*（《比利·巴德》）是Herman Melville（赫尔曼·梅尔维尔）的作品；*Sea Wolf*（《海狼》）的作者是Jack London（杰克·伦敦）；*Dangling Man*（《晃来晃去的人》）是Saul Bellow（索尔·贝娄）的小说。

3. C　《喧哗与骚动》是福克纳第一部成熟的作品，讲述的是南方没落地主康普生一家的家族悲剧。长子昆丁绝望地抱住南方所谓的旧传统不放，因妹妹凯蒂风流成性、有辱南方淑女身份而恨疚交加，竟至溺水自杀。次子杰生冷酷贪婪，三子班吉则是个白痴，三十三岁时只有三岁小儿的智能。本书通过这三个儿子的内心独白，围绕凯蒂的堕落展开，最后则由黑人女佣迪尔西对前三部分的"有限视角"作补充，归结全书。小说大量运用多视角叙述方法及意识流手法，是意识流小说乃至整个现代派小说的经典名著。

4. B　在福克纳的小说中，《押沙龙，押沙龙!》的题目是和圣经有关的，因为押沙龙是旧约里的一个人物，是大卫的儿子。

5. B　《丧钟为谁而鸣》的作者是海明威。选项D《村子》是福克纳的斯诺普斯三部曲的第一部。

6. C　福克纳小说中虚构的地方与他长大的地方有很多相似之处，被他称为"乡土的微型邮票"。

7. D　《喧哗与骚动》中涉及到了家族的衰落、南方与北方、过去与现在的主题，但是种族主义不是主要方面。

8. A　托马斯·塞德潘（Thomas Sutpen）是威廉·福克纳小说《押沙龙，押沙龙!》中的主人公。

9. B 《押沙龙，押沙龙!》是最复杂、深奥，最具史诗风格的一部作品。它讲述的是美国南方一个家族从1860年到1910年左右所经历的激烈的分崩离析的故事，深刻地表现了人与人、人与自己内心的种种冲突，触及与人类境遇有关的诸多普遍性的问题。

10. D 福克纳称《押沙龙，押沙龙!》是一部历史小说。

Ⅲ. Explain the following terms.

1. The Southern Renaissance (also known as Southern Renascence) was the reinvigoration of American Southern literature that began in the 1920s and 1930s with the appearance of writers such as William Faulkner, Caroline Gordon, Elizabeth Madox Roberts, Katherine Anne Porter, Allen Tate, Tennessee Williams, and Robert Penn Warren, among others. The major themes in their works are: the South's conservative culture; the South's troubled history in regards to racial issues and the burden of history in a place where many people still remembered slavery, Reconstruction, and a devastating military defeat. These writers also brought new modernistic techniques such as stream of consciousness and complex narrative techniques to their works.
2. Yoknapatawpha is a fictional county created by American author William Faulkner as a setting for many of his novels. It is widely believed by scholars that Lafayette County, Mississippi is the basis for Yoknapatawpha County. Faulkner would often refer to it as "my apocryphal county." Yoknapatawpha is located in northwestern Mississippi and its seat is the town of Jefferson. This fictional county is bounded on the north by the Tallahatchie River and on the south by the Yoknapatawpha River.
3. Point of view is the vantage point from which a narrative is told. Novels sometimes, but infrequently, mix point of views. The American writer William Faulkner is a master at presenting multiple points of view, showing within the same story how characters react differently to the center and various points of view radiating from it. This technique makes it difficult for the reader to see the truth of the story.

Ⅳ. Read the following quotations and answer the questions.

Passage 1

(1) The title of the work is "A Rose for Emily".

(2) The main theme of "A Rose for Emily" is the decline of the Old South after the Civil War. Emily was treated as the monument of the tradition. After the Civil War, the south began to crumble under the crash of northern industrialization. The old buildings were torn and the old social system collapsed. The most important was that people's ideas were changed. Another theme of this story is community vs. isolation which is related to the relationship between Emily and the town people. Emily's seemingly eccentric behaviors were actually evidence that she was alienated by the whole town.

Passage 2

(1) The passage is taken from "A Rose for Emily" by William Faulkner.

(2) "us" in this passage refers to the townspeople in Jefferson.

(3) The iron-gray hair is Emily's.

(4) Emily sleeps every night besides Homer—her lover's corpse. It is her head that causes the indentation in the pillow.

(5) The story is a tragedy.

V. Short answer questions

1. In my opinion, *The Sound and the Fury* is the most impressing novel of William Faulkner. It tells a story of deterioration from the past to the present. The past is idealized to form a striking contrast with the loveless present. There is enough despair and nihilism but not much love and emotion in this novel.
2. Faulkner usually located his stories in a fictional town called Jefferson in the fictional Yoknapatawpha County.

   With his imagination, Faulkner turned the land, the people and the history of the place into a literary creation and a mythical kingdom, which stands for the American South. The Yoknapatawpha County fiction has an overall pattern in which Faulkner's protagonists collide with the twentieth century society. Most of the major themes are directly related to this confrontation in Faulkner's fiction.
3. Faulkner is called a Southern writer in that most of Faulkner's works are set in the South. His works have managed to show a panorama of the experience and consciousness of the whole Southern society both before and after the Civil War. Though Faulkner set his works in the South, his concern was always with the general human situation.
4. William Faulkner is among the most challenging American writers of the twentieth century. He is known as a novelist of great importance. His novels are exclusively celebrated for the narrative technique he has employed in his works. He always structures his stories in his original fashion and is proficient in employing a distinctive narrative method of gradually fitting in and withholding or even giving confusing information. Gradually confusions vanish as context and periphery are defined and the center is revealed. Faulkner also used a naturalistic or more conventional prose form as well for much of his work. Most of his novels and stories offer a combination between naturalistic prose and stream-of-consciousness. There are a lot of interior-monologues; the modern stream of consciousness technique is frequently and skillfully used. Words often run together, with no capitalization and no proper punctuation. Faulkner is well-known for his stylistically complex sentence structure. The complicity of sentence structures parallels the complexity of the thoughts of his characters. Sentences are not always clearly indicates; many long ones are pushed together in peculiar ways. One fragment runs into another without proper notice, and added to all this, is the use of pronouns which often causes irritating perplexity. For his handling of language, Faulkner's prose ranges from colloquial, regional dialects to highly charged courtroom rhetoric, covering a variety of registers of the English language. Faulkner was a master of his own particular style of writing.

VI. Essay questions

1. Emily Grierson, the main character in "A Rose for Emily" by William Faulkner, represents the tradition of the south. Firstly, she is the representative of the high class of southern society which is crumbling. Social class is the typical production of southern tradition and her family is a typical upper-class family. Her father did a special contribution to the town during the war which gained respects of government. Her family members have eccentric temper which is thought understanda-

ble for royal family. Standing in the garages and cotton gins, her house is the only building of the old time. Secondly, she is living in a traditional way which is worshiped by old men in the town. She lived with a black servant, having no tax to the town. Thirdly, she has the hereditary obligation upon this town which is the spirit core of the southern tradition. According to her obligation, she can't marry man from north and low class, which buried her love at last. This is the root of her tragedy. Fourthly, she rejects advance of society, new life value and locks herself in her big, old house as the only rejection in the whole town. Though people all begin to live in a new way ignoring the old tradition, they sent Emily as their representative of the vanishing past. Faulkner saw the north industrialization eroding the south tradition day after day and set Emily as the monument to fight against it which is in vain finally.

2. According to Faulkner, Caddy Compson is the true hero of *The Sound and the Fury*. She is the second Compson child, a strong-willed yet caring woman. She is Benjy's only real caregiver and Quentin's best friend. Caddy never develops a voice, but rather allows her brothers' emotions towards her to develop her character.

    The first section of the novel is narrated by Benjamin Compson, a source of shame to the family due to his mental retardation; the only characters who evidence a genuine care for him are Caddy, his older sister; and Dilsey, a matriarchal servant. From Benjy's memory we know that Caddy is very kind and caring.

    In the second section, we understand Quentin's feeling about Caddy. He is obsessed with southern ideals of chivalry and is strongly protective of women, especially his sister Caddy. He could protect his sister by joining her in whatever punishment she might have to endure. He is depressed on hearing the sexual affairs of Caddy, and finally kills himself.

    Through the memories of her brothers, the voice of Caddy becomes clear. In fact, the whole story is told by different people, all around Caddy. She is the most active and attractive one of the Compson family, as well as the favorite character of Faulkner in the novel.

3. *The Sound and the Fury* is William Faulkner's best novel. The title is taken from Macbeth's lines in Shakespeare's *Macbeth* "It (life) is a tale / Told by an idiot, full of sound and fury, / Signifying nothing." There is enough despair and nihilism but not much love and emotion in this sad story of the Compsons. One of the overarching themes of the book is the decline of the Compson family, which also acts as a symbol of the decline of the South itself. Mr. Compson is disenchanted with life and the society he lives in. Unable to find meaning in the moral verities he was brought up with, he escapes into alcoholism and cynicism. Mrs. Compson is spiritually effete and has little love to spare for her children. Of the four children, Caddy is the only one capable of loving, but she loses her virginity. The youngest brother, Benjy, is an idiot, a curse on the family. Another, Quentin, lives in the ideal world of his youth with his dreams of love, honor, and integrity, and, when he fails to keep off the intrusion of the "loud, harsh world", he destroys himself. The life of the eldest brother, Jason, is empty and meaningless. Love is alien to him, and so are other traditional humanistic values.

    It is one of the first modernist works to apply the stream of consciousness and objective correlative literary techniques. The nonlinear story is told from the perspectives of the three Compson brothers between 1910 and 1928: Benjy, Jason, and Quentin. A fourth unnamed narrator gives a third-person account of the family's live-in maid, Dilsey. It is a story of deterioration from the past to the present. The past is idealized to form a striking contrast with the loveless present. There is in the book an acute feeling of nostalgia toward the happy past. Through Benjy' narration Faulkner highlights the theme of loss. Quentin's suicide could be regarded as an example of a thorough negation of the present. To some extent, Quentin's value system may reflect Faulkner's own view towards an ideal way of life, that of an antebellum society. It is through the selfish and heartless individual Jason, the triumph of rationalism over feeling and compassion is best illustrated.

第16章 安德森·斯坦·刘易斯·凯瑟·沃尔夫

16.1 复习笔记

I. Sherwood Anderson (1876 –1941)	I. 舍伍德·安德森
1. Life Sherwood Anderson was in born in Ohio. At the age of 36, he had a successful career and a happy family. But he always feels uneasy and obsessed with literary creation. Therefore, he later engaged in business during the day and wrote in the evening. One day, he suddenly left the office in the middle of a dictation and never came back. People found him in poor mental state and wandering around. He then was sent to the hospital. After that, he gave up business and started his literary career.	**1. 生平** 舍伍德·安德森出生于俄亥俄州。36岁时他已经事业成功，家庭幸福。但是他总觉内心不安，着迷于文学创作。故后来白天从事经营事业，晚上时间写作。一天，他在默写时，突然停下来离开了办公室，然后再也没有回来。人们发现他精神混乱、四处游荡，并把他送到了医院。之后，他永远地告别了商界，并开始了他的文学生涯。
2. Literary contributions (1) In terms of themes, Anderson showed the courage to explore the new material of novel creation, namely the psychological and emotional aspects of life in small American towns. He focuses on low-level figures, such as losers, fallen ones, and people who are not good at expressing. His classic work *Winesburg, Ohio* is a good example. (2) In terms of technique, Anderson was an original writer who relies on inspiration to create. He observes the grotesque behaviors of human beings from the perspective of Freudian psychoanalysis, thus trying to accurately reveal the abnormal psychological conditions of the characters. (3) Anderson was probably the first writer who used oral language to create after Mark Twain. He believed that everyday language was a reliable medium. His writing style was known for being clear, direct and deceptively simple. This style had a great influence on Hemingway and Faulkner.	**2. 文学贡献** (1) 在主题方面，安德森勇于挖掘小说创作的新素材，即美国小镇生活中的心理和情感层面。他着重关注底层人物，诸如失败者、堕落者和不善表达的人等。他的经典作品《小城畸人》就是很好的例证。 (2) 技巧方面，安德森是原创性的作家，他依靠灵感进行创作。他从佛洛依德心理分析的角度观察人类的怪诞行为，从而试图准确地揭示人物反常的心理状况。 (3) 安德森是继马克·吐温之后运用口头语言进行创作的首位作家。他认为日常用语是一种可靠的媒介。他的写作风格以清晰，直接和貌似简单著称。这种风格对后来的海明威和福克纳产生了很大影响。

3. Major works

Windy McPherson's Son
Marching Men
Winesburg, Ohio
The Triumph of the Egg
Horses and Men
Death in the Woods
Poor White
Many Marriages
Dark Laughter
Kit Brandon
A Story-Teller's Story
Tar: A Midwest Childhood
"Hands"
"Paper Pills"
"Mother"
"I Want to Know Why"

Ⅱ. Gertrude Stein (1874 – 1946)

Gertrude Stein is famous in the history of literature. First, because of her work, and second, because she was a patron of art and literature.

1. Life

Gertrude Stein was born in a rich family. Relying on her inheritance, she was able to live a comfortable life in Paris. She graduated from Radcliffe College, and her amazing abstract thinking left a deep impression on writing teachers. She also studied psychology courses offered by William James, the brother of novelist Henry James. She worked hard throughout her life and created more than 50 works. She often gave lectures on her literary theory at Cambridge University and Oxford University. In 1934 she returned to the United States to give a lecture tour.

2. Literary contributions

Stan did several things to make her a name in the history of American literature.

(1) She had a keen mind and was aware of the trend of the age and subtle changes. She believed that life after the First World War was different, in this way, art and literature should also make corresponding changes in the way of expressing life. She made many contributions in leading the new modern era of literature.

3. 主要作品

《饶舌的迈克逊的儿子》
《前进中的人们》
《小城畸人》
《鸡蛋的胜利》
《马和人》
《林中之死》
《穷白人》
《许多婚姻》
《暗笑》
《吉特·布兰登》
《讲故事人的故事》
《中西部的童年》
《双手》
《纸团》
《母亲》
《我想知道为什么》

Ⅱ. 格特鲁德·斯坦

格特鲁德·斯坦在文学史上出名一是因为她的作品，二是因为她是艺术和文学的赞助人。

1. 生平

格特鲁德·斯坦生于富贵之家。依靠继承的遗产她得以在巴黎过着舒适的生活。她毕业于拉德克利夫学院，大学时其惊人的抽象思维给写作老师留下很深的印象。她还听过小说家亨利·詹姆斯的哥哥威廉姆·詹姆斯开设的心理课程。她终生笔耕不辍，共著有50余部作品。她经常在剑桥大学和牛津大学举办讲座阐述她的文学理论。1934年她回美国做了一次巡回演讲。

2. 文学贡献

斯坦做过的几件事情足以让她在美国文学史上留名。

(1) 她思想敏锐，意识到了时代趋势和微妙的变化。她认为一战后的生活与战前不一样了，因此艺术和文学在表现生活的方式上也应作出相应的改变。她在引领新的文学现代时期上做出了很多贡献。

(2) Another thing worthy of praise is her literary theory and practice. Her literary theories were well explained in her work *How to Write*. Her works show the spirit and modernity of her courage to experiment.

3. Major works

Three lives
"The Good Anna"
"The Gentle Lena"
"Melanctha"
Tender Buttons
The Making of Americans
How to Write
Four Saints in Three Acts
The Autobiography of Alice b. Toklas
"Sacred Emily"
"Picasso"

Ⅲ. Sinclair Lewis (1885 – 1951)

1. Life

Sinclair Lewis was the first American author to win the Nobel Prize for literature. He was born in a middle-class family in central Sauk, Minnesota. Lewis has been ruthlessly satirizing this class all his life while at the same time affirming some of its virtues. He started writing when he was in college. After graduating from Yale University, he spent a few years in a row, during which he had been working hard to write and tried to publish novels. From 1912 to 1919, his five novels were published. It was not until the publication of his sixth novel *Main Street* in the summer of 1920. He then became famous all over the world. In next ten years, Lewis was on the rise. He became famous in Europe and won the Nobel Prize in 1930. He reached the pinnacle of his literary career in 20 years. However, after that, he started to go downhill. He is now known as the worst important writer in the history of American literature.

2. Literary contribution

Lewis is a sociological writer, and his works are an integral part of American social history. Lewis learned and introduced the American middle class in decades. He explained the American middle class to the world and coined a word, "Babbit", which has been included in the English dictionary as a synonym for "vulgar and low-level businessman".

（2）另一件值得称道的是她的文学理论与实践。她的文学理论在其作品《写作指南》上得到了很好地阐释。她的作品显示出其勇于尝试的精神和现代性。

3. 主要作品

《三个女人》
《好人安娜》
《温和的丽娜》
《米兰克莎》
《温柔的纽扣》
《美国人的成长》
《写作指南》
《三幕剧里的四仙人》
《爱丽丝 · B. 托克拉斯的自传》
《神圣的艾米莉》
《毕加索》

Ⅲ. 辛克莱 · 刘易斯

1. 生平

辛克莱 · 刘易斯是第一位获得诺贝尔文学奖的美国作家。他出生在明尼苏达州索克中心镇一个中产阶级家庭。刘易斯一生都在对这个阶级进行无情的讽刺，同时又肯定它的某些美德。他在大学时便开始写作。他从耶鲁大学毕业以后，闯荡了一些年，然而他一直努力写作并试图发表小说。从 1912 年到 1919 年，他共发表了五部小说，直到 1920 年夏天他的第六部小说《大街》问世，他才得以闻名天下。此后十年间，刘易斯平步青云。他开始享誉欧洲，并于 1930 年获得诺贝尔奖。他在 20 年间爬到了文学生涯的顶峰。然而，在那以后，他就开始走下坡路。现在他被称作美国文学史上最差劲的重要作家。

2. 文学贡献

刘易斯是位社会学型作家，他的作品是美国社会史的组成部分。刘易斯在几十年内了解和介绍了美国中产阶级。他向世人解释了美国中产阶级，并且创造了一个词，"巴比特"，这个词已经作为"庸俗低级的商人"的同义词而被列进英文字典里。

3. His limitations

On the subject, he affirmed certain virtues of the middle class, which seems to be too outdated. In terms of style, his novels are too scattered, lacking order and artistry. In addition, his external description is very accurate, but lacks psychological exploration. In the atmosphere of post-war experimentalism, Lewis appeared to be too conservative and outdated. Even now, critics and readers still have the same impression of him.

4. Major Works

Main Street

Babbitt

Arrowsmith

Dodsworth

Elmer Gantry

Ⅳ. Willa Cather (1873 –1947)

1. Life

Willa Cather was born in Virginia. At the age of 9, she moved with her family to Nebraska and grew up in the western prairie town. In her later novels, the lifestyle in the Old West became the moral judgment standard for measuring the current living conditions. She was a traditional writer who refused to accept the modern life. She once claimed that around 1922, the world had been divided into two. She seemed to live between the two worlds, trying to escape to the past. All her main works were portrayals of her ambivalence in life.

2. Major works

My Antonia

The song of the Lark

A Lost Lady

The Professor's House

Death Comes for the Archbishop

Shadows on the Rock

Ⅴ. Thomas Wolfe (1900 –1938)

1. Characteristics

(1) Wolfe's works are mostly autobiographical, which reveal his personal emotions. Therefore, his writing art is close to confession.

3. 局限性

在主题方面，他肯定中产阶级的某些美德，这使他显得太过时。在风格上，他的小说过于散乱，缺乏秩序和艺术性。此外，他对外在的描写十分准确，但缺乏心理上的探究。在战后实验主义的氛围中，刘易斯显得过于守旧和过时。即便是现在，评论家和读者对他的印象仍是如此。

4. 主要作品

《大街》

《巴比特》

《阿罗斯密斯》

《多兹沃斯》

《艾尔默·甘特里》

Ⅳ. 薇拉·凯瑟

1. 生平

薇拉·凯瑟生于弗吉尼亚州，9岁时随家人移居到内布拉斯加州，在西部大草原乡镇里长大。在其后来的小说中大西部成为衡量现在生存状况的道德评判标准。薇拉是传统型的作家，她拒绝接受现代生活。她曾说过，在1922年前后，世界已一分为二，她似乎生活在两个世界之间，力图逃避到过去的日子里去。她的主要作品都是她在生活中这种矛盾心理的写照。

2. 主要作品

《我的安东妮亚》

《百灵鸟之歌》

《迷途的女人》

《教授的住宅》

《大教主之死》

《磐石上的阴影》

Ⅴ. 托马斯·沃尔夫

1. 特点

(1) 沃尔夫的作品多是自传性质的，其中表露了他个人的情感，因而他的写作艺术接近于自白性质。

(2) He is an extremely aspiring writer. He takes every aspect of American life as his novel writing material. (3) As an original writer, he shows his unique strengths and weaknesses.	(2) 他是一个极有抱负的作家，他把美国生活的方方面面都当做他的小说写作范畴。 (3) 他是一位原创性的作家，他的写作中有力之处与薄弱之处都是属于他个人独有的。
2. Major works *Look Homeward, Angel* *Of Time and the River* *The web and The Rock* *You Can't Go Home Again*	**2. 主要作品** 《天使望故乡》 《时间与河流》 《网与石》 《你不能再回家》

16.2 考研真题与典型题详解

I. Fill in the blanks.

1. *Winesburg, Ohio* was written by __________. (大连外国语学院 2007 研)
2. Two writers played important roles in making Faulkner what he later became. __________ helped him to write and publish his first novel *Soldier's Pay* and __________ was his idol and inspired him to write creatively.
3. The author of *Main Street* is __________.

II. Multiple Choice

1. Which of the following pairs concerning the writer and the main setting in his/her works is incorrect? (天津外国语学院 2009 研)
   A. Kate Chopin——Louisana　　B. Willa Cather——Georgia
   C. O Henry——New York　　D. Sherwood Anderson——Ohio
2. Among the following writers, __________ is best known for his sensitive depiction of the American small-town life. (首师大 2007 研)
   A. Henry James　　B. Sherwood Anderson
   C. Stephen Crane　　D. Ernest Hemingway
3. Which of the following techniques is NOT typical of Gertrude Stein's?
   A. Automatic writing
   B. Minimalist style
   C. Frequent use of repetition and reiteration
   D. Circular movement in story-telling
4. Sinclair Lewis' *Babbitt* presents a documentary picture of the narrow and limited __________.
   A. up-class mind　　B. middle-class mind
   C. proletarian　　D. ordinary people
5. The first American to win the Nobel Prize for Literature was a sharp social critic, whose name was __________.
   A. Sinclair Lewis　　B. Thomas Steams Eliot
   C. Ernest Hemingway　　D. William Faulkner

6. Which of the following works is NOT written by Willa Cather?

A. *The Song of the Lark*　　B. *O Pioneers*

C. *House of Mirth*　　D. *Shadows on the Rock*

III. Essay questions

1. Comment briefly on the contribution Sherwood Anderson made to American literature.
2. Comment on the contribution of Gertrude Stein to American Literature.

参考答案及解析

I. Fill in the blanks.

1. Sherwood Anderson

(《俄亥俄州的温斯堡》(或译《小城畸人》)是美国二十世纪早期小说家舍伍德·安德森(Sherwood Anderson)的一部著名小说。)

2. Sherwood Anderson; James Joyce

(安德森和乔伊斯对福克纳的文学创作产生了很大影响。)

3. Sinclair Lewis

(《大街》的作者是辛克莱·刘易斯，他是第一个获得诺贝尔文学奖的美国人。)

II. Multiple Choice

1. B　薇拉·凯瑟是美国著名女作家，以自幼所熟悉的西部边疆生活为题材，创作富有地方特色的作品，而 Georgia 是美国东南部的州。凯特·肖邦是美国女作家，出生于美国圣路易斯，小说背景为路易斯安那。欧·亨利的作品构思新颖，语言诙谐，结局常常出人意外，善于描写美国社会尤其是纽约百姓的生活。舍伍德·安德森出生在中西部俄亥俄州克莱德镇的一个贫寒家庭，作品背景为自己所熟悉的俄亥俄州。

2. B　舍伍德·安德森擅长描写美国小镇的生活。

3. B　极简风格不是斯坦的写作技巧。

4. B　刘易斯的《巴比特》表现了中产阶级的狭隘性和局限性。

5. A　辛克莱·刘易斯(Sinclair Lewis)是第一位获得诺贝尔文学奖的美国作家。刘易斯不仅是小说家，还是一位敏锐的社会观察家和批评家。他以犀利的文笔触及20世纪上半叶美国社会的许多方面，成为当时最有影响力的人物之一。

6. C　《欢乐之家》的作者是伊迪斯·华顿。

III. Essay questions

1. Sherwood Anderson did a few things for which he is remembered today.

In terms of themes, Anderson showed the courage to explore the new material of novel creation, namely the psychological and emotional aspects of life in small American towns. He focuses on low-level figures, such as losers, fallen ones, and people who are not good at expressing. His classic work *Winsburg*, *Ohio* is a good example.

Technically, Anderson was an original writer who relies on inspiration to create. He observes the grotesque behaviors of human beings from the perspective of Freudian psychoanalysis, thus trying to accurately reveal the abnormal psychological conditions of the characters.

Then there is his style to consider. Anderson was probably the first writer who used oral language to create after Mark Twain. He believed that everyday language was a reliable medium.

His writing style was known for being clear, direct and deceptively simple. This style had a great influence on Hemingway and Faulkner.

2. Gertrude Stein is famous in the history of literature. First, because of her work, and second, because she was a patron of art and literature. She worked hard throughout her life and created more than 50 works. These include *Three Lives*, *Tender Buttons*, *The Making of Americans*, *How to Write and Four Saints in Three Acts.*

Stan did several things to make her a name in the history of American literature. She had a keen mind and was aware of the trend of the age and subtle changes. She believed that life after the First World War was different, in this way, art and literature should also make corresponding changes in the way of expressing life. She made many contributions in leading the new modern era of literature.

Another thing worthy of praise is her literary theory and practice. Her literary theories were well explained in her work How to Write. One of the hallmarks of her writing is her repetition of words. She believes that these words can eliminate their superficial meaning and reveal their practical meaning. Her work is full of obscure abstractions and cryptic language, which she believes will help describe reality. In most of her works, she breaks the conventional word order and coherence. She connects sounds to sounds, the taste, smell and rhythm of individual words. Her works show the spirit and modernity of her courage to experiment.

第17章 20世纪30年代·多斯·帕索斯·斯坦贝克

17.1 复习笔记

Ⅰ. The 1930s	**Ⅰ. 20世纪30年代**
1. Historical background	**1. 历史背景**
The social atmosphere in the 1930s was very depressing. On October 24, 1929 "the bottom dropped of the stock market" and the Great Depression began. For the next ten years, Americans struggled in the dark. The situation did not change until the outbreak of World War Ⅱ. The 1930s were dark times. Banks and factories closed. Agriculture was also poorly developed. Millions of unemployed people flocked to the streets, waiting long lines for food. Extreme poverty has become an indisputable fact. As the Great Depression spread further, for many people, survival itself became a cruel struggle.	20世纪30年代的社会氛围十分压抑。1929年10月24日纽约华尔街证券交易所"掉穿了底盘",大萧条至此开始。在其后长达十年间的时间里,美国人在黑暗中挣扎。直到二战爆发情况才有所改观。20世纪30年代是真正黑暗的时代,银行关门,工厂倒闭,农业凋敝。数百万失业者涌上街头,等待救济食物的队伍像长龙一般,极度贫困成为不争的事实。随着大萧条的进一步蔓延,对于许多人来是说生存本身成为一场不折不扣的搏斗。
2. Overview of literature in 1930s	**2. 20世纪30年代文学简介**
If Eliot tries to express the spiritual wasteland in his famous poem *The Wasteland*, then the writers of the 1930s had to depict the material wasteland of America. Obviously, for most writers, social attention has become a top priority, and the social participation has become the main feature of literature in the 1920s. The three branches of literature, novels, poetry and drama all did their best to face the challenges of history.	如果艾略特试图在其著名诗歌《荒原》中表现精神上的荒原,那么20世纪30年代的作家则面临着描绘美国这个物质上的荒原。显然,对大多数作家来说,社会关注成为头等大事,社会参与成为30年代文学的主要特点。文学的三大分支——小说,诗歌,戏剧——都竭尽全力应对历史的挑战。
(1) The 1930s was a great era of novels. Dreiser's naturalistic style became the mainstream during the Great Depression. John Doss Passos and John Steinbeck became famous figures in the novel world. Dos Passos' *U. S. A*, Steinbeck's The *Grapes of Wrath*, and other writers' works together reflect American society during the Great Depression.	(1) 20世纪30年代是小说的伟大时代。德莱赛的自然主义风格成为大萧条时期作家的典范。约翰·多斯·帕索斯和约翰·斯坦贝克成为这一成为小说界的著名人物。多斯·帕索斯的《美国》和斯坦贝克的《愤怒的葡萄》以及其他作家的作品真实地反映了大萧条时期美国的经历。

(2) The dramas in 1930s were also excellent. Although no one could match O'Neill during this period, many talented scholars tried their best to add luster to the stage of the times. These playwrights include Clifford Oditz, Maxwell Anderson, Lillian Hellman, Thornton Wilder, etc.

(3) Possibly because there were many great masters such as Eliot, poetry in this period was not as prosperous as novels and dramas. There was no new great poet in this age.

Ⅱ. John Dos Passos (1896 –1970)

1. Life

John Dos Passos was born in Chicago. After graduating from Harvard University in 1916, he went to Spain to study architecture. He later participated in the First World War in France. He then became a journalist. He is a special figure in the history of American literature in the 20th century. Among all the major writers who are closely related to the turbulent modern American life, he showed a drastic change in political views from left to right. John Dos Passos was born in Chicago. After graduating from Harvard University in 1916, he went to Spain to study architecture. He later participated in the First World War in France. After the war, he became a journalist. He is a peculiar figure in the history of American literature in the 20th century. Among all the major writers who are closely related to the turbulent modern American life, he has shown a drastic change in political views from left to right. He began his writing career by depicting the situation of the lower class. In 1917, he claimed to be a "red radical revolutionary". His works had a communist tendency for a long time. In 1936, he became a supporter of the "New Deal". At the same time, he still strongly criticized capitalism. It was not until the 1950s that he completely turned to conservatism. Dos Passos later showed his approving attitude towards large companies and supported the Vietnam War.

2. Major works

U. S. A

The 42nd Parallel

1919

The Big Money

District of Columbia

Adventures of a Young Man

3. Analysis of major work

◆*U. S. A*

(2) 20 世纪 30 年代的戏剧也是丰富多彩的。诚然，这一时期没有人能与奥尼尔相媲美。但是许多有才学之士都竭尽全力，为时代的舞台添彩。这其中包括克利福德·奥德茨，马克斯威尔·安德森，莉莲·海尔曼，索顿·怀尔德等。

(3) 可能是因为有诸如艾略特等大师们的掩盖之故，这一时期诗歌没有像小说和戏剧那样繁盛。诗歌舞台上没有出现新的大诗人。

Ⅱ. 约翰·多斯·帕索斯

1. 生平

约翰·多斯·帕索斯生于芝加哥。1916 年毕业于哈佛大学，然后赴西班牙学建筑。后赴法参加第一次世界大战。大战结束后，他成为新闻工作者。他是 20 世纪美国文学史上的一位奇特人物，在所有与动荡的现代美国生活紧密联系的主要作家中，他的政治观点经历了从左向右的最突出的激烈转变。他是从描绘下层人的境遇开始他的写作生涯的。1917 年，他曾自称是"红色的激进革命者"。他的作品在很长时间内具有共产主义倾向。而 1936 年他成为"新政"的支持者。与此同时，他对资本主义的抨击仍然非常强烈，直到 20 世纪 50 年代，他彻底转向保守主义。多斯·帕索斯后期对大企业表现出赞许态度，支持美国对越南的侵略战争。

2. 主要作品

《美国》

《北纬四十二度》

《一九一九年》

《赚大钱》

《哥伦比亚特区》

《一个年轻人的冒险》

3. 主要作品分析

◆《美国》

(1) *U. S. A* contains *The 42nd Parallel*, *1919* and *The Big Money*. The first work depicts the formation process of the American capitalist "machine", as well as its dictatorship and destruction of individuals. The second work is a record of American life in World War I. It continues to describe the "depersonalizing" process mentioned in the first novel, laying the foundation for the next novel to describe the prosperity of the 1920s.

(2) *U. S. A* was a "collective" novel, which describes the lives of 11 main characters and more than 30 minor characters. Its purpose is to expose the social reality of how capitalist "machines" influence individual physical and mental development.

(3) In *U. S. A*, the author portrayed the lower class with a touching and sad tone.

(4) This trilogy shows the creative spirit of Dos Passos. In his novels, he cited techniques such as "Newsreels," the "Biographies," and the "Camera Eye".

(5) In addition, Dos Passos' language was concise with touching image and full rhythm. He used many parallel sentences. His language has some typical characteristics of the American colloquial style as a unique style writer.

(1)《美国》由《北纬四十二度》《一九一九年》和《赚大钱》组成。第一部《北纬四十二度》描绘了美国资本主义"机器"的形成过程以及它对个人的专制和摧残。第二部《一九一九年》是第一次世界大战中美国生活的记录，继续描写第一部小说中提到的"非人格化"过程，为下一部小说《赚大钱》记述"繁荣"的20世纪20年代奠定了基础。

(2)《美国》是部"群体小说"，它描述了11位主要人物和30余位次要人物的生活。其中心意图在于揭露资本主义"机器"如何左右个人身心发展的社会现实。

(3) 在《美国》里作者对下层人民的刻画具有一种动人的伤感色调。

(4)《美国》三部曲表现了多斯·帕索斯勇于创新的精神。在其小说中，他引用了"新闻片""人物传记"及"照相机镜头"等手法。

(5) 此外，多斯·帕索斯的语言简练，意象感人，句子富有节奏感，结构多排比句，其语言具有美国口语风格的一些典型特点，他是独具特点的文体家。

Ⅲ. John Steinbeck (1902 –1968)

1. Life

John Steinbeck was born in Salinas, California. He loved literature since he was a child and read a lot of English and French literature at home. He later studied at Stanford University, but did not graduate. For a while, he felt confused and didn't know what to do. He did a lot of work during this period. This experience was very helpful to him and became the basic material for his outstanding works in the future. Later, with the support of his father, he decided to specialize in literary creation. He wrote some romantic works. But none of these works produced any repercussions in the literary world. His masterpiece *The Grapes of Wrath* was published in 1939 and he won the Pulitzer Prize for Fiction. In his later years, Steinbeck became extremely conservative. He won the Nobel Prize for Literature in 1962.

Ⅲ. 约翰·斯坦贝克

1. 生平

约翰·斯坦贝克出生于加利福尼亚州的萨利纳斯。他自幼喜爱文学，在家读了不少英国和法国文学作品。后来他就读于斯坦福大学，但未毕业。之后一段时间，他感到迷茫，不知何去何从。这期间他做过很多零工。这段时间对他有教育意义，因为这成为他日后优秀作品的基本素材。后来在父亲的资助下，他决定专门从事文学创作。他写了一些浪漫主义作品。但这些作品在文坛上都未产生任何反响。1939年他的代表作《愤怒的葡萄》出版并获得了普利策小说奖。晚年的斯坦贝克变得极为保守。1962年他获得了诺贝尔文学奖。

2. Major works

Cup of the Gold

The Pastures of Heaven

To a God Unknown

Tortilla Flat

In Dubious Battle

Of Mice and Man

The Grapes of Wrath

The Moon is Down

East of Eden

The Winter of Our Discontent

Travels with Charley

3. Analysis of major work

◆*The Grapes of Wrath*

(1) *The Grapes of Wrath* is an important novel in the history of American literature. Its title is taken from a few lines in "The Battle Hymn of the Republic," a war song of the Civil War, "Mine eyes have seen the glory of the coming of the Lord, / He is tramping out the vintage where the grapes of wrath are stored."

(2) This novel depicts the process of Joads and other families moving westward. What Steinbeck wants to say is that when most people are hungry and cold, they will resort to violence to get what they need. The days of anger are coming. The anger in people's souls is growing more and more heavy. If no measures are taken to prevent them, the social revolution will occur.

(3) In terms of structure, this novel consists of two parts, the westward trek of the Joads and the dispossessed Oklahomans, and the general picture of the Great Depression. The inserted chapter provides the social and historical background for the character's activities. In addition, the structure of the novel draws on the outlines of the biblical story. There are many places in the novel that are obviously influenced by the Bible.

(4) This novel shows the difference between Steinbeck and other writers who reflected on the economic crisis in the 1930s. Depression and defeatism permeated the works of that era. But in such an atmosphere, Steinbeck believed in human nature and thought that people would overcome difficulties in the future and the situation could get better.

2. 主要作品

《金杯》

《天堂里的牧地》

《致无名之神》

《薄饼坪》

《胜负未决的战斗》

《鼠与人》

《愤怒的葡萄》

《月落》

《伊甸园以东》

《我们的不满的冬天》

《查理和我》

3. 主要作品分析

◆《愤怒的葡萄》

(1)《愤怒的葡萄》是美国文学史上一部重要的小说。它的题目取自美国内战时期的《共和国战歌》中的几句"我的眼睛已看到了上帝到来的光环，/他在走遍储存愤怒葡萄的葡萄园。"

(2) 这部小说描绘了乔德等家庭西迁的过程。斯坦贝克想要说的是，当大多数的人们处于饥寒交迫的情况时，他们就会付诸暴力，取其所需。愤怒的日子正在到来，在人们的灵魂中愤怒的葡萄正在成长得越来越沉甸甸，倘不采取措施阻止，某种社会革命将会发生。

(3) 在结构上，这部小说由两部分材料组成，乔德一家和被迫迁移的俄克拉荷马人集体西迁的过程，以及大萧条的概貌。插入章节为人物活动提供了社会和历史背景。另外，小说的结构借鉴了圣经故事的构思轮廓。小说中有很多地方明显受到圣经的影响。

(4) 该小说显示了斯坦贝克和其他20世纪30年代反映经济危机的作家有不同之处。那个年代的作品中弥漫着沮丧与失败主义，但在这样的氛围之中，斯坦贝克相信人性，相信未来人们能克服困难，情况能有所好转。

17.2 考研真题与典型题详解

I. Fill in the blanks.

1. The novel, set in the American Dust Bowl region, that shows the social significance of the migrant labor problem was written by ________ and the title is ________. (大连外国语学院2007研)
2. The ________ of the 1930s greatly weakened the American nation's self-confidence.
3. In the short novel ________, John Steinbeck portrayed the tragic friendship between two migrant workers.
4. ________ is generally regarded as John Steinbeck's masterpiece.
5. In 1935, John Steinbeck published ________, a collection of short stories which vividly described the life of poor Mexican-Americans with affection and humor.
6. John Steinbeck's post-war novel ________ reflected his bitter feelings against those greedy, rapacious elements of society which made the war possible.
7. ________ was the foremost novelist of the American Depression of the 1930s.

II. Multiple Choice

1. The American social upheavals and the literary concerns of the Great Depression years ended with the prosperity and turmoil brought by the ________.

   A. First Word War　　B. Second World War

   C. Civil War　　D. War of Independence

2. ________ tells the Joad family's life from the time they were evicted from their farm in Oklahoma until their first winter in California.

   A. *Of Mice and Men*　　B. *The Grapes of Wrath*

   C. *The Great Gatsby*　　D. *For Whom the Bell Tolls*

Ⅲ. Explain the following term.

1. Camera eye

Ⅳ. Essay questions

1. What are the major artistic features of John Steinbeck? (北航2007研)
2. Analysis of John Steinbeck's *The Grapes of Wrath*.

参考答案及解析

I. Fill in the blanks.

1. John Steinbeck, *The Grapes of Wrath*

   (20世纪30年代中期，由于受到沙尘暴的侵袭，美国中部大平原地区变成"尘谷"(Dust Bowl)，受此影响，大批居民迁徙到加利福尼亚州，被称为"沙尘暴移民"，美国小说家John Steinbeck的小说《愤怒的葡萄》正是以此为背景。)

2. Great Depression

   (20世纪30年代的经济危机Great Depression极大地削弱了美国整个民族的自信心。)

3. *Of Mice and Men*

   (约翰·斯坦贝克在1937年发表小说《鼠与人》(*Of Mice and Men*)，描写了两个无家可归、无地可耕、相依为命的流动农业工人的悲惨遭遇。)

4. *The Grapes of Wrath*

(《愤怒的葡萄》(*The Grapes of Wrath*)是约翰·斯坦贝克的代表小说。该小说通过乔德一家从俄克拉荷马向西迁徙的过程，描绘了在30年代经济危机和特大旱灾影响下大批农民破产的真实面貌，揭示了人们在苦难历程中精神上的变化。)

5. *Tortilla Flat*

(1935年约翰·斯坦贝克发表了小说《煎饼坪》(*Tortilla Flat*)。在这部小说里斯坦贝克用幽默的语言善意地描写了居住在蒙特雷城郊煎饼坪的一群贫穷墨西哥裔美国人的生活。)

6. *The Pearl*

(1947年约翰·斯坦贝克的著名中篇小说《珍珠》出版。这部小说文字洗练，寓意深刻，无情地鞭挞了人世间有钱人的贪婪和凶恶。)

7. John Steinbeck

(约翰·斯坦贝克是20世纪30年代美国文坛上最活跃、最引人瞩目的作家之一，也是经济大萧条期间最重要的小说家。他的小说《愤怒的葡萄》(*The Grapes of Wrath*)以大萧条为背景，具有史诗般的规模和气魄。)

II. Multiple Choice

1. B 第二次世界大战结束了大萧条带来的美国的社会动荡和文学对这方面的关注。

2. B 《愤怒的葡萄》(*The Grapes of Wrath*)通过乔德一家从俄克拉荷马州向西迁至加利福尼亚州的过程，描绘了在30年代经济危机和特大旱灾影响下大批农民破产的真实面貌，揭示了人们在苦难历程中精神上的变化。

Ⅲ. Explain the following term.

1. ①Dos Passos developed the literary device. Corresponding to the time of the narrative, the novel shows his life autobiography. ②With the stream-of-consciousness style, the author's activities and thinking are reflected while the fictional narrative takes place. ③These narratives which show his changing mood in the chaotic era indicate that his private experience is part of the complexity of social culture.

Ⅳ. Essay questions

1. John Steinbeck was a significant Depression writer. He did all kinds of jobs when he was young. This experience was very helpful to him and became the basic material for his outstanding works in the future. He gives a vivid picture of his time. His works examined the lives of the working class and migrant workers during the Dust Bowl and the Great Depression.

His novels showed the difference between Steinbeck and other writers who reflected on the economic crisis in the 1930s. Depression and defeatism permeated the works of that era. But in such an atmosphere, Steinbeck believed in human nature and thought that people would overcome difficulties in the future and the situation could get better.

Steinbeck uses many literary devices such as metaphors, similes, symbols and imagery to develop his characters and describe the scenes. The structures of Steinbeck's novels are well-arranged. For example, there is an inherent unity in his *The Grape of Wrath*. Its structure is dictated by the Bible. The 30 chapters fall neatly into three sections, which correspond to "The Exodus" story in the Old Testament.

2. John Steinbeck's *The Grapes of Wrath* is one of the major American books. The title of the book comes from "The Battle Hymn of the Republic", a war song of the Civil War. The implication of the title is that as injustice is building up and up, something is going to explode into violence.

The Grapes of Wrath is a crisis novel. It is Steinbeck's clear expression of sympathy with the dispossessed and the wretched. This novel depicts the process of Joads and other families moving westward. What Steinbeck wants to say is that when most people are hungry and cold, they will resort to violence to get what they need. The days of anger are coming. The anger in people's souls is growing more and more heavy. If no measures are taken to prevent them, the social revolution will occur. In terms of structure, this novel consists of two parts, the westward trek of the Joads and the dispossessed Oklahomans, and the general picture of the Great Depression. The inserted chapter provides the social and historical background for the character's activities.

The novel is structurally interesting for another, perhaps more important, reason, that its structure is dictated by the Bible. There are suggestions that the author was thinking about the Bible when writing the novel. Steinbeck is not stating this very explicitly, but the suggestion is very strong, and is supported by symbols such as that of the grapes.

This novel shows the difference between Steinbeck and other writers who reflected on the economic crisis in the 1930s. Depression and defeatism permeated the works of that era. But in such an atmosphere, Steinbeck believed in human nature and thought that people would overcome difficulties in the future and the situation could get better.

第 18 章　波特·韦尔蒂·麦卡勒斯·韦斯特·新批评

18.1　复习笔记

Ⅰ. Katherine Anne Porter (1890 – 1980)

1. Life

Born in India Greek, Texas, Katherine Anne Porter had worked as a news reporter, an actress and ballad singer before her writing career. Later she traveled to Europe and Mexico, which was very useful for her later writing. Her major works are short stories, among which *Collected Stories* helped her win a Pulitzer Prize, as well as a National Book Award. Honorary doctorates were sent to her, and she also gave lectures at many universities, with her works being selected and collected as the standard textbooks for college students. From 1950 to 1952, she was hired as the vice president of the National Institute of Arts and Letters.

2. Major works

Flowering Judas

"The Flowering Judas"

"The Jilting of Granny Weatherall"

Pale Horse, Pale Rider

Leaning Tower and Other Stories

Ships Of Fools

3. Analysis of major work

◆*Ships Of Fools*

This novel came out from her travel on the trip from Mexico to Europe in 1931. She believed that her bovel is the true reflection of the gradual decline of the western civilization. The novel is divided into three parts: "Embarkation", "High Sea" and "The Habours". Here the boat represents the whole life and world of human beings. What we can learn from the novel is the truth of our life, which is really depressing. In this novel, man is described as a fool with various shortcomings, and his behavior is really sickening. Life is cold, lonely

Ⅰ. 凯瑟琳·安·波特

1. 生平

凯瑟琳·安·波特出生于得克萨斯州印第安河市。她曾做过报社记者，演员和民谣歌手。后来她到过欧洲和墨西哥。这段经历对她日后的写作很有帮助。她主要是短篇小说家。她的《短篇小说集》获得了普利策奖和全国图书奖。她曾到许多大学做讲座，收到了许多机构授予的荣誉博士学位，作品也被节选为大学的标准教材。从 1950 年到 1952 年她担任美国国家艺术与文学协会副主席。

2. 主要作品

《开花的犹大树》

《开花的犹大树》

《风霜老奶奶的婚变》

《灰色骑士灰色马》

《斜塔及其他》

《愚人船》

3. 主要作品分析

◆《愚人船》

该小说是作者根据 1931 年从墨西哥到欧洲的航行经历写成的。她曾说她的小说讲的是西方文明逐渐衰落的情况。小说分为三部分，即《上船》《海上》和《港口》。船本身便是人类世界的缩影。小说讲述了关于人及人生的真谛，但是这真谛确实令人感到憋闷。小说描述了人类的缺点不足以致其显得像个十足的傻子。他们的行为令人沮丧。而人生则苍凉、落寞、病态，

and disgusting, and human beings are living without any aims or targets. The final destination of man's voyage lies in a dark and cold place. It can be easily concluded from the novel that the author is a misanthropist.

人活着毫无意义。人们的航行最终驶向黑暗、阴冷之地。读这本小说很容易看出作者的厌世情绪。

Ⅱ. Eudora Welty (1909 – 2001)

1. Life

Eudora Welty was born into a rich family in Jackson, Mississippi. She received a good education and was exposed to a wide range of social life, and her first short story "Death of a traveling Salesman" helped her gain a good reputation. Later she kept her writing habit and produced many pieces of short stories, novellas and novels, thus she won various kinds of awards including the Pulitzer Price. She was well-known for her short stories.

2. Literary theory

Great significance has been attached to the place where the works are produced. In her "Place in Fiction", Welty has emphasized that "place" is a treasure house of an author's emotions, enabling them to focus on details, to depict everything accurately, and to explore the nature of life. She thinks that only if the art is being molded clearly, directly and passionately from its original place can it be remained and understood forever. She is known for her loyalty to the South and for presenting readers with a broader picture of America.

3. Major themes

The relationship of traditional southern family is the main topic of Welty's works. She concentrates on the inner world of man, relationships between people and the power of love instead of describing the ups of downs of a family.

In some pieces, she focuses on the theme of loneliness, estragement and other sides of family life.

4. Major works

"Death of a Traveling Salesman"
"Place in Fiction"
Delta Wedding
"A Worn Path"
"Why I Live at the P. O."
"Lily Draw and Three Ladies"
"The key"

Ⅱ. 尤多拉·韦尔蒂

1. 生平

尤多拉·韦尔蒂生于密西西比州杰克逊市一个较富裕的家庭。她受过良好的教育，并且广泛地接触社会生活。1936 年她发表了第一篇短篇小说《旅行推销员之死》，这使得她声名鹊起。这之后她笔耕不辍，创作了多篇短篇小说、中篇小说和长篇小说，并获得了普利策奖等奖项。她因短篇小说方面的成就而知名。

2. 文学理论

韦尔蒂强调文学创作中地点的重要性。她在《小说里的地点》一文中指出：地点是作者情感的宝库，能使他们关注细节，确切地描绘事物，并且能使他们看清事物的本质。她认为出自其发源地，并以清晰、明确、直接和热情的方式所表达的艺术最能长久地为人们所理解。她以忠于美国南方、并向读者展示了更为广阔的画面著称。

3. 主题

韦尔蒂作品的主要主题是传统南方社会家庭关系。她的重点并不在于描述家族的兴衰、变化无常，而在于探索人物的内心世界，人际关系以及爱的力量等。

她的一些作品强调孤立、疏远及其他家庭生活方面等主题。

4. 主要作品

《旅行推销员之死》
《小说里的地点》
《三角洲婚礼》
《熟路》
《我为什么住在邮局》
《莉莉和三位女士》
《钥匙》

"The Whistle"

"Flowers for Marjorie"

5. Analysis of major work

◆"Death of a Traveling Salesman"

The significance of family has been emphasized in the short story "Death of a Traveling Salesman". Alienation has been pictured in this novel though Bowman's lonely life. Without love and sense of belonging, Bowman lives along and cannot find the meaning of life, while the farmer and his wife love each other and enjoy mutual trust. Poverty has not eroded their positive attitude towards life and expectation for the future. Their life has illustrated the coordination of inside and outside world, as well as the balance between sense and sensibility. These are exactly what is lacking in the bleak life of the salesman.

Ⅲ. Carson McCullers (1917 – 1967)

1. Life

Carson McCullers was born in Columbus, Georgia, with astonishing talent, strong character but little friends. The themes of isolation, violence and terror in her later works were probably related to her intense sense of loneliness. She was imaginative and wanted to be an author. She was an omnivorous reader and once took place in the fiction-writing class of Columbus University. Her glorious writing career began with her first novel *The Heart Is a Lonely Hunter* being published. Before she became mentally exhausted and died at the age of 50, she had written several bestsellers and gained both fame and wealth. Although she was weak and sickly, she was versatile and perseverant, which was very impressive.

2. Major themes

Carson McCullers holds a Gothic view of human life, which is being described as "sense of awful" by her friend Tennessee Williams. She seems to believe that some people are bound to live a horrible and isolated life. And the existence of these people with physical and spiritual problems represents the power that will destroy lives of human beings. She has showed special preference to the incongruity in life. Loneliness, the outcast and the lack of belonging are the focus of her novel. She believes love is significant, but it also leads to

《哨子》

《送给玛朱莉的花》

5. 主要作品分析

◆《旅行推销员之死》

《旅行推销员之死》生动地表达了家庭的重要性。在这篇短篇小说中韦尔蒂通过对鲍曼的刻画描绘了一幅孤立的画面。鲍曼与世隔绝，生活中没有爱，没有意义，没有归属感。与此相反，农夫和他的妻子珍爱彼此、互相信任。他们尽管贫穷，但是思想积极，行动积极。总是憧憬着美好的未来。他们阐释了内心与外界、理智与情感的协调一致，而这些正好是推销员鲍曼凄凉的生活中所缺乏的。

Ⅲ. 卡森·麦卡勒斯

1. 生平

卡森·麦卡勒斯生于佐治亚州的哥伦布市，幼时天资过人，性格坚定，但朋友不多。强烈的孤立感和她日后作品中经常写疏远、暴力和恐怖等主题有关。她想象力丰富并立志成为作家。她阅读广泛，曾在哥伦比亚大学上过小说创作课。1940年她的第一部小说《心是孤独的猎人》出版，她辉煌的文学创作生涯自此开始。她写了一些畅销书，名利双收，但后来精神起伏不定，在50岁时去世。麦卡勒斯多才多艺多产，虽然体弱多病，但坚持创作，颇令人叹服。

2. 主题

卡森·麦卡勒斯对生活持有一种"哥特式"的观点，他的好友田纳西·威廉姆斯称之为"对可怕事物的感知"。她似乎认为，世上有些人注定要过可怕、与世隔绝的生活。这些身心方面的怪异人物的存在代表了摧毁人类生活的力量。她对生活中的怪异、奇特、不协调的现象情有独钟。她的小说重点描绘孤独、遗弃和没有归属感。她认为

pain and death when it creates problems.

爱情是重要的，但它带来无法解决的问题，导致痛苦甚至死亡。

3. Major works

The heart Is a Lonely Hunter
Reflections in a Golden Eye
The Ballad of the Sad Café
The Member of the Wedding
Clock Without Hands

3. 主要作品

《心是孤独的猎人》
《金眼里的映像》
《伤心咖啡馆之歌》
《婚礼的成员》
《没有指针的钟》

4. Analysis of major work

◆ *The Ballad of the Sad Café*

Love and pain are the main themes of the whole story *The Ballad of the Sad Café*, which reflects the life and people's behavior of McCullers' works. The story can be divided into three parts, and in the second section, she declared that love is bound to bring pain to both sides because of the insoluble conflicts between them. Hate emerges when the lover and the beloved have different experience and comprehension about love, and the hate will lead to violence, death and pain. The love-hate complex exists in the relationships of the three couples, among which the character Lyman perfectly explains the author's notion of love.

4. 主要作品分析

◆《伤心咖啡馆之歌》

《伤心咖啡馆之歌》反映出麦卡勒斯作品里生活的基调和人物的行为模式。爱情与痛苦这一主题贯穿着整个故事。这个故事分为三个部分，麦卡勒斯在第二部分中解释道，爱情必定给双方都带来痛苦，因为他们之间的矛盾无法解决。爱与被爱者对爱的体会不同，结果必然产生仇恨。仇恨导致暴力、死亡和痛苦。在这部小说中爱恨情结存在于三对恋爱关系中，其中里曼这个人物代表了作者对爱的理解。

Ⅳ. Nathanael West (1903－1940)

1. Life

Nathanael West, born to a wealthy New York family, was one of the most important figures in American literature in the 1930s. He was familiar with the classics of world literature and tried his best to introduce the avant-garde of European literature and art to America. He went to Paris in 1920s, where he came into contact with French symbolism, aestheticism and surrealism, and he also got acquainted with several modernists' writers. During the Great Depression of the 1930s, he met left-wing writers and expressed his support for the Spanish people in their struggle against fascism, later he died in a car crash in 1940.

Ⅳ. 纳撒尼尔·韦斯特

1. 生平

纳撒尼尔·韦斯特出生于纽约一个富有之家，是20世纪30年代出现在美国文坛上的重要人物之一。他熟读世界文学经典作品，竭力把当时欧洲文艺界的先锋主义介绍到美国。他在20世纪20年代去了巴黎，在那结识了一些现代派作家，并他接触到法国象征主义、唯美主义和超现实主义。在30年代的大萧条时期，他结识了左翼作家，并对西班牙人民的反法西斯斗争表示支持。他在1940年死于车祸。

2. Major works

The Complete Works of Nathanael West
The Dream Life of Balso-Snell
Miss Lonelyhearts
A Cool Million: The Dismantling of Lemuel Pitkin
The Day of the Locust

2. 主要作品

《纳撒尼尔·韦斯特全集》
《巴尔索·斯乃尔的梦幻生活》
《孤心小姐》
《整一百万：莱缪尔·皮特金的肢解》
《蝗灾日》

V. The new Criticism

As a school of poetry writing and literary criticism, New Criticism became an orthodox school in American academic circles in the 1940s. Until today, it still has a great influence in the literary world and college teaching. The new Criticism arose in the early 1920s, and was acknowledged in the 1930s and 1940s, becoming the dominant school in poetry writing and literary criticism. But it was confronted with rebellion in the 1950s and 1960s when it gradually ceased to be a school.

V. 新批评

20 世纪 40 年代新批评作为诗歌创作和文学批评的一个流派，在美国成为学术界的正统学派。时至今日，它仍然在文学界和大学教学中有重要影响。这个学派在 20 年代开始兴起，通过 20 年的时间，于 30 年代和 40 年代获得认可，在诗歌创作和文学批评中占统治地位。它在 50 年代和 60 年代遭到反对，渐渐失去作为正统学派的地位。

1. Features of the New Criticism

The New Criticism is a school of formalist criticism, being famous for its outstanding features:

(1) It emphasizes the text itself instead of analyzing the external factors such as its social background and influence, as well as the writer's intention and political attitude.

(2) It tries to find out the structure of the work instead of the framework of writer's mind or the reader's reaction.

(3) It emphasizes the careful reading of the texture and regards a literary piece as an organic entity with the combination of content and form.

1. 新批评的特点

新批评作为形式主义的一个流派，因其突出特点而著称。

(1) 它集中分析文本本身，而不关注诸如社会背景、作者的意图和政治态度、其对社会的影响力等外部因素。

(2) 它挖掘作品本身的艺术结构，而不是作者的思想框架及读者的反应。

(3)它把文学作品视为一个有机的实体，是内容和形式的统一。并且强调细读文本。

2. Features of the New Critical poem

(1) The new critical poem remained the basic characteristics of Modernist, such as concision, irony, humor, impersonality and the usage of antiphrasis, while other features like fragmentation, parallel sentences, ellipsis, symbolism and myth are being deserted or weakened.

(2) The new critical poem is the cohesion of attitude and views, with the forms, images, quotations, rhymes and stanzas being regulated and combined together.

2. 新批评诗歌的特点

(1) 新批评诗歌保留了现代派的基本特点，如简练、幽默、运用反语、非个人化、注重形式等。但同时摈弃或弱化了现代派的一些其他特征，如凌乱、并连句式、省略、象征与神话的运用、跨文化多语言的出现以及通篇用典等。

(2) 新批评诗歌形式、意象、典故、韵律、诗节等整齐而连贯，也有非人格化的特点，态度和观点统一。

3. Major New Critics

(1) John Crowe Ransom (1888 –1974)

◆Major works

Poems about God

Chills and Fever

3. 主要的新批评家

(1) 约翰·克劳·兰塞姆

◆主要作品

《关于上帝的诗歌》

《发冷与发烧》

Two Gentlemen in Bonds *God without Thunder* *I'll Take My Stand* *The New Criticism* **(2) Allen Tate (1899 – 1979)** **◆Major works** *I'll Take My Stand* *Mr. Pope and Others* *Three Poems* *Collected Poems: 1922 – 1947* *Collected Poems* "Ode to the Confederate Dead"	《契约中的两个绅士》 《没有雷声的上帝》 《我要坚持我的立场》 《新批评》 **(2) 艾伦·塔特** **◆主要作品** 《我要坚持我的立场》 《蒲柏先生及其他诗篇》 《三首诗》 《诗集：1922 – 1947》 《诗集》 《南方同盟烈士颂》

18.2 考研真题与典型题详解

I. Fill in the blanks.

1. In her essay "Place in Fiction", Eudora Welty emphasizes the importance of ________ for literary creations. She is noted for her fidelity to the American South, so her major theme relates to ________.
2. Carson McCullers was said to touch William Fanlkner in writing, and her well-known novels are ________ and ________.
3. One of the important figures in the 1930s who tried to adapt European avant-gardism to American writing is ________.
4. The New Criticism first emerged in 1920s as a reaction against the prevailing time-honored critical tendency to focus on the theme often in disregard of the form of the work. The name is given by John Crowe Ransom's collection of critical essays ________.

II. Multiple Choice

1. Which of the following works by Katherine Anne Porter is a novel?

A. *Pale Horse, Pale Rider*　　B. *The Leaning Tower*

C. *Ship of Fools*　　D. *The Big Tree*

III. Explain the following term.

1. new criticism (厦门大学2008研)

参考答案及解析

I. Fill in the blanks.

1. place, traditional southern family relationships
(美国女作家尤多拉·韦尔蒂(Eudora Welty)在其论文《小说中的地点》中强调地点在文学创作中的重要性。她以对美国社会的忠诚而著称，其作品主要的主题是传统南方社会的家族观念和家庭关系。)
2. *The Heart Is a Lonely Hunter*, *The Ballad of the Sad Café*.

(卡森·麦卡勒斯(Carson McCullers),20 世纪美国最重要的女作家之一,重要作品是《心是孤独的猎手》(*The Heart Is a Lonely Hunter*)和《伤心咖啡馆之歌》(*The Ballad of the Sad Café*)。)

3. Nathanael West

(纳撒内尔·韦斯特(Nathanael West)是 20 世纪 30 年代美国文学上的重要人物。他试图将欧洲的新潮主义引入美国文学。)

4. *The New Criticism*

("新批评"一词,源于美国文艺批评家约翰·克劳·兰塞姆(John Crowe Ransom)1941 年出版的《新批评》(*The New Criticism*)一书。新批评于二十世纪二十年代在英国发端,三十年代在美国形成,并于四五十年代在美国蔚成大势。它反对只关注文学作品主题而忽视文本本身的批评倾向。)

II. Multiple Choice

1. C 《愚人船》是凯瑟琳·安·波特根据 1931 年从墨西哥到欧洲的航行经历写成的小说。

III. Explain the following term.

1. It's an approach to literature made popular between the 1940s and the 1960s that evolved out of formalist criticism. New Critics suggest that detailed analysis of the language of a literary text can uncover important layers of meaning in that work. Critics such as John Crown Ransom, I. A. Richards, and Robert Penn Warren are commonly associated with New Criticism.

第 19 章　美国戏剧

19.1　复习笔记

Ⅰ. Overview of American drama

American drama started in the year 1916 when Eugene O'Neil's first play, *Bound East for Cardiff* was produced by the Provincetown Players. It is true that there were no great masters in the field of theater comparable to such figures in fiction as Melville or James, but there had been people who made effort to prepare for the rise of American drama in the 1920s. There was a renaissance of drama in the 1920s. American drama began to develop and became a branch of American literature which is as significant as poetry and the novel. Theaters during the Depression were not depressing at all. Like other departments of literature, the drama also paid much attention to social concern. In the year 1945, the staging of Tennessee Williams' *The Glass Menagerie* on Broadway was of unusual significance, marking American drama entered the age of maturity. A temporary decline in dramatic productions occurred to American drama in the late fifties, but soon it resumed its energy in the next decade. As time went by, the tendency of "decentralization" became more obvious, which means more and more plays staged Off-Broadway and Off-Off-Broadway. At the end of the sixties. American theater entered a new growth stage where diversity became one of its primary features.

Ⅱ. Eugene O'Neill (1888 – 1953)

1. Life

Eugene O'Neill was America's greatest playwright. He was born in New York. His father was a well-known actor, which made O'Neill could travel around with his father's group a lot. He used to study at Princeton for a year but then got expelled for misbehavior. Then he started his experience of wandering which was of great significance to his writing. O'Neill got tuberculosis and was sent to a sanitarium in the winter of 1912 – 1913, during which he read plenty of dramatic

Ⅰ. 美国戏剧概述

美国戏剧开始于 1916 年普罗文斯顿剧团演出奥尼尔第一出戏《东航卡迪夫》之时。19 世纪没有戏剧大师问世，戏剧界没有声名如麦尔维尔或詹姆斯那样的大手笔，但是不能由此而忽视，在戏剧领域有不少人在辛勤耕耘，为 20 世纪 20 年代美国戏剧的复兴进行着准备工作。20 世纪 20 年代美国戏剧经历了一场复兴。美国戏剧成为美国文学中独立的分支，与诗歌和小说相媲美。大萧条期间的戏剧并不沉闷。像文学的其他分支一样，戏剧较多地关注社会生活。1945 年田纳西 · 威廉姆的《玻璃动物园》的上演具有重大的意义，它标志着美国戏剧的成熟。50 年代后期美国戏剧经历了短暂的衰落。但是在 60 年代美国戏剧获得了新的能量。随着时间的推移，出现了远离百老汇的趋势。越来越多的剧目在外百老汇和外外百老汇上演。在 60 年代末美国戏剧进入了新的发展阶段，多样化已成为它的显著特点之一。

Ⅱ. 尤金 · 奥尼尔

1. 生平

尤金 · 奥尼尔是美国最伟大的剧作家。他出生于纽约市，他的父亲是当时有名的演员。幼年时奥尼尔常随父亲的剧团演出。他曾就读于普林斯顿大学，但一年后因行为不端被校方开除。之后他开始了漂泊生涯，这段经历对其创作意义重大。1912年到1913年冬天奥尼尔

literature of the world. In 1916 his one-act play *Bound East for Cardiff* was staged, which marked the beginning of O'Neill's long-lasting and successful career as a playwright, as well as the coming of American Theater modernization. O'Neill obtained a number of prizes as a playwright. For example, he was awarded the Pulitzer Prize of 1920 1922 for his *Beyond the Horizon* and *Anna Christie* and was honored with the Nobel Prize in Literature in the year 1936.

因肺结核不得不疗养治病。这段时间他广泛阅读世界戏剧名著。1916年他的独幕剧《东航卡迪夫》上演。这标志着奥尼尔漫长且成功的戏剧生涯的开始，也标志着美国戏剧现代化时代的到来。奥尼尔的一生赢得了众多奖项。1920 年到 1922 年间，他的《天边外》和《安娜·克里斯蒂》分别获得普利策奖，1936 年他获得了诺贝尔文学奖。

2. Artistic characteristics

(1) O'Neill was a persistent experimentalist in drama. He liberated drama from the traditional shackles of the 19th century and made it deeply rooted in real life. He was the first who introduced realism or even naturalism into the American theater. his writing style is known for its diversity and proficiency.

(2) The spirit of innovation in him allowed him to borrow from the best traditions of European drama, such as Greek tragedies, Ibsen's realism, or Strindberg's expressionism and integrated them into the art of his own in an organic manner. He also borrowed from modernist literary techniques such as the stream-of-consciousness, which helped him better reveal the emotional and psychological complexities of modern people.

(3) Moreover, he paid much attention to the use of setting and stage property in his dramatic representation. O'Neill's unremitting experimentation enriched American drama and influenced later playwrights. He was regarded as the American Shakespeare.

2. 艺术特点

(1) 奥尼尔坚持不懈地革新戏剧艺术，他把戏剧从 19 世纪的传统束缚中解放出来，使之深深地扎根于现实生活。他首次把现实主义乃至自然主义的手法引进美国戏剧中，他的艺术以多样化及精深圆熟而著称。

(2) 他大胆借鉴欧洲戏剧传统中的精华，诸如希腊悲剧、易卜生现实主义及斯特林堡表现主义等，并把它们融入到自己的艺术中。他还大胆借鉴现代派文学技巧，如意识流手法，这有助于他揭露现代人情感及心理上的复杂性。

(3) 此外，他还特别重视布景和道具的使用。奥尼尔不懈的创新丰富了美国戏剧、影响了后来的剧作家。他被誉为“美国的莎士比亚”。

3. Major works

Bound East for Cardiff
Beyond the Horizon
The Emperor Jones
Anna Christie
The Hairy Ape
Desire under the Elms
All God's Chillun God Wings
The Great God Brown
Lazarus Laughed
Strange Interlude

3. 主要作品

《东航卡迪夫》
《天边外》
《琼斯皇帝》
《安娜·克里斯蒂》
《毛猿》
《榆树下的欲望》
《上帝的儿女都有翅膀》
《大神布朗》
《拉萨路笑了》
《奇异的插曲》

Marco Millions	《马可百万》
Dynamo	《发电机》
Morning Becomes Electra	《悲悼》
Ah, Wilderness	《啊，荒野》
Days without End	《日子没有尽头》
The Iceman cometh	《送冰的人来了》
Long Day's Journey into Night	《进入黑夜的漫长旅途》
A Moon For the Misbegotten	《月照不幸人》
A Touch of the Poet	《诗人的气质》
Ⅲ. Elmer Rice (1892 –1967)	**Ⅲ. 艾尔默·赖斯**
◆Major works	**◆主要作品**
The Adding Machine	《计算器》
On Trial	《审判》
Street Scene	《街景》
Left Bank	《左岸》
Judgment Day	《审判日》
Dream Girl	《梦幻女孩》
The Grand Tour	《周游》
The Winner	《获胜者》
A Voyage Purilia	《小溪之旅》
Ⅳ. Susan Glaspell (1882 –1948)	**Ⅳ. 苏珊·格拉斯伯尔**
◆Major works	**◆主要作品**
The Verge	《边缘》
Alison's House	《爱丽森之家》
Fidelity	《忠贞不贰》
The Morning Is Near Us	《清晨在靠近我们》
Trifles	《琐事》
Ⅴ. Clifford Odets (1906 –1963)	**Ⅴ. 克里夫德·奥德茨**
◆Major works	**◆主要作品**
Waiting For Lefty	《等待老左》
Till the Day I Die	《到我死之时》
Paradise Lost	《失乐园》
Awake and Sing!	《觉醒而唱歌》
I Can't Sleep	《我睡不着》
Golden Boy	《金孩子》
Rocket to the Moon	《飞往月球》
Night Music	《夜里的音乐》
Clash by Night	《夜冲突》
The Big Knife	《大刀》

Ⅵ. Tennessee Williams (1911 – 1983)

1. Life

Tennessee Williams was one of the greatest American playwrights. His original name was Thomas Lanier Williams, but was then changed to "Tennessee" in 1939. He was born in Columbus, Mississippi, in 1911. Several years later after his birth, the family moved to the University City neighborhood of St. Louis, Missouri. He attended the University of Missouri in 1929, dropped out in 1932 for poverty, but in the end acquired a degree in 1938 from the University of Iowa. His first play, *Battle of Angels*, proved to be a fiasco that kept him unknown to the world until 1945 when *The Glass Menagerie* won him international recognition. After that, he released new work for an average of two years and enjoyed popularity all along. He was also a novelist and a poet. He wrote a novel, two volumes of poetry, and six volumes of prose, including three collections of short story.

2. Major works

American Blues
Battle of Angels
A Streetcar Named Desire
Summer and Smoke
The Rose Tattoo
Cat on a Hot Tin Roof
Suddenly Last Summer
Sweet Bird of Youth
Period of Adjustment
Night of the Iguana
The Milk Train Does Not Stop Here Anymore
Red Battery Sign
Vieux Carre
The Glass Menagerie

Ⅵ. 田纳西·威廉斯

1. 生平

田纳西·威廉斯是美国最伟大的剧作家之一。他的原名是托马斯·拉尼尔·威廉斯，1939年他把"托马斯"改为"田纳西"。他于1911年出生在密西西比州的哥伦布市。几年后随全家移居密苏里州的圣路易斯城。1929年他进入密苏里大学学习，但是在1932年因贫困被迫辍学。后来又入大学，1938年从爱荷华大学获得学士学位。他的第一部剧本《天使之战》遭遇惨败。直到1945年《玻璃动物园》的上演，他才得以扬名世界。这之后，他平均两年推出一部新作并且一直广受欢迎。他同时还是小说家和诗人。他著有一本长篇小说，两本诗集，六本散文集，其中包括3本短篇小说集。

2. 主要作品

《美国布鲁斯》
《天使之战》
《欲望号街车》
《夏日烟云》
《玫瑰纹身》
《热铁皮屋顶上的猫》
《夏天的突变》
《可爱的青春小鸟》
《调整时期》
《鬣蜥之夜》
《牛奶车不再在此停留》
《红色的炮台信号》
《维厄·卡雷》
《玻璃动物园》

Ⅶ. Arthur Miller (1915 – 2005)

1. Life

Arthur Miller was a great playwright in the 1940s. He was born in New York. He grew up during the Depression when he witnessed his father' s business failure. In the mid-1930s he studied journalism at Michigan University, where he

Ⅶ. 阿瑟·米勒

1. 生平

阿瑟·米勒是40年代出现的伟大剧作家。他出生于纽约市，成长于经济大萧条时期。他目睹了父亲生意上的失败。30年代中期他就读于密西根大学，并开始写剧本

began to write plays and radio scripts. His first play, *The Man Who Had All the Luck*, was completed in 1944, and his first important work, *All My Sons*, helped him acquired his reputation as an Ibsenian playwright. The staging of *Death of a Salesman*, helped him win the Tony Award and the Pulitzer Prize and strengthened his position as a genius playwright. In 1965 he was elected the president of the international P. E. N.. It was the first time for a writer from American who got this position. Arthur Miller is a friend of the Chinese people. He once visited China in 1978 and in 1983 to help stage his Death of Salesman, and its stage finally acquired a big success around the country.

2. Major themes

A typical theme of Arthur Miller's work is the plight of modern people in family and work. In his plays, the protagonist often finds himself under a pressure from his society and moral norms. He is caught in a mental and material predicament, which he has been trying to get rid of but found that everything was a futile, and only suicide, either mentally or physically, can save himself. The world is harsh. There is no choice for the protagonist. Either he submits to the impossible demands of society, or he rejects them. He dies in either case. Miller is, however, not completely pessimistic. Reading his plays, one feels a faith in human and in life, however vague it may be, though very often gloom overweighs hope.

3. Major works

The Man Who Had All the Luck
All My Sons
Death of a Salesman
The Crucible
A View from the Bridge
Collected Plays
After the Fall
Incident at Vicky
The Price
The Creation of the World and Other Business
The Archbishop's Ceiling
The Last Yankee
Broken Glass

和广播剧脚本。第一个剧作《鸿运高照的人》创作于1944年。他的第一个意义重大的剧作,《全是我的儿子》为其赢得"易卜生式剧作家"的美名。《推销员之死》公演后,为其赢得了托尼奖和普利策奖,并坚定了其戏剧界天才作家的地位。1965年他当选为国际笔会的首任美国主席。阿瑟·米勒是中国人民的朋友。他曾在1978年访问中国,1983年他又亲自到中国指导话剧《推销员之死》,该剧在中国大获成功。

2. 主题

阿瑟·米勒作品典型的主题是现代人在家庭与工作方面的困境。在他的剧作中,主人公经常处于社会及其道德规范的压力之下。他陷入了精神及物质上的困境,他竭力摆脱却发现一切只是徒劳,真实或精神上的自杀才能使之解脱。主人公别无选择,对于社会的需求,他要么服从要么拒绝,两种情况下都是死亡。然而,米勒并不是完全悲观的。虽然他的剧本中阴郁多过希冀,但是我们能感受到一种对人类、对生活的信念,尽管这种信念可能不太明确。

3. 主要作品

《鸿运高照的人》
《全是我的儿子》
《推销员之死》
《炼狱》
《桥头眺望》
《戏剧集》
《堕落之后》
《维希事件》
《代价》
《创世纪及其他》
《大主教的天花板》
《最后一个美国佬》
《破碎的镜子》

Ⅷ. Edward Albee (1928 –)

1. The Theater of the Absurd

Albee was closely tied with the tradition of the Theater of the Absurd which prevailed in the 1950s and 1960s. The theater of absurd refers to those plays focusing on the theme such as the meaninglessness of life with its pain and sufferings that looks ridiculous. The typical works includes Samuel Becket's *Waiting for Godot and Endgame*. In these works the playwright tries to force the audience to face up to the human condition as it is, instead of making a false depictions in order to satisfy the needs of the public. Edward Albee has written in this spirit. His plays seem to only focus on the one problem only, namely, the absurdity of human life based on a fragile illusion and spiritual emptiness. *Who is Afraid of Virginia Woolf ?* is a good example.

2. Major works

The Zoo Story
The Death of Bessie Smith
The Sandbox
The American Dream
Who's Afraid of Virginia Woolf ?
The Ballad of the Sad Cafe
A Delicate Balance
Box and Quotations from Chairman Mao TSe-Tung
All Over
Seascape
The Lady from Dubuque
The Man Who Had 3 Arms
Three Tall Women

Ⅸ. Sam Shepard (1943 –)

The two eminent playwrights that have impacted contemporary American theater are Sam Shepard and David Mamet.

◆Major works

Buried Child
Fool for Love
A Lie of the Mind
Paris, Texas

Ⅷ. 爱德华·阿尔比

1. 荒诞派戏剧

阿尔比与20世纪五、六十年代盛行的荒诞派戏剧的传统紧密相关。荒诞派戏剧是指一些集中反映人生的虚无、痛苦及折磨是滑稽、荒谬的等主题的剧作。典型的例子是塞缪尔·贝克特的《等待戈多》和《终局》。在这些作品里作者试图迫使观众正视人类的生活状况，而不是为迎合公众需要而进行虚假描绘。爱德华·阿尔比正是在这种精神下进行创作的。他的作品似乎只集中反映一个问题，即建筑在脆弱的幻想及精神的空虚之上的人类生活的荒诞性。《谁害怕弗吉尼亚·伍尔夫?》就是很好的例证。

2. 主要作品

《动物园的故事》
《贝西·史密斯之死》
《沙盒》
《美国梦》
《谁害怕弗吉尼亚·伍尔夫?》
《伤心咖啡馆之歌》
《脆弱的平衡》
《匣子和毛主席语录》
《一切皆已过去》
《海景》
《杜布克的女人》
《三臂人》
《三个高个女人》

Ⅸ. 塞姆·谢泼德

当代美国戏剧界富有影响力的两位剧作家是塞姆·谢泼德和大卫·马麦特。

◆主要作品

《被埋葬的孩子》
《爱情傻瓜》
《心之谎》
《德州巴黎》

Motel Chronicles	《旅店纪实》
Geography of a Horse Dreamer	《马塞梦测者的地理》
States of Shock	《震动》
X. David Mamet (1947 –)	**X. 大卫·马麦特**
◆Major works	**◆主要作品**
House of Games	《娱乐之家》
Sexual Perversity in Chicago	《芝加哥的性变态》
American Buffalo	《美国水牛》
Glengarry Glen Ross	《拜金一族》
The Woods	《树林》
The Shawl	《披肩》
Speed the Plow	《快耕》

19.2 考研真题与典型题详解

I. Fill in the blanks.

1. Early in the 1920s, the most prominent of the new American playwrights, whose name is __________, established an international reputation. (人大 2006 研)
2. Eugene O' Neill borrowed freely from the best traditions of __________ drama, be it Greek __________, or the __________ of Ibsen, or the __________ of Strindberg. (国际关系学院 2010 研)
3. __________ is the first master in the American history of drama.
4. The magic of Eugene O' Neill' s power lies in his never ceasing attempt to improve his art in step with the spirit of the times. He began writing in a __________ vein, then, he moved on and became obsessed with devices such as __________ and __________. During the 1940s, he turned back to what he had started with. Thus, his career came full circle.
5. Of all the plays that O' Neill wrote, most of them are __________, dealing with the basic issues of human existence and predicament such as life and death.
6. __________ is the one who dares to deal with themes such as violence, sex, and homosexuality on the stage in the postwar period.
7. __________ in the 1950s and 1960s refers to some plays, some of which center on the meaninglessness of life with its pain and suffering that seems funny, even ridiculous, __________ is one of the representatives.

II. Multiple Choice

1. __________ is NOT written by Eugene O' Neill. (首师大 2009 研)
   A. *Beyond the Horizon* B. *The Iceman Cometh*
   C. *Long Day' s Journey into Night* D. *The Crucible*
2. The author of *Long Day' s Journey into Night* also wrote __________. (北二外 2010 研)
   A. *Death of a Salesman* B. *The Hairy Ape*
   C. *A Streetcar Named Desire* D. *Looking Back in Anger*

3. "American Shakespeare" refers to ________.

A. Elmer Rice
B. Edward Albee
C. Eugene O'Neill
D. Tennessee Williams

4. "He got me, aw fight. I'm trou. Even him didn't rink I belonged." In these sentences taken from *The Hairy Ape*, the words "he" and "him" both refer to ________

A. Yank
B. God
C. The ape in the zoo
D. A person unnamed

5. Which of the following works is NOT written by Tennessee Williams?

A. *The Class Menagerie*
B. *A Streetcar Named Desire*
C. *Cat on a Hot Tin Roof*
D. *A Moon for the Misbegotten*

6. Which of the following statements concerning Tennessee Williams is NOT correct?

A. He has been influenced by Anton Chekhov, D. H. Lawrence and Hart Crane.
B. His last Broadway play is named *Clothes for a Summer Hotel.*
C. The recurrent themes in many of his plays are loneliness and desire.
D. He was awarded Nobel Prize for his brilliance as a dramatist.

7. *Death of a Salesman* is written by ________.

A. Tennessee Williams
B. Arthur Miller
C. Elmer Rice
D. Clifford Odets

Ⅲ. Explain the following terms.

1. Theatre of Absurdity
2. Monodrama
3. Parody
4. Tragic hero
5. Willy Loman

Ⅳ. Short answer questions

1. Which play of Eugene O' Neill's is autobiographical?（国际关系学院 2007 研）
2. Analyze the character of Willy Loman in *Death of a Salesman* by Arthur Miller.（南京大学 2008 研；厦门大学 2010 研）
3. What is Yank struggling for in Eugene O'Neill's *The Hairy Ape*? And how does his struggle reflect the universal dilemma of the modern man?

Ⅴ. Essay question

1. Highlight Nobel Prize Laureate Eugene O'Neill.（北航 2010 研）

参考答案及解析

I. Fill in the blanks.

1. Eugene O'Neil

（美国文学史上最伟大的戏剧家尤金·奥尼尔在 20 世纪 20 年代确立了国际声望。）

2. European; tragedies; realism; expressionism

（尤金·奥尼尔被称为"美国戏剧之父"，其戏剧融合欧洲戏剧传统的精华，包括希腊的悲剧，易卜生现实主义剧作和斯特林堡的表现主义。）

3. Eugene O'Neill

（尤金·奥尼尔(Eugene O'Neill)是美国最伟大的剧作家，他在1936年获得诺贝尔文学奖，被誉为“美国戏剧之父”。）

4. naturalistic, symbolism, expressionism

（尤金·奥尼尔是一位不断创新的剧作家，创作初期他倾向于自然主义风格，而后转向运用象征主义和表现主义的手法。）

5. tragedies

（奥尼尔大部分剧作是悲剧，探讨人类生存及生与死等困境。）

6. Tennessee Williams

（田纳西·威廉姆斯(Tennessee Williams)的戏剧勇于探讨暴力、性和同性恋等主题。）

7. The Theater of the Absurd, Edward Albee

（20世纪五、六十年代的荒诞派戏剧(The Theater of the Absurd)集中表现现实的丑恶与恐怖、人生的痛苦与绝望，达到一种抽象的荒诞效果。爱德华·阿尔比(Edward Albee)是荒诞派戏剧的代表作家之一。）

II. Multiple Choice

1. D *The Crucible* 的作者是 Arthur Miller(阿瑟·米勒)，其余都是奥尼尔的作品。
2. B 《进入黑夜的漫长旅程》是美国伟大剧作家 Eugene O'Neill(尤金·奥尼尔)的代表作，他的其他作品有 *The Emperor Jones*(《琼斯皇帝》), *The Hairy Ape*(《毛猿》), *Desire Under the Elms*(《榆树下的欲望》), *The Great God Brown*(《大神布朗》)。
3. C 尤金·奥尼尔(Eugene O'Neill)是美国最伟大的剧作家，他被誉为“美国的莎士比亚”(“American Shakespeare”)。
4. B 这句话选自奥尼尔的《毛猿》，其中“他”指代上帝。
5. D D项《月照不幸人》是奥尼尔的作品。
6. D 田纳西·威廉斯并未获得诺贝尔奖。
7. B 《推销员之死》(*Death of a Salesman*)是阿瑟·米勒(Arthur Miller)的代表作，该剧获得了纽约剧评奖和普利策奖。

III. Explain the following terms.

1. Theatre of Absurdity referred to a kind of plays written mainly in France from the mid-1940s to the whole 1950s. These works usually employ illogical facts, unconventional dialogues, and very simple plots to express the obvious absurdity of human society. This term was first used, in 1961, by British scholar Martin Esslin. Samuel Beckett and Eugene Ionesco are two of the leading figures of Theatre of Absurdity movement.
2. monodrama, a play or a scene in which only one character speaks; or a series of dramatic monologues all made by one single character. Many plays written by Samuel Beckett, including *Krapp's Last Tape* (first performed 1958) and *Happy Days* (1961), are monodramas. Monodrama also refers to a dramatic expression of what a person's thought in his or her mind, or refers to a musical drama in which there is only one solo performer.
3. Parody is a mocking imitation of the style of literary works, ridiculing the typical writing style of an author or school by exaggerated imitation. Henry Fielding and James Joyce are two of the leading parodists in English literature. Poets in the 19th century, especially William Wordsworth and

Robert Browning suffered lots of parodies of their works.

4. A privileged, heroic character of high repute, who, by virtue of tragic flaws and destiny, ultimately suffers a downfall from glory into suffering. A tragic hero is usually a protagonist. Sophocles' Oedipus is an example.
5. Willy Lowman is the protagonist of Arthur Miller's play *Death of a Salesman*, which is a sad representation of the American dream. Willy Lowman, the salesman of the title, is as "phony" as Mark Twain's Colonel Sellers but more diligent and honest. He is as tragic as F. Scott Fitzgerald's Great Gatsby but not as successful and "great". It seems that Willy has never been aware of how suffocating the modern world he's living and never stopping on dreaming of success. He is all the time governed by the desire for success. His dreaming is certainly a symptom of his illusion and craziness. The mind of Willy eventually falls apart under too much pressure.

Ⅳ. Short answer questions

1. *Long Day's Journey into Night* is regarded as Eugene O'Neill's autobiographical play. the drama written in 1956 is widely welcomed, leading to O'Neill's winning of the 1957 Pulitzer Prize. The action depicts a fateful, heart-rending day from about 8:30 in the morning to midnight, in August 1912, at the seaside Connecticut home of the Tyrones—the autobiographical representations of O'Neill himself, his older brother, and their parents at their home, Monte Cristo Cottage.
2. In the play, Willy Loman keeps on dreaming of success and living in illusions and lies. He desires to build up his own business and own a big house. He dreams of a "big" future for his children. The success in his mind is something that can be measured only in terms of dollars. In fact, the dreaminess of Willy is a symptom of the craziness which is absorbing him. The mind of Willy is finally falling apart under the pressure of this much. All he can think of day and night is his global success, thus making him mentally unprepared for the impending tragedy. Willy never came to realize that it was the problematic social system that had made it impossible for him to achieve success and that the American obsession with financial success had ruined him. Willy is a typical example of a tragic hero.
3. Throughout the play, Yank is struggling to find the place where he belongs. However, he is rejected by the whole society. He attempts to make friends with the ape and calls him brother, but finally crushed by the gorillas and dies in the cage. Identity is what Yank has been struggling with, but no matter how he struggles, he can only finds himself an outsider, a freak.

Ⅴ. Essay question

1. Eugene O'Neill was considered the greatest American playwright of the first half of the 20th century, and was called "founder of the American drama". Some of his famous plays are: *Beyond the Horizon*, *The Emperor Jones*, *The Hairy Ape*, *Desire Under the Elms*, *The Great God Brown*, *Long Day's Journey Into Night*. His plays have been translated and staged all over the world.

   He was the first playwright to touch serious themes in the theater and to carry out his constant and bold experiments with theatrical traditions. Most of his works are tragedies, dealing with human existence and predicament: life and death, illusion and disillusion, alienation and communication, dream and reality, self and society, desire and frustration, etc.

As the nation's first important playwright with forty nine published plays, he did a great deal to establish the modes of the modern theatre in the country. He employed sets, lighting and sound to enhance emotion rather than to represent a real place. He often ignored normal play divisions of scenes and acts, paid little attention to the expected length of plays, made his character wear masks, split one character between two actors, reintroduced ghosts, chorus, monologue and direct addresses to audience.

He successfully introduced the European theatrical trends of realism, naturalism, and expressionism to the American stage as devices to express his comprehensive interest in life and humanity. He grounded his works in personal experience and reflected the life of his country and his time.

第 20 章　二战后诗歌 · 20 世纪 40 年代的诗人

20.1　复习笔记

Ⅰ. Social background The world after the war has undergone tremendous changes. The new experience in the new stage makes the way of literary expression more unique. The great changes include the threat of nuclear weapons, the madness of McCarthyism, the upsurge of the civil rights movement, the outrage caused by the Vietnam War, the feminist movement and sexual liberation, the contemporary information explosion, the improvement of the self-awareness, as well as the economic development and social abundance. All these have caused great changes in people's attitudes and values regarding life and the world. Human experience has become more and more individualized, and the way of expression has become more and more individualized and even unusual.	**Ⅰ. 社会背景** 战后的世界发生了重大的变化。新阶段的新的经历使得文学表达方式更具独特性：核武器的威胁，麦卡锡主义的疯狂，民权运动的高涨，越战所引起的民情激愤，女权运动及性解放，当代信息大爆炸以及人们自我意识的提高，加上经济的发展和社会的富足等等，这些都使人们看待生活与世界的态度以及价值观方面发生了很大变化。人的经历变得越来越个体化，表达方式也越来越个人化甚至不同寻常化。
Ⅱ. Postmodernism Postmodernism shows a new way of understanding and creation. In terms of poetry, it tries its best to maintain opposition to the new critical poetry fashion and modernism decades ago. In terms of creative themes, postmodernism sees the world as invisible and unpredictable, rather than something to be shaped. Postmodernism does not strive to exert influence on life and reality. It tends to accept life and reality as it is. It often uses topics and objects which reflect personal nature or even forbidden nature to create. In terms of form, postmodernism seeks freedom of literary expression. For example, it tends to use colloquial and informal language rather than always pursuing the grammatical correctness and coherence of sentences. Postmodern novels show its unique characteristics including metafiction, black humor and avant-garde forms. Postmodernism is still developing as the dominant literary form.	**Ⅱ. 后现代主义** 后现代主义代表了一种新的理解方式和创作方法。在诗歌方面，它尽量与新批评诗歌的风尚及几十年前的现代主义保持对立。在创作主题方面，后现代主义将世界看成是无形的、不可预知的，而非有待塑造的。后现代主义并不竭力对生活和现实施加影响，而是乐于接受生活和现实本来面貌。它往往使用反映个人本性甚至是被禁止的本性的话题和对象进行创作。在形式方面，后现代主义寻求文学表达上的自由。例如，它更倾向于使用口语和非正式用语，而并不总是追求句子的语法正确和连贯性。后现代小说展示了它独有的特点，如超小说、黑色幽默和先锋派的形式。后现代主义现在仍是作为主导的文学形式前进发展着。

III. Elizabeth Bishop (1911 –1979)

1. Life

Elizabeth Bishop was born in Worcester, Massachusetts. When she was eight months old, her father died. When she was five years old, her mother was sent to a mental hospital. So she was raised by her grandparents and grandparents. She graduated from Vassar College. She won many awards, including the Pulitzer Prize for poetry and the National Book Prize.

2. The features of her poems

Bishop's poems are mostly the portrayal of her personal experience. For example, the loss of her parents in her childhood, her travels in Europe, South America and her home country, and the encounter with Marianne Moore and T. S. Eliot, all these events are reflected in her works. She is a postmodernist who not only accepts life as it is, but also pursues the openness of poetry themes and forms.

3. Major Works

Questions of Travel
Geography III
"Sestina"
"One Art"
"Over 2000 Illustrations and a Complete Concordance"
"The Fish"
"At the Fish House"

4. Analysis of major work

◆"The Fish"

The poem can be divided into several sections. The poet said that she caught a big fish. The first 20 lines describe its appearance to the reader objectively and informatively. The next 25 lines have emotional intervention and further specific subjective emotions. The poet gradually developed admiration and awe, and finally put the fish back into the water. The poet first admired the wisdom and heroism of fish. After that, she felt immensely proud and happy, because she felt that she was the same as the fish. The reason why the poet released the fish is that she had a sense of identity with the fish either consciously or subconsciously, the notion of "Heroes love heroes".

Ⅲ. 伊丽莎白·毕肖普

1. 生平

伊丽莎白·毕肖普出生于马萨诸塞州的伍斯特。在她八个月大的时候，父亲去世了。而在她五岁时，母亲又被送进了精神病院。所以她先后由外祖父母和祖父母抚养。她毕业于瓦萨学院。她曾获得过很多奖项，其中包括普利策诗歌奖和国家图书奖。

2. 诗歌特点

毕肖普的诗歌大多是她个人经历的写照。比如她童年时代失去双亲，她在欧洲、南美洲和自己祖国的旅行，以及与玛丽安·穆尔与T. S. 艾略特的相遇，所有这些事件都被浓缩在她的作品中。

她是一位后现代主义者，不仅对生活的坦然接受，而且追求诗歌主题与形式的开放。

3. 主要作品

《旅行的问题》
《地理Ⅲ》
《六行诗》
《一种艺术》
《两千多幅图解》
《鱼》
《渔屋》

4. 主要作品分析

◆《鱼》

这首诗可以分为几节，诗人说她钓到一条大鱼，前20行向读者客观而翔实地描绘它的外观，在接下来的25行有情感上的介入和进一步具体的主观情感上的描述，诗人逐渐产生敬佩之情，肃然起敬，最后把鱼又放回水中。诗人首先钦佩鱼的智慧和英雄主义，之后她感到莫大的自豪和快乐，觉得自己和鱼是一样的。诗人为什么将鱼放生是因为意识中或者潜意识中与鱼有认同感，"英雄惜英雄"，出于尊

She protected the dignity of her opponent out of respect and sympathy. This poem shows people's gradual process of understanding reality, and reflects the poet's idea of "the perpetually changing integration of what has been written with what is being written."

重和同情来保全对手的尊严。这首诗显示出人对现实的循序渐进的认识过程，体现出诗人的写作是“对已有的作品和创作中的作品所进行的不断变化的整合”的思想。

Ⅳ. Richard Wilbur (1921 –)

Ⅳ. 理查德·威尔伯

1. Life

Richard Wilbur is an American poet and literary translator. He was born in New York. He then attended Amherst College and Harvard University. He participated in World War II in Europe.

1. 生平

理查德·威尔伯是美国诗人和文学翻译家。他生于纽约，在艾姆赫斯特学院和哈佛大学接受过教育。二战期间在欧洲参战。

2. Writing style

Wilbur was the most elegant poet in the new criticism era. He paid attention to pace and rhythm. His poems had a beautiful rhythm and left a very pleasant impression on the readers. In terms of form, Wilbur accepted any form which is conducive to creation. Although his style is always witty and elegant, his form is flexible. He rejected dogma and extremist models. His language style is casual and relaxed.

2. 写作风格

威尔伯是新批评时代文风最优雅的诗人。他注重步格和韵律，韵律优美，给读者留下了很愉悦的印象。

在形式上，威尔伯对任何有助于创作的形式都采取开放的态度。尽管他的风格总是机智、优雅的，形式总是灵活的，但他拒绝教条和极端主义的模式。语言风格很随意轻松。

3. Major works

The Beautiful Changes and Other Poems
Ceremony and Other Poems
Things of This World
Complaint
The Mind-Reader: New Poems
Verses on The Times
New and Collected Poems
Bone Key and Other Poems

3. 主要作品

《美好的变化及其他诗》
《礼仪及其他诗》
《世事的诗歌》
《抱怨》
《知心人：新诗》
《时代之歌》
《诗集》
《骨头钥匙及其他诗》

Ⅴ. John Berryman (1914 –1972)

Ⅴ. 约翰·贝里曼

1. Life

John Berryman was an American poet. He was the main representative of American poetry in the second half of the 20th century. He was regarded as the originator of confession poems. When he was 12 years old, his father committed suicide with a bullet. He tried to use his life and poetry creation career to get rid of the shadow but failed. When he couldn't bear the great despair and pain, he finally suffered a nervous breakdown and committed suicide.

1. 生平

约翰·贝里曼是美国诗人。他是20世纪下半叶美国诗歌的主要代表人物。他被视作“自白诗的鼻祖”。当他12岁时他父亲饮弹自尽。这件事对他造成极大的伤害。他试图用一生的时间和诗歌创作生涯来摆脱阴影，但没成功。当无法忍受巨大的绝望和痛苦之时，他最终精神崩溃自尽身亡。

2. Themes

The theme of Berryman's poems was largely related to his father's suicide. Whether consciously or unconsciously, he was always tortured by this event. He could not overcome his guilt, nor could he escape the pain and anger in his heart. He constantly struggled with his despair. His inner conflicts were also exacerbated by the chaos of his personal life: his desire for love, sexual guilt, alcoholism, etc. In addition, he was anxious because of his desire for the recognition of his work. In short, he must always face his naked inner world. So his poems were full of details of his life, or the heavy cargo.

3. Major Works

The Dream Songs

77 Dream Songs

His Toy, His Dream, His Rest

Ⅵ. Randall Jarrell (1914–1965)

1. Life

Randall Jarrell was born in Nashville, Tennessee, in 1914. He received bachelor's and master's degrees from Vanderbilt University. From 1937 to 1939 he taught at Kenyon College, where he met John Crowe Ransom and Robert Lowell. He joined the navy in 1942. Then he joined the army as a control tower operator. This experience provided a lot of material for his poetry creation.

2. Theme

Jarrell's poetry creation can be roughly divided into three stages: early childhood emotional frustration, wartime poems about war, and the similar themes of his early poems after the war. The content of his poems is always related to the childhood. His poems all contain his memories, or the meaning of thinking about mother or looking for mother. His best works always have memories of his childhood.

3. Major Works

Blood for a Stranger

Little Friend, Little Friend

The Woman at the Washington Zoo

The Lost World

2. 主题

贝里曼诗歌的主题大体和他父亲的自杀有关。无论是有意识或无意识地，他总是受到这个事件的折磨，不能克服自己的负罪感，也摆脱不了内心的痛苦和气愤，他不断地与自己的绝望情绪做斗争。他的内心矛盾也由于他个人生活的混乱而加剧了：他对爱情的渴望、性方面的负罪感、酗酒成性等，此外还有他在艺术上渴求承认的忧虑。总之他必须时刻面对他的赤裸裸的内心世界。所以他的诗充满了他生活的细节，或者说沉重的负荷。

3. 主要作品

《梦之歌》

《77 首梦之歌》

《他的玩具，他的梦想，他的安息》

Ⅵ. 兰德尔·贾雷尔

1. 生平

兰德尔·贾雷尔于 1914 年在田纳西州的纳什维尔出生。在范德堡大学获得学士和硕士学位。1937 年至 1939 年间在肯尼恩学院执教，在那儿遇见约翰·克劳·兰塞姆和罗伯特·洛威尔。1942 年加入空军。不久又加入陆军，做控制塔操作员，这一经历给他的诗歌创作提供了大量的素材。

2. 主题

贾勒尔的诗歌创作大体可以分作三个阶段：早期儿时感情受挫，战时关于战争的诗歌，战后又返回早期诗作的主题。他的诗歌内容总和幼儿时期有关。他的诗作都有某种回首往事，或思母或寻母的意味。他最好的作品总是有关于他的童年及对幼时的回忆。

3. 主要作品

《给陌生人的血》

《小朋友，小朋友》

《华盛顿动物园的女人》

《失去的世界》

VII. James Merrill (1926 – 1995) **1. Life** James Merrill grew up under the influence of new critical concepts. In his career as a poet, he insisted on using this concept to create. His parents divorced when he was young, and this incident left a heavy shadow in his life. He always wrote about this in his poetry creation. Many of his poems touched this topic directly or indirectly.	**VII. 詹姆斯·梅里尔** **1. 生平** 詹姆斯·梅里尔在新批评观念的影响下成长。在他的诗人生涯中也坚持用这种观念进行创作。幼时父母离异，这件事在他的一生中留下浓重的阴影挥之不去。在他的诗歌创作中，常常情不自禁地写到此事，他的不少诗作直接或间接地触及这个题目。
2. Major features of his works He focuses on writing romantic love, family, memories of the past, and science as a potential threat to human life. He also pays attention to form and believes that art is form. He can be described as versatile and well-rounded in the use of traditional poetry forms, such as sonnets, six-section poems, plain-style poems, and three-line rhyming poems. Merrill's puns, overtones, word games, and sense of humor are all well-known.	**2. 作品的主要特点** 他注重写浪漫的爱情，家庭，回忆往昔以及科学是人类生活的潜在威胁等题材。他也注重形式，认为艺术就是形式。他在运用传统诗歌形式方面可谓多才多艺，精深圆熟，比如十四行诗，六节诗，素体诗，三行隔句押韵诗等。 梅里尔的双关语、弦外音、文字游戏及幽默感等都相当闻名。
3. Major Works *First Poems* *The Country of a Thousand Years of Peace* *Nights and Days* *Braving the Elements* *Changing Lights at Sandover*	**3. 主要作品** 《处女作》 《千年和平之国》 《夜与日》 《搏击风雨》 《桑多弗变化的光》

20.2 考研真题与典型题详解

I. Essay questions

1. Write a short essay (in no more than 200 words) about the basic features of Postmodernism. (上海交大 2007 研)

参考答案

1. Postmodernism is a disputed term that has occupied much recent debate about contemporary culture since the early 1980s. As applied to literature and other arts, the term is notoriously ambiguous, implying either that modernism has been superseded or that it has continued into a new phase. Postmodernism shows a new way of understanding and creation. In terms of poetry, it tries its best to maintain opposition to the new critical poetry fashion and modernism decades ago. In terms of creative themes, postmodernism sees the world as invisible and unpredictable, rather than something to be shaped. Postmodernism does not strive to exert influence on life and reality. It tends to accept life and reality as it is. It often uses topics and objects which reflect personal

nature or even forbidden nature to create. In terms of form, postmodernism seeks freedom of literary expression. For example, it tends to use colloquial and informal language rather than always pursuing the grammatical correctness and coherence of sentences. Postmodern novels show its unique characteristics including metafiction, black humor and avant-garde forms. Postmodernism is still developing as the dominant literary form.

第 21 章　自白派·垮掉的一代

21.1　复习笔记

Ⅰ. The Confessional School

The term is usually used to certain poets of the United States from the late 1950s to the late 1960s. Broadly, the poetry of this group of poets share common features such as a merciless, painful self-analysis of one's own history, one's own most secret desires and illusions etc., and the urgent "I'll-tell-it-all-to-you" impulse. In a sense, Lowell's merciless dissection regenerated Confessional poetry and made it more fashionable than ever before. Representatives of the Confessional School are Robert Lowell, Anne Sexton, Sylvia Plath.

Ⅰ. 自白派

这一术语用来指 20 世纪 50 年代末到 60 年代末的一些美国诗人。广义上讲，这些诗人的诗歌具有以下共同特点，如对自己的历史，内心深处的欲望和幻想等进行无情的、令人痛苦的自我分析，以及一种急切的“我将告诉你一切”的冲动。从某种程度上讲，洛威尔无情的自我剖析使自白诗获得新生也使其成为新时尚，并远超以往。自白派代表人物是罗伯特·洛威尔、安妮·塞克斯顿、西尔维娅·普拉斯。

Ⅱ. Robert Lowell (1917 – 1977)

1. Life

Lowell came from a distinguished New England family. This background endowed him with culture and taste in his poetic nature, and meanwhile enabled him to examine and dissect the decline of his New England tradition. He received an excellent education at Harvard and then at Kenyon College, Ohio under the famous New Critical poet and critic John Crowe Ranson. Lowell's poetic career peaked when he won the 1946 Pulitzer for his second poetry volume, *Lord Weary's Castle*. In 1959 his *Life Studies* came out. At that time his poetic style was no more the New Critical but open form, and had unintentionally started a new school of poetry, the Confessional School poetry. He won the National Book Award for *Life Studies*. In 1967 he was once arrested for his part in the march on the Pentagon against the Vietnam War.

Ⅱ. 罗伯特·洛威尔

1. 生平

洛威尔来自显赫的新英格兰家族。这样的家族背景赋予了他文化和品味上的诗人气质，同是也使得他能审视新英格兰传统衰败与剖析其衰败的原因。他接受了良好的教育。先在哈佛大学就读，后又进入俄亥俄州的肯尼恩学院师从著名的新批评主义诗人、评论家约翰·克洛·兰森。1946 年洛威尔因其第二部诗集《威尔利老爷的城堡》获得普利策奖，他的诗歌生涯达到顶峰。1959 年他的新作《生命研究》问世。那时他的诗作风格已不再是新批评主义，而是开放自由的了，他也在不经意间开创了一个新的诗歌流派，自白派。他也因为这部新作而获得国家图书奖。1967 年，他曾因为参与在五角大楼举行的反越战游行而被捕。

2. Comments on Lowell

(1) Lowell at first strictly adhered to the New Critical school in the 1940s. His poetry before *Life Studies* had a regular form, witty, tight, and delicate . Stunned at "all the horrors of this age," Lowell was constantly concerned with human's existence and salvation.

(2) However, at the end of the 1950s Lowell started his painful introspection He left his "City of God" and set foot in the "City of Man" of which he was a member. He examined his social and family background and the potential of art as a means to his own salvation.

(3) What made Lowell great is that he dissects his national culture. It seems that a sense of historic mission always inspires Lowell and endows his poetry with an epic quality.

3. Major works

Land of Unlikeness

Lord Weary's Castle

The Mills of the Kavanaughs

Life Studies

For the Union Dead

History

Day by Day

4. Analysis of major work

◆*Life of Studies*

(1) It is regarded as the masterpiece of Confessional poetry, which is made of four parts.

(2) Part one, four poems, defines the situation of human behavior and offers a reference framework for ensuing revelations. Part two is the book's prose section, entitled "91 Revere Street." Strictly speaking, it is an autobiography, disclosing the poet's concern over the declining New England culture. The third part, consisting of four poems, is aimed to explore whether aesthetic redemption is possible. Part four, entitled "Life Studies," which includes two parts of altogether 15 poems. Section one is a series of 11 poems related to failure. The first 7 poems are centered on the Lowell family's failure. The later 4 poems are centered on his own failure.

2. 对洛威尔的评价

(1)起初，洛威尔在20世纪40年代的时候严格遵守新批评主义的诗学主张。出版《生活研究》之前，他的诗歌形式规整，不失机智、紧凑、精美。惊讶于“这个时代的所有令人惊恐的事情”，洛威尔一直对人类的生存和救赎感兴趣。

(2)然而，20世纪50年代末，洛威尔转向内心世界，开始他痛苦的自我反省。他离开“上帝之城”，进入自己也是其中一员的“人类之城”。他分析了自己的社会和家庭背景，及将艺术作为自我救赎的可能性。

(3)洛威尔之所以伟大在于他剖析了自己国家的文化。似乎总有一种历时使命感激励洛威尔去创作，他的诗歌也因此具有了史诗的品质

3. 主要作品

《不一样的国度》

《威尔利老爷的城堡》

《卡瓦纳家族的磨坊》

《生命研究》

《为联邦军阵亡将士而作》

《历史》

《日复一日》

4. 主要作品分析

◆《生命研究》

(1)这首诗被看作是自白派诗歌的代表作，由四个部分组成。

(2)第一部分由四首诗组成，给人类行为划定了界限，并为同时带来的启示提供了参照框架。第二部分是散文，题目为《里维尔街91号》。严格来说，这部分属于自传，它反映出诗人为衰败的新英格兰文化深深忧虑。诗歌的第三部分有四首诗组成，旨在探索艺术救赎是否可能。第四部分标题为《生命研究》，包括两部分，共15首诗。其中，开始的7首诗全都讲述了洛威尔家族的失败。之后的4首诗讲述了自己的失败。

(3) *Life Studies* concludes with "Skunk Hour", which may be his most well-known one. The poem's title is interesting. The hour of skunks' out eating is the hour when humans realize their embarrassments and predicaments, when the poet is at the lowest circle of hell, and achieves self-realization and prophetically appeals humankind to follow.

(3)《臭鼬时刻》是《生活研究》的最后一首诗，也可能是洛威尔最为著名的一首诗。诗的题名也很有意思。臭鼬外出觅食的时刻是人类意识到自己卑微与自身困境的时刻。诗人意识到自己处于地狱的底层，并获得自我认识，同时向人类发出先知般的呼吁，呼吁大家认识自我。

Ⅲ. Sylvia Plath (1932 – 1963)

Ⅲ. 西尔维娅·普拉斯

1. Brief introduction on Sylvia Plath's writing

1. 创作简介

For Sylvia Plath writing was a relief, a process of removing her keen "existential anxiety," caused by her self-consciousness of being a German descendant, her father's death, her fierce subconscious distaste for her mother, and the hurt of her husband's infidelity which she failed to ease for herself. Thus, death along with suffering and agony became the central among her major works. Her poetic art transmutes her individual experience to made it accessible to most people. This is where her excellent art lies.

对西尔维娅·普拉斯来说，创作是减轻痛苦的过程，是驱除她剧烈的"生存焦虑"的过程。这焦虑源于她是德国后裔的自我意识、父亲之死、潜意识里对母亲的厌恶以及丈夫不忠带给她的无法缓解的伤害。因此死亡和痛苦、苦恼一并成为她重要作品中的主题。她创作的完美艺术在于她能确保通过自己的诗歌创作艺术能力来再现其个人的经历，使作品获得一定的普遍适用性。她的诗歌艺术再创了其个人经历，尽力使得更多的人明白诗歌的内容。这就是她诗歌艺术高明之所在。

2. Major works

A Winter Ship
The Colossus and Other Poems
Ariel
Crystal Gazer and Other Poems
Winter Trees
Fiesta Melons
Crossing the Water
Lyonesse: Hitherto Uncollected Poems
Pursuit
The Bell Jar

2. 主要作品

《冬天的船》
《巨人及其他诗歌》
《爱丽尔》
《水晶球占卜师及其他》
《冬天的树》
《瓜果节》
《渡河》
《莱昂尼斯：迄今为止未收录的诗歌》
《追求》
《钟形坛》

Ⅳ. Anne Sexton (1928 – 1974)

Ⅳ. 安妮·塞克斯顿

1. Brief introduction about Anne Sexton's writing

1. 创作简介

Anne Sexton was a leading light among Confessional poet. Her urgent desire to unleash her suppressed internal pressure is clearly shown in her poetry. Madness, victimization, a

安妮·塞克斯顿是一位非常重要的自白派诗人。她的诗歌生动展示了她急迫地想要倾泻自己的情感

sense of engulfing chaos, fascination with suicide and death, incest, adultery, illegitimacy, guilt, and addiction constitute her fundamental themes. Her work represents her emotionally dramatic life journey where she struggled for survival but reached no salvation.

以释放内心的压抑。她创作的基本主题包括精神错乱、欺骗、吞噬一切的混乱感、迷恋自杀和死亡、乱伦、通奸、私生、罪恶和吸毒。她的作品代表了她所经历的生命历程，一个诸多情感变故的历程，一个她奋力生存最终却没得到救赎的经历。

2. Major works

Live or Die
To Bedlam and Part Way Back
All My Pretty Ones
Transformations
The Death of Notebooks
The Awful Rowing toward God
"Her Kind"
"Housewife"
"Young"
"The Farmer's Wife"
"Death Baby"

2. 主要作品

《生或死》
《去精神病院中途返回》
《所有我可爱的人》
《变形》
《死亡笔记》
《庄重地划向上帝》
《她那一类》
《家庭主妇》
《年幼》
《农夫的妻子》
《死亡宝贝》

V. The Beat Generation

The 1950s witnessed a sweeping discontentment among the postwar generation, who protested against all the American mainstream culture They have become known as the Beat Generation. Ginsberg and his friend Jack Kerouac picked "beat" from one of their junkie friends. The word "beat" represented a rebellious attitude toward traditional values toward sex, religion, the arts, and the American way of life. Depression, despair, and the need to flee into an unconventional, sometimes communal, living mode shaped this rebellious attitude. "Beat" literature refreshed prose and poetry of the 1950s and 1960s. Representatives of the Beat Generation are Jack Kerouac, William Burroughs, Allen Ginsberg, Lawrence Ferlinghett, and Gary Snyder.

V. "垮掉的一代"

20 世纪 50 年代，二战后一代人中普遍存在着一种不满情绪，他们反对美国的一切主流文化。他们被认为是"垮掉的一代"。金斯堡和他的朋友杰克·凯鲁亚克从一个吸毒的朋友那儿听来了"垮掉"一词，它代表了一种不遵从传统价值观的叛逆态度，有关性、宗教、艺术和美国的生活方式。沮丧和厌倦感，想逃入一种非传统的、有时是团体的生活方式的需求塑造了这种反叛的态度。"垮掉派"文学在 20 世纪 50 年代和 60 年代是诗歌和散文界刮起一阵新的强风。"垮掉的一代"的代表有杰克·凯鲁亚克、威廉·巴罗斯、艾伦·金斯堡、劳伦斯·费尔林希提以及加里·斯奈达。

VI. Allen Ginsberg (1926 –1997)

1. Brief Introduction

A rebel, a trailblazer, and an explorer of the unknown, and the poet laureate of the Beat Generation may best conclude

VI. 艾伦·金斯堡

1. 简介

叛逆者、开拓者和对未知的探索者，"垮掉的一代"的桂冠诗人这

Allen Ginsberg. He was born in Newark, New Jersey. Both of his parents both influenced his literary career. Ginsberg went to Columbia University and met Lucien Carr, William Burroughs, and Jack Kerouac there and formed the heart of the Beat Generation. Kerouac and Burroughs introduced him to taking drugs and the illusion of drug's exceeding human consciousness. Columbia suspended him for his graffiti on classroom windows.

些名号也许最能概括艾伦·金斯堡其人。他出生于新泽西州的纽瓦克。父母对他的文学生涯有一定的影响。金斯堡就读于哥伦比亚大学，在那里遇到了卢辛·卡尔、威廉·巴罗斯、杰克·凯鲁亚克，组成了“垮掉的一代”的核心。凯鲁亚克和巴罗斯带着他吸毒，给了他超越人类正常意识的幻象。他由于在教室窗户上涂鸦而被哥伦比亚大学勒令退学。

2. Ginsberg's Literary Points of View

To Ginsberg, the fullest art, the most individual, uninfluenced, unrepressed, uninhibited expression of art, is true expression and the true art. William Carlos Williams' literary doctrine of portraying contemporary life in daily speech was advocated and practiced by Allen Ginsberg.

2. 文学观点

对金斯堡来说，最完美的艺术，最个人的、不受影响的、不受压抑的、不受限制的艺术表达才是真实的艺术表达、真实的艺术。他崇尚威廉·卡洛斯·威廉斯用生活语言再现当代生活的原则。

3. Major works

Howl

"America"

The Fall of America

3. 主要作品

《嚎叫》

《美国》

《美国的衰落》

4. Analysis of major work

◆*Howl*

(1) *Howl* is typical of Ginsberg's life. It consists of three sections. Section one sums and glorifies the Beat Generation with all its features: its anti-mainstream way of living, its vision and its power, its ambition and a sense of historical mission and the depth of their despair in face of the threat of failure. Section two digs out the root cause of their plight and their nightmarish experience. This section focuses its attack on America's mechanical civilization. The last section is at once an elegy about the possible defeat at the hands of fate and an effort to brace for the future.

(2) In formal terms Ginsberg imitated the cataloging form of Whitman's prose poetry and William Carlos Williams's tone and rhythm.

4. 主要作品分析

◆《嚎叫》

(1)《嚎叫》整体上以金斯堡的生活为原型，由三部分组成。第一部分勾勒了“垮掉的一代”显著且不可磨灭的特征：他们反主流的生活方式、他们的视野和力量、他们的雄心壮志和使命感和他们面对失败时那极度失望的感受。第二部分深入挖掘了带给他们困境和噩梦般经历的根本原因，这一部分集中抨击了机械化的美国文明。最后一部分既是命运手中可能出现的失败的挽歌，又是支持未来的努力。

(2) 在形式上，金斯堡借鉴了惠特曼散文诗中的列举形式和威廉·卡洛斯·威廉斯的音调和节奏。

Ⅶ. Gary Snyder (1930 –)

In the mid-1950s and early 1960s, the "Beats" included Snyder among whom he was only second to Ginsberg in reputation.

Ⅶ. 加里·斯奈达(1930 –)

在20世纪50年代中期和60年代早期，斯奈达是垮掉派中的一员。在这派中，他的名声仅次于金斯堡。

1. Snyder's literary points of view (1) For Snyder the wilderness can always stimulate human. He tries to hold history and wilderness in his mind so that his poetry may approach the true measure of things and stand against the unbalance and ignorance of his time. (2) The "stillness" among the dynamic universe is fundamental to Snyder's poetic concern. (3) Snyder believes in the mission of the poet is to find poetic which is exclusive to nature.	**1. 文学观点** (1) 对于斯奈达来讲，荒野总是人类的兴奋剂。他总是将历史和荒野牢记脑海以使他的诗歌接近事物的真实面貌，并使之与他那个时代的紊乱和无知作对。 (2)"静止"是斯奈达诗歌关注的中心。他试图在变动不居的雨中中寻找"静止"之物。 (3) 斯奈达似乎认为诗人的职责就是要看到诗歌的哲学，而诗学就蕴藏于自然界。
2. Major works "Mid-August at Sourdough Mountain Lookout" "Stillness" "Straight-Creek—Great Burn" "Riprap" "It Was When" "Song of the Taste"	**2. 主要作品** 《八月中旬的苏德尔山瞭望点》 《静止》 《笔直的小溪——伟大的燃烧》 《砌石》 《就在那时》 《品味之歌》
Ⅷ. Other poets **1. W. S. Merwin (1927 –)** The theme of Merwin's poetry is generally concerned with the dilemmas of humankind and the wholesome effect of the natural world. The general theme of Merwin's poetry is the difficulties of humankind and the healthy influence of nature.	**Ⅷ. 其他诗人** **1. W. S. 默温** 默温诗歌的主题通常是关于人类的困境和大自然有益健康的功效。
◆Major works "The Asians Dying" "For a Coming Extinction" "Summer Doorway" "The Drunk in the Furnace"	**◆主要作品** 《亚洲人正在死亡》 《为即将到来的灭亡而作》 《夏天的门洞里》 《炉边醉汉》
2. Robert Bly (1926 –) Aside from surrealism, he thinks that the poet should liberate himself form ration and reveal the lurking consciousness in the mind. Also, modern poetry should grasp the flowing spiritual power. His opinion on imagery is "deep image". Bly's poetry is generally sad.	**2. 罗伯特·布莱(1926 –)** 关于布莱的诗学，除了他对超现实主义的观点外，他还认为诗人必须将自己从理性的自我中解放出来，释放出潜藏在脑海中的思想。现代诗也要抓住流动的精神力量。他对意象的观点被称为"深层意象"。布莱的诗歌通常比较忧郁。
◆Major works *Silence in the Snowfields* *The Light around the Body* *This Tree Will be Here for a Thousand Years*	**◆主要作品** 《雪地里的寂静》 《身体周围的光》 《此树在此待千年》

<table>
<tr>
<td>

3. James Wright (1927 –1980)

Wright began writing poems in traditional forms. But later he abandoned it, and turned to a new poetry of leaping images and free verse of American colloquial speech.

◆Major works

The Green Wall

Saint Judas

To a Blossoming Pear Tree

This Journey

</td>
<td>

3. 詹姆斯·赖特

赖特开始是以传统的方式创作诗歌。后来他放弃了以前的写作方式，创作了具有跳动意象的新诗和美国口语化的自由诗。

◆主要作品

《绿墙》

《圣犹大》

《致鲜花盛开的梨树》

《此行》

</td>
</tr>
</table>

21.2 考研真题与典型题详解

I. Fill in the blanks.

1. In the 1950s, there was a widespread discontentment among the postwar generation, whose voice was one of protest against all the mainstream culture that America had come to represent. This generation was known as the __________ generation. (天津外国语学院 2009 研)
2. Author __________ Title __________(南京大学 2009 研)
   What thoughts I have of you tonight, Walt Whitman, for I walked down the sidestreets under the trees with a headache self-conscious looking at the full moon.
3. The publication of Robert Lowell's *Life Studies* marked the coming of the age of __________, which represents a new mode of perception and a way of writing.
4. __________ is the spokesman of postwar Beat Generation in American literary history.
5. Gary Snyder has been placed next to Allen Ginsberg among the Beat Generation. He seems to think that the job of the poet is to catch sight of __________, which resides nowhere but in __________.

II. Multiple Choice

1. Of the following poets, who is NOT remembered as a confessional poet?

   A. Anne Sexton　　B. Sylvia Plath

   C. Robert Lowell　　D. Elizabeth Bishop

Ⅲ. Explain the following terms.

1. confessional poetry (厦门大学 2009 研)
2. The Beat Generation (北航 2007 研；北二外 2010 研)

参考答案及解析

I. Fill in the blanks.

1. beat

   (垮掉的一代：第二次世界大战后风行于美国的文学流派。该流派的作家都是性格粗犷豪放、落拓不羁的男女青年，他们生活简单、不修边幅，喜穿奇装异服，厌弃工作和学业，拒绝承担任何社会义务，以浪迹天涯为乐，反对一切世俗陈规和垄断资本统治，抵制对外侵略和种族隔离，讨厌机器文明，他们永远寻求新的刺激，寻求绝对自由，纵欲、吸毒、沉沦，以此向体面的传统价值标准进行挑战，因此被称作“垮掉的一代”。代表作家有金斯堡及其作品《嚎叫》。)

2. Allen Ginsberg; *A Supermarket in California*
(题目选自金斯堡的 *A Supermarket in California*。)
3. Postmodernism
(罗伯特·洛威尔(Robert Lowell)《人生探索》(*Life Studies*)是一部里程碑式的诗集，它的发表标志着后现代主义(Postmodernism)时代的到来。)
4. Allen Ginsberg
(美国当代诗人艾伦·金斯堡是20世纪50年代末美国“垮掉派”文学运动的中心人物。他的代表作是《嚎叫》(*Howl*)。)
5. the poetic, the natural world
(加里·斯奈德(Gary Snyder)，二十世纪美国著名诗人、“垮掉派”代表人物之一。所以喜欢沉浸于自然，在大自然中，他既是劳动者也是思考者，因此他的诗“更加接近于事物的本色以对抗我们时代的失衡、紊乱及愚昧无知”。)

II. Multiple Choice

1. D　伊丽莎白·毕肖普属于20世纪40年代的诗人，她不是自白派诗人。

Ⅲ. Explain the following terms.

1. Confessional poetry traffics in intimate, and sometimes unflattering, information about details of the poet's personal life, such as in poems about illness, sexuality, and despondence. The confessionalist label was applied to a number of poets of the 1950s and 1960s. John Berryman, Allen Ginsberg, Robert Lowell and Anne Sexton have all been called "Confessional Poets".
2. The Beat Generation is a group of American writers in the late 1950s, led by the poet Allen Ginsberg and the novelist Jack Kerouac. Writers of the "beat generation" dropped out of middle-class society in search of "beatific" ecstasy through drugs, sex, and Zen Buddhism. Their loose styles favor spontaneous self-expression and recitation to jazz accompaniment. The principal works of the group are Ginsberg's *Howl* (1956) and Kerouac's *On the Road* (1957).

第22章　纽约派诗人·沉思型诗歌·黑山派诗人

22.1　复习笔记

Ⅰ. The New York School

1. Features of the New York School

The so-called New York School became famous with Donald Allen's anthology published in 1960. The New York School poets have different pursuits, but their poems all share the same characteristics.

(1) First, they both strongly oppose the dominant New Critical values such as the presentation of objective imagery, and both seek to express their individual poetic characteristics.

(2) They also introduced popular, more vulgar features of life, such as popular songs, cartoon comic strips and Hollywood movies, into their poetry.

(3) Third, they both display a strong sense of humor, and their works are not without their vulgar and sentimental elements.

(4) Finally, they both experimented with surrealism for a period of time.

2. Representatives of the New York School

Frank O'Hara

Kenneth Koch

John Ashbery

James Schuyler

Ⅱ. Frank O'Hara (1926–1966)

1. Features of O'Hara's poetry

(1) A large part of O'Hara's work is of the "occasional" variety, such as birthday tributes and thank-yous. His poems are full of names of people, places, and works, with no particular commentary.

(2) Much of O'Hara's early poetry is surrealistic. Although quite Zen, they are usually obscure and difficult to understand.

Ⅰ. 纽约派诗人

1. 纽约派诗歌的特点

所谓的纽约派是随着唐纳德·艾伦1960年发表的文集而出名的。纽约派诗人的追求各异，但他们的诗歌都有相同的特点。

(1)首先，他们都强烈反对占主导的新批评价值观如客观意象的展现，都力图表达个人的诗歌特点。

(2)他们也把大众化的，比较低俗的生活特色，如通俗歌曲，卡通连环画和好莱坞电影等引入诗歌中。

(3)第三，他们都展现了浓郁的幽默感，他们的作品中也不乏粗俗和伤感成分。

(4)最后，他们都在一段时期内尝试过超现实主义。

2. 纽约派代表诗人

弗兰克·奥哈拉

肯尼斯·科克

约翰·阿什贝里

詹姆斯·舒伊勒

Ⅱ. 弗兰克·奥哈拉

1. 奥哈拉诗作的特点

(1)奥哈拉的很大一部分作品都是“即景生情”类，例如致生日、致谢等。他的诗满是人名、地名、作品名，没有特别的注释。

(2)奥哈拉早期的诗歌大部分都是超现实主义的。因此虽颇有禅机，却通常晦涩难懂。

(3) In his poetry, O'Hara has a kind of tragic thought.

(4) His poetry is famous for its language. His language is colloquial, leisurely, casual and unrefined, so he is absolutely in tune with the anti-literary and anti-art tradition.

(3) 在其诗歌中，奥哈拉有种悲剧思想。

(4) 他的诗歌因其语言而著名。他的语言通俗、闲适、随意、不经雕琢，因此他与反文学反艺术的传统绝对搭调。

2. Major works

The Lunch Poems

"Second Avenue"

"Why I Am Not a Painter"

"The Day Lady Died"

"Joe's Jacket"

2. 主要作品

《午餐诗》

《第二大街》

《我为何不是一个画家》

《黛女士死的那天》

《乔的夹克》

III. John Ashbery (1927 –)

For a long time, John Ashbery was seen as a member of the New York School. But as he reached a mature stage in his career, his poetry increasingly showed the prominent characteristics of contemplative thought. Today Ashbery is one of the most contemplative contemporary American poets.

Ⅲ. 约翰·阿什贝里

很长一段时间以来，约翰·阿什贝里被看作是纽约派的成员。但当他在事业上走向成熟阶段，他的诗歌越来越显示了沉思型思想的突出特征。如今阿什贝里已成为当代美国最有沉思型特色的诗人。

1. Features of his poems

(1) Ashbery is probably the most obscure and unknown poet of our time. When reading his poetry, the reader does not need to make much effort to understand its literal meaning; it is the underlying meaning represented by the structure of the words that is difficult.

(2) Ashbery's poetry reflects on mistakes and makes a record of these indulgent "spiritual acts". His ideas operate in a unique and distinctive way, often breaking with widely accepted logical principles.

(3) His poems, no matter how long or short, are generally recorded in a stream-of-consciousness style. His poetry observes anything temporarily appealing while engaging in a great deal of commentary, using its own imagery and language, and thus appears to be drawn out, irrelevant, uninformative and mysterious. They are a combination of reason and fallacy.

1. 诗歌特点

(1) 阿什贝里可能是当代最隐晦不明的诗人。读他的诗歌，读者并不需费大力去理解它的字面意思，困难的是文字结构所代表的潜在意义。

(2) 阿什贝里的诗歌对错误进行反思，做这些放纵的"精神行为"记录。他的思想运作方式独特，别具一格，通常会打破广为接受的逻辑原则。

(3) 他的诗歌，无论长短，一般都是意识流式的记录，观察任何暂时吸引人的东西，同时进行大量的评论，运用自身意象和语言，因此显得东拉西扯，毫不相干，寓意不明，神秘莫测，是理性和谬误的结合。

2. Major works

Some Trees

The Tennis Court Oath

Rivers and Mountains

The Double Dream of Spring

2. 主要作品

《一些树》

《网球场誓言》

《河与山》

《双重春梦》

Self-Portrait in a Convex Mirror *The Vermont Notebook* *Houseboat Days* *As You Know* *Shadow Train* *A Wave* *Selected Poems* *April Galleons* *Flow Chart* *Hotel L' Autreamont* *Can You Hear, Bird*	《凸镜中的自画像》 《佛蒙特笔记本》 《船家日子》 《如你所知》 《影子列车》 《波浪》 《诗选》 《四月的古帆船》 《流程图》 《洛特雷阿蒙酒店》 《鸟儿，你能否听见》
Ⅳ. A. R. Ammons (1926 –) Ammons is another major contemporary poet of the contemplative type. He often writes in the Romantic tradition.	**Ⅳ. A. R. 阿蒙斯** 阿蒙斯是当代另一位主要的沉思型诗人。他常以浪漫主义的传统方式写作。
◆Major works "Corson Inlet" "Mountain Talk" "So I Said I am Ezra"	**◆主要作品** 《科尔森水湾》 《山地语言》 《我说我是艾兹拉》
V. The Black Mountain Poets The Black Mountain School refers to a group of poets active in the contemporary era, including Charles Olson, Denis Levertov, Robert Duncan, and Robert Creeley. These people were either associated with the Montenegrin Academy or with the *Black Mountain Review* magazine, and were therefore called "Black Mountain Poets". The Black Mountain poets have left a brilliant page in contemporary American literature.	**Ⅴ. 黑山派诗人** 黑山派指的是活跃在当代的一群诗人，包括查尔斯·奥尔森、丹尼斯·莱弗托夫、罗伯特·邓肯和罗伯特·克瑞里。他们这些人要么与黑山学院有关，要么与《黑山评论》杂志有关，因此被称为"黑山派诗人"。黑山派诗人在当代美国文坛留下了辉煌的一页。
VI. Charles Olson (1910 – 1970) **1. Brief Introduction about Olson** Charles Olson was born and raised in Worcester, Massachusetts, and did his doctoral research at Harvard University. He is a distinguished scholar in the fields of archaeology, education and anthropology. As a poet and critic, his writing contributed greatly to moving American poetry away from the traditions of T. S. Eliot and New Criticism and to elevating the status of Williams and Pound's poetry. Olson had a strong sense of mission. He was almost alone in his fight to resist the New Criticism's monopoly on the publishing world and to promote the birth of new poetry. He was the first American poet to call for a new poetic style after World War II and remains highly influential in the contemporary American poetry scene.	**Ⅵ. 查尔斯·奥尔森** **1. 奥尔森简介** 查尔斯·奥尔森出生并成长于马萨诸塞州的沃斯特在哈佛大学做了博士研究。他是考古学、教育学和人类学领域的杰出学者。作为诗人和批评家，他的写作对促使美国诗歌脱离 T. S. 艾略特和新批评的传统，对提升威廉斯和庞德诗歌的地位作出了极大贡献。奥尔森有种强烈的使命感。为了反抗新批评对出版界的垄断，促进新诗的诞生他几乎是孤军奋战。他是二战后呼唤新诗体的美国诗歌第一人，在当代美国诗坛仍有很大的影响力。

2. Major Works "Projective Verse" *In Cold Hell, In Thicket* *The Distances* *The Maximus Poems* *Call me Ishmael* "Human Universe"	**2. 主要作品** 《投射体诗》 《在冰冷的地狱中，在灌木丛中》 《距离》 《马克西姆诗集》 《叫我以实玛利吧》 《人类的宇宙》
VII. Robert Creeley (1926 – 2005) **1. Literary points of view** (1) In terms of content, he fully subscribes to Williams' idea of "no ideas but in things". He also agrees with Pound's stance that "any tendency to abstract general statement is a greased slide." (2) In terms of form, Creeley feels that the criterion of "form" should not continue to be seen as a necessary criterion, since form is an extension of content. His literary criteria are clearly open-ended. (3) The themes of Creeley's poetry are usually love, marriage, complex human relationships and the connection between individuals of both sexes. **2. Major works** *For Love: Poems 1950 – 1960* *Words* *The Charm: Early and Uncollected Poems* *Pieces* *A Day Book* *Thirty Things* *Away* *Later* *The Collected Poems 1945 – 1975* *Mirrors* *The Memory Gardens* *Windows*	**Ⅶ. 罗伯特·克瑞里** **1. 文学观点** (1) 在内容方面，他完全赞同威廉斯"没有观点，只有事实"的思想，也认同庞德"任何抽象概括陈述的倾向就如爬一个油滑的斜坡。" (2) 在形式方面，克瑞里觉得"形式"的准则不该继续被看作是必要标准，形式不过是内容的延伸。克瑞里的文学标准显然是开放式的。 (3) 克瑞里诗歌的主题通常是爱情、婚姻、复杂的人际关系和两性个体之间的联系。 **2. 主要作品** 《致爱情：1950 – 1960》 《文字》 《早期杂诗的魅力》 《碎片》 《一日记》 《三十件事》 《离开》 《后来》 《1945 – 1975 诗选》 《镜子》 《记忆花园》 《窗》
VIII. Denise Levertov (1923 – 1997) **1. Features of Levertov's Poetry** (1) Over the years Levertov has developed her own poetic views and aesthetic. As a poet, she has a strong sense of mission. Her works have a strong religious dimension.	**Ⅷ. 丹尼斯·莱弗托夫** **1. 莱弗托夫诗歌的特点** (1) 多年来莱弗托夫形成了自己的诗学观点和审美。作为一名诗人，她有种强烈的使命感。她的作品中有浓厚的宗教色彩。

(2) Levertov's poetry demonstrates a clear social purposefulness. She has always been interested in humanitarian politics. Her passion responds to a wide variety of issues, such as the status of women, marriage, eroticism, war, etc.

(2) 莱弗托夫的诗歌展现了一种明确的社会目的性。她一直都对人道主义政治感兴趣。她的热情在各种各样的问题上都有反应,例如女性的地位,婚姻,情欲,战争等。

(3) Many of her poems focus on subjects that are more personal and more directly related to nature.

(3) 她的许多诗歌聚焦于更个人化、更直接贴近自然的题材。

(4) Levertov's differences in the perception of men and women are also very interesting and worth mentioning. This perception is not quite feminist in nature, but very close.

(4) 莱弗托夫对男女认知的差异也是非常有趣值得一提的。这种感知本质上讲不太像女权主义,却很接近。

2. Major works

The Double Image
Here and Now
The Jacob's Ladder
Overland to Islands
With Eyes at the Back of Our Heads
O Taste and See
The Sorrow Dance
Relearning the Alphabet
To Stay Alive
Footprints
The Freeing of the Dust
Life in the Forest
Candles in Babylon
Oblique Prayers
Breathing the Water
A Door in the Hive
Evening Train

2. 主要作品

《双重形象》
《此时此地》
《雅各的梯子》
《群岛之路》
《追随的目光》
《哦,尝尝看看吧》
《悲伤之舞》
《重学字母表》
《活着》
《足迹》
《解放灰尘》
《林中生活》
《巴比伦之烛》
《不虔诚的祷告》
《水中呼吸》
《闹市中的门》
《晚间列车》

IX. Robert Duncan (1919–1988)

1. Literary Points of View

(1) Duncan argues that poetry comes from life and that language is capable of renewal and reordering because of its regenerative power.

(2) Duncan is a love poet. He points out that poetry is the soul of life, a way to give and receive love, and that the most perfect form of life is love. Love is divine.

(3) Throughout his writing career, Duncan believed in the reality of myth and used it to define his role as a poet and the nature of poetry.

IX. 罗伯特·邓肯

1. 文学观点

(1) 邓肯认为,诗歌来源于生活,语言因其再生能力能够进行更新,重列新秩序。

(2) 邓肯是位爱情诗人。他指出诗歌是生命的灵魂,是给予和获得爱的方式,生命最完美的形式就是爱。爱是神圣的。

(3) 在他整个写作生涯,邓肯相信神话的真实性,并用神话来定义自己作为诗人的作用和诗歌的本质。

2. **Major works**	2. **主要作品**
Heavenly City Earthly City	《天国之城与世俗之城》
The Opening of the Field	《开垦土地》
Passages	《路》
Roots and Branches	《根与枝》
Bending the Bow	《开弓》
Ground Work: Before the War	《地基：战前》
Ground Work II: In the Dark	《地基Ⅱ：黑暗中》
"A Poem Beginning with a Line by Pindar"	《以品达诗行开始的诗》
"Often I am Permitted to a Meadow"	《我常回到草地》
"Dove"	《鸽子》

22.2 考研真题与典型题详解

I. Fill in the blanks.

1. The Black Mountain Poets are so called because these poets are associated with ________, or with ________.

II. Multiple Choice

1. Which of the following poets is NOT a member of the New York School?

A. William Burroughs　B. John Ashbery
C. Frank O'Hara　D. Kenneth Koch

2. Which of the following poets is NOT member of the Black Mountain poets?

A. Robert Creeley　B. Robert Duncan　C. Theodore Roethke　D. Charles Olson

Ⅲ. Explain the following terms.

1. Black Mountain poets
2. The New York School

参考答案及解析

I. Fill in the blanks.

1. Black Mountain College; Black Mountain Review

(黑山派诗歌是美国当代的一个诗歌流派。20世纪50年代初，在马萨诸塞州黑山学院任教的查·奥尔逊、罗·邓肯、罗·克瑞利等人创办《黑山评论》杂志，提倡与40年代流行的传统格律体相反的"放射体"诗歌，逐步形成一个流派。)

II. Multiple Choice

1. A　威廉·勃洛斯是垮掉派作家之一。

2. C　西奥多·罗特克是自白派诗人之一。

Ⅲ. Explain the following terms.

1. A loosely associated group of poets that formed an important part of the avant-garde of American poetry in the 1950s, publishing innovative yet disciplined verse in the Black Mountain Review (1954 –57), which became a leading forum of experimental verse. Their experimental yet disci-

plined style took its impetus from the essay "Projective Verse" (1950) by Charles Olson. The Black Mountain School is linked with Charles Olson's theory of "projective verse," which insisted on an open form based on the spontaneity of the breath pause in speech and the typewriter line in writing. The group grew up around the poets Robert Creeley, Robert Duncan, and Charles Olson while they were teaching at Black Mountain.

2. Unlike the Beat and San Franciso poets, the poets of the New York School are not interested in overtly moral questions, and, in general, they steer clear of political issues. They have the best formal educations of any group. The major figures of the New York School are John Ashbery, Frank O'Hara, and Kenneth Koch. They are quintessentially urban, cool, nonreligious, witty with a poignant, pastel sophistication. Their poems are fast moving, full of urban detail, incongruity, and an almost palpable sense of suspended belief. New York City is the fine arts center of America and the birthplace of Abstract Expressionism, a major inspiration of this poetry. Most of the poets worked as art reviewers or museum curators, or collaborated with painters. Perhaps because of their feeling for abstract art, which distrusts figurative shapes and obvious meanings, their work is often difficult to comprehend, as in the later work of John Ashbery (1927 –), perhaps the most influential poet writing today.

第23章　二战后美国小说(1)

23.1　复习笔记

Ⅰ. Overview of postwar novel **1. Historical Background** The optimism in the post-World War II generation was quickly eroded by the Cold War between the great powers. McCarthyism fundamentally poisoned people's lives in the 1950s. The civil rights movement, the emergence of a counter-culture, and the rise of feminism greatly enriched life in the 1960s. And the Vietnam War weighed heavily on people's minds. Life has been complicated by political or radical acts of violence, such as the assassinations of John. F. Kennedy and Martin Luther King, Jr. Everything is caught up in being skeptical. Advances in science and technology have made people feel empowered, but they have also taken the mystery out of life.	**Ⅰ. 二战后小说简介** **1.历史背景** 在二战后的一代中的乐观情绪，很快就被大国之间的冷战削弱了。麦卡锡主义从根本上毒害了人们的50年代的生活。民权运动，反主流文化的出现，女权主义的风起云涌则极大地丰富了60年代的生活。而越南战争使人们的思想沉重。生活因政治上的或激进的暴力行径而变得错综复杂，例如，肯尼迪和马丁·路德·金的遇刺身亡。一切都陷入被质疑中。科学技术方面的进步使人们感觉到力量，但同时也使生活失去了神秘感。
2. Features of postwar novels Between the end of the war and the end of 1960, war novel, Southern novel, Jewish novel, the Beat novel, the Black novel, satire and secular fiction, attracted a great deal of attention. This was followed by fantastic and surrealist fiction, nonfiction, science fiction, dark or absurd humor, parody and popular novel, and experimental novel-writing techniques. Themes included social tyranny, the subjugation of the individual, the search for personal identity, and the writer's self-indulgence in a self-imposed environment.	**2. 战后小说特点** 战末至1960年末期间，战争小说、南方小说、犹太小说、垮掉派小说、黑人小说、讽刺与世俗小说，引起了人们的广泛关注。这之后，又有梦幻与超现实主义小说、非虚构小说、科幻小说、黑色或荒诞幽默小说、模仿与通俗小说、试验小说等。主题则包括社会专制，个人被征服，寻求个人认同，作家在自我环境下的自我放纵等。
Ⅱ. Saul Bellow (1915-2005) **1. Life** Saul Bellow is one of the most famous contemporary American novelists. He was born in Canada to a family of Russian Jewish immigrants and grew up in Chicago. His published his first book, *Dangling Man* in 1944. Over the next half century or so, he wrote a large number of full-length novels, short	**Ⅱ. 索尔·贝洛** **1. 生平** 索尔·贝洛是当代美国最著名的小说家。他出生于加拿大一个俄国犹太移民家庭。他在芝加哥长大。他的第一部小说《摇来晃去的人》发表于1944年。在接下来的半个多世纪，他创作了大量的长篇小

stories and plays, winning numerous awards. His creative career reached its peak in 1976, when he was awarded both the Pulitzer Prize and the Nobel Prize for Literature.

说、短篇小说和剧本，赢得了众多的奖项。1976 年他的创作事业到达巅峰，他同时被授予普利策奖和诺贝尔文学奖。

2. His Themes

Saul Bellow's themes are divided into three main areas. First, he believes that contemporary society is a threat to people's lives and independent personalities. As a result, people living in this environment are prone to paranoia, nervousness, weakness and incompetence to the point of losing their minds. Finally, there is always the theme of the search for truth and values in his works. The process of the search is difficult and painful, but the end result is successful.

2. 主题

索尔·贝洛的主题主要是如下三方面：首先，他认为当代社会对人们的生活和独立人格是个威胁。因此，生活在这种环境中，人们容易偏执多疑、精神紧张、虚弱无能以至失去理智。最后，他的作品中总会有追寻真理及价值观的主题，追寻的过程是困难的、痛苦的，但最终结果却是成功的。

3. Major works

Dangling Man
The Victim
The Adventures of Augie March
Seize the Day
Henderson the Rain King
Herzog
Mosby's Memoirs
Mr. Sammler's Planet
Humboldt's Gift
The Dean's December
More Die of Heartbreak
The Bellarosa Connection
A Theft
Something to Remember Me
The Last Analysis

3. 主要作品

《摇来晃去的人》
《受害者》
《奥吉·马奇历险记》
《只争朝夕》
《雨王汉德森》
《赫索格》
《莫斯比的回忆》
《塞姆勒先生的行星》
《洪堡的礼物》
《院长的十二月》
《更多的人死于伤心》
《贝拉罗莎暗道》
《偷窃》
《以此记住我》
《最后的分析》

Ⅲ. Norman Mailer (1923 – 2007)

Norman Mailer was a multifaceted genius. In addition to being a novelist, he was a metaphysical philosopher, poet, playwright, filmmaker, journalist, politician, and actor. His best-known work is *The Naked and the Dead*.

Ⅲ. 诺曼·梅勒

诺曼·梅勒是多方面的天才。除了是小说家之外，他还是形而上学哲学家、诗人、剧作家、电影制作人、记者、政治家、演员。他最知名的作品是《裸者与死者》。

◆Major works

The Naked and the Dead
Barbary Shore
The Deer Park
The Armies of the Night

◆主要作品

《裸者与死者》
《北非之岸》
《鹿园》
《夜幕下的大军》

Marilyn: A Novel Biography
The Execution's Song
Ancient Evening
Tough Guys Don't Dance
Harlot's Ghost
The Gospel According to the son
Advertisement for Myself
An American Dream
Why Are We in Vietnam?
Miami and the Siege of Chicago
Existential Errands
Genies and Lust
"The White Negro"

《玛莉琳：小说体传记》
《刽子手之歌》
《古老的夜晚》
《硬汉不跳舞》
《哈洛特的鬼影》
《圣子福音》
《我自己的广告》
《美国梦》
《我们为什么在越南?》
《迈阿密和芝加哥之围》
《存在主义的使命》
《天才与欲望》
《白色黑人》

Ⅳ. J. D. Salinger (1919 – 2010)

1. Life

J. D. Salinger was born in New York City to a Jewish middle-class family. Shy and unsociable as a child, he entered the Valle Foch Military Academy at the age of 15, where he felt uncomfortable. This school later became the model for *The Catcher in the Rye*. Many aspects of the protagonist Holden's life replicate Salinger's experiences at this school. Salinger is a unique writer. He has written only one full-length novel, for which he has become famous. For decades afterward, he lived in seclusion in his New Hampshire home, refusing interviews and other means of contact with the media and the outside world. He died on January 27th, 2010, at the age of 91.

2. Major works

The Catcher in the Rye
"The Young Folks"
"Slight Rebellion off Madison"
"I'm Crazy"
Nine Story
Franny and Zooey
Raise High the Roof Beam, Carpenters; and Seymour: An Introduction

Ⅳ. 杰罗姆·大卫·塞林格

1. 生平

塞林格出生于纽约市一个犹太中产阶级家庭。他幼时腼腆、不爱交际。15岁时进入瓦利福奇军校，在这里他感觉不能适应。这所学校后来成为《麦田里的守望者》的原型。主人公霍尔顿生活的诸多方面复制了塞林格在这所学校的经历。塞林格是一位独特的作家。他只写过一部长篇小说，并因此而扬名。之后数十年，他隐居在新罕布什尔的家中，拒绝采访和其他与媒体及外界联系的方式。他死于2010年1月27日，享年91岁。

2. 主要作品

《麦田里的守望者》
《年轻人》
《麦迪逊街边的小乱子》
《我疯了》
《九篇故事》
《弗拉尼和佐伊》
《木工们，升高顶梁；及西摩介绍》

Ⅴ. Bernard Malamud (1914 – 1986)

Bernard Malamud is considered one of the major Jewish writers of the postwar period. Most of his works are about Jews and their lives.

Ⅴ. 伯纳德·马拉穆德

伯纳德·马拉穆德被认为是战后时期主要的犹太作家之一。他的大多数作品都是关于犹太人及其生活。

◆**Major works**	◆**主要作品**
The Natural	《天生有才能的人》
The Assistant	《店员》
A New Life	《新生活》
The Fixer	《基辅怨》
The Tenants	《房客》
Pictures of Fidelman	《费德尔曼写照》
Dubin's Lives	《杜宾的生活》
God's Grace	《上帝的恩惠》
The People	《人们》
The Magic Barrel	《魔桶》
Idiots First	《白痴第一》
Rembrandt's Hat	《拉姆布兰特的帽子》
Ⅵ. John Updike (1932 – 2009)	**Ⅵ. 约翰·厄普代克**
◆**Major works**	◆**主要作品**
The Centaur	《半人半马》
Couples	《夫妻们》
Marry Me	《同我结婚》
Gertrude & Claudius	《格特鲁德与克劳迪斯》
Rabbit, Run	《兔子快跑》
Rabbit Redux	《兔子归来》
Rabbit Is Rich	《兔子阔了》
Rabbit at Rest	《兔子歇了》
Licks of Love	《怀念兔子》
Ⅶ. John Cheever (1912 – 1982)	**Ⅶ. 约翰·契弗**
◆**Major works**	◆**主要作品**
The Stories of John Cheever	《约翰·契弗短篇小说集》
The Wapshot Chronicle	《维普肖特记事》
The Wapshot Scandal	《维普肖特丑闻》
Bullet Park	《布里特公园》
Falconer	《猎鹰者》
Oh What a Paradise It Seems	《啊，那多么像天堂》
"Swimmer"	《游泳者》
Ⅷ. Flannery O'Connor (1925 – 1964)	**Ⅷ. 弗兰纳里·奥康纳**
◆**Major works**	◆**主要作品**
Wise Blood	《慧血》
A Good Man Is Hard to Find	《好人难寻》
The Violent Bear It Away	《暴力得逞》
Everything That Rises Must Converge	《水到渠成》

Ⅸ. William Styron (1925 – 2006) ◆**Major works** *Lie Down in Darkness* *Set This House on Fire* *The Confessions of Nat Turner* *Sophie's Choice* *The Long March*	**Ⅸ. 威廉·史泰伦** ◆**主要作品** 《在黑暗中躺下》 《放火烧屋》 《奈特·特纳的自白》 《索菲的选择》 《长途行军》
Ⅹ. Truman Capote (1924 – 1984) ◆**Major works** *Other Voices, Other Rooms* *The Grass Harp* *A Christmas Memory* *Breakfast at Tiffany's* *In Cold Blood*	**Ⅹ. 杜鲁门·卡波特** ◆**主要作品** 《其他声音，其他房间》 《草竖琴》 《圣诞回忆》 《蒂凡尼早餐》 《冷血》
Ⅺ. Philip Roth (1933 –) ◆**Major works** *Goodbye, Columbus and Five Short Story* *Portnoy's Complaint*	**Ⅺ. 菲利普·罗斯** ◆**主要作品** 《再见，哥伦布，及五个短篇故事》 《波特诺伊的抱怨》
Ⅻ. Joyce Carol Oates (1938 –) ◆**Major works** *Them* *Wonderland* *Do with Me What You Will*	**Ⅻ. 乔伊斯·卡罗尔·欧茨** ◆**主要作品** 《他们》 《奇境》 《对我爱怎样就怎样》

23.2 考研真题与典型题详解

Ⅰ. Fill in the blanks.

1. *Seize the Day* was written by ________. （大连外国语学院 2008 研）
2. A very influential book to come out of the post-war world is a novel by J. D. Salinger entitled ________.（南开大学 2008 研）
3. John Cheever has written some of the finest short stories, and he wrote mainly about the ________ people.

Ⅱ. Multiple Choice

1. The post-World War Ⅱ period wasn't a peaceful one for America. The life of the 1950s was poisoned at the root by ________, and that of the sixties enriched by ________. Whereas ________ weighted all the time on the consciousness of the people, life was complicated by violence, political or racial, including the assassination of ________ and ________.
2. The experimental feature of *The Naked and the Dead* merits attention. In it, Norman Mailer wedges ________ and ________ into otherwise normal narrative.
3. The title of J. D. Salinger's novel *The Catcher in the Rye* comes from ________ poem "if a

body catch a body coming from the rye".

A. William Wordsworth　　B. William Black

C. Alfred Tennyson　　D. Robert Burns

4. Which of the following is NOT a southern writer in the USA?

A. Saul Bellow　　B. Tennessee Williams

C. Eudora Welty　　D. Flannery O' Connor

Ⅲ. Explain the following term.

1. Modernism

Ⅳ. Short answer question

1. Comment briefly on Saul Bellow's theme.

参考答案及解析

I. Fill in the blanks.

1. Saul Bellow

（索尔·贝洛，美国作家，1976 年荣获诺贝尔文学奖，瑞典皇家学会授奖时特别提及他的小说《只争朝夕》，认为是现代典型作品之一。）

2. *The Catcher in the Rye*

（《麦田里的守望者》是塞林格最著名的作品，描写的是一个叛逆的中学生霍尔顿。）

3. suburban middle class

（约翰·契弗(John Cheever)当代美国著名的短篇小说家，其小说主要描写郊区中产阶级生活。其最著名的短篇小说为《游泳者》"The Swimmer"。）

II. Multiple Choice

1. McCarthyism; the Civil Rights Movement; the Vietnam War; John F. Kennedy; Martin Luther King

（二战后美国并不太平。50 年代麦卡锡主义(McCarthyism)，60 年代的民权运动(the Civil Rights Movement)，越战(the Vietnam War)，及约翰·肯尼迪(John F. Kennedy)和马丁·路德·金(Martin Luther King)的遇刺都使美国人的思想不断经历着冲击。）

2. "chorus"; "the time machine"

（诺曼·梅勒(Norman Mailer)的作品《裸者与死者》(*The Naked and the Dead*)成为美国战争小说史上里程碑式的作品，其主题在于表现兽性与理想在人类心灵中的搏斗。该小说中诺曼·梅勒成功地运用了"副歌"("chorus")和"时间机器"("the time machine")的手法。）

3. D　J. D. 赛林格代表作是《麦田里的守望者》(*The Catcher in the Rye*)。这部小说的题目选自于罗伯特·彭斯的诗句"if a body catch a body coming from the rye"。

4. A　索尔·贝洛是著名的犹太作家，他出生于加拿大，在芝加哥长大，因而不是南方作家。

Ⅲ. Explain the following term

1. It's a general term applied to the wide range of experimental and avant-garde trends in literature of the early 20th century, including Symbolism, Futurism, Expressionism, Imagism, Vorticism, Dada, and Surrealism. Modernist literature is characterized chiefly by a rejection of 19th century

traditions: the conventions of realism, for instance, were abandoned by Franz Kafka and other novelists, and by expressionist drama, while several poets rejected traditional meters in favor of free verse. Modernist writers tended to see themselves as an avant-garde disengaged from bourgeois values, and disturbed their readers by adopting complex and difficult new forms and styles. In fiction, the accepted continuity of chronological development was upset by Joseph Conrad, and William Faulkner, while James Joyce and Virginia Woolf attempted new ways of tracing the flow of characters' thoughts in their stream-of-consciousness styles. In poetry, Ezra Pound and T. S. Eliot replaced the logical exposition of thoughts with collages of fragmentary images and complex allusions. Modernist writing is predominantly cosmopolitan, and often expresses a sense of urban cultural dislocation, along with an awareness of new anthropological and psychological theories. Its favored techniques of juxtaposition and multiple point of view challenge the reader to reestablish a coherence of meaning from fragmentary forms.

Ⅳ. Short answer question

1. Saul Bellow's themes are divided into three main areas. First, he believes that contemporary society is a threat to people's lives and independent personalities. Modern civilization tends to dehumanize, making people lose their distinction and turning them into what he calls "fat goods". Material abundance distracts people and separates them from each other. As a result, people living in this environment are prone to paranoia, nervousness, weakness and incompetence to the point of losing their minds. Bellow's characters are most likely to suffer from certain psychosis. They go through a phase before they regain their mental balance and serenity. F Finally, there is always the theme of the search for truth and values in his works. The process of the search is difficult and painful, but the end result is successful. To Saul Bellow, human's search for affirmation should have a happy ending, and people should see light in the end. The emotions of his characters are a mixture of sadness and joy, but in the end, they are all happy. He is indeed a very human writer.

第 24 章　二战后美国小说(2)

24.1　复习笔记

Ⅰ. The Postmodernist Novel

1. Historical Background

Social, political, and artistic life in America are in turmoil when America moves into the 1960s. A wide range of social, political and artistic restlessness disturbed the thinking minds in the decades of 1960s and 1970s (It is necessary to remember a few things listed in the book such as the Vietnam war). American are more concerned about their society with the help of flooding information from various channels. The principles of democracy, individualism, and the credibility of the government all changed evidently in nature. So does popular awareness. It is noted that there is only a faint line or none between fact and fiction.

2. Postmodernist Novel

There was the novel of the absurd, metafiction, and avant-gardism.

(1) Old-fashioned novelistic devices are usually satirized by the novelists of the absurd. They believe it is impossible to grasp a certain truth and reality and that it is invalid for any traditional literary form to be faithful to reality. Their works often portrays the tragic absurdity of the human condition as a huge joke. Therefore, their works share some common devices such as black humor or black comedy. It is probable to see a feeling of frustration and dilemma as well as a sense of suffering comes through the laughter.

(2) Metafiction is fiction about fiction. It opposes realism but makes readers aware of fiction is fiction and makes readers to shape a reality for themselves. Text within text, authorial personae, and undecidability with no real story are among a series of metafictional approaches.

Ⅰ. 后现代主义小说

1. 历史背景

自美国步入 20 世纪 60 年代，美国社会、政治和艺术生活都处在不安动荡之中。一系列动荡不安的社会，政治和艺术生活现象强烈冲击着人们的思想(有必要识记书中列举的几种事件，比如越战)。信息通过各种渠道涌来，这使得大众对社会的关注更加强烈。民权主义、个人主义、政府的可信度等都发生了质的变化，公众的意识也发生了相似的改变。人们发现事实和虚幻之间的界限不再那么明显，甚至是不再存在了。

2. 后现代小说

后现代主义出现了荒诞小说，元小说和先驱小说。

(1) 荒诞主义小说家常常嘲弄传统小说技巧。他们认为真理和现实都是多样的、捉摸不透的、不稳定的；他们觉得任何自称能真实展现现实的传统形式都是不合逻辑、具有误导性的。人类境况的悲剧荒诞性在他们的作品中经常表现为特大笑话。小说家多采用的黑色幽默或是黑色喜剧。通常笑声传递出的更多的是悲哀和痛苦，苦恼和被困的感觉。

(2) 元小说以小说形式写作，又是一种有关小说的写作形式。它反对现实主义，使用小说的叙述风格，力图告诉读者小说就是小说，让读者自己去找到一种现实。重要的元小说技巧包括互为文本、原著者人物和没有真实故事的不可判定性。

(3) Avant-gardism is a usual term for postwar writing which possesses forefront literary techniques. An avant-garde novel departs from novelistic norms, often not readable, even insulting to middlebrow taste.

(3) 先驱主义被用来指具有先驱位置的战后作品。先驱小说代表着与普通小说标准的完全脱离，通常很少或几乎没有故事趣味性，不仅枯燥无味，而且不为受过一般教育的读者所喜欢，大都没有可读性。

Ⅱ. Joseph Heller (1923–1999)

Ⅱ. 约瑟夫·海勒

The most important American novelist of the absurd after the second World War is Joseph Heller. His famous *Catch-22* is based on his war experience, the title of which now is an English phrase.

约瑟夫·海勒是美国二战后最杰出的荒诞派小说家。著名的《第二十二条军规》是以其战争经历为基础写就的，其标题已经成为英语语言中的一个新的词汇。

1. Major Works

Catch-22

Something Happened

We Bombed in New Haven

Good as Gold

God Knows

1. 主要作品

《第二十二条军规》

《出了毛病》

《我们轰炸纽黑文》

《好的不得了》

《上帝知道》

2. Analysis of major work

◆*Catch-22*

(1) *Catch-22* was the first book in America to employ absurdist techniques to portray absurdity. The military power structure in the book is an objection to the absurdity of modern America.

(2) The protagonist, Yossarian, is afraid of death. He is no longer faithful to God, and feels insecure. The sight of death and absurdity frightens him and his fellow pilots.

(3) The world of Yossarian is absurd. The way Heller reveals it is through parody. Three major features satirize fully the military unreason: the structured turmoil of the military organization, the military logic (the typical symbol is the rule "Catch-22"), and the ubiquitous absurdity.

(4) The absurd depth of the modern world is reflected by Joseph Heller's absurd linguistic superficial appearance. The absurdity of the mad world is exposed deftly by the following devices: "circular conversations", constructions with their

2. 主要作品分析

◆《第二十二条军规》

(1)《第二十二条军规》是美国第一部以荒诞技巧表现荒诞主题的著作，它以对军队情景的具体描述抗议现代美国社会的荒诞性。

(2) 故事的主人公，飞行员尤索林，害怕自己会死去，他对上帝失去了信仰，再也没有了安全感。他和其他伙伴一起惊恐地目睹了发生在身边的死亡和荒诞事件。

(3) 尤索林所在的是一个荒诞的世界，通过三个特点，海勒对军队的荒谬性进行了残酷讽刺：即军队结构中的组织混乱，军事逻辑（其象征之一就是"第二十二条军规"）和各个层面上分布的荒诞性。

(4) 约瑟夫海勒运用了荒诞的语言表象来反映现代社会的荒诞程度之深。许多文学手法，如"循环式对话"问答极其幽默并出人意料；"套语"的运用，即把俗语中关键字眼换成能产生荒谬效果的字词；谈话语气的突然变化，即由严肃话

funny, unexpected responses, the "wrenched cliché" which is a consequence of the change of "a key word in an otherwise hackneyed expression," juxtaposed incongruities, sudden tonal changes from seriousness to triviality.

题到琐细话题的突然跳跃和转换等等诸如此类的文学修辞手法。这些手法的巧妙结合，使小说的文字呈现一种荒诞状貌，有力地表现了一个疯狂世界缺乏理智和逻辑以及不可预料的特点。

Ⅲ. Kurt Vonnegut (1922 –2007)

Vonnegut is basically a science fiction writer. His short stories are also famous where he skillfully combines black humor with science fiction.

1. Major Works

Player Piano

Mother Night

Cat's Cradle

Slaughterhouse-Five

Breakfast of Champions

Slapsticks

Jailbird

Deadeye Dick

Galapagos

Bluebird

Hocus Pocus

Canary in a Cathouse

Welcome to the Monkey House

2. Analysis of major work

◆*Slaughterhouse-Five*

(1) *Slaughterhouse-Five* is an antiwar novel. It not only delineates life and history but also disapproves human's brutality against human during the war, which is the root cause of life's misery.

(2) Death is a common phenomenon in the novel and is always concluded by "So it goes", a phrase that mixes so many emotional shades such as anger, agony, apathy, helplessness, and cynic distaste at life and history. He implies that history is either meaningless or purposeless, and the human dilemma does not bother God. Life is so absurd that the people's attitude toward life is nihilistic.

Ⅲ. 库尔特·冯内古特

冯内古特基本上是一位科幻作家。他同时也是一位短篇小说家。他善于在短篇作品中将黑色幽默和科幻相结合。

1. 主要作品

《自动钢琴》

《黑夜母亲》

《猫的摇篮》

《第五号屠宰场》

《冠军的早餐》

《滑稽剧》

《囚鸟》

《神枪手迪克》

《加拉帕戈斯群岛》

《蓝鸟》

《咒语》

《猫舍里的金丝雀》

《欢迎来到猴子屋》

2. 主要作品分析

◆《第五号屠宰场》

(1)《第五号屠场》是一部反战小说。它不仅描述了生活和历史如何如何，也谴责了战争中人类对彼此的野蛮残酷。后者使得生活变得悲惨。

(2) 小说中一百次提到了死亡，而且每次都伴随着"就这么回事"的语句，这个短语包含了对生活和历史的愤怒、痛苦、冷漠、无助、愤世嫉俗的厌恶这样多种感情色彩。作者暗示着历史既没有意义，也没有目的，上帝对人类的困境丝毫没有兴趣。生命是荒诞的，偶然的和尴尬的，所以人们似乎不在意它的结束。

(3) The structure of the book confirms the absurdity in the book. The stream of consciousness dealing with time strengthens the absurdity. (4) Black humor also strengthens the absurdity in the book. **Ⅳ. Ken Kesey (1935 – 2001)** Ken Kesey was another well-known novelist of the absurd. **◆Major Works** *One Flew Over the Cuckoo's Nest* *Sometimes a Great Notion* *Demon Box* *Sailor Song* **Ⅴ. John Barth (1930 –)** He is a highly significant writer of the period. His credited 1967 essay "The Literature of Exhaustion" marked the beginning of postmodern and metafictional fiction in America and claims the end of conventional realism. **◆Major works** *The Floating Opera* *The End of the Road* *The Scot-Weed Factor* *Lost in the Funhouse* *Letters: A Novel* *Sabbatical: A Romance* *The Tidewater Tales* *The Friday Book* *Giles Goat-Boy* **Ⅵ. Donald Barthelme (1931 – 1989)** Barthelme was a short story writer, a novelist, and a writer of children's literature. **◆Major Works** *Come Back, Dr. Caligarri* *Unspeakable Practices, Unnatural Acts* *City Life* *Sadness* *Guilty Pleasures* *Amateurs* *Great Days* *Overnight to Many Distant Cities*	(3) 生活的荒诞主题通过其结构得到加强，处理时间的方式是使用了意识流。 (4) 黑色幽默使得这部作品的荒诞特点得到加强。 **Ⅳ. 肯·克西** 肯·克西是另一位著名的荒诞派小说家。 **◆主要作品** 《飞越疯人院》 《永不让步》 《恶魔的盒子》 《水手之歌》 **Ⅴ. 约翰·巴思** 他是这一时期重要的作家。其为人称道的一件事是，他在 1967 年写了一篇文章《枯竭的文学》，这篇文章标志着美国后现代和超小说的开端，也宣布了传统现实主义的死亡。 **◆主要作品** 《浮动的歌剧》 《路的尽头》 《烟草代理商》 《迷失在娱乐场中》 《书信集》 《假日浪漫史》 《湖边的故事》 《星期五札记》 《羊孩贾尔思》 **Ⅵ. 唐纳德·巴塞尔姆** 巴塞尔姆是一位短篇故事家、小说家、儿童文学作家。 **◆主要作品** 《回来吧，卡里加利博士》 《不可言说的做法，不自然的行为》 《城市生活》 《悲伤》 《心感内疚的娱乐》 《业余爱好者》 《美好的日子》 《通宵畅游许多遥远的城市》

Snow White
The Dead Father
The King
The Slightly Irregular Fire Engine

《白雪公主》
《亡父》
《国王》
《不太规则的消防车》

Ⅶ. Thomas Pynchon (1937 –)

Ⅶ. 托马斯·品钦

Thomas Pynchon is a contemporary writer with his life unknown. The publication of the *Gravity's Rainbow* won him the National Book Award and has since received enormous critical attention. It ensured Pynchon's prominence in American postmodern fiction.

托马斯·品钦是当代作家中生平鲜为人所知的一个。他的作品《万有引力之虹》获得了国家图书奖并吸引了评论界的关注，这奠定了他在美国后现代小说界的杰出地位。

1. Literary theories

1. 文学理论

Scientific and technologic theories, which helps to explain Pynchon's thematic worries, play a principal role through Pynchon's writing career. These include entropy and the quantum theory. Entropy is a physics term, denoting the tendency of the universe toward uniformity. Quantum theory thinks that uncertainty is immanent in everything, and that human's knowledge is false. His entropic vision sees the mechanical civilization puts humans at risk. It leads to dehumanization of humans and reduces them into "inanimate automation".

品钦在写作生涯中借鉴了科学技术理论，并将它们作为作品中传递消息的原理，包括熵和量子理论。熵是物理名词，指示着宇宙走向统一的趋势。品钦也同样对量子理论着迷，根据该理论，所有的事物包含一定程度的不确定性，扩充来说，人类的知识是不准确的。这些理论很好地反映了品钦的主题思想。在他关于熵的看法里，机械文明的威胁会使人们失去人性，将他们变为灰暗的"死气沉沉的自动机器"。

2. Major Works

2. 主要作品

V.
The Crying of Lot 49
Gravity's Rainbow
Vineland
Mason & Dixon
Slow Learner: Early Stories

《V.》
《第四十九组拍卖邮票的呼唤》
《万有引力之虹》
《葡萄园》
《梅森和迪克森》
《笨鸟集》

Ⅷ. William Burroughs (1914 – 1997)

Ⅷ. 威廉·勃洛斯

William Burroughs was the oldest of the Beat writers.

威廉·勃洛斯是"垮掉的一代"作家中最为年长的一位。

1. Features of his works

1. 作品特点

Drugs, perverse ways of living, violence, and homosexuality are the themes of his works which are devoted to portraying life in its oddest form. He likes to think and communicate distinctly from accepted standards. Burroughs enjoyed shocking his readers out of their accustomed perceptive patterns and delighted in distracting them from their self-satisfaction.

他只写毒品、变态生活、暴力和同性恋题材，总之，就是关于生活最奇异和古怪的形式。他的作品展示了不同于普通标准的思考和交流状态。博罗斯喜欢使读者震惊，脱离他们的常规理解方式，他非常着迷于将让他们从舒适自得中转移注意力。

2. Major works

Junkie

The Exterminator

The Wild Boys

Cities of the Red Light

Queer

Mind Wars

The Naked Lunch

Place of Dead Roads

Ⅸ. Jack Kerouac (1922 – 1969)

Jack Kerouac was, along with Ginsberg and Burroughs, representative of the Beat generation of the 1950s.

1. Writing style

Kerouac is famous for his "spontaneous prose", an experimental style that made him disregard accepted rules and restraints in writing. He declared that he found this style in 1951. It is rapid writing like jazz, emphasizing improvisation and neglecting steadiness. *On the Road* is a good example of "spontaneous prose".

2. Major Works

The Subterraneans

Maggie Cassady

The Lonesome Traveler

On the Road

3. Analysis of major work

◆*On the Road*

Tensions, conflicts, and abnormal themes in the book are attractive to the imagination of the readers, though it has neither an obvious dramatic interest nor an obvious plot line. Alcoholics, junkies, and jazz musicians are common characters in the book. Although the two protagonists, Dean Moriarty and Sal Paradise, are both depraved drug addicts they still grope for their truth. *On the Road* is a story immune to life pressure, featuring a sympathetic first-person narrator and a confessional style.

2. 主要作品

《吸毒者》

《灭虫者》

《放荡的人们》

《红夜城》

《同性恋》

《思想战争》

《裸露午餐》

《死路之地》

Ⅸ. 杰克·凯鲁瓦克

杰克·凯鲁瓦克和金斯堡、勃洛斯一起，是20世纪50年代年轻骚动一代的代表人物。

1. 写作风格

克鲁亚克的实验性写作风格叫做"自发式散文"，这使得他能摆脱一般写作规则和局限，自由地写作。他宣称在1951年发现了这种方式。这种写作方式基本不用时间思考、较少进行修改，像爵士乐一样自由、快速，没有固定的音调。《在路上》是这种写作风格的典型例子。

2. 主要作品

《地下者》

《麦吉·凯萨迪》

《孤独的旅行者》

《在路上》

3. 主要作品分析

◆《在路上》

作品属于散文叙述体，没有多少戏剧性，也没有什么情节，有的只是悬而未决的紧张局面，让人身心疲惫的冲突，和非传统的主题，明显地吸引着读者的想象力。作品中许多角色都是酒鬼、瘾君子和爵士音乐家等。迪恩莫里亚蒂和萨尔帕拉斯蒂两个主角都是吸毒成瘾者，虽然堕落却还仍在摸索着属于他们的真理。《在路上》由一位富有同情心的第一人称叙述者讲述，使用忏悔式风格，是一个关于从生活的重压下得到自由的故事。

X. Vladimir Nabokov (1899 – 1977)	X. 弗拉基米尔·纳博科夫
He was from a wealthy family in St. Petersburg of Czarist Russia. He studied Romance languages and literature in Trinity College, Cambridge University. His immigration to America in 1940 indicated a turning point of his career. He was a classic postmodern and metafiction writer. ◆**Major Works** *Lolita* *Dar, or the Gift* *Pale Fire*	弗拉基米尔·纳博科夫出生在沙皇俄国圣彼得堡的一个富有家庭。他在剑桥大学三一学院学习罗曼语言和文学。1940 年移居美国成为他事业的转折点。他是一位典型的后现代和超小说作家。 ◆**主要作品** 《洛丽塔》 《献礼，又名天赋》 《微暗的火》

24.2 考研真题与典型题详解

I. Fill in the blanks.

1. ________ by Joseph Heller is the representative novel of black humor. (南开大学 2008 研)
2. A great postmodern writer, ________ became the cult figure of the counterculture generation at that time, known as "a gum for the youth" in supporting the students in their anti-war movements.

II. Multiple Choice

1. ________ wrote the essay "The Literature of Exhaustion" and was the first to announce that the traditional novel is dead, and that traditional novelistic resources have been exhausted.
   A. Donald Barthelme　　B. John Barth
   C. Kurt Vonnegut　　D. Vladimir Nabokov
2. Out of the fifty-two paragraphs that make up the story of *Lost in the Funhouse* by John Barth, five consist wholly of the author's chat about fiction writing, which is the typical feature of ________.
   A. metafiction　　B. poststructuralist fiction
   C. dystopian fiction　　D. black humor fiction
3. Which of the following is not Thomas Pynchon's works?
   A. *V.*　　B. *The Crying of Lot 49*
   C. *Gravity's Rainbow*　　D. *Letters*
4. William Burroughs and Jack Kerouac belong to ________.
   A. the Confessional School　　B. the Black Mountain Poets
   C. novelists of absurdity　　D. the Beat Writers
5. Which beat-poet wrote the work *On the Road*?
   A. Allen Ginsberg.　　B. Jack Kerouac.
   C. William Burroughs.　　D. Charles Bukowski.

III. Explain the following terms.

1. Postmodernism (北航 2010 研)
2. Yossarian (from: *Catch-22*) (厦门大学 2008 研)

3. Surrealism
4. Expressionism
5. Black humor（厦门大学 2010 研）
6. Metafiction

Ⅳ. Short answer questions

1. What are the formal characteristics of postmodern writings (list at least three).
2. What ideas does Thomas Pynchon want to express by the obscure identity of V in the novel *V.*?

Ⅴ. Essay questions

1. What brought the change from Modernism to Postmodernism in postwar American literature?
2. How do you understand the novel of the absurd of the 1960s?

参考答案及解析

Ⅰ. Fill in the blanks.

1. *Catch-22*

（《第二十二条军规》是约瑟夫·海勒的著名小说，也是黑色幽默的代表作。）

2. Kurt Vonnegut

（在上世纪 60－70 年代的美国大学里，年轻学生们常常把库尔特·冯内古特的书揣在牛仔裤兜里，他让前卫小说变得好读、有趣，成为美国黑色幽默文学代表人物。）

Ⅱ. Multiple Choice

1. B　约翰·巴斯在 1967 年写了一篇文章《枯竭的文学》，这篇文章标志着美国后现代和超小说的开端，也宣布了传统现实主义的死亡。

2. A　超小说（metafiction）是有关小说的小说：是关注小说的虚构身份及其创作过程的小说。小说的叙述往往在谈论正在进行的叙述本身，并使这种对叙述的叙述成为小说整体的一部分。

3. D　D 项不是品钦的作品。

4. D　美国作家威廉·巴勒斯（William Burroughs）与艾伦·金斯堡（Allen Ginsberg）及杰克·凯鲁亚克（Jack Kerouac）同为"垮掉的一代"文学运动的创始者。

5. B　《在路上》是"垮掉的一代"作家杰克·凯鲁亚克的代表作。

Ⅲ. Explain the following terms.

1. Postmodernism: Postmodernism is a disputed term that has occupied much recent debate about contemporary culture since the early 1980s. It is said to be a culture of fragmentary sensations, eclectic nostalgia, disposable simulacra, and promiscuous superficiality, in which the traditionally valued qualities of depth, coherence, meaning, originality, and authenticity are evacuated or dissolved amid the random swirl of empty signals. It seems to have no relevance to modern poetry, and little to drama, but is used widely in reference to fiction, notably to the novels (or anti-novels) and stories of Thomas Pynchon, Kurt Vonnegut, Italo Calvino, Vladimir Nabokov, William S. Burroughs, and Angela Carter.

2. In *Catch-22*, Yossarian is a 28-year-old Captain in the 256th squadron of the Army Air Forces where he serves as a B-25 bombardier stationed on the small island of Pianosa during World War

II. Throughout the novel, Yossarian's main concern is the idea that people are trying to kill him, and he goes to great lengths to try to prevent his death.

3. Surrealism is a literary and art movement, influenced by Freudianism, dedicated to expressing the imagination as revealed in dreams, free of the conscious control of reason and convention. Founded in Paris by Andre Breton with his Manifesto of Surrealism, it can be traced back to Rimbaud, and Baudelaire. In literature, surrealism was confined almost exclusively to France, and was based on the associations and implications of words. Surrealism was a major intellectual force between the wars.
4. The term refers to a movement in Germany early in the 20th century, in which a number of painters sought to avoid the representation of external reality and instead, to project a highly personal vision of the world. The main principle involved is that expression determines form, and therefore imagery, punctuation, syntax, and so on. In belief, any of the formal rules and elements of writing can be bent or disjointed to suit the purpose. Theatrically, expressionism was a reaction against realism in that it tends to show inner psychological realities. O'Neill's plays are some of the best examples.
5. It is a kind of writing that places grotesque elements side by side with humorous ones in an attempt to shock the readers, forcing him or her to laugh at the horrifying reality of a disordered world. It is a humor out of despair and laughter out of tears. Black humor conveys anguish and fury at conditions in which institutionalized absurdity gets the upper hand. It intends to satirize hypocrisy, racial prejudice, and above all the dehumanization of the individual by a modern society. Black humor prevails in modern American Literature. Joseph Heller's Novel *Catch-22* is considered a superb example of the use of Black humor. Kurt Vonnegut's *Slaughterhouse Five* is also a case in point.
6. Metafiction is a literary term popularized by Robert Scholes to describe novels that specifically and self-consciously examine the nature and status of fiction itself and that often contain experiments to test fiction as a form in one way or another. Postmodernist writers tend to apply metafiction in their works, for instance, John Barth's *Lost in the Funhouse* and John Fowles's *The French Lieutenant's Woman.*

IV. Short answer questions

1. Postmodern writers tend to (1) apply metafictional techniques; (2) use parody; (3) employ literary collage; (4) aim at the deconstruction of genres; (5) have fragmented narratives; (6) discontinuity, uncertainty, and disorder in time and plot, etc.
2. V is the person/thing that the protagonist wants to seek in the story. V seems to have many identities, which puzzles the protagonist. The author wants to show that the world is full of uncertainties and that it is impossible to gain access to the truth.

V. Essay questions

1. In terms of the idea of art, in the 1890s and the first years of the 20th century art and poetry were regarded as the finished products of the creative process, closed in form, with rhymes and stanzas, coherent images and figures, and completed in plot enacted. While art and poetry of Post-

modernism are seen as open, on-going, not as the end of thought, but as the process of the mind thinking, stressing motion, created on the impulse of the moment, and not previously well-planned. And there is not much of the finely metered Modernist poem in the new verse that, instead of aiming at an elite readership, endeavors to the common people as much as possible.

Thematically, the new poetry normally portrays everyday experiences, events, and emotions. It envisions man as vulnerable and helpless and at the mercy of overwhelming odds. It accepts life for what it is, feeling resigned, painfully aware of its inability to control and contain life. Instead of trying to "give shape and significance to the immense panorama of futility and anarchy that is contemporaneous history" (as Eliot puts it), the new verse tries to represent life as it is with its strengths and weaknesses, as something inconsistent, ever changing, and never wholly knowable. The poets' job is, seen by some people, to seize the moment and make the best of it for themselves as well as for the world at large.

As regards formal considerations, the new verse embraces open form, "the perfect, easy discipline of the swallow's dip and swoop, without east to west" (as Gary Snyder puts it). It repudiates the Eliotic, New Critical values of impersonality and objectivity as distancing art from life. It refuses to use "persona" as they feel it separates the writers from their readers. In the new verse, there is very often autobiographical; the tone is personal and emotional; the emotions are often intense though qualifies: there is ambivalence and humor amid remorse, disgust of anguish. The diction of the new verse is mostly from daily speech, its style is conversational, colloquial, discursive and meditative, and its mood generally casual and relaxed. It is necessary to note here that contemporary American poetry is not always easy to read. In fact, much of this poetry is very hard to understand. Possible reasons for this may include the private nature of the poet's thinking and expression, and their self-indulgence encouraged by the postmodern tendency of extreme individualization.

2. The notion that the universe is absurd was not really new to American authors. But the "absurd" novelists of the sixties tend to regard the conventional novel as "literature of exhaustion". To them the old ways of presentation are no longer good enough, and even obsolete. To reflect the new, stupefying and sickening reality, these conventions must be updated, while at the same time new devices should be found. The 1960s and 1970s proved to be a period in which the common run of humanity had also come to sense absurdity existing on all conceivable levels of life, and it fell to the "absurd" novelists to discover a new rhetoric effective enough to voice that feeling in literature.

The novelists of the absurd tend to burlesque traditional novelistic devices. They parody other novels, other styles and forms and take them with highly equivocal attitudes: they want to prove the artificiality of any literary art which, by pretending to bring order to reality, falsifies it and keeps people from comprehending its absurdity. The universe is out of joint. It is a tragic place to live in. The response they intend to provoke in the reader to the blackness of modern life is laughter that is, laughing in face of a tragic situation. Hence black humor, or black comedy, is one of the commonly employed devices of the novelists of the absurd. What occurs oftener is a sense of grief and pain coming through the laughter, a feeling of frustration and being bottle up.

The writers of the absurd tend to accept the world as it is. They regard these features of modern existence as normal and locate themselves within the messiness of their world. They attempt to generate meaning in the face of, but without denying chaos and absurdity. For them uncertainty is the rule. Because they believe that the self constitutes part and parcel of the world, involvement, immersion, and participation become their ethic.

第25章 多种族文学(1)

25.1 复习笔记

Ⅰ. Overview of African American Literature 1. African American literature develops from oral tradition in the form of songs, ballads, and spirituals. The folk literature in its various manifestations contributes to Afro-American literature. 2. The abolitionist movement and the Civil War inspired African American literature. After the Emancipation, the Great Migration occurred in full swing in the years between 1890 and 1920. Large numbers of sharecroppers moved from the south to the north and poured into the cities. Harlem New York City became the hub of black life after the Great Migration attracted artists and intellectuals. 3. The Harlem Renaissance was an intellectual and cultural revival of African American literature in the 1920s and 1930s. Shortly after the first world war, a new black intelligentsia appeared on the scene. They sought a better standard of living and relief from the institutionalized racism in the South. They began a search for a distinct tradition of their own lives and values and tried to solicit the attention of their African American people as well as the whites. The movement continued to be an important cultural force in the United States. 4. The 1960s turned out to be a chaotic period for the United States when the African Americans awoke to the pursuit for Black power. It also proved to be a period of spectacular growth in African American literature. 5. Contemporary writers such as Toni Morrison and Alice Walker contribute to the development of African American literature. **II. Frederick Douglass (1817 – 1895)** Frederick Douglass was born a slave, who saw his own folks born enslaved and lived a brutal life himself.	**Ⅰ. 非裔美国文学发展概貌** 1. 非裔美国文学从口头传说发展而来，包括歌曲、民谣、圣歌等形式。各种各样表现形式的民间文学促进了非裔美国文学的发展。 2. 废奴运动和美国内战为非裔美国文学注入了新活力。黑人奴隶解放后，1890 年到 1920 年间，大规模的迁移进行得如火如荼。大量的佃农从南向北迁移涌入城市。大迁徙吸引了大批黑人艺术家和知识分子，而纽约的哈莱姆区也成为黑人文化中心。 3. “哈莱姆文艺复兴”是 20 世纪 20 和 30 年代的由非裔知识分子主导的美国非裔文学的复兴运动。一战后不久，出现了一个新的黑人知识分子阶层。他们试图从南方奴隶制度的阴影中得到解脱，寻求更好的生活方式。他们开始追寻能确立非裔身份的传统生活与价值，并试图让美国黑人和白人都注意到这一点。哈莱姆文艺复兴作为一种文化力量持续影响着美国社会。 4. 20 世纪 60 年代是美国社会的动荡时期，这一时期美国黑人觉醒和黑人权力斗争。它同时也是美国非裔文学茁壮成长、颇受关注的时期。 5. 当代作家托尼·莫里森和爱丽丝·沃克为非裔美国文学做出了突出的贡献。 **Ⅱ. 弗雷德里克·道格拉斯** 弗雷德里克·道格拉斯生来就是奴隶，他亲眼目睹了他的种族受奴役的生活，也亲身体验过那种残酷的生活。

◆**Major work**

My Bondage and My Freedom

The Life and Times of Frederick Douglass

◆**主要作品**

《我的枷锁和我的自由》

《弗雷德里克·道格拉斯的生平及时代》

Ⅲ. W. E. B. Dubois (1868 –1963)

As the first African American intellectual to receive a Ph. D. , Dubois helped to found the National Association for the Advancement of Colored People. His major works includes *The Souls of Black Folks: Essays and Sketches.*

Ⅲ. W. E. B. 杜波依斯

杜波依斯是第一位获得博士学位的美国黑人。他还协助建立了"全国有色人种发展协会"。他的主要作品包括《黑人的灵魂》。

Ⅳ. Langston Hughes (1902 –1967)

Langston Hughes was a key figure in the Harlem Renaissance and known as African Americans' poet laureate. Hughes was an important speaker at the American Writers' Conference in 1935. As an influential writer, he wrote novels, poems, plays, and autobiography that encouraged writing of other African American writers. During the Depression, he helped the founding of the black theater in the Federal Theater Project. He was the editor of many literary anthologies of African American literature.

Ⅳ. 兰斯顿·休斯

兰斯顿·休斯是哈莱姆文艺复兴运动的核心人物，也是众所周知的美国黑人桂冠诗人。1935 年成为美国作家协会的主要发言人之一。此后，作为一名有影响的作家，他的小说、诗歌、戏剧和自传鼓励了其他黑人作家的创作。他还是大萧条时期联邦剧院工程中黑人剧院的创始人之一。他也为许多美国黑人文学作品选集担任编辑。

1. Features of his writing

(1) Hughes wrote in praise of the October Revolution and encourage the Chinese in their revolutions. He visited Spain and wrote to support the Spanish people in their fight against the Fascist regime of Franco.

(2) In form, Hughes Hughes' poetry is famous for its fresh simplicity and its notable features of the free verse of Whitman, Sandburg, and Paul Dunbar.

1. 写作特点

(1)休斯在写作中歌颂十月革命，并对中国人民及其革命深表同情，他访问西班牙，发文支持西班牙人民反抗弗朗哥法西斯统治的斗争。

(2)在形式上，休斯的诗歌以其清新简约和运用惠特曼、桑德堡和保罗·顿巴的自由诗体的显著特征而著称。

2. Major works

The Weary Blues

The Ways of White Folks

Simple Speaks His Mind

Montage of a Dream Deferred

The Best of Simple

Simple's Uncle Sam

"The Negro Speaks of Rivers"

"As I Grew Older"

"Dream Variation"

2. 主要作品

《疲惫的布鲁斯》

《白人的行径》

《辛普尔倾诉衷情》

《缓梦蒙太奇》

《辛普尔集锦》

《辛普尔的山姆叔叔》

《黑人谈河》

《当我长大》

《梦的变奏》

Ⅴ. Richard Wright (1908 –1960)

Wright was a power writer who appeared in the 1940s. Much of Wright's literary works concerns racial themes, especially related to the plight of African Americans during the late 19th to mid-20th centuries. He exerted a great influence over subsequent African American writers. He began the contemporary African American literary tradition of violent self-assertion.

1. Major works

Uncle Tom's Children: Four Novellas

Native Son

Black Boy

2. Analysis of major work

◆*Native Son*

(1) Centering on an African American adolescent's growth, *Native Son* consists of three sections, subtitled respectively, "Fear," "Flight," and "Fate."

(2) *Native Son* is an extremely fascinating book. It deals with one of the thorniest problems with which American had been beleaguered, the racial question.

(3) he novel tells the story of 20-year-old Bigger Thomas, a black youth living in utter poverty in a poor area on Chicago's South Side in the 1930s. Bigger Thomas embodies a new type of African American personality and a higher level of African American racial awareness. Rebellious by nature, he is never able to feel at peace with the world in which he finds himself. His actions represents African American identity and the obligation of the whites. In the end, he committed violent crimes and was executed to death sentence. The author denotes that there is no escape from this destiny for Bigger or any other black American since they are the product of the mainstream society that formed them.

Ⅵ. Ralph Ellison (1914 –1994)

1. Major works

Invisible Man

Shadow and Act

Going to the Territory

Ⅴ. 理查德·赖特

赖特于20世纪40年代创作的文学作品主要围绕种族议题，尤其讲述了非裔美国人从19末期到20世纪中叶期间所面临的困境。赖特对后来的黑人作家影响深远，他开启了现代美国文学极端彰显自我的传统。

1. 主要作品

《汤姆叔叔的孩子们》

《土生子》

《黑孩子》

2. 主要作品解析

◆《土生子》

(1)《土生子》是一个美国黑人青年觉悟成长的故事，有三部分组成，副标题分别为"恐惧""逃跑"和"命运"。

(2)《土生子》是一部极具吸引力的作品。它着手于美国最为苦恼和棘手的种族问题。

(3) 小说主人公比格·托马斯是一位20岁的美国黑人青年，成长于20世纪30年代芝加哥南部的贫穷地区。比格·托马斯展现了新非裔青年的特点和美国黑人更高层次的民族认知。他本性叛逆，在发现自我的世界里他感受不到安宁。他的行为代表了黑人自身的定位和白人的责任。他最终因犯下暴力罪行而被判死刑。作者借此指出比格及其他非裔美国人都难逃悲剧性命运，因为他们都是主流社会价值下的产物

Ⅵ. 拉尔夫·埃里森

1. 主要作品

《看不见的人》

《影子与行动》

《走向领域》

2. Analysis of major work

◆*Invisible Man*

(1) *Invisible Man* tells atypical modern existential story. The protagonist-narrator is nameless apparently because he is invisible. He was brought up in Deep South. As a teenager he attended a horrifying "battle royal" where black men were reduced to fighting animals. After he journeyed to the streets of Harlem, he joined a Communist rally where black men were elevated to the status of trophies. He had to hide in basements to avoid policemen.

(2) The novel's ending is significant, which can be particularly seen from the fact that the narrator constantly refers to "you", humanity at large. He transcends the physical limits of an African American individuality and speaks for all men in the world. His dilemma, generalized and magnified, assumes a universal magnitude.

(3) In addition, the novel's writing style and techniques are amazing. Its language is more or less naturalistic in the beginning, then changes into something expressionistic, and ends with a surrealistic texture.

Ⅶ. James Baldwin (1924 – 1987)

James Baldwin has been seen as Richard Wright's successor. Like Wright he stayed in Europe for some nine years to escape intolerable racial discrimination in America. Baldwin was a serious writer and an honest man. He criticized his country due to patriotism. He considered this his greatest responsibility in life.

◆Major works

Go Tell It on the Mountain

Notes of a Native Son

Giovanni's Room

Nobody Knows My Name

The Fire Next Time

Another Country

Blues for Mister Charlie

Tell Me How Long the Train Been Gone

Ⅷ. Toni Morrison (1931 –)

Morrison inherited the legacy of African American literature. She has been recognized by the highest awards, including

2. 主要作品分析

◆《看不见的人》

(1)《隐形人》是一个典型的现代存在主义的典型故事。叙事者主人公无名无姓显然是因为人们对他视而不见。他生长于美国南方，在白人俱乐部里参与黑人少年之间残忍血腥的格斗，而后他流亡到纽约哈莱姆区，投身"兄弟会"牵头的激进政治运动，为警察的追捕隐居地下。

(2) 书的结尾十分重要，尤其是叙事者时常提及"你们"，这里的"你们"广泛指全人类。他叙事者由此超越了美国黑人个体身份的界限，骤然成为所有人的代表，他的困境推及到全人类，放大到了全世界的层面。

(3) 此外，这部小说的写作方式和技巧令人震撼。小说的语言开头多少有些自然主义的特征，后来转为表现主义，最后则是以超现实主义结尾。

Ⅶ. 詹姆斯·鲍德温

詹姆斯·鲍德温被看作是理查德·莱特的接班人。他与莱特一样，由于无法忍受美国的种族歧视逃到欧洲，并在那里生活了九年。鲍德温是位非常严肃的作家和诚实的人。他出于爱国主义精神而批判国家不合理的制度。他认为这是生命中最大的责任。

◆主要作品

《向苍天呼吁》

《土生子札记》

《乔万尼的房间》

《没有人知道我的名字》

《下一次将是烈火》

《另一个国家》

《为查理先生唱的布鲁斯》

《告诉我火车已经开多久》

Ⅷ. 托尼·莫里森

莫里森继承了非裔美国文学的传统。她曾摘得无数重要文学奖项，

the National Book Award, the National Book Critical Circle Award, the Pulitzer Prize and the Nobel Prize in 1993.	包括国家图书奖、国家图书批评奖、普利策奖以及1993年的诺贝尔文学奖。

1. Major works

The Bluest Eyes
Sula
Song of Solomon
Tar Baby
Beloved
Paradise

1. 主要作品

《最蓝的眼睛》
《秀拉》
《所罗门之歌》
《柏油孩子》
《宠儿》
《天堂》

2. Analysis of major works

◆*Song of Solomon*

(1) Morrison won her literary position in contemporary American literature with the novel *Song of Solomon* (1977). This novel is seen as another great work in African American literature after *Native Son* and *Invisible Man*. It tells the story of an African American trying to recover his family roots.

(2) Morrison praises the history and civilization of the African Americans and expose the cruelty of racism. She uses folk myths, legends and magic realism to achieve her theme.

(3) The greatness of this novel lies in its interlocking plotlines, varieties of language, and colorful folktales, legends, magic, and fantasy.

◆*Beloved*

(1) *Beloved* is based on the true antebellum story of a slave mother, Margaret Garner, who killed her own children just to spare them from the tragedy of slavery. "Beloved" in Morrison's novel is the word inscribed on the tombstone of the child killed by its mother.

(2) The novel reconstructs horrible slavery history through black folk culture and folk tales. It is a powerful book: it not only sympathize with African Americans but compels the white to face history.

2. 主要作品分析

◆《所罗门之歌》

(1) 莫里森凭借《所罗门之歌》的发表奠定了在当代美国文坛的地位。这部小说被看作是继《土生子》和《隐形人》之后非裔美国文学的又一里程碑。它讲述了一个美国黑人试图寻找家族根源的故事。

(2) 在《所罗门之歌》中莫里森颂扬美国黑人文明及其悠久的历史，展现种族主义的罪恶可耻。她通过使用民间神话传奇和魔幻现实主义来点明主题。

(3) 这部作品的伟大之处在于它交错纵横的情节，多种多样的语言，以及丰富多彩的民间故事、传说、魔法和幻想。

◆《宠儿》

(1)《宠儿》根据内战前一个真实的故事创作而成。一个奴隶母亲，玛格丽特·加纳，杀死自己的孩子以免他们沦为奴隶。莫里森小说中的“宠儿”就是孩子母亲在墓碑上刻的文字。

(2) 这部小说通过黑人民俗文化和民间故事重建和再现可怕的奴隶历史。这是一部极具影响力的作品：它不仅与美国黑人的经历共情，也迫使白人面对历史。

Ⅸ. Alice Walker (1944 –)

1. Major works

The Third Life of Grange Copeland
Meridian
The Color Purple
The Temple of My Familiar
Possessing the Secret of Joy

Ⅸ. 爱丽丝·沃克

1. 主要作品

《格兰奇·科普兰德的第三次生命》
《子午线》
《紫色》
《殿堂》
《拥有快乐的秘密》

2. Analysis of major work ◆*The Color Purple* (1) As an epistolary novel, *The Color Purple* consists of 90 letters, of which over two thirds are written to God by Celie, 14 to her sister Nettie, and 15 from Nettie to Celie. The story centers on Celie's life, with Nettie's African adventure as complementary. (2) *The Color Purple* describes African American women's growth against social and familial oppression. From the perspective of feminism, the book relates a story of solidarity between the oppressed women in a sexist, racist world. (3) *The Color Purple* marks a new dawn in the growth of African American consciousness. It raises questions for the African Americans: they need to know themselves better and get ready for their own responsibility. (4) The title of the novel is symbolic. The purple color denotes self-dignity, love, human fellowship, and surviving in spite of suffering and pain. It represents God's creation as well as common humanity.	**2. 主要作品分析** ◆《紫色》 （1）《紫色》是一部书信体小说，共有 90 封信，其中三分之二是希莉写给上帝的，14 封是写给妹妹南蒂的，15 封是南蒂写给希莉的。故事以希莉的生活为中心，以南蒂的非洲冒险为辅。 （2）从主题上来看，《紫色》第一次深入分析美国黑人女性在社会和家庭的双重压迫下的成长。从女性主义角度出发，这本书讲述了有关置身性别和种族歧视、压迫世界里的女性之间的团结互助。 （3）《紫色》标志着美国黑人意识成长的新阶段。它提出了美国黑人需要思考的问题：他们得更了解自己，得为自己生活中的责任和义务做好准备。 （4）小说的标题深含寓意。紫色象征尊严、爱、人类同胞之情，与痛苦和苦难时时相伴。它同时代表了上帝造物和普通人性。
X. Maya Angelou (1928 –) **◆Major works** *I Know Why the Caged Bird Sing* *Gather Together in My Name* *Swingin' and Swingin' Merry Like Christmas* *The Heart of a Woman* *All God's Children Need Traveling Shoes*	**X. 玛雅·安吉洛** **◆主要作品** 《我知道囚鸟为何歌唱》 《以我的名义集合》 《摇啊摇，像圣诞节一样快乐》 《女人心》 《上帝的孩子都需要旅行鞋》
XI. Gloria Naylor (1950 –) **◆Major works** *Linden Hills* *Mama Day* *Bailey's Café* *Sophhira Wade* *Women of Brewster Place* *Men of Brewster Place*	**XI. 格洛丽亚·奈勒** **◆主要作品** 《林顿山》 《母亲节》 《贝利的咖啡馆》 《索菲拉·韦德》 《布鲁斯特地的女人们》 《布鲁斯特地的男人们》

25.2 考研真题与典型题详解

I. Fill in the blanks.

1. Author ____________ Title ____________ (南京大学 2007 研)

It goes a long way back, some twenty years. All my life I had been looking for something, and everywhere I turned someone tried to tell me what it was. I accepted their answers too, though they were often in contradiction and even self-contradictory. I was naive. I was looking for myself and asking everyone except myself questions which I, and only could answer.

2. African American literature is patterned on a myth of ____________ from slavery, that of the Hebrew prophet Moses leading the Jews in their flight from the bond age in Egypt.

3. African American literature has undergone a long process of evolution. Its early form was ____________, including ____________, ____________ and ____________, in short, folk literature in its various manifestations.

4. In the 1920s, there was a new upsurge of African American literature, which has come to be known as ____________.

5. DuBois helped to found a movement and established the organization ____________ which fought more than any other for civil right.

6. By far the most important person in the Harlem Renaissance was ____________ known as African Americans' poet laureate, who ultimately outgrew the movement, and developed into one of the major African American authors to help make African American culture.

7. Alex Haley's ____________ marked a new level of self-awareness of the African American people as a race.

8. In the 1940 Richard Wright's ____________ came out as a watershed in the tradition of the African American novel.

9. Native Son by ____________ is a story about an African American adolescent's growth of awareness. It consists of three sections, namely ____________, ____________ and ____________.

10. African American literature attained a higher degree of maturity in 1952 when Ralph Ellison's ____________ appeared in print.

11. In 1993, ____________ became President Clinton's inaugural poet (the second person ever to do so for a president in history, the other being ____________).

II. Multiple Choice

1. The most popular and versatile of all the writers connected with the Harlem Renaissance is ____________. (大连外国语学院 2008 研)

A. Richard Wright　　B. W. E. B. Du Bois

C. Langston Hughes　　D. James Baldwin

2. ____________, Booker T. Washington, and Frederick Douglass are generally regarded as the three greatest African American writers in the 19th century.

A. Ralph Ellison　　B. Langston Hughes

C. Toni Morrison　　D. W. E. B. Du Bois

3. One of the most noticeable elements of Harlem Renaissance writing is its use of dialect and folk-

lore and its identification with the spirit of ___________.

A. rap　　B. jazz　　C. blues　　D. R&B

4. Among the African American writers of the fist half of the 20th century, ___________ was the most durable and versatile: he was a poet, playwright, novelist, song writer, biographer, editor, newspaper columnist, translator and lecturer.

A. Countee Cullen　　B. Claude McKay

C. Jean Toomer　　D. Langston Hughes

5. Which of the following is not said of Langston Hughes?

A. The first African American to support himself as a professional writer.

B. National Book Award winner.

C. Poet Laureate of Harlem.

D. O. Henry of Harlem.

III. Explain the following term.

1. Harlem Renaissance（北外 2009 研；北师大 2007 研；南开大学 2007 研；山东大学 2018 研）

IV. Read the following quotations and answer the questions.

Passage 1

I've known rivers:
I've known rivers ancient as the world and older than the
Flow of human blood in human veins.
My soul has grown deep like the rivers.
I bathed in the Euphrates when dawns were young.
I built my hut near the Congo and it lulled me to sleep.
I looked upon the Nile and raised the pyramids above it.
I heard the singing of Mississippi when Abe Lincoln
Went down to New Orleans, and I've seen its muddy bosom turn
All golden in the sunset.
I've known rivers.
Ancient, dusky rivers.
My soul has grown deep like the rivers.

Questions:

(1) What is the title of the poem?

(2) What is the name of the poet?

(3) What does "I" stand for in the poem?

(4) What is the theme of the poem?

Passage 2

I am an invisible man... I am invisible, understand, simply because people refuse to see me. Like the bodiless heads you see sometimes in circus sideshows, it is as though I have been surrounded by mirrors of hard, distorting glass. When they approach me they see only my surroundings, themselves. Or figments of their imagination—indeed, everything and anything except me... You often doubt if you really exist... You ache with the need to convince yourself that you do exist in the real world.

Questions:

(1) Which novel is this passage taken from?

(2) What is the name of the author?

(3) At the end of the novel, the author writes "even an invisible man has a socially responsible role to play.., who knows but that, on the lower frequencies, I speak for you?". What does "you" refer to here? What does the author want to convey by applying this pronoun?

V. Short answer question

1. What are the major themes of *Native Son* by Richard Wright (give at least three)?

Ⅵ. Essay questions

1. Discuss one significant Jewish writer or Black writer in American literature.（大连外国语学院 2007 研）

2. Searching for identity is always a dominant theme in African American literature. Discuss how this theme is developed in one specific African American book.（天津外国语学院 2007 研）

3. Toni Morrison is considered the best and the most representative of the contemporary African American writers. Discuss her art of fiction.

参考答案及解析

I. Fill in the blanks.

1. Ralph Waldo Ellison; *Invisible Man*

（题目节选自埃利森的《看不见的人》，本书是当代美国黑人文学中的经典之作，具有西方当代小说的许多特点：思想内容上提出了个人在荒谬的宇宙里的处境问题并探索自我本质；艺术上大胆创新，现实主义与超现实主义相结合，在运用黑色幽默手法上开美国后现代派文学的先河。）

2. deliverance

（美国黑人文学是建筑在摆脱奴役的神话之上的，即希伯来先知摩西率领犹太人反抗埃及的奴役和压迫。）

3. oral, songs, ballads, spirituals

（美国黑人文学经历了长期的演变。其早期主要是口述形式的，包括：歌曲、民谣和圣歌。）

4. the Harlem Renaissance

（哈勒姆文艺复兴（the Harlem Renaissance）是 20 世纪 20 年代黑人文学充满活力和创造力的时期，其中心在纽约市哈勒姆黑人聚居区。）

5. the National Association for the Advancement of Colored People

（1910 年 5 月，全国黑人委员会与杜波依斯领导尼亚加拉运动合并，定名为全国有色人种协进会(the National Association for the Advancement of Colored People)。协进会的目标，是通过改良的道路，使黑人享有完全的公民权、法庭公平裁判权。）

6. Langston Hughes

（兰斯顿·休斯(Langston Hughes)在美国文坛，尤其是黑人文学方面，是一个举足轻重的人物。他主要以诗歌著称，被誉为"黑人民族的桂冠诗人"。）

7. *Roots*

（1976年，美国出版了黑人作家亚历克斯·哈利(Alex Haley)所写的一部家史小说《根》(*Roots*)。该小说标志着美国黑人整个民族新的自我觉醒。）

8. *Native Son*

（1940年美国黑人作家理查德·赖特(Richard Wright)发表了小说《土生子》(*Native Son*)，该小说成为美国黑人文学的分水岭。）

9. Richard Wright, "Fear", "Flight", "Fate"

（美国黑人作家理查德·赖特(Richard Wright)的小说《土生子》(*Native Son*)讲述了一个美国黑人青年觉醒的过程。小说共分三部分：《恐惧》("Fear")、《逃跑》("Flight")和《命运》("Fate")。）

10. *Invisible Man*

（拉尔夫·艾里森(Ralph Ellison)的小说《看不见的人》(*Invisible Man*)是当代美国黑人文学中的经典之作。它的出版标志着美国黑人文学的成熟。）

11. Maya Angelou; Robert Frost

（1993年，黑人女作家玛娅·安杰洛(Maya Angelou)应总统比尔·克林顿的邀请，在其就职仪式上朗诵献诗《清晨的脉搏》("On the Pulse of the Morning")，成为美国历史上继罗伯特·弗罗斯特之后的官方诗人。）

II. Multiple Choice

1. C　兰斯顿·休斯，美国著名黑人诗人，"哈莱姆文艺复兴"的代表，《黑人谈河》是其最脍炙人口的作品。
2. D　杜波依斯、布克·华盛顿及弗雷德里克被认为是19世纪美国最伟大的3位非裔文学作家。
3. B　哈莱姆文艺复兴最突出的特点之一是运用方言及民歌，以及展现了爵士乐的精神。
4. D　兰斯顿·休斯是哈莱姆文艺复兴运动的核心人物，也是众所周知的美国黑人桂冠诗人。1935年成为美国作家协会的主要发言人之一。此后，作为作家他的影响力无处不在，作品产量惊人。小说、诗歌、戏剧、散文、译著、自传——他轻松地写出这一切。
5. B　休斯并未获得国家图书奖。

III. Explain the following term.

1. Harlem Renaissance: The Harlem Renaissance refers to the flowering of African American cultural and intellectual life during the 1920s and 1930s. At the time, it was known as the "New Negro Movement", named after the 1925 anthology The New Negro edited by Alain Locke. Centered in the Harlem neighborhood of New York City, the movement impacted urban centers throughout the United States. Challenging white paternalism and racism, African-American artists and intellectuals rejected imitating the styles of Europeans and white Americans and instead celebrated black dignity and creativity.

IV. Read the following quotations and answer the questions.

Passage 1

(1) The poem is entitled "The Negro Speaks of Rivers".

(2) The poet is Langston Hughes.

(3) "I" stands for the Blacks throughout history.

(4) The poem writes about the wisdom, courage and the powerful aspirations of a race suffering mistreatment and injustice throughout history.

Passage 2

(1) *Invisible Man*

(2) Ralph Ellison

(3) By using the pronoun "you", the author is addressing his readers. By doing so, he transcends the physical limits of an African American individuality. "You" in the novel refers to all the modern people, whether they are black or white. The author wanted his readers to realize that all the modern people with their aspirations for self-identity are suffering from alienation and frustration in a dehumanized society.

V. Short answer question

1. The major themes of *Native Son* by Richard Wright are racism, protest, alienation, frustration, and the mentality of African Americans.

VI. Essay questions

1. Toni Morrison is a great contemporary American writer, she won the Nobel Prize for Literature in 1993, the first African American writer who won this prize.

Toni Morrison is known for "magical realism" in that she uses magic, folktales, and the supernatural in her novels. Her style combines unrealistic (supernatural) dements with a realistic presentation of life and characters.

For Morrison, "all good art has been political" and the Black artist need to be responsible for the Black community. She aims at capturing "the something" that defines what makes a book "Black." All her fictions bear witness to the experience of the Black community. Sense of loss, roots, community, and identity of the Blacks are usual themes of her works. In her works Toni Morrison has shaped roles of black women in a racist and male dominated society. In the center of her complex and multilayered narratives is the unique cultural inheritance of African-Americans.

Morrison's prose has the quality of speech. She deliberately strives for this effect, which she calls "aural literature." Morrison wants readers to participate in her novels, to be involved actively. Readers are encouraged to create the novel with her and to help construct meaning. She is known for her epic power, unerring ear for dialogue, and her poetically-charged and richly-expressive depictions of Black America.

2. Searching for identity is a dominant theme of *Invisible Man*, a novel written by Ralph Ellison. The novel addresses many of the social and intellectual issues facing African-Americans in the early twentieth century, as well as issues of individuality and personal identity.

Invisible Man is narrated in the first person by the protagonist, an unnamed African American man who considers himself socially invisible. Speaking from the basement of Harlem which he says is "like a grave," he relates his bitter experience of having lived a horrible life for decades until he discovered his social invisibility. He tells readers how he held great expectations and won the approval of the whites who, satisfied with his docile character, sent him with a scholarship to a state college for Negroes. There he became the apprentice of Dr. Bledsoe, the black president, who, however, expelled him for having shown a white sponsor the dark secrets of the place. Next he went to New York where blacks are forced to be "invisible." What he tried to do was to be seen. At last, his dreams were failed and he had to hide in an underground cellar. It is from the basement that he narrates. The book ends with the narrator's awareness that "even an invisible man has a socially responsible role to play." The whole story is about a black man searching for his identity in a country dominated by the white.

3. Toni Morrison is a great contemporary American writer.

   Toni Morrison is known for "magical realism" in that she uses magic, folktales, and the supernatural in her novels. Her style combines unrealistic (supernatural) dements with a realistic presentation of life and characters.

   For Morrison, "all good art has been political" and the Black artist has a responsibility to the Black community. She aims at capturing "the something" that defines what makes a book "Black." All her fictions "bear witness" to the experience of the Black community. Sense of loss, roots, community, and identity of the Blacks are usual themes of her works. Her sympathy is especially given to the Black women who suffer from both the Whites and Black men.

   Morrison's prose has the quality of speech. She deliberately strives for this effect, which she calls "aural literature." Morrison wants readers to participate in her novels, to be involved actively. Readers are encouraged to create the novel with her and to help construct meaning.

第 26 章　多种族文学(2)

26.1　复习笔记

Ⅰ. Native American Literature

1. Brief Introduction

For a long time, Indians in American literature have been a distorted image. No matter how they are portrayed in mainstream literature, their images will be more or less distorted. As the American Indian writer N. Scott Momaday pointed out, "American Indians were once caught in a crisis in which the Indians left a rigid image in Americans' minds." So far, the Indians have been telling their stories from their own point of view for a long time, and they successfully changed the original image and made it a real and vivid existence. In 1968, N. Scott Momadai published *House Made of Dawn* and won the Pulitzer Prize, which inspired the well-known "Renaissance of Native American Literature" in the late 1960s. Nowadays, the works of American Indian writers flood the book market, and their literature has become a unique part of American literature.

2. D'Arcy McNickle (1904 – 1977)

McNickle devoted his whole life to improving the fortunes of his fellow American Indians.

◆**Major Works**

Native American Tribalism: Indian Survivals and Renewal
The Surrounded

◆**Analysis of *The Surrounded***

The Surrounded is a milestone in the history of Native American literature. The novel tells a tragic story of cultural dislocation and identity division, and reveals the painful process of the disintegration of the Native American culture. It also directly accuses the invasion of Indian traditional life by the whites.

Ⅰ. 美国本土印第安文学

1. 简介

很长一段时期内，美国文学中的印第安人一直是一种被歪曲的形象。无论主流文学如何刻画，他们的形象都会或多或少有些失真。正如美国印第安作家 N. 司各特·莫玛戴所指出的，“美国印第安人曾一度陷入这样一种危机，即印第安人在美国人的脑海中留下的是一种僵化的形象。”迄今为止，印第安人长期以来一直从自己的角度出发讲述自己的故事，他们成功的改变了了原先的形象，使之成为一种真实鲜活的存在。1968 年 N. 司各特·莫玛戴发表了《黎明之屋》，获得普利策奖。这激发了 20 世纪 60 年代末众所周知的“美国本土印第安文学复兴”。如今美国印第安作家的作品充斥书市，他们的文学也已成为美国文学中独特的一部分。

2. 德·安塞·麦克尼克(1904 – 1977)

麦克尼克一生都在致力于改善他的印第安同胞的命运。

◆**主要作品**

《美国印第安部落文化：印第安的幸存者与再生代》
《被包围者》

◆**《被包围者》分析**

《被包围者》是美国本土印第安文学历史上的一个里程碑。小说讲述了一个文化错位、身份分裂的悲剧故事。它揭示了美国本土文化分崩离析的悲恸过程。它将控诉的矛头直指白人对印第安传统生活的入侵。

3. N. Scott Momaday (1934 –)	**3. N. 司各特·莫玛戴(1934 –)**
◆Major Works	**◆主要作品**
House Made of Dawn	《黎明之屋》
Angle of Geese	《鹅的视角》
The Names	《名字》
The Gourd Dancer	《葫芦舞者》
The Ancient Child	《远古的孩子》
In the Presence of the Sun: Stories and Poems	《在太阳面前：故事和诗歌》
4. James Welch (1940 –)	**4. 詹姆斯·韦尔奇(1940 –)**
◆Major Works	**◆主要作品**
Winter in the Blood	《血中的冬天》
The Death of Jim Loney	《吉姆·洛尼之死》
Fools Crow	《伏厄斯·克洛》
The Indian Lawyer	《印第安律师》
5. Leslie Marmon Silko (1948 –)	**5. 莱斯利·马尔蒙·希尔科(1948 –)**
◆Major Works	**◆主要作品**
Laguna Women	《拉姑纳妇女》
Ceremony	《典礼》
Storyteller	《说故事者》
Almanac of the Dead	《死者年鉴》
Sacred Water	《圣水》
Yellow Women and a Beauty of the Spirit	《黄皮肤的女人与神灵美人》
6. Louise Erdrich (1954 –)	**6. 路易斯·厄德里齐(1954 –)**
◆Major Works	**◆主要作品**
Love Medicine	《爱药》
The Beet Queen	《土著皇后》
Tracks	《痕迹》
The Bingo Palace	《宾果宫》
Tales of Burning Love	《燃情故事集》
The Antelope Wife	《羚羊妻》
Ⅱ. Asian American Literature	**Ⅱ. 亚裔美国文学**
1. Brief Introduction	**1. 简介**
Asian American literature is usually subdivided into Chinese American literature, Japanese American literature, Indian American literature, Korean American literature, and Filipino American literature. Because these Asian American writers incorporate different cultural and historical backgrounds in their creations, Asian American literary works present a highly diverse feature. In the 1970s, Asian American literature began	亚裔美国文学通常细分为华裔美国文学、日裔美国文学、印度裔美国文学、韩裔美国文学和菲律宾裔美国文学。由于这些亚裔美国作家在创作中融入了不同的文化和历史背景，因此亚裔美国文学作品呈现出高度多样化的特点。20 世纪 70 年代，亚裔美国文学才作为美国

to receive attention as a branch of American literature. It was the civil rights movement of the 1960s that aroused the national independence spirit of the various minorities in the United States. Courses on university campuses become "ethnical" and Asian American academic research projects emerged. The Immigration Reform Act of 1965 brought a new round of highly educated immigration to make the cultural atmosphere more oriented, leading Asian American writers to develop further.

文学的一个分支开始被关注。那是60年代的民权运动激起了美国各少数民族的民族独立精神。大学校园里的课程变得"民族化"。美国亚裔学术研究项目出现。1965年的《移民法案》带来了新一轮的高学历移民使文化氛围更有导向性，引领亚裔美国作家进一步发展起来。

2. Maxine Hong Kingston (1940 –)

Kingston was born and grew up in a dual cultural environment: during her growth, the conflict and integration of Chinese and American cultures were very obvious, which also made identity, race and ethnic issues the themes of her writing.

◆**Major Works**

The Woman Warrior: Memoirs of a Childhood among Ghosts

China Men

Tripmaster Monkey: His Fake Book

2. 汤婷婷(1940 –)

汤婷婷出生并成长在一个双重文化环境中：她的成长过程中中美文化冲突与融合非常明显，这也使得身份、种族和民族问题成为她的写作主题。

◆**主要作品**

《女勇士》

《中国佬》

《孙行者》

3. Amy Tan (1952 –)

Amy Tan's first novel, *The Joy Luck Club*, has set off a lot of waves in contemporary American literary circles, enabling readers and critics to conduct a comprehensive review of Asian American literature.

◆**Major Works**

The Joy Luck Club

The Kitchen God's Wife

The Bonesetter's Daughter

3. 谭恩美(1952 –)

谭恩美的第一部小说《喜福会》在当代美国文坛掀起了不小的波浪，使读者和评论界对亚裔美国文学进行全面审视。

◆**主要作品**

《喜福会》

《灶神之妻》

《接骨师的女儿》

4. Bharati Mukherjee (1940 –)

Mukherjee's novels are all exploring the nature of the assimilation of cultures in foreign countries like North America. Assimilation means transformation and self-innovation. She studied this issue from a female perspective. So far, all the protagonists in her novels are women or Indian women.

◆**Major Works**

The Tiger's Daughter

Wife

Jasmine

The Holder of the World

4. 巴拉蒂·幕克吉(1940 –)

幕克吉的小说都在探究在北美这样的异乡文化同化的本质。同化意味着变形和自我创新。她从女性的角度研究了这个问题。迄今为止，她小说的所有主人公都是女性，或是印度女性。

◆**主要作品**

《老虎的女儿》

《妻子》

《贾思敏》

《世界的拥有者》

5. Garrett Hongo (1951 –) Hongo is a Japanese American poet. He has won many awards, including the Guggenheim Fellowship, the Hopwood Prize for Poetry, and the Pushcart Prize. ◆**Major Works** *The Buddha Bandits Down Highway 99* *Yellow Light* *The River of Heaven*	**5. 加勒特·本乡(1951 –)** 本乡是一位日裔美国诗人。他获得过多个奖项。他曾荣获古根海姆奖、霍普伍德奖和普士卡奖。 ◆**主要作品** 《99号公路上的佛陀劫匪》 《黄光》 《天堂河》
III. Chicano Literature **1. Brief Introduction** The term "Chicano" is derived from "Mexicano". Chicano literature is a kind of work about the Mexican-American experience created by American Mexicans and Mexicans in America. For Chicano writers, the sense of nationality is a vital part of their literary perception, portraying the experience of the Chicanos' nation in America and the main issues they are concerned about. This literary tradition dates back to the mid-19th century, but it was not obvious before the mid-1960s. The civil rights movement among Mexican Americans introduced Chicano literature to a new stage. Chicano families, groups and their struggle for civil rights became the subject of Chicano writers. The Chicano Renaissance emerged from the mid-1960s to the early 1980s. The writing theme of Chicano literature is to seek to confirm the national identity and tell the national experience.	**III. 奇卡诺文学** **1. 简介** "奇卡诺"一词衍生自"Mexicano"。奇卡诺文学是美国墨西哥人后裔和在美国的墨西哥人创作的关于美国墨西哥人经历的作品。对卡奇诺作家来说，民族感是他们文学感知至关重要的一部分，刻画卡奇诺民族在美国的经历是他们关注的主要问题。这个文学传统可追溯至19世纪中期，但在20世纪60年代中期以前并不明显。墨西哥裔美国人间的民权运动将卡奇诺文学引入新阶段。卡奇诺家庭、团体和他们为民权而斗争成为卡奇诺作家的创作主题。20世纪60年代中期到80年代初期兴起了卡奇诺文艺复兴。卡奇诺文学的写作主题就是寻求印证民族身份，讲述民族经历。
2. Tomas Rivera (1935 – 1984) ◆**Major Work** *Y no se lo trago la tierra* (*And The Earth Did Not Part*)	**2. 托马斯·里维拉(1935 – 1984)** ◆**主要作品** 《大地不会分开》
3. Luis Omar Salinas (1937 –) ◆**Major Works** "*Aztec Angel*" "*Quixotic Expectations*"	**3. 路易斯·奥玛·萨林纳斯(1937 –)** ◆**主要作品** 《阿兹泰克天使》 《狂想》

26.2 考研真题与典型题详解

I. Fill in the blanks.

1. The most famous of the Asian American writers is ________, whose *The Woman Warrior*: *Memories of a Childhood among Ghosts* won ________ for nonfiction for 1976 and established her as a preeminent contemporary American writer.
2. Another important Asian American writer is Amy Tan, whose first novel, ________, made quite a stir on the contemporary American literary scene and brought Asian American literature to

the intensive scrutiny of readers and critics alike.

3. The four parts of *The Joy Luck Club* are: ________, ________, ________ and ________.

Ⅱ. Essay question

1. Analysis of *The Joy Luck Club* by Amy Tan.

参考答案及解析

Ⅰ. Fill in the blanks.

1. Maxine Hong Kingston, the National Books Critics Circle Award
（美国最著名的亚裔作家是汤婷婷（Maxine Hong Kingston），她的第一部作品是回忆录式的小说《女勇士》（*The Woman Warrior : memoirs of a girlhood among ghosts*），此书于1976年出版后，获当年美国全国书评界奖。这部作品的文学成就和热销的程度在美国文学史上是空前的。她从而蜚声美国文坛。）
2. *The Joy Luck Club*
（著名华裔美国女作家谭恩美（Amy Tan）的第一部小说《喜福会》一经出版就在美国文坛上引起很大轰动，并引起读者和评论家们对亚裔美国文学的强烈关注。）
3. "Feathers From a Thousand Li Away", "The Twenty-Six Malignant Gates", "American Translation", "Queen Mother of the Western Skies"
（谭恩美的小说《喜福会》分为四部分"千里鹅毛"（"Feathers From a Thousand Li Away"），"二十六扇凶门"（"The Twenty-Six Malignant Gates"），"美国翻译"（"American Translation"），"西方天空的母后"（"Queen Mother of the Western Skies"）。）

Ⅱ. Essay question

1. Amy Tan's first novel *The Joy Luck Club* has set off a lot of waves in contemporary American literary circles, enabling readers and critics to conduct a comprehensive review of Asian American literature.

   It is interesting both in theme and form. Thematically speaking, this is a story about eight two-generation women from four families telling their different stories. These stories share a common connection with each other as connective tissues. It consists of four parts, each of which begins with a vignette or preface, in short italics, and is narrated by one of the four mothers, pointing out the theme of this section. A dividing line can be drawn between the two generations of women. The mothers on one side tell their stories of their experiences in China while the daughters talk about their lives in America. The relationships between the mothers and their daughters are sometimes tense and even confrontational not only because of the generation gap but also mainly due to their different growth and cultural experiences. These stories eventually bridge the gap and represent the efforts of American-born daughters to understand and accept Chinese traditions.

   The format of the book is also very interesting. The sixteen stories are all narrated in the first person. Each of the eight characters has two stories, except Jin Mei, who tells four stories, two of her own and two of her mother. The variety of the voices seems dizzying, but inspires imagination. And there is almost no sense of misalignment between different parts. Everything is in place at the right time and fits well with the overall situation.